Praise fo

"Through Susan, Slabach crafts a ɪ .... no doubt resonate with those at a similar station in life: women who love their families yet yearn for just a little more--to feel wanted rather than needed, to feel passion rather than complacency."

—Kirkus Reviews (starred review)

"Susan's personal decisions and consequences feel familiar and real in this smart and sensual novel."

—Publishers Weekly

"This is an extraordinarily well-written book that will leave readers turning the pages as fast as they can to see how it will all turn out."

—San Francisco Book Review, 5 Stars

"*Degrees of Love* will take readers on an emotional journey as we watch Susan explore the different roles in her life, working to discover what it is she truly wants most."

—RT Review, Top Pick

"*Degrees of Love* is an astounding depiction of love, marriage, family and what life could be if different choices were made... The plot is distinctive and unpredictable. With an ending that will not disappoint."

—Chick Lit Cafe

This is an author to watch out for and I will eagerly be waiting for her next novel. *Degrees of Love* will be added to my best of 2018 list!

—Library of Clean Reads

The ending made me sit back and think. I couldn't just move on to the next book. This is a novel that had me talking to my girlfriends about it, going through the scenarios of the main character's life, asking each other what we would do.

—Readers' Favorite

Ten Thousand I Love Yous

A Novel

Lisa Slabach (signature)

Lisa Slabach

Published by Olivarez Media, Inc.

2022

Ten Thousand I Love Yous

Olivarez Media, Inc.
Davis, California
USA

ISBN: 978-1667811185

The weaker partner in a marriage is the one who loves the most.
—Eleonora Duse

Chapter 1

I SAT NEXT TO my husband in the Davis High School stadium bleachers with the sun beating on my face, and like almost everyone else, fanned my graduation program back and forth in a vain attempt to tease a Delta breeze out of the still air. Scanning the crowd, I noted all the sane people had dressed for heat. Jay had insisted on dressing for the occasion, so I followed suit and sweated in a dress that constricted my middle. He pulled a handkerchief out of his pocket, swiped at a bead of sweat gathering on his brow, and then pulled on his collar.

"Take your tie off," I whispered.

"I'm fine."

He and I squinted as we watched a sea of blue caps and gowns flow onto the field while the school band played *Pomp and Circumstance.* They all appeared so gleeful, smiling, giggling, and waving as they weaved their way to the waiting chairs. I wondered if they were happier about shedding the tediousness of high school, or about the journey ahead—college, leaving Davis, and testing their independence. I wondered what futures were in store for these children—yes, I still thought of them as children. Most would be heading to college. (The highly educated Davis community expected their children to go to college.) Many were headed to Ivy League schools and other prestigious institutions. Maybe, just maybe, there were a handful thinking about marriage and parenthood.

Jay and I had missed our high school graduation. We'd spent the night in the delivery room. At the time, missing the ceremony had seemed insignificant compared to the enormity of becoming parents. We hadn't understood why not marching was such a colossal disappointment to both my and Jay's parents; we had graduated after all. Now I got it. The ritual formally celebrated and marked the end of day-to-day parenthood. It was an accomplishment, an end, and a beginning rolled into one life-changing moment.

I spotted Haley's black hair shining in thick waves down her back and pointed. "There she is."

"Yep, that's our girl. Hard to miss that hair."

She had Jay's hair and olive skin and my blue eyes—the perfect blend of the two of us. Everyone had thought we were too young to get married, let alone be parents. *Their marriage will never last—and their daughter. What will happen to their poor daughter?* I glanced down and unashamedly beamed at all the asterisks following *Haley Braxton* in the program. Each tiny black dot denoted a huge win. As smart as she was beautiful, graduating with a 4.2 and attending U.C. Berkeley in the fall, she planned to be an attorney, like her daddy. That was what happened to us and our daughter. Our lives were a success and about as perfect as anyone could reasonably expect.

Jay smiled down at me. "You did a good job, Kimmy."

"So did you, Mr. Braxton."

His eyes glistened, and from nowhere, tears trickled down my cheeks. "Sorry, totally blindsided by the tears." I swiped at them and rummaged through my purse for the small tissue package I'd purchased earlier that day.

He shook his head with a chuckle. "Wrong usage."

"What?"

"Blindsided. You used the term wrong. You knew you'd cry."

"I didn't feel the tears coming."

"Why was Kleenex in your purse, then?"

"Fine. I thought I *might* cry." *Jeesh.* Mr. Litigator always had to be right.

The beginning of the speeches put an end to our bicker. The joy and excited energy of the graduates kept me from shedding another drop. After the ceremony, Jay took pictures of Haley and her friends until it was time for them to board the bus for their Senior Class party.

With the whooping and laughter fading behind us, we walked home in silence, each of us absorbed with our own thoughts. Haley had only been four years old when we'd moved to Davis for Jay to attend the University of California-Davis School of Law. We'd fallen in love with the sunny college town, with its endless bicycle paths and easy pace, and felt so lucky to be raising our daughter in a community that valued education and family. Now, she was technically an adult. When had that happened?

As we turned up our walkway I asked, "Feeling a little sad?"

"Not sad. Wistful."

Wistful described my mood exactly. We were moving to a different stage, but it would be exciting. We could do things like make love on the couch or on the kitchen table if we wanted. As much as I loved, and would miss Haley, I looked forward to nights alone with Jay.

Once in the house, I suggested we open a bottle of champagne. Jay's mood lightened and he popped the cork while I got down our crystal champagne bowls. Delicately etched with swirls and flowers, they were our go-to glasses for special occasions. My grandmother had given them to us as a wedding gift. My parents had boycotted our wedding, but Gran had defied them by supporting my choice. She and my grandfather had toasted with them on their wedding day, and she thought they would bring us good luck. So far, they had.

We met at the kitchen table. He poured and then lifted his glass. "Every ending is a beginning. Cheers." We tapped our glasses together and simultaneously sipped.

The bubbly tickled my nose, and I smiled at my husband. "Can you believe Haley has graduated? Her life really is just beginning."

"So's ours."

What an odd comment. We had been married for eighteen years. I understood we would be entering a new phase, but our life wasn't just beginning. "What do you mean?"

"With Haley going to college, the day-to-day responsibility is over. You and I will be free in a way." His voice was shaky. He took a sip and stared at his glass. "It's a chance to reboot ... try new things."

"What kind of 'things'?" Jay was very athletic. One time he had wanted to be dropped by a helicopter on top of a mountain to ski down. I'd talked him out of it because it was so needlessly dangerous and hoped he had some-thing else in mind.

"Adventurous things. Things we never got to do because we were parents when everyone else was young and having fun. Don't you agree?"

As high schoolers, we'd contemplated taking a summer and traveling around Europe or possibly Australia, but now we were a little old for back-packing Europe or dancing at clubs until two in the morning. "Not really, I think that stage has come and gone."

"Why? We're still young."

I laughed. He was close to being made a named partner at the law firm, and we had an eighteen-year-old daughter for crying out loud. "Fine, but no motorcycles."

"Don't laugh at me," he growled. "I'm serious."

"Okay, honey," I said apologetically. "Let's have some fun. We can join a bowling league," I joked, expecting him to grin and confess what he thought we should try or where we should go. Instead, his leg bobbed a few times, and he refilled our glasses. He probably had something in the works and was wait-ing for the right moment to spring it on me, like when he'd secretly planned a Caribbean cruise for our fifteenth wedding anniversary.

I walked behind his chair and draped my arms on his shoulders. He smelled good. Haley was out of the house. "What would you like to try?" I whispered as I nuzzled his neck.

He jerked, knocking his champagne glass. Time slowed as I watched it roll off the table, drop to the floor, and shatter. I don't know why I didn't try to stop it.

"I'm so sorry. I'll clean it up," Jay said as he pushed out of his chair. "Why don't you get ready for bed?"

"Okay," I murmured, blinking back my tears. It was only a glass for goodness sake.

To distract myself while waiting for Jay, I flipped through Modern Mom magazine. Without fail, my spirits lifted seeing my name on a byline. Kimberly Braxton wasn't a household name, but I was regularly published in women's magazines.

About thirty minutes later he shuffled in. I asked, "Tired, honey?"

"Yeah." Poor baby. He'd had a rough day. As a litigator, he'd battled in court before racing home to get ready for Haley's graduation.

I watched him undress and admired the way his muscles flexed and moved as he stripped to his briefs and pulled on an old t-shirt. His six pack wasn't as defined as it once had been, but he was still plenty fit. I loved this man and all I wanted at that moment was to feel close to him.

He crawled in bed, reached for his book, and settled in to read. I snuggled up next to him and rested my head against his bicep. He kept reading.

"Hey," I said, "Let me in?"

He sighed, lifted his arm, and let me nestle into him. I knew he was exhausted, but I really wanted to make love with my husband, so while he read, I slipped my hand under his t-shirt and ran my fingertips in small swirls over his stomach.

Less than a minute later, he reached over and turned off the light. Lately he'd insisted on making love in the dark, but I missed gazing into his eyes and seeing his body move with mine. I wished he wasn't so self-conscious about getting soft. I loved his body and always had. I was the one who'd packed on the pounds, but the extra weight added a cup size to my figure; Jay, being a breast man, couldn't complain about that.

His lovemaking was particularly wham-bam-thank-you-mam fast and furious—the kind of sex we used to have when he'd been in law school and needed a quick stress release. It left us both sweaty. I got up to take a shower, and he was asleep before I got back to bed.

The sound of a key turning in a lock woke me sometime after two. Haley. I found her in the kitchen digging in the refrigerator.

"Hi, honey. Did you have a good time?"

Haley emerged with a bottle of water, and the smile on her face told me she'd had an exceptionally good time. "Yeah. Derek asked me out."

"Told you the boy was smitten," I teased.

"Mom, *please*," she groaned.

"Alright, alright, but tell what happened."

She took a swig of water and her smile returned. "He asked me to dance about ten minutes after we got there, and we ended up hanging out all night."

Ah, young love. "So, did he kiss you?"

Her eyes went dreamy and she sighed. "Yeah, he kissed me. Please, don't tell Dad. He'll be merciless with Derek if he knows."

"Don't worry, I won't."

Jay expounded countless times on the unbridled horniness of teenage boys and was determined his daughter would not follow in my footsteps. I agreed, but it made him overly strict when it came to Haley's natural desire to date. Some things she and I kept just between us.

"How's Daddy? He seemed kind of bummed."

"He's fine. I suspect he's planning something."

Haley giggled. "I caught him packing a suitcase and stashing it in the garage. Think he's going to surprise you with another trip?"

I smiled and raised my eyebrows. "Could be. We should go to bed. We'll have to head out around seven to get you to the airport on time."

The next morning, I woke Jay a few minutes before it was time to leave. Haley was going with a group of friends to Disneyland for a few days. We were hesitant to let her go without a chaperone, but she reminded us we were married at her age and her godmother, who also happened to be my best friend, lived less than twenty miles from the park.

Jay quickly pulled on an old t-shirt and pair of shorts, grabbed his camera, and asked to have a few minutes alone with Haley. I loaded her luggage and waited in my SUV while they talked, knowing whatever he said to her she would repeat as soon as we drove away.

He took Haley's picture, and she yelled, "Come on, Mom. I want one with you."

I got back out of the SUV and after a couple snaps, had Haley on her way. As we pulled out of the driveway, Jay watched us from the front porch, and Haley waved to him until we turned the corner.

"Dad's planning something for sure," she said.

"What'd he say?"

"First, he gave me his standard lecture about boys and drinking and then he slipped me this." Haley grinned and held up five, one hundred-dollar bills.

"Nice."

"Very nice. Then, he said he'd miss me and told me he wouldn't be home when I got back. So, it sounds like you two are going somewhere."

For most of the drive we speculated on where he might take me. Her money was on Hawaii, but given Jay's recent mood, I bet on Vegas.

After I set her bags on the curb, I squeezed her tight. I wanted to tell her to be safe, not to talk to strangers, and to call me, but checked my impulses. Instead, I said, "Have fun, kiddo."

"You, too." She laughed. "Oh hey, Dad asked me not to say anything about the suitcases or about not being home when I get back, so please don't say anything."

On the way home, I stopped for a latte. I wanted alone time to catch my breath and take in how my life was changing, how Haley was changing, and how I would have to loosen my mommy reins and let her become an adult. I missed my girl already and needed to get control of the aching feeling in my chest before going home to whatever Jay had planned. Recently, he'd been acting oddly, but it had only been a year since his mother had died, and now, we were coming to the end of a huge chapter of our lives. I could feel him gearing up for a change, antsy to flip the page and see where life would lead us next. If he wanted to be dropped by a helicopter on top of a mountain, I had to be prepared to do it with him—metaphorically speaking, of course.

Seeing our suitcases lined up i   ⁓tle faster. I smiled in anticipation of what   Jay walked into the living room.

My smile slipped as I registered the tense, straight line of his lips. His deep brown eyes, which were usually soulful and warm, glanced at me, cold and detached.

He gestured toward the couch. "You should sit down."

My stomach dropped and my mind raced with possibilities as I sunk onto the cushion. Had someone died? Had something happened to his father? What? What?

I stared up at him, terrified of his answer. "What's going on?"

He sat on the ottoman, facing me. "I haven't been happy for a long time."

"I know, but your mom died a year ago. I thought you were better and moving past it."

"I am—I have. It's not my mom. It's us, our marriage. I'm not happy with us."

Marriages have peaks and valleys. I've written about it, but we hadn't been fighting. We hadn't had a major fight in a long time. "I don't understand."

"I'm not in love with you anymore."

What? What did he just say? Of course, he loved me. We were soul mates; he'd said so more times than I could remember. I must have misheard him, and I opened my mouth to object.

He held up his hand. "Kim, listen. Please, listen to me." He kept going, and like some surreal nightmare, his words jumbled and blurred as they attacked my heart with stabs of pain. Something about not loving me … had done his duty … needed to be free … our marriage suffocated him … best thing for both of us … would always, always care about me. He was sorry … so sorry, but he didn't love me as a husband anymore.

"But we made love last night," I said still not believing him. If he needed more romance and passion, I could give it to him. Things would be different with Haley gone.

"We had sex. It had nothing to do with love."

What he'd said wasn't true. I knew in my heart it wasn't true. Before I could voice my thoughts, he pulled an envelope out of his back pocket and thrust it toward me. "Here, it's a roundtrip ticket to LAX. I thought it'd be a good idea if you spent a few days with Valerie."

I shook my head, refusing to take it. I didn't want my friend. *I wanted my husband.*

He set the ticket on the ottoman and stood. "I'll call you in a few days."

As I watched him turn his back to me, my mind flashed to my grandmother's champagne glass smashing to the ground, not trying to save it. Next thing I knew, my body blocked the front door. "You're not going anywhere! Whatever is going on, we'll work it out."

"Kim, move out of the way. I don't want to hurt you, but I am leaving."

"No, not until you tell me why! Did you meet someone else?" My face flamed and my pulse raced, waiting for his answer.

His jaw clenched and he shook his head. "No, dammit. Now *move*."

"No, I love you!" I said, widening my stance while tears flooded down my face. "I'm not letting you leave without a fight, not until you tell me why."

In one quick move, he hoisted me over his shoulder and dropped me on the couch. As he reached for the door, I scrambled back to my feet and launched at him, wrapping my arms around his legs. "You can't tell me because you still love me. You love me," I sobbed.

He toppled to the floor and yelled, "The only way I can stand making love to you is with the lights off! Doesn't that tell you enough?"

I let go and crumpled, all s   an I'd loved for twenty years, the man I'd l   didn't love me. I repulsed him, and he left n   : or breathe.

Hours later, I lay curled in the same spot, unable to move, feeling like I'd been hit by a Mack truck—marriage roadkill, kicked to the curb and abandoned with my heart so shattered I wasn't sure if I was alive or dead. What a sad story it would make on the evening news that Kimberly Braxton literally died of a broken heart.

Blindsided. I now knew what it meant to be blindsided.

Chapter 2

One Year Later

MIRACLE OF MIRACLES, I continued to breathe despite my heartbreak. I used to relish having a quiet house all to myself, but now that entire days passed without me speaking to anyone, solitude had become my unwelcome companion. Sometimes I talked to myself just to ensure my voice still worked. I hadn't realized how much I'd depended on Jay for socialization until he'd left, but the reality was Jay had been our social planner. I had loved hosting dinner parties and going to get togethers, but without Jay, I doubted an invitation from me would be welcome, and not many invites came my way.

Thus, to be around people without imposing on friends, I developed a habit of frequenting my local grocery store. I loved my Nugget Market. In addition to bargains and staples, the store carried items like duck fat, Meyer lemon infused oil, and exotic cheeses. As a bonus, the employees were exceptionally cheerful and friendly. I was a pleasant place and the faces of the college students working at the store had become increasingly familiar. So there I was, on the anniversary of Jay's flight, at a place of comfort, at the Nugget.

When I got out of the car, the sky was beginning to dim. The cars, the grocery carts, and the people coming and going were bathed in a pinkish-purple glow of pre-twilight. It made everything have a filtered, out of focus, not quite real, quality. The glass of wine I'd had, combined with my mood, made me feel sensual, hyperaware of colors, the summer heat radiating from the asphalt, the sounds around me.

I'd heard an interview on the radio with a sociologist who did a study on the way women walk. Supposedly, he could tell by the way a woman walked if she was regularly having sex. God knows I wasn't, but dang, I'd love to get laid. I consciously swayed my hips—just in case anyone was watching.

I wondered if I'd see Joshua. He was one of the college kids who worked at the store. I had no memory of the first time I'd seen him but could vividly recall the day he popped out of the background and into the forefront of my Nugget experience.

When I'd pushed my cart to his line that day, I'd been distracted thinking about a dinner party I was hosting and had been perusing the food magazines by the checkout stand with the hope some scrumptious looking cover would inspire me to culinary greatness.

A checker from the adjacent line had grabbed my cart.

"I'll take you over here," the helpful clerk offered.

"No worries, I got her," Joshua said, reclaiming my cart.

I glanced up and big hazel eyes met mine, stunning me. I'd never locked eyes with anyone but Jay, and accidently doing so with a stranger completely unnerved me.

He pulled my cart through and closed the line behind me. "I'm supposed to be going on break, but you've waited in line a long time. I hate turning you away."

"How nice of you."

"Yeah, I'm a sweetie," he joked, and smiled, showing perfectly straight teeth.

He was a sweetie, and ever since that day, I'd kept an eye out for him.

The crash of breaking glass snapped me out of my daydream, and I turned in the direction of the sound. Joshua, with his mop of dark hair, was crouched by a car, and his eyes were on me—or were they? I probably imagined his wide-eyed gaze. The scent of cranberry juice wafted toward me as I walked past, and he bent over to pick up the remains of the broken juice bottle. He had a nice butt. In my semi-wine-buzzed state, I fantasized running my hand over it.

Bad, bad thoughts. I forced Joshua out of my head, grabbed a cart, and wheeled into the store. *Strawberries were on sale, salad fixings, what else?* Joshua's butt flashed in my mind again. *Meat.* I automatically went to the family pack section. Ribeyes were four dollars a pound cheaper if I bought the three pack. A familiar pang rippled through my chest.

Would that feeling ever stop? Jay wasn't coming back. I'd heard he was dating a twenty-something cocktail waitress from Sacramento. I pictured her with bleached hair and ginormous fake boobs that compensated for her miniscule I.Q.—not that I was bitter or anything.

Haley hadn't come home for the summer. She said there wasn't enough to do in Davis and stayed in Berkeley. I couldn't blame her. And I couldn't eat three steaks by myself ... maybe I could, but I could not afford it.

I selected a single, perfectly marbled ribeye. It was a splurge, but I hadn't sunk my teeth into a hunk of beef in a while, and if I made two meals out of it, my budget wouldn't be completely blown. It irked me having to be so cost conscious while Jay was probably wining and dining Miss Booby at one of our favorite restaurants this very evening.

With my cart finally filled with the things I needed and a few items I absolutely did not need—including a pint of Ben & Jerry's which I justified because Cherry Garcia was on sale—I rounded the corner to the checkout lanes and big hazel eyes locked on me. What could I do? His line was open. It would be rude to push past to another check stand. My chest tightened and inexplicably, my hands shook. Gripping the cart and willing my hands to still, I wheeled to him.

He grinned at me, grabbed the Ben & Jerry's, and scanned it. "I thought that was you in the parking lot earlier."

The way he'd said *you* felt intimate—as if I were someone special, or someone he knew. *He noticed me in the parking lot?* Stop. He was simply making polite conversation.

Despite my thick and uncooperative tongue, I managed to answer, "Yep, it was me."

He picked up my ribeye and examined it. "Nice cut. If you marinate it in beer for about an hour before you grill, it'll melt in your mouth like butter."

"I've never heard that before. I will, thanks."

"No problem." He grinned again and kept scanning. "So what did you do today?"

I binge-watched Outlander and struggled with how much I craved the weight of a man's body on top of me. "I wrote."

"Wrote?"

And I fantasized about hunky men in kilts. "Pretty much that's it. I just wrote." I expected him to ask me what I wrote about, but he just nodded and kept scanning. *Say something.* "So are you taking any classes this summer?"

"No, I graduated last December, but I'll probably go back to school this coming fall."

Thank God, I wasn't completely depraved. Still too young for me to lust after, but at least he wasn't a college kid. "Oh? Are you going to grad school?"

"Possibly. I was accepted to an M.A. in Education program."

"Have you always wanted to be a teacher?"

"Not really, but I majored in History. I figure I can either teach high school or keep working here. Not that working here is bad, but you know, I need to do something."

"You have a lot more options than you think. You're great with customers and you work hard. There are a lot of things you can do."

He stopped scanning. "You've noticed me?"

Dang. The wine and daily isolation weakened my filter. Embarrassed, I fessed up. "Yes, I've noticed you."

I peeped up at him. A huge, open smile spread across his face and his eyes shined. "Wow. That makes me feel good; someone like you noticed me."

His lack of artifice was endearing. People thought those things. They didn't voice them. He wasn't playing it cool. He was open and honest. He was sweet. I smiled back.

Wait a second. Someone like me? What did he mean? Someone beautiful and sexy? Probably not. Someone older and wiser—someone motherly.

The mom in me kicked into gear and vomit mouth ensued. As he bagged my groceries, I spewed a plethora of unsolicited advice: he should put together a resume, ask for references, utilize the campus career center, apply for internships, et cetera.

He set the last bag in my cart and smiled. "Thanks for the suggestions."

"Oh, well I'm sure you'll do great with whatever you pursue," I said, starting to go.

"Wait. I'll walk you out."

"Can you leave your station? I don't want you to get in trouble."

He shrugged and glanced behind him. "No one's in line."

We chatted as he walked me to my car and loaded the groceries into the back of my SUV. I could swear even though he grinned down at me, his eyes glazed over from my yammering. I talked too much, but it felt so good to talk to someone after being alone all day.

"Thanks for your help. I hope you have something fun planned for when you get off work," I said, wrapping up.

"Yeah, I'm going to hang with this girl."

My heart twinged with an inner sigh. Of course, he'd be hanging out with a girl. Why had I imagined his friendliness meant anything other than he was polite? As a grown woman, I should be fantasizing about having my hands on a man's butt—Jamie Fraser's would do nicely.

Monday morning, my editor called. I had met Wendy years ago at a San Francisco writers' conference. She'd been launching a new online magazine for working mothers called *OTG*, which stood for "On The Go." I had proposed a series of "How To In 15 Minutes or Less" articles. She loved it. I took the "15 Minute" challenge and came up with 15 Minute Meals, 15 Minute Halloween Costumes, 15 Minute Desserts That Impress, and even How to Wow Your Man in 15 Minutes or Less. (Jay had been quick to volunteer as my research partner.)

Irony of ironies, my reputation for marriage advice and entertaining family anecdotes had given me an entree to freelance for other women's magazines. I continued to write the articles even though Jay and Haley no longer lived with me. Jay covered our mortgage but writing paid the rest of my bills.

I knew why she was calling and bit the bullet. "Sorry, sorry I know I usually have my piece to you by now. I've had writer's block, but I promise to make the deadline."

"That's fine. I'm actually calling because we need to chat. Do you have a minute?"

Wendy requesting a "chat" was never good. A sinking sensation hit my chest. "Sure, I have a few minutes. What's up?"

"I know you've had a rough year, with your divorce and all, and it pains me, but you're not right for *OTG* anymore. When your contract expires, we won't renew."

"Has my writing been lacking?"

"Kim, you know I adore you, but part of your charm has always been the reality and human factor you bring to the readers. Lately, your articles sound false."

Tears stung my eyes, and I fought against boohooing to Wendy. Over the last year, I had struggled to write about working mom and marital issues. What could I say? I lived alone with two cats. I didn't even like the cats.

"Okay, well, if that's all," I squeaked.

"No, it's not all. I want you to write for another site I'm launching."

Thank goodness, I wasn't being flat out dumped. "Who's the target audience?"

"Divorced women."

"Ah, something which rings true?" I couldn't keep the sarcasm out of my voice.

"Before you say no, at least hear me out."

It would be foolish not to. Wendy had given me my first break. "I'm sorry. I was taken off guard. I am interested. What did you have in mind?"

"A dating and sex column."

"Are you serious?" If Wendy knew I had gone on a grand total of one date since Jay walked out, she wouldn't be asking me to write anything.

"Of course I'm serious. You're only, what, thirty-five?"

"Thirty-seven."

"Fine. My point is you're still young. You can't tell me you're not back on the market."

I didn't feel young, but more importantly, did I dare tell her about my one date? My "friend" set me up with a fifty-three-year-old divorced dentist who had a receding hairline which started mid-scalp. The nicest thing I could say about him was he had good teeth.

"Kimberly? You there?"

"Yes, I'm here. It's a rather personal subject."

"So were the articles you wrote about trying to conceive. They were very personal."

"True." If I didn't take it, I'd have to hunt down other writing gigs, which meant sending submissions and dealing with a barrage of rejections before finding a taker or get a nine-to-five job. On the other hand, I wasn't dating or having sex, and I wasn't ready. Jay was still too much a part of me. I had yet to pass a single day without thinking about him. I might sound just as *false*. Besides, I wasn't divorced yet. "Can you give me a few days to think about it?"

"Sure, but this will be a weekly column, and you'll have to come up with an angle. I want something unique, like the 15 Minute series. I don't want a standard dating blog."

Wendy reinforced what I'd been told by practically everyone. I should get back in the market and accept Jay wasn't coming back. For months, I'd pretended that he was on a business trip. I even bought a bottle of his favorite cologne. The whiff of ocean breeze combined with a hint of citrus mingled with Jay's natural scent perfectly. I'd spray his side of the bed with it, hug his pillow, and tell myself he'd be home the next day.

A visit by Jay a few days after I'd been served with divorce papers ended the charade. He'd dropped by the house to pick up more of his clothes and sundries, saw the bottle, and pocketed it. That inconsequential, mindless act made me explode like a volcano spewing hot lava rage—rage like I'd never felt before. I'd been so infuriated about the way he'd left, refusing even to discuss counseling, and then to waltz in and start grabbing things … ugh. It hadn't mattered that he thought he'd left the damn bottle. It shot me over the roof. I'd demanded it back and chased him out of the house screaming, "Get out! Get out!" like a crazed lunatic. When he'd gotten to his car, I'd hurled the bottle at him. Instead of hitting him, Jay had caught it with one hand. He'd coolly sat it on the edge of the planter box, got in his car, and driven away.

It was a shaming moment that I wished I could purge from my memory. I'd acted abominably and looked my absolute worst to boot. I'd gained so much weight that I could barely zip my jeans and had to wear an oversized sweatshirt to mask my rolls. Even worse, my face had been bloated from months of drinking too much. The good thing that came out of it was that I cut back on the wine, dug out my old Beach Body workout DVDs, and started moving.

Since then, I've lost thirty pounds, but Jay still hasn't seen me. My little freak-out prompted him to insist we communicate via our attorneys going forward. I'd attempted to halt the proceedings by making high financial demands. At the very least, I'd hoped to force a meeting, but Jay agreed to everything I'd requested: the house, alimony, half of his 401K, and his treasured Porsche Panamera, which he had bought used and insisted was a bargain. He'd be responsible for Haley's tuition and our consumer debt—lucky for him I was credit card adverse.

I'd been furious with him in spurts and had hated him in waves. Lately, I simply missed him. He had to have days when he missed me, too. How could he not?

One more day and our divorce would be final.

I sat by my phone the rest of the afternoon, seized by a crazy, irrational feeling he would change his mind. I was sure he would. He didn't. The next day I received the first of my consolation prizes: Jay's Porsche sitting in my driveway and an alimony payment padding my bank account. At least I was no longer broke.

———

Convinced I reminded Joshua of his mother, I stayed away from Nugget until the following Saturday. I prayed I wouldn't bump into him, but I was running low on groceries and couldn't bring myself to shop anywhere else. I had just begun to relax when I turned a corner, and big hazel eyes locked on me. *My God, he has beautiful eyes.* Was I staring or was he staring? After a couple beats, I smiled and kept going, my palms sweaty, nervous as a teenager.

"Hey, I thought about what you said." I stopped and faced him. "I really want to thank you. I've been treading water because I really don't want to be a teacher. You've inspired me to get moving with something else."

I inspired him? Warmness tingled my stomach. "That's so sweet of you to say."

We stood grinning at each other for a moment. Then he put his hand on my arm, gave me a squeeze—no, more like a hug—and said in a low, intimate voice, "Thanks again."

His confident—dare I say seductive—touch surprised me, and I left the store in a glowy haze, certain of the growing attraction between us. If he knew how old I was, that I was divorced, and had a daughter old enough for him to date, he would probably be horrified. As flattering as his notice was, Joshua was too young and that was that.

Nonetheless, it had been over a year since I'd felt desired by a man. The thrill of it boosted my battered ego, and Joshua filled my thoughts for hours after I got home.

He was undeniably attractive, but his warmth of spirit pulled on me more. I couldn't help imagining how it would feel to wrap my legs around his slim frame, to run my hands down his back, and grip his butt, or to kiss him in the small space between his jaw and ear. I was so used to Jay's muscled frame that I found the idea of the Joshua's slimness exciting, if only in the contrast to Jay. Would he have any bedroom skills? Maybe.

The only way I can stand having sex with you is with the lights out for Christ's sake.

The happiness that had blossomed in my heart withered.

I stripped naked and stared in the mirror. Six months of working out to *Shaun T Hip-Hop Abs* had transformed my body. Look at me, Shaun T! Say, hey! I had a figure again. The *Brazilian Butt Lift* worked. I might not ever be model thin, but my stomach was flat and muffin top gone, leaving a curvy toned shape. Take that, Jay Braxton!

How old did I look? Could I pass for twenty-seven? Twenty-eight? Not in this town where I knew people, people who knew Haley and Jay, but what about strangers? Why not sell the house, move to a big city, and start over? I could be twenty-eight and no one would know. I could have a one-night stand with a twenty-five-year old hottie, and no one would know. I could experience the youth I'd never had with Jay.

I scrutinized the image in the mirror. Mrs. Braxton stared back at me.

Chapter 3

AT LAST, AN invitation! For years, Jay and I had been part of a group of friends consisting of four couples. Despite job changes, kids, and two of the couples moving out of Davis, we stayed close. When we were younger, we'd meet at someone's house, make popcorn, drink cheap booze, and play games or just talk and talk all night. As everyone became more affluent, our gatherings escalated to weekends in Carmel, wine tasting in Napa, trips to Tahoe, and the like.

I had barely spoken to any of the wives since Jay left. I wasn't sure if it was me or them. I didn't want to burden any of them with my perennial tears; nor did I want to be pitied or grilled on the mortifying particulars of Jay's exodus, so I didn't reach out. On the other hand, none of the women had called me either. I liked to think they thought I had a contagious disease—matrimonium morbis or something—and they were afraid their husbands would catch it. After not hearing from any of them for a good nine months, I couldn't stop my trembly heart from concluding they only had been friends with me by extension of Jay.

In any event, I was pleasantly surprised when I got a call from Carol. The men were headed to Oakland for an A's game, which meant the gals were free. She suggested we take the opportunity to celebrate my singlehood. My new status wasn't something I particularly wanted to whoop about, and Jay and I undoubtingly would be missing out on a couple's outing the next day but planning something for Jay and me separately was cheering. I hoped it meant our friendship could continue. Instead of couple events, it would be girls' nights.

So Friday night I drove Jay's beloved Porsche, my car now, across town to Carol's house, bolstered with the knowledge I had value as a friend without Jay. She greeted me at the door. One look at her khaki shorts, flip-flops and t-shirt, and I knew I'd over-dressed.

Her eyes scanned me over too. "Wow, Kimberly. You look great. Love the dress."

"Thank you, I just came from a dinner date," I fibbed, not wanting to admit I'd gussied up because I thought it would be more of a party, and there was a chance I might see Jay after the men returned from the game, which was also the reason I drove over in the Porsche.

I handed her the bowl in my hand.

"You shouldn't have but thank you. Your shrimp dip is divine." I smiled. She had always loved my cooking. "Paige and Liz are already here," she said, leading me to her kitchen.

I'd met them while Jay had attended law school. Carol and Paige had been in his class. Liz and I had been supportive spouses keeping our husbands pumped with caffeine, and paying bills, while they struggled through Torts and the California Bar.

"What can I get you? We have margaritas, vodka, wine—pick your poison."

"I'll start slow. How about a glass of wine?"

Carol's phone rang and she left me in her kitchen to get my own drink. Liz and Paige were already seated around a table on Carol's patio. I inwardly groaned. The temperature was ninety degrees despite the sun going down. Of course, she would want to show off her new pool and stone slab patio, which reminded me of half a dozen other backyards in the more exclusive Davis neighborhoods. Jay would agree it was attractive, but too generic for us.

But that was Carol. She went with the latest trends and her kitchen fell in line with modern grey cabinets and white quartz counters, a starkness and absolute absence of color that reminded me of an Apple store. As I reached for a wine glass, I could hear Paige's strident voice chatting away. In fairness, she didn't know I'd arrived. "Jay met her at some club. She was his cocktail waitress and apparently has big tits. So typical—I'm not surprised he walked out."

"Why?" Liz asked, "What do you mean?"

"Appearance is important to Jay, and Kimberly let herself go."

"Poor Kimberly."

Poor Kimberly. She let herself go, which inarguably justified her husband walking out on her so he could boink a cocktail waitress with big tits. I never thought the health of my marriage was dependent on the size of my waist.

The hell with the wine. I poured a margarita. Now, I was glad I'd worn my sexy red, spaghetti-strap dress. I looked forward to their jaws dropping.

"Hey, I see you decided to go for something a little stronger," Carol observed as she walked back in the kitchen.

"What the heck. We're having a celebration, right?"

"Absolutely. Come on, let's go outside."

Grabbing the pitcher of margaritas, I followed her. The shock on Paige's face was my revenge: surprise, disbelief, and yes, *envy*.

"Wow, Kimberly! You look fantastic. Turn around and let me see," Liz said.

Leave it to Liz to make my day. I loved Liz. Vain of me, terribly vain, but music to my ears. I put the pitcher down and did a quick spin.

"You've lost weight," Paige said surprised.

"Actually, I lost thirty pounds. So how is everyone?" I asked taking a seat.

Liz smiled sympathetically. "We're fine. The question is, *how are you?*"

"I'm great. I just nailed a new writing assignment."

"Oh? What is it?" Carol asked.

"A divorcee dating column for a new online magazine."

"Are you dating?" Why did even a simple question sound bitchy coming from Paige? At heart, she wasn't a bad person—there were times when I really liked her—but for some reason her question made me feel like I was being cross-examined.

I loathed lying, but I hated even more being judged as sad and pathetic while Jay was cavorting with a cocktail waitress. "Of course," I said, faking a laugh. "Why wouldn't I be?"

Liz squealed and asked, ready for a vicarious thrill, "Anyone in particular?"

Hmmm …. If I'm going to lie, I might as well invent someone drool worthy. "There's this med student I've been out with a few times."

Liz squealed a second time, "Ooh la la, a younger man. Love it! What's he look like?"

"He has blond hair and blue eyes like sea glass. And his body ... let's just say he can eat crackers in my bed anytime."

"What's his name?" Paige asked.

Dang! She didn't believe me. Knowing Paige, she'd check if my hot med student was enrolled at UCD. Why did I feel the need to lie to my friends? I was being adolescent. "I'd rather not say. I might write about him. No names, of course." I smiled and turned to Carol. "I love your pool! Which design company did you use?"

Hallelujah, the conversation jumped from my non-existent dating life to home improvements. Paige didn't get a chance to object, and by the end of my second margarita, we were laughing and dishing just as we always had. Then, the Jay subject came up.

"Jay's being an idiot," Carol stated firmly.

"Can you believe he claimed we had only been in puppy love?"

"What denial!" I appreciated the contempt in Paige's voice. "A man doesn't stay married as long as you two were because of puppy love."

Carol asked gingerly, "Yes, but didn't you get married because you were pregnant?"

Her question hit like a punch. What had Jay told her husband? "No, it was why we married so young, but Jay had given me a promise ring months before. He loved me pregnant. He'd walk me to class with his arm around me, so proud to be a procreator."

Liz tittered. "Sounds like Jay."

"It wasn't all show." We'd talk for hours with his head on my breasts. I'd run my hand through his hair, and he would run his hand over my stomach. "He wanted us to be a family."

"He did love you." Liz sighed. "I used to envy the way he'd gaze at you. You seemed like the perfect couple."

I thought we were too. How many times had he told me he loved me? Multiple times a day for years and a minimum of once a day for the last few years of our marriage meant at least ten thousand I love yous had passed his lips. Ten thousand I love yous counted for something.

Tears pooled at the edge of my eyes, and I blinked quickly, trying to push them back.

Carol handed me a tissue and put her arm around my shoulder, giving me a quick squeeze. "You're entitled to a few tears."

"Jay's just going through a mid-life crisis." Paige wasn't so bad. "He bought a fifty-thousand-dollar Camaro. Can you believe?"

"I can't believe he's taking Amber wine tasting with us tomorrow," Liz grumbled.

Whoa. Back up. "Jay's taking *who* wine tasting with *whom?*"

Liz paled. "I'm sorry. I assumed you knew. Carol, you told her, right?"

Carol hissed at Liz, "Why would I tell her?"

"Are all of you going to Napa tomorrow with Jay and his cocktail waitress?" None of them answered. I stared at their guilty faces. There definitely would be a couples outing. *Wow, I mean, just wow.* "I see." No one said anything. What more was there to say? Sobering instantly, survival mode kicked in. "Well, it's getting late." I faked a yawn. "I should go."

"Kimberly, Jay's our friend too," Paige tried to explain.

"Sure, of course." *Kimberly is out and the cocktail waitress is in. I get it.* I pushed away from the table, picked up my purse, and forced my lips to smile. "Thank you for the drinks, Carol. I hope you ladies have a lovely time tomorrow. The weather should be perfect."

Their pinched and strained expressions told me they were all holding their breath, waiting for me to leave; waiting to heave a sigh of relief that I was gone, their duty done, and they'd be free to dissect everything I'd said, the tears I'd shed, and how I'd exited from their lives. I walked out with as much dignity as I could muster, only stopping to collect my bright orange Bauer bowl that sat empty, looking out of place in the colorless kitchen.

Dazed, I slid into the Porsche, started the engine, and headed home, guided by a blur of streetlights through the darkness. I had years of memories with those couples. I'd considered the women close friends—not that I spent a great deal of time with them, but whenever I did see them, it was easy and comfortable. Now I was divorced from the pack, but Jay wasn't. How had that been decided? Flip of a coin or a group vote? A stop light loomed ahead. I very consciously took my foot off the gas and eased to a stop. Despite the shock, I was remarkably calm. Maybe my heart had been shattered in so many pieces that there was nothing left to break.

Nugget Market came up on my left. Something inside of me snapped, and I flipped on the turn signal and pulled into the parking lot. Out of habit, I parked the longest distance possible from the entrance of the store. It was one of my calorie burning techniques.

A few minutes later, I peeked at the checkout stands. He was there, checking opposite the pet food aisle. I quickly threw some things in my cart and purposely wheeled to the cat food section last. I tossed in a few cans of Friskies even though a month's supply sat in my garage.

When I emerged from the aisle—what a coincidence—he was right in front of me, and he only had one customer in his lane. An incoming cart appeared on my left. I cut her off, cringing at my rudeness, but if I let her go first, I'd be expected to go to another line.

Please be happy to see me. He turned his head toward me. His eyes widened and then his face broke into a huge hey-it's-you smile.

"Hey, you're shopping late."

"I guess I am."

He gave me an appreciative once over. The unmistakable admiration in his eyes warmed me. "Like the dress. Were you at a party?"

If he only knew what kind of party. "Yeah, a friend of mine had a little margarita party."

"Sounds like fun."

"It was."

"Guess what I did this week?"

"You got a haircut?"

He colored, obviously pleased I had noticed. "That too." He ran his hand through his hair. "Too short?"

I liked the way his hair used to flop in front of his eyes, and he'd shake it back, but the shorter cut made him appear more mature, more hot than cute. "No, your hair looks great."

"Thanks. I was shooting for a more professional image."

"It works. So, tell me what you did."

"Oh, I applied for two management training programs."

"Joshua, that's wonderful!"

"You know my name?" He seemed so astonished and pleased.

I couldn't help laughing. "It's on your name tag."

His cheeks instantly flushed. "Right. Of course."

"By the way, I'm Kimberly."

"Nice to meet you, Kimberly." Something about the way he said *Kimberly* made my heart jump. We both laughed, and he finished bagging my groceries.

I boldly asked, "Are you going to walk me out?"

He grinned, glanced at his nonexistent line, and turned off the light. "Lead the way."

The store was about to close, so the parking lot was dark and almost empty. Joshua usually walked briskly, but tonight he took his time strolling me to my car. It had been a scorching day and heat from the asphalt swept up my legs, making my skin sticky. I desperately hoped my deodorant was holding up.

"What management training programs did you apply for?"

"Macy's and a Bay Area grocery chain."

"I didn't realize Macy's had a program."

"I didn't either until I checked out at the campus career center. You know, talking to you changed my perspective. I realized there are a lot of things I can do."

He was so young. I needed to stop viewing him sexually.

I opened my trunk, and we both grabbed a bag of groceries. Our arms rubbed when we simultaneously bent into the trunk. I glanced over and his face turned toward mine. Just like a movie running in slow motion, time suspended as our eyes met.

"You smell good," he whispered.

"I'm wearing Chanel."

We were frozen, leaning in the trunk, close enough I could hear him breathing. His face somehow got closer. Then I did it. I kissed him. He kissed me back. His lips were warm, and heat flashed through my body as our tongues entangled for a few glorious seconds.

What am I doing! I jerked back. His head sprang up, hitting the trunk hood.

"Oh my God." I asked, "Are you okay?"

I wasn't sure if he was more stunned by knocking his head or the kiss. He rubbed the back of his head. "I'm uh, I'm fine. Kimberly—"

"I have to go."

I raced into the driver's seat and started the engine. He wheeled the cart out of my way, and I backed out. Through the rearview mirror, I could see him watching me as I drove away.

I had officially lost my mind. I'd kissed a checkout boy in the parking lot. Was I crazy?

Worst of all, Jay really, truly wasn't coming back. He was taking his girlfriend wine tasting with our friends—my God, our friends. He'd publicly—humiliatingly—replaced me. For weeks, I'd told myself he wasn't coming back, but deep down I hadn't believed it. Reality slammed through my chest, and the remnants of my heart shattered into even smaller pieces.

Somehow, I managed to drive home through my waterworks. I grabbed my purse and stumbled into the house. What now? What the hell was left for me now? I couldn't shop at Nugget anymore. My friends turned out to be Jay's friends. I was the hanger-on who could easily be replaced. Collapsing into a chair, the tears fell harder. Maybe it would make it easier on everyone if I didn't exist ... if I went *poof* and was gone.

Oh hell, I'd never kill myself. Haley would miss me. Who would feed the cats?

I had to talk to someone. I called the one person who was always there for me. She'd been with me when I was seventeen and took a pregnancy test. She stood by my side when Jay and I had exchanged vows. She'd been there when Haley was born, and when Jay and I had had our nastiest fights. I needed my friend. Although late, she'd be up.

"I'm in a club. Can't hear a thing," she said. "Call you right back."

Of course, Valerie was in a club. She wasn't married, lived in L.A., and was a celebrity stylist. She didn't take drugs or drink excessively, but she considered it part of her business to keep up with the club scene. A few minutes later, she called back.

"What's going on? Why are you calling this late?"

"Jay's taking his girlfriend on a couples' outing with our friends."

"Asshole. Jay has a girlfriend?"

"Apparently, and he bought a fifty-thousand-dollar Camaro."

"You have got to be shitting me! What an idiot."

"It gets worse. Tonight I kissed a Nugget checkout boy in the store parking lot."

She laughed, so I did too. "How old is he?"

"I'm guessing twenty-three."

"Then he's legal. Don't beat yourself up."

"Val, he isn't coming back. I loved him so much, and I've been waiting for him to get things out of his system. Now, I know he won't and I ... I ... I feel so alone and lost ... oh, Val ..." I couldn't talk and swiped at the snot running out of my nose. I took a deep breath. "I'm sorry. Shit. I think I'm going crazy."

"You are not crazy, and you'll get through this. Now, I want you to put on your pajamas, pour a glass of wine, and watch the funniest, most ridiculous movie you have, okay?"

"Okay."

"I'm taking the first flight I can book to Sacramento tomorrow. Just stay away from those checker boys until I get there."

I chuckled. "Okay." I could make it through the night by myself.

Chapter 4

*T*RY AS I might to follow Val's advice, I didn't have the focus for a movie. Had I imagined how much Jay and I had been in love in high school? I had never questioned that we would have married even if I hadn't been pregnant. It was only a question of when, but maybe Carol had been right. Maybe I had an idealized recollection of our relationship. Maybe Jay had the better memory. I had no idea what enlightenment or assurance I'd find, but I went to the garage and dug out my old scrapbook from a dusty box. It chronicled the golden summer Jay and I had fallen in love.

The first page had "before" and "after" pictures of me. I'd been a text-book geek in high school. My blonde hair had been too curly, and I'd had braces. Even better, I'd sported a pair of cats-eye glasses—not because I needed them, but because I was convinced they counteracted the blue-eyed-blond stereotype.

For some reason, Valerie Sturgis befriended me at the end of my sophomore year. Val had been popular, but in a good "Everyone Loves Val" way. School had been out for the summer about a week when she'd called, wanting to give me a make-over. The next night she had bleached, plucked, or waxed all the hair on my body and taught me the proper way to apply make-up. After that night, we were BFFs.

I flipped the page of the scrapbook and stared at a picture of Jay and me at Stinson Beach. Val had taken the picture a few days after she'd given me the makeover. I couldn't remember the particulars about anyone other than Jay, but I had a very clear memory of him. I had been bending over, shoving clothes into my beach bag when I'd heard his voice.

"Hey, Val, who's your friend?" Jay asked.

"You know Kimberly," she answered.

Great. Jay Braxton would walk up when I was bent over with my butt sticking up. I spun around. Having just come out of the water, his tan chest glistened, and his usually neat black hair was a tangle of sea-salt-matted locks. He grinned and looked like a toothpaste ad with his dimples and white teeth practically glowing in the sun.

He tilted his head with a twinkle in his eyes. "I didn't recognize you without your clothes," he teased, making my cheeks flame. "Hey, wanna grab a beer with me?"

I glanced at Valerie, unsure what to do. She smiled, quite pleased, and whispered, "Go."

I'd never drunk alcohol before, but I took a can of Bud from him and pretended to like it.

"Did you do something to your hair?" he asked as we strolled away from the crowd.

"Valerie highlighted it for me. Did you really not recognize me?"

He laughed. "Nah, I was just teasing. I was surprised to see you though. I thought you spent your weekends working math puzzles and reading."

I giggled. "I like to have fun."

"That's good. I hate to think you're serious all the time. Hey, how come you won't talk to me in class? Afraid talking to a jock will ruin your smart girl reputation?" Of course, we both knew he was no academic slouch.

"I'm talking to you now," I said, smiling confidently.

"Yeah, that's probably because none of your smart friends are watching."

I teased back, "True, I do have a reputation to maintain."

"Hey, you got your braces off."

"Oh, yeah." I ran my tongue over my teeth, still unused to the smoothness. "I got them off a few days ago."

He turned to face me. "Let me see. Smile again." I smiled and ours eyes connected, really connected. My stomach whooshed and my knees threatened to buckle. "I've always thought you were pretty, but without your braces and glasses you're like … wow."

Hearing his compliment made me feel like Cinderella at the ball. He offered me another beer. I drank it, laughing with him. Then, my teeth numbed, the sand moved under my feet, and my body wobbled.

"Hey Kimberly, what's wrong?"

I fessed up. "I've never drunk beer before." I hiccupped. "I don't feel good and I'm dizzy." I started to cry. "I'm sorry."

"Hey, hey, don't cry. Come on, I'll take care of you."

He walked me away from the crowd, found us a spot to sit down, and put his arm around me. He smelled like an ocean breeze, and I snuggled against his solid chest. The soothing sound of waves breaking on the shore competed with voices and laughter from the party, but soon Jay's heartbeat drowned out everything else.

I woke up about an hour later, mortified, having completely embarrassed myself in front of Jay Braxton. He arranged for someone else to drive his car and insisted on driving Valarie and me home in my car. Jay dropped Val first and then asked directions to my house. He pulled over when we were a block away.

"It probably wouldn't be cool for your parents to see me drive you home. Think you can handle it from here?"

My parents would freak, especially my dad. He'd bought me the brand spanking new Honda Civic for my sixteenth birthday and given specific instructions about boys and alcohol. Besides, Jay was our school's star quarterback. My dad put football players in the same category as boys who had tattoos and rode motorcycles. As a surgeon, he'd witnessed too many tragedies in emergency surgeries to trust his daughter with young men who he considered indulged in reckless behavior.

"I'll be okay, but how will you get home?"

"I'll walk. It's no big deal."

"Okay. Well, it was super nice of you to drive me. I'm sorry I ruined the party for you."

"Nah, you didn't. I liked hanging out with you." He leaned over and gave me a sweet kiss—no tongue, only warm, soft lips pressing tentatively against mine. His gentle touch sent delicious tingles through my body that were absolutely electrifying. When he pulled back, a shy smile lit his face. "I've wanted to kiss you all day."

I couldn't believe Jay Braxton kissed me ... me, Kimberly Kirby. I'd always thought him out of my league, so never considered liking him, but now I knew he liked me. Enveloped in a warm, heady glow, I was afraid of saying something stupid, so I grinned and said nothing.

He took my hand and played with it before he asked, "Is it okay if I call you tomorrow?"

Halfway through that magical summer, Jay confessed he'd had a crush on me since seventh grade and claimed to have fallen in love with me while I slept leaning against him on the beach that day. By the end of the summer, I had fallen wildly in love with him, too. My life had seemed perfect—our love had felt perfect—and I'd thought the only thing I needed in life to be perfectly happy was to spend the rest of my life with Jay.

I closed the scrapbook. As all-consuming as my love for him had felt, maybe it had been puppy love. If I hadn't gotten pregnant, maybe our love would have died quickly after high school. I would have gone to Bryn Mawr or Vassar, possibly Smith, and he would have headed to a Southern California school. I could have fallen in love with someone else ... married someone else. Who's to say what could have happened. The one certainty I had was that I wasn't crazy. Puppy love or not, our love had been real, and it had been intense.

⌒

"Valerie, over here!" I called and waved my arm. Valerie pushed up her Versace sunglasses and waved back. Tall and slender, she could pass as a runway model with her Pucci print dress and white Gucci sandals—way too chic for the Sacramento International Airport. She only was supposed to stay a couple nights, but she dragged a huge Louis Vuitton suitcase behind her.

She gave me a quick hug. "You look fantastic!"

"Thanks. Jeez, Val, how long you planning to stay?"

"Two nights, but I brought you some things." She laughed when I opened my trunk and asked suspiciously, "Did you go grocery shopping this morning?"

"Shoot. I forgot to unload the groceries last night. Told you I was going crazy." I wedged the grocery bags into the tiny backseat and heaved her luggage into the trunk.

As soon as we got in the car, Valerie turned to me. "So, how was it?"

"How was what?"

"The kiss! Kissing Checker Boy."

"Mmmm … nice."

"Just nice? Was there any tongue action?"

Even though Valerie was my best friend, I still blushed. "Yes, there was 'tongue action.' It didn't last long, but long enough to know he's a good kiss-er—I mean *really* good."

"Are you going to see him again?"

"No. He's probably fourteen years younger than me, for heaven's sake."

"Don't let the age difference stop you. The whole cougar thing is hot."

"Aren't I too young to be a cougar?"

"Technically, you're a puma. You're not a cougar until you hit forty."

"Great. I'm a *puma*. I feel so much better. Honestly, I don't even know if he would want to see me. It's not as if we were on a date. I kissed him when he was helping me load groceries into the trunk."

"Oh baby, we have got to get you laid."

"I'm ready to hire a gigolo just so I can get it over with."

Valerie snorted.

"You think I'm joking? I'm not. Something inside of me snapped last night. I think it's why I kissed Joshua." I reached over and squeezed her hand. "I'm so glad you're here. I need to figure out what's next." My voice cracked and hot tears pricked my eyes.

"You will, but you seem tired."

"I am. Couldn't sleep again last night."

"Let's go get one of those yummy crepes from the place by the park; then you can take a nap. You'll feel better after you catch up on some sleep."

———

Despite Farmer's Market being in full swing across the street, we got lucky with a parking spot right in front of Crepeville. The ultra-casual vibe of the restaurant eased my tension, and my basil crepe tasted especially good with Valerie keeping me company. She always had a way of making me feel better.

Eating also made me feel better, but I'd worked too hard to get back in shape to blow it on a depressive eating binge. I pushed my plate aside.

Valerie eyed my leftovers. "Are you going to eat those potatoes?"

"I thought no one from L.A. ate carbs. Last time you were here, you wouldn't eat bread."

"New diet. I eat carbs until noon and then not for the rest of the day."

I glanced at my watch. "You have ten minutes."

As I slid over the plate, my eye caught a glimpse of a slim muscular body passing the window, and he was holding hands with a girl. I hated the jealousy heating my face.

Valerie noticed my flushed cheeks and raised her brows. "What's going on?"

"Nothing. Just thought I saw someone I know, but it wasn't him."

"Who him? Jay?"

"No. No one you know. Let's go."

We got up to leave, and I sidestepped to avoid colliding into Joshua and the girl, who were now in the restaurant. I kept my head down. At the last second, I snuck a peek and our eyes met. His eyes widened and his face froze midway to a smile. I kept going.

"Who was that?" Valerie asked as we walked out the door.

"Checker Boy," I whispered.

She twisted to turn around. I grabbed her arm. "Will you please not stare?"

"He has a nice butt."

"Come, on," I groaned and bee-lined for the car.

As I unlocked the door, Joshua called, "Hey, Kimberly? Can we talk a sec?" He was striding toward me and his voice came out slightly high-pitched. The poor guy's face was red.

Valerie smirked, but she got into the car and shut the door. I stepped back onto the sidewalk and gazed up at him.

Keeping his voice low he said, "I ... I want to apologize. I had no right to kiss you. You smelled so good and you were right there. Anyway, thanks for not slapping my face."

He thought he initiated the kiss? Maybe he had. "You have no reason to apologize."

"Thank you. I've been worried you'd complain to my manager."

I smiled reassuringly at him. "It'll be our secret."

"Awesome." Happiness washed over his face and he grinned. "Would you like … well, I was hoping …." He stared questioningly at me with those big eyes of his.

My stomach tingled and warmed up to *whoosh.* Then my eye caught his girl watching us through the window of the restaurant. Her brow was creased. She was a beautiful girl, in a very wholesome, all-American sort of way. I was sure she was a nice person. I looked down and saw Joshua sported a pair of bright yellow Converse covered with Manga drawings. Haley would consider them "hella dope." *Shame, shame, shame on me.*

"Is she your girlfriend?"

He colored again and shoved his hands in his pockets. "Not exactly. I've hung out with her a few times, but she's not an official girlfriend."

Bet the girl didn't view herself as "not exactly" a girlfriend, officially or otherwise. "Well, she's waiting for you and my friend is waiting for me … so …."

"Right. Yeah, so I'll see you at the store?"

"Sure, I'll see you around."

He opened his mouth, but nothing came out. Ultimately, he nodded and turned around with the girl still watching. I got into the car, started the engine, and pulled out.

Valerie gave me a minute before she said, "He's a cutie—slim, but nice Y-shape bod and a good height. I'm guessing six feet."

"Mm-hmm."

"I liked his kicks, shows some fashion daring."

I glanced at her and rolled my eyes. Grown men do not wear florescent sneakers. Jay would snigger if he saw them.

"He'd do you."

"Val! He has a girlfriend. Besides, how would you know? You don't even know him."

"His body language told me everything I need to know." She snickered and teased, "That boy pitched a tent for you. You should go for it."

"No, I shouldn't. He's too young. I wouldn't want to hurt him or his girlfriend."

"You're right. What you need is a *man.*"

"Yep, I do." I shook my head, trying to clear it. "I feel like I need to bust loose and do something crazy ... something fun ... something I've never done before."

"Good. I'm taking you out tonight."

"Hate to disappoint you, but the only places I know of are The Grad if you want to hang out with college kids or a wine bar us Davis moms like."

"No worries. I found a club in Sacramento. And before you say anything, I brought club clothes for you, so no arguments."

When she used that tone, I didn't dare object.

Chapter 5

*M*Y DIGITAL CLOCK said six. The last time I'd checked, it had said three. No wonder I was groggy and disoriented. A part of me wished I had never woken up. After Haley had left for college, there had been a lot of days when I contemplated never getting out of bed. I hadn't had the energy or the desire to do anything. Thank God I'd had deadlines to meet. I'd rather force myself to face another day than risk Wendy's wrath for missing a deadline. That and fear of being eaten by my cats had motivated me to at least get up and feed them. Even so, I'd spent a large portion of those days in bed. For months, I only got dressed when I ran out of wine or ice cream and had to go to the store.

The cologne incident had shaken me out of complete lethargy. After he'd left that day, I'd taken a hard look in the mirror. The image staring back had looked like one of those photos flashed on the internet of stars of yesteryear that make you gasp with horror and pity, not believing this was a gorgeous starlet only a few years ago. My face had been pudgy and bloated, my skin sallow, my clothes were too tight, I needed a haircut—in short, I'd looked like hell. Why would Jay want me? Why would anyone want me?

That night I'd vowed that even if I felt like crap on the inside, my outward appearance wouldn't show it. Maybe if I worked on my outward appearance, my insides would catch up. Maybe the next time Jay saw me, he would think twice about who he was giving up. Six months of religiously working out to transform my body, for what purpose? I was still divorced, Jay had moved on to someone else without ever seeing the new me, and it was still hard to get out of bed.

I thought about trying to go back to sleep, but I'd neglected my guest long enough. The good hostess in me sat up and planted feet on the ground. I went to the kitchen, poured two tall glasses of iced tea, and found Val reading on the patio.

"Hey, Sleepyhead," she said, putting her book down. "I was wondering if I should wake you. Do you crash like this often?"

"Told you I've had a hard time sleeping. Every few days my sleep deficit catches up with me." I handed her a glass and sat down in the lounge chair next to her.

She took a sip. "Mmmm, that's good. Peach mint?"

"Yep, it's my new diet drink, zero calories and no fizzies to bloat my tum."

She laughed. "Well, you seriously look great. You should have men lining up."

They hadn't so far. What if I simply wasn't desirable anymore? If whatever I'd *had*, I'd lost, and no amount of weight loss could bring back? "I think my prime has passed."

"Are you kidding? Even at your heaviest, you were always beautiful. These days you're back to being a knockout. Think about it. You sure turned on Checker Boy."

"I guess." Joshua was a cutie, but maybe he had a thing for older women? "I haven't seen Jay in six months ... wonder what he'd think?"

"Who cares? Your weight wasn't the reason he left."

"I know it's more complicated, but at least it's something to point to. I hated him being so worried about appearances: the house, the cars, dressing well."

"Okay, pot. You're a bit of a perfectionist yourself."

I frowned, taken aback. "What are you talking about?"

"I've never seen your house a mess."

"Pshaw," I joked. "You weren't here six months ago. And so what if I like a clean house? For Jay, it goes deeper."

"Trying to prove something to your dad?"

"Or himself, but all that was years ago."

"Debatable, but that's another topic," she said, dodging what could be an all-night discussion. "Honestly, did you really not see it coming?"

Tears crept into my eyes. *No more tears.* I swallowed hard. "Now I see all the clues, but I swear I didn't at the time. I'd thought he was still mourning. His mom had been so young and vibrant. Perfectly fine one day and dying of a heart attack the next. It was such a shock."

"Sure as hell was." Val took a sip of her tea.

"Did you know, I never saw Jay cry? He just clammed up and walked around in a daze."

"You were just as out of it for a while after she died, too. Maybe that's why you didn't see it coming?"

"Possibly, but now, he's having the time of his life, and everything's changed. I mean everything—the way I sleep, my daily routine, friends, my relationship with Haley—everything. It's like living in this surreal alternate reality. All I want is to feel normal."

"I don't think you will until you let go." Val reached over and squeezed my hand.

"I'm ready. I meant it when I said something finally snapped. I'm tired of having my life on hold. I want to start living again, and I want to get laid."

Valerie whooped. "That's my girl."

I lifted my sluggish body out of the chair. "Let's have some fun."

"You're going to love what I brought." Her devilish grin scared me. Val had studied and worked hard, paying her dues to build her reputation and celebrity client list. A perk was being sent clothes gratis from up-and-coming designers and picking up discards from various sources.

While she unloaded her suitcase, I cranked up the stereo and opened a bottle of Chardonnay. It had been years since she'd used me as her Barbie Doll. I walked into my bedroom expecting to see something edgy, but what Valerie held up dropped my jaw.

"What are those?"

"A failed Japanese trend: thong jeans. Some people call them bikini jeans."

Held up by ties at the hip, like a string bikini, the pants were essentially a denim bikini bottom sewn onto a pair of jeans which had been cut off two inches above the crotch.

"Unbelievable. Who actually wears them?"

"Skinny bitches who want to get laid." Valerie snickered. She tossed me the jeans and a midriff top. "Here try this with it. I brought my camera."

"Okay, but no posting online. Which shoes should I try with them?"

She handed me a pair of three-inch high wedge sandals. "I have everything laid out by outfits. Where do you want to have your fashion show?"

The living room had better lighting, since it faced south, but was in the front of the house. The family room windows faced the backyard. "Family room."

I needed a dose of liquid courage before trying the thong jeans. My first choice was a pair of leggings, over-the-knee high-heeled suede boots, a billowing gauze shirt, and a wide hip belt. As Valerie instructed, I kept the shirt unbuttoned halfway down the front.

Doing my best attempt at a catwalk strut, I made my entrance.

Valerie whistled. "I like it!"

"Actually, I do too. If I swapped out the pirate shirt for a black turtle-neck, it would make a great Cat Woman costume for Halloween." I clawed the air. "Meow."

"Oh, stop it. Seriously, it's a perfect outfit for hanging out in San Francisco."

"Yeah, for all the times I'm hangin' in the City." I giggled, struck a couple silly poses and let her snap my picture.

A glass of wine and a pile of clothes later, I wiggled into the thong jeans and tied the strings. They were debauched and licentious, but sexy. I could give Jay's girlfriend a run for her money. All I needed was a belly ring and a tattoo slapped on the small of my back.

I shouted, "I'm ready to be sexy!"

The stereo blared out, "Are you feeling seeexxxyyyy? … That's right, Mama … Do that strut, shake that butt … uh huh, uh huh …" Swaying my hips in time with music, I sashayed into the family room.

Valerie whooped and got up to dance with me. I cranked up the stereo even louder and we sang at the top of our lungs, "Do that strut, shake that butt … uh huh, uh huh …." Shaking my booty with joyous abandon, I let loose for the first time in over a year.

The song ended and was replaced by clapping hands and a deep masculine laugh filling the room. All the joy flew out of me along with the air in my lungs. Jay stood in the exact same spot, grinning exactly as he had the last time Valerie and I had played dress up. He looked the same too, handsome as ever with his toothpaste ad smile. While I stared at him absolutely paralyzed, unable to speak or move, Valerie turned off the stereo. Part of me wanted to run my hands up his chest, touch his face, and make sure he was real, while another part, a dominant part, wanted to scream at him to get out of my house.

Once my heart started beating again, I found my voice. "This isn't your house anymore. You can't just walk in."

His smile slipped. "Sorry, I did knock. I heard the music and you two singing … door was unlocked, so … yeah." He smiled uneasily at Valerie. "Hey, Val. How've you been?"

"Alright. Yourself?"

"I've been great."

"Sorry to hear it." Valerie's glare matched her glacial tone.

Jay had the decency to appear ashamed. "Can I have a minute alone with Kim?"

She raised her brows at me, and I nodded. Walking out, she threw Jay a parting sneer. I loved Val. Even though she and Jay had been pals longer, she was unshakably loyal to me.

He peeked over his shoulder toward the hallway and dropped his voice to almost a whisper. "Paige told me you were pretty upset last night."

I didn't care if Valarie heard us and asked louder than necessary, "Like you care?"

"Come on, Kimmy. Of course I still care about you."

"You *care* about me? What the hell does that mean?"

"It means I was worried about you. I didn't want to hurt you more than I already have."

"Then why would you take your little girlfriend wine tasting with our friends?"

"She's not my girlfriend. It was only a date. I didn't think it was a big deal."

Only a date? Not a big deal? How clueless could he possibly be? "Whatever. I don't need your shoulder to cry on, and I sure as hell don't need your pity." I threw up my hands. "As you can see, I'm fine."

He scanned over my body. "You look …." He swallowed. "Wow."

His eyes did their droopy, sleepy turned-on thing. His reaction was what I'd worked for when I'd crunched my abs. I couldn't resist a little revenge and rubbed my hand over my flat stomach, knowing it would push his buttons in more ways than one. "Val and I are going to a club tonight."

His jaw twitched. "You're not going out dressed like that, are you?"

I smiled. "You're not the only one who's single."

He let out a loud grunt. "I didn't come here to fight. This last year has been hard on both of us." He paused. For the first time since he walked out, I saw pain in his eyes. It gave me no pleasure to see, but at least I knew he had some grief for the life we'd shared. "I was hoping now that our divorce is final, we can be friends."

Oh hell and no. I shook my head. "No, oh no."

"Why not? What's so bad about being friends?"

"Lest you've forgotten, we did not consciously uncouple. You walked out with no warning! You knew how to hurt me more than anyone else in the world and you did it. You god damn did it, Jay, and you've never apologized. So no, you are not my friend."

"I'm sorry. I didn't mean everything I said. You were clinging to me. I was trying to get you to let me go. I had to leave."

"Why? Why did you have to? You've never explained a damn thing!"

"I can't explain, but I really am sorry. It kills me knowing how much I hurt you."

"Right." I turned to walk out of the room. He grabbed my arm.

"*Kimmy*, I *am* sorry, and I'd like us to be friends."

He was sincere, but he confused me. I jerked my arm away. "Why now?"

"We're divorced now. I didn't want to give you the wrong impression before. Just because I don't want to be married, doesn't mean I don't want you in my life."

Was he insane? I couldn't believe what he was asking. "So what? You want to have brunch on Sundays and compare notes on the hotness of our Saturday night dates?"

"You know that's not what I mean. I miss talking to you sometimes. I don't know, I was hoping we could all have dinner together when Haley is in town."

"I see. You want the freedom to sleep around, but you miss a home cooked meal and a sympathetic ear from good old Kimmy, that it?"

"You know what? Forget it. You're still too pissed off."

"Don't you think I have a right to be?"

He heaved a sigh and said with an anguished voice, "I know I handled things badly, and I truly am sorry. I'd hoped you'd forgiven me at least a little bit."

The anger boiling inside of me cooled to a simmer. I softened my tone. "You were my first love. You'll always be a part of me, but we can't be friends."

"It's too soon, isn't it?"

"No, it's too late. I'm not blindly in love with you anymore. The Jay I loved wouldn't have done the things you've done. I honestly don't know who you are anymore."

He winced and shook his head. "Guess I'll go then."

When he reached the front door, I stopped him. I had to know the truth. "Hey, I need to ask you something, and I hope you'll be honest."

"What do you want to know?"

"Did you cheat on me?"

"No, but it got to a point where I thought about it. I'm sorry."

What did he mean? Had he already met someone? Or had he wanted the freedom to explore? Either way, he'd stopped loving me, wanting to be with me. I'd heard enough.

"Thank you for being honest."

"You'd know if I was lying. I haven't changed that much," he said defiantly. "Will you be honest with me too?"

What did he think I'd done? I shrugged. "Sure."

He frowned. "Are you really wearing that outfit tonight?"

How ludicrous to ask something so inconsequential. I shook my head and shut the door.

Chapter 6

*A*PPRAISING THE LINE at Club Violet, my legs wobbled mutinously, my antiperspirant broke ranks, and my courage retreated. The girls, and they were *girls*, all looked so nubile in their flesh-revealing minis and stilettos. How was I supposed to compete with them? No man would be interested in me with all the little chickadees strutting around in their mate-with-me-now attire. I left the house feeling sophisticated and flirty in the Dolce & Gabbana summer dress Valerie had picked out, but now I felt matronly. Maybe I should have worn the bikini jeans.

Besides, no one appeared much older than twenty-five, too young of a crowd for me, and there had to be at least fifty people in front of us.

"Val, maybe we should forget it and go home."

Her face scrunched with exasperation and determination. "Okay, this place isn't what I expected, but we're here and you said you wanted to try something new."

I pointed to a huge guy with a shaved head and burly arms covered with tattoos. "He's only letting in cute young things with lots of cleavage. We're not getting in."

"Kimberly, you look great and we'll get in."

I stumbled after her as she strode up to the bouncer. I stopped her steps before she reached him. "Aren't we being rude trying to cut ahead?"

"No. This is how to get into clubs. When we get to the bouncer, smile. Got it?" I didn't seem to have a choice. On cue, I smiled, and Valerie asked, "How long is the wait?"

"Could be an hour. We're at capacity. No one goes in until someone comes out."

Valerie shook his hand. "Thanks for letting us know."

A group of four walked out. The bouncer glanced at his hand and grinned. He pointed his finger at Valerie and then jutted his thumb toward the door. "You two have fun."

"That's the plan. Thanks," she said as we walked through the entrance.

I was impressed. "What did you do?"

"It wasn't me. It was your smile."

"Come on …."

"I slipped him a fifty."

Club Violet was an apropos name; the back wall of the circular main bar glowed with backlit amethyst light and the bar stools were covered with purple zebra stripes. I hadn't been in very many bars, let alone nightclubs; Jay and I had been too broke to go out when we were younger. Funny, clubbing never seemed the thing with a daughter at home. I never thought I'd missed out, but gazing around, I began to think I had.

Bodies gyrating and swaying with the music packed the dance floor. No one seemed to have a particular partner. It was free for all. Groups huddled around tables and the bar, with girls laughing and guys flirting. Not all the men were eye-catching. Not all the women were beautiful. Still, there was plenty to attract.

The energy of the room and music coming from all sides pulsed through me. Thump, thump, thump. Fun, fun, fun. The beat of the club was I'm-here-to-have-fun. More than fun. Sex, sex, sex. I'm-here-to-find-sex. Mating rituals were at play everywhere. Women were dressed to arouse. Men puffed their muscles to impress. Bodies moved to entice, and the air hung thick with pheromones.

Valerie nudged me. "Let's get a drink." I followed her to the bar and ordered a glass of wine, but Valerie vetoed my order. She bought us each an appletini.

Taking a sip, the liquor burned as it made its way down my throat. I shuddered when it dropped and made a warm splash in my stomach.

Val lifted her glass. "What do you think?"

"Delicious." I wasn't talking about the drink.

My eyes were drawn to a table with four men crammed around it. They were very male, probably in their early to mid-thirties, and there was nothing boyish about them. I wasn't sure who was hotter: the blond with short hair, a soul patch, and bulging biceps or the dark-haired guy with a day's growth of whiskers on his face. His biceps weren't lacking either. Both were sexy as sin, but I leaned toward the dark-haired guy. There was definitely something about him. I hoped drool wasn't running down my chin. I took a bigger sip.

"Now what?" I asked.

"Cruise and check out the place."

Valerie moved us toward an exit leading to other areas of the club. We passed the table with the sexy men, and I snuck another peek at the ruggedly handsome, dark-haired guy. He caught me gawking and winked. I quickly diverted my eyes and caught up with Valerie.

There were three dance floors, each with a different style of music: hip-hop, contemporary pop, and retro, where they played dance music from the 1980s-1990s. A sizable patio in the back was lit with string lights and had a fire pit, but instead of a fire, the center of the pit flickered with multiple color changing neon tongues. Most amazing were the day beds with canopies arranged around the perimeter of the courtyard. Gauzy white curtains were held in place by a tie on each corner posts of the beds. Men and women lounged on them laughing and talking. One couple groped and made out as if they were in the privacy of their own bedroom, not even bothering to close the curtains. I had an image of a spontaneous orgy rivaling the antics of the ancient Romans.

Valerie and I got another drink and went to the retro room. After the second appletini warmed its way through my system, I was buzzed and ready to dance. Like a sign from God, Eurythmics' *I Need A Man* blared through the room. Valerie and I grinned at each other and headed to the dance floor. Next, *Love Shack* kept me moving. I lost Valerie, having been separated by the crowd. I was about to leave the floor to search for her when a hand touched my arm. I turned and faced a cute guy with wavy blonde hair and a wide smile.

"Dance with me?" he mouthed. He must have used his vocal cords, but I couldn't hear him over the music. He had the sweetest expression.

Without a word, we danced. He was a playful partner and a good dancer. Dang, he had a great smile. He seemed familiar, but I couldn't place him. Although, he was too old to be a college student, he could have gone to UCD. I could've seen him around town.

Sexy dark-haired guy made his way into the room. He was watching me and in response, I swirled my hips in what I hoped was liquid fluidity before turning my attention back to my dance partner.

Sweat dripped from my partner's brow, and he wiped his forehead with the back of his arm. Leaning toward me, he shouted over the music. "Want a drink?"

I nodded and followed him. I wasn't sure what the rules were regarding the acceptance of a drink, but it seemed safe. I wasn't getting any weird vibes and, *dang*, I loved his smile.

"My name's Kimberly. What's yours?" I asked when we reached the bar.

He blinked a few times and chuckled. I had no idea what was so amusing about asking his name. Had I made some clubbing faux pas? "I'm Bill. What can I get you?"

Never mix, never worry. "Appletini, please."

After Bill ordered our drinks, he suggested we go to the patio to cool off. I was hesitant to leave the retro room without Valerie, but I didn't see her anywhere. She could have already wandered off to another room. I agreed and we pushed our way to the exit.

On the way out, I saw Sexy Guy again. He was holding a beer and talking to a girl wearing a short black halter dress and heels that had to be four inches high. The corner of his mouth lifted, and he winked as I walked by. The man had mastered the art of the wink. Emboldened by the alcohol, I smiled flirtatiously over my shoulder.

Bill found us a table. It was a relief to sit down. I wasn't used to dancing or wearing heels, and my feet were killing me.

"So Kimberly, do you come here often?"

"No, this is my first time. How about you?"

"I've been here a few times, but I live in San Diego. I'm only here for the weekend visiting my parents."

"Did you grow up around here?"

He laughed at some private joke. "Yep. Not too far from here. I noticed you're not wearing a ring. That mean you're not married?"

I held up my ring free left hand. "Trust me, I wouldn't be here if I were. And you?"

He held up his left hand. "Still single."

Bill was a talker and easy company. When we finished our drinks, he asked, "So hey, can I get your number? I make it up here about every month or so."

He was cute and a nice guy, but something seemed off. "You want to take me out?"

He laughed at my disbelief. "Yes. So how about it? You gonna give me your number or what?"

He did have a certain charm and I laughed too. "Do you have a pen?"

"Even better." He pulled his I-phone out of his pocket. "Fire a way."

"530—"

"Billy! Hey, I heard you were here!" A cute little blond bounced over and threw her arms around Bill.

He laughed and hugged her back. "Hey, Ash. How's it going?"

"Going good." The girl stepped back and registered Bill was not alone. She peered at me, and her face lit up with surprise. "Mrs. Braxton?" she questioned.

Oh my God. Ashley Simms, the girls' youth leader for the poodle skirt dancers the year Haley participated in the Davis Community Nutcracker. Every year about two hundred Davis children under the age of twelve performed everything thing from a snowflake ballet to the hula as the Nutcracker and the Sugar Plum Fairy entertained Clara. The youth leaders were teenagers who had performed the same dance routines when they had been in elementary school. Haley had idolized Ashley and had a huge crush on the boy who was the youth leader for the leather jacket boys dancing with the poodle skirt girls. His name was Billy.

Oh my God, it hit me. *"Billy Peterson?"*

He smiled a little sheepishly, but not much. "Yes, *Mrs. Braxton.*"

Puzzled, Ashley eyeballed us. "What's going on?"

I was tipsy … no, not tipsy … closer to inebriated and the whole encounter felt like a bizarre dream. The last time I'd seen Billy he had been a junior in high school. He obviously had grown up, but it was still too freaky for me. I tried to sober and sound like a responsible mother. "Nothing, Ashley. I'm actually not Mrs. Braxton anymore."

"Oh. I forgot. I heard about you and Mr. Braxton splitting up. I'm sorry."

"Don't be. How've you been?"

"Good. I got engaged last week." She held out her ringed hand as proof.

"How wonderful. Congratulations." I admired her ring and then declared, "Well, it's been great seeing you kids. I should probably go find my friend."

Billy stopped me just before I made it back inside. "Hey, I'd still like to call you."

"Did you know who I was?"

"Yeah, I knew."

"And you still hit on me?"

He laughed and his cheeks slightly reddened. "You were my teenage fantasy. I gotta say you still look good."

I was his teenage fantasy? "Billy, you're very sweet. Thanks for the drink."

I turned back into the club. That was close. What would Haley think if she found out her mom got drunk and hooked up with Billy Peterson? I needed another drink.

I could hear Jay's voice in my head, *"You've had enough, Kimmy."*

"Shut up, Jay," I mumbled. A hangover was in my future anyway.

Weaving through the crowd to the main bar, I kept an eye out for Valerie. After downing another appletini, I was past tipsy. I should have listened to the voice in my head. I needed to go home. I needed to find Valerie.

Instead, I ventured to the closest dance floor. On my way, I saw Sexy Guy again. This time he was back with his buddies at their table. He grinned and stood when he saw me. I winked at him. The alcohol made me do it. I never wink. I was such a dork. I kept going and resisted the temptation to check if he was following.

The lights pulsated with the beat of the music. *Sex on Fire* flowed through me, and I danced with my eyes closed, letting the music have its way with me. My eyes fluttered open when I felt a strong warm body close to me, swaying with me. My heart beat a little faster.

Sexy Guy smiled and tilted his mouth close to my ear. His deep voice penetrated through the cacophony of music and voices and laughter. "I like the way you move."

His warm breath sent a wave of heat rippling through me. I bet sex with him would be on fire. I had an urge to grind against him.

Closing Time started up. Sexy Guy pulled me close. He didn't ask permission—he just did it, making my knees wobble like jello. He was all hard muscle and smelled of sandalwood and spice, smelled like sex.

He sang softly, right next to my ear, "I know who I want to take me home …." His whiskers prickled my cheek. This was what I had wanted—a man, a deeply masculine man holding me, moving with me, singing to me.

My arms draped around his neck. His hand moved from my waist to the small of my back and he tugged me closer. Our stomachs brushed teasingly, and I tipped my head back to gaze at his handsome face. His head bent down, and his lips barely met mine before his cool tongue was in my mouth. He tasted like beer and virility. He tasted good.

Have to get out of here. Must find Valerie.

I pulled away. "Thanks for the dance."

He followed me. "Where are you going?"

"I need some air, and I have to find my friend."

"I'll help you."

Sexy Guy took my hand. He had big rough hands. We passed a light fixture, and I could discern he had beguiling green eyes. My instinct told me he was someone who would help.

He led me around the club searching for Valerie through the crowds. We interrupted our hunt to dance a few times. I think he bought me a drink. I know he made me laugh. It was like a game of *Where's Waldo. Where's Valerie?* There were so many people. After a while, it made my head dizzy. I was so tired and had to sit down. Sexy Guy took me outside.

I know he told me his name, but I couldn't remember it. I think I told him my name, but I couldn't remember for certain. I couldn't remember anything we discussed.

The next thing I knew, we were on one of the daybeds, *the orgy beds*, with the billowy curtains closed around us. Sexy Guy was nuzzling my neck and his whiskers tickled.

He pulled away and gazed down my body. "God, you're luscious."

He kissed me again and my head spun. I closed my eyes to make it stop.

When I opened my eyes again, my face was raw from his stubble grazing my skin. His jeans were unzipped, and his baby maker was in my hand.

Oh God, no. I have to get out of here. My body listened and I shot upright.

"Please don't leave me this way. I'm so close," he practically whimpered.

Part of me was disgusted and sick. Part of me was frightened of not finishing what I'd started. I gripped him more firmly and stroked him faster until his muffled groans vibrated against my neck.

His breathing was ragged. He whispered, "Thank you," in my ear and kissed my cheek.

I stared at the mess in my hand, not knowing what to do with it.

He took the tail of his shirt and gently wiped my hand clean. Then he kissed my knuckles. The act was strangely tender. "You have the softest hands."

"I have to go to the ladies' room," I said getting up.

"Are you okay?"

I'm going to be sick. "Yeah."

"Are you coming back?"

No. "Yeah."

As soon as I got away from him, tears ran down my face. I had groped him and unzipped his pants like an out of control slut. Was he the pig, or was I the pig? We were both pigs. I was drunk. No, I wasn't drunk or inebriated or intoxicated … I was wasted. I couldn't even remember his name. I wanted Valerie and to go home.

Something jerked in my stomach, demanding release. I raced to the closest ladies' room and mercifully, a woman let me cut ahead of her. The stall door wasn't even shut when my stomach erupted.

A group of women walked in laughing and talking loudly.

"Will you fucking stop telling people I have fake boobs?"

"Well, you do."

Their voices hurt my ears.

"Eeewww. Disgusting. Someone drank too much."

"Should we help her?"

"Hey, do you need some help?"

I croaked, "No. I'm fine."

My stomach stopped heaving and they left. I felt a little better and staggered to the sink. I washed my hands with soap twice before cupping water in my hand to wash out my mouth. Could I get a disease from having his fluids on my hand? Looking in the mirror, I didn't recognize the face staring back, so pale and distorted with black smudges under puffy eyes. The door opened again.

"Kimberly, where the hell have you been?"

Thank God, Valerie. Black blobs rolled down my face. "I wanna go home."

"What happened?"

"I got sick."

"Shit, you poor thing. Why didn't you answer your phone or my text messages?"

I opened my purse. My cell phone wasn't there. "I can't drive."

"Don't worry. I can."

A cocktail waitress poked her head in and asked, "Anybody in here named Kimberly?"

"I'm Kimberly."

"There's a guy out here asking for you. He wants to know if you're okay," she said.

"Please, tell him I found my friend and I'm fine."

As soon as the waitress shut the door Valerie quizzed, "Who's looking for you?"

"Just a guy I met."

She took a tissue out of her purse and cleaned up the mascara running down my face. She handed me another tissue so I could blow my nose. "Come on, let's get you home."

To my horror, Sexy Guy was leaning against the wall opposite the bathroom, waiting for me. His front shirttail was wet, as if he had rinsed it in a sink. I had expected him to leave once he knew I'd met up with my friend.

He pushed away from the wall and stood right in front of me. I craned my neck gaping up at him. "Hey, I was worried about you. You didn't look too good when you left."

"I'm okay. I found my friend. We're going home."

He nodded and smiled self-consciously. "Well, hey. It was fun." He dipped his head and pecked my cheek. "I'll call you." It seemed a gratuitously chaste gesture considering our lewd dalliance.

He'd call me. Right, as if I believed him, as if I wanted him to call. I wanted to purge the entire evening from my memory. No, I wanted to delete the entire last two days. I wished there was a way to backspace or hit an undo key … undo, undo, undo.

Chapter 7

*E*XCRUCIATINGLY HUNG-OVER AND unable to move without risking a head explosion, I lolled in bed thinking about the night Jay proposed. His parents had been out of town for the weekend, and I'd told my parents I was staying the night with Valerie. We were lying on his twin bed, his desk lamp providing the only light, with our naked bodies entwined and Goo Goo Dolls' *Iris* playing on the radio. Unlike most memories, my memory of that night never faded.

Jay stroked my back while the song spoke to us in a deep and life-changing way. We gazed at each other knowing we would give up forever just to touch the other a moment longer, and in that moment, we understood each other in a way no one else ever would.

Jay said with a quiet voice, "Cancel the appointment. You can't do it."

He'd said what I'd longed to hear. I loved him so much, and our baby already felt real. My throat tightened, strained between joy and fear. "I can't give up our baby."

"Let's get married. Now that football season is over, I can work full-time at the warehouse and support us. We can still go to college. It won't be easy, but we can do it."

"You're serious."

"Hell yeah." His eyes warmed and liquid swirled at the brims, threatening to spill. "I love you so much it hurts. I swear I'll always take care of you and our baby. I want us to be a family—what do you say?"

He had believed what he'd said, and I had believed in him.

So much for taking care of me. My whole body ached: my head and eyeballs throbbed, my stomach rolled with nausea, my thigh muscles were sore from dancing, and my feet hurt from being in heels too long. Worst of all, my self-image had taken a beating, leaving my ego badly bruised. My sole comfort was being horizontal in bed.

Before Jay, I only had one brief romance in the tenth grade. He was a senior named Mitchell Mayer. We had made out in the back seat of his mom's Lexus, but I wouldn't let him in my pants. It'd been the reason why he asked Lara Olvera to his Senior Prom instead of me. Although crushed to have missed the Classic Hollywood themed dance (I'd envisioned myself waltzing in like Grace Kelly in her iconic baby-blue satin gown) I'd been consoled by knowing I had self-respect, unlike some of my classmates.

Now I had a list of who I'd French kissed: Mitchell Mayer, Jay Braxton, Joshua, and Sexy Guy. I doubled my list in two nights. The list of men I'd touched below the waist doubled in one night. I didn't know Joshua's last name. I didn't even know Sexy Guy's first name.

My memory slowly came back. I recalled giving Sexy Guy my number and he'd told me his name, but I truly couldn't remember it. I was certain he'd said he and his buddies were firemen. He was the one who suggested we go outside, but I'd been the one who proposed sitting on the bed. I remembered making out. He'd felt so big rubbing against me, and I'd wanted to touch him; then, well ….

I didn't want to remember any more. Besides, it was time to face Valerie. The slightest movement sent darts ricocheting through my head. I rallied and found her sitting at the kitchen table sipping coffee and reading the paper.

"Morning," I greeted.

"Actually, it's afternoon." She went to the refrigerator, pulled out a tumbler and handed it to me. "It'll help."

I took a sip, expecting to gag, but the drink was surprisingly refreshing. "What is it?"

"Ginger juice, coconut water, and a banana blended with vitamins and a drop of honey. It really will help. You drink and I'll fix you some eggs."

I sipped the concoction and watched Valerie putter in my kitchen. Usually when she visited, I'd whip up a frittata or my special crème brulee French toast, topped with peach compote and fresh cream. I was supposed to be the hostess with the mostest. Today I couldn't even manage to make a pot of coffee for my guest.

Valerie set a plate of scrambled eggs and toast in front of me. The smell made my stomach jerk. I forced myself to take a bite of egg and swallow.

The night before, I'd passed out on the way home. She had roused me just enough to get me into bed, so I hadn't given her any more details about Sexy Guy.

"Aren't you going to ask about last night?"

She smiled and shrugged. "Crazy enough for you?"

"Enough to know clubbing isn't for me."

She laughed. "If you'd remembered your phone, I would've rescued you sooner."

"Sorry. I left it charging and forgot to put it in my purse."

I tried the toast. It scratched down my throat, and my stomach didn't reject it. Valerie's hangover smoothie helped, but only time would completely restore me.

She still hadn't asked about Sexy Guy. I wasn't sure how much I wanted her to know. It occurred to me that we'd never discussed our sex lives in any kind of detail. I asked, "Have you ever had a one-night stand?"

She chuckled. "Yeah, I have."

"Why haven't you ever told me about it?"

She sighed. "You lost your virginity to the man you married. I didn't think you'd want to hear about my sexcapades."

In truth, I hadn't. "I guess that's right, but now I'm curious."

"Does this have anything to do with the guy who was waiting for you?"

I took a deep breath. "I gave him a hand-job last night." Instead of being shocked by my depravity, she burst out laughing. "What's so funny?"

"Oh, honey. I'm sorry. It's just so high school. You didn't do him in a back room or go down on him. You gave him a hand-job," she tried to explain through her giggles. "No wonder he looked so sheepish. You brought him back to his teenage years."

I snickered. When she put it that way, I was able to appreciate some of the humor. "I know it sounds funny, but I feel so dirty ... so wanton."

"Are you worried he's not going to respect you?"

"Yes," I admitted with a fresh wave of humiliation.

She waved her hand dismissively. "You'll probably never see him again."

"He called me 'luscious.' That's what really got me."

Valerie giggled again. "So do you remember what Mr. Luscious does for a living?"

"He's a fireman."

"Oh my. Did he have a big hose?"

"Yes, and he spouted all over my hand."

She snorted with laughter. "Oh my God, what did you do with it?"

I laughed too. "Wiped it on his shirt."

Her eyes bugged, horrified. "Was he pissed?"

"No. It was his idea. He cleaned me up and then kissed my hand."

"You know, in a weird way, it was kind of decent of him ... and he did seem sincerely worried about you. He's probably not a total asshole."

"No, he was nice to me. He said he'd call me, but he probably won't, right?"

"Not likely." Valerie poured herself another cup of coffee. "Can you handle some?"

"Please." She poured me a cup too. "So, how many one-nighters have you had?"

She sat back down and took a sip. "Six ... the first two times were alcohol-induced when I was in my early twenties. The other four times were purely for a little fun with no strings. I knew it. The men knew it."

"Oh my God!" It popped out before I had a chance to check my reaction.

"Close your mouth, Kim. Look at what you did last night. I bet you would've jumped the guy's bones if there'd been a bedroom handy."

I wasn't proud of what I'd done and was taken aback by her nonchalance. It flabbergasted me. I had no idea she had such a casual attitude about sex. I did my best to sound intrigued, rather than judgmental. "Did you feel bad afterwards?"

"No—except one time when the sex was plain bad."

"So how many men have you been with?"

She hesitated again. "Somewhere around twenty-five."

What do you say when you find out your best friend is a sex addict? We both took a sip of our coffee. "I'm not judging, but whoa, Val ...."

"It's really not a big number when you think about it."

Twenty-five wasn't a big number? A titter escaped my lips. I glanced at her quickly, hoping I hadn't offended her. She snickered, too.

"Okay, I give," I said. "Please, explain your logic."

"First of all—as you know—I've never been interested in marriage. Secondly, I lost my virginity when I was eighteen, which means I've averaged one to two lovers a year. Excepting the occasional one-offs, I'd dated all the rest. Does less than two a year sound excessive?"

"I don't know." What I did know was that I missed having sex more than I ever imagined I would. I could give myself an orgasm, but there was no battery-operated substitute for being close to someone—for a warm body touching me, for intimacy. The regularity of Jay and my sex life had been off and on, but we had never gone more than a week or so without making love. Most nights we had at least cuddled before going to sleep. How long could I go without the tender touch of another person? "I don't want to talk about this anymore."

"Hold on, I'm not trying make you feel worse, but we aren't teenagers. Most men expect something after a handful of dates. Some guys will say and do almost anything to have their itch scratched. It's only sex. You can't even expect a second date."

"You know what? Enough. I'm a grown woman and not completely naïve."

"Hey, I don't want you to get hurt. If you're looking for more, then you need to be more careful. That's all."

Damn, Jay! It wasn't supposed to be like this. The most intimate physical acts we had shared only with each other, but now, even though I didn't want to think about it, I knew other women had touched my husband. Now I knew what another man's penis felt like in my hands. I had joked about wanting to get laid, but the reality of having a stranger inside of me was unsettling. I wanted my husband back. Not the Jay who showed up last night—that man was practically a stranger. I wanted *my husband*. I wanted the man who loved and cherished me.

Getting air past the fist-sized lump in my throat took effort. "I'm going back to bed."

"No, you need to shower and get dressed."

"Why?"

"Because you just do. Last night was a little freaky but get over it. Stop feeling sorry for yourself and woman up!"

"What does that mean?"

"It means it's time to stop playing the victim. It's unhealthy and depressing."

"Excuse me, but I am the victim. I didn't ask for this!"

"Maybe not, but do you really think you have zero responsibility for what's happened? Why do you think Haley didn't want to come home this summer?"

Ouch. I couldn't speak. I stared at Val while tears streamed down my cheeks. She pulled me into her arms and let me have a good cry. Once I calmed, she said, "You know I've had my share of knocks. One thing I've learned is that there's a lot in life you cannot control, but you can control your reaction to it."

I couldn't argue. It was one thing to take time to lick my wounds. It was another to indulge in a pity party to a point where I'd alienated Haley. Jay did what he did, but I was responsible for how I'd handled things since. I couldn't blame him for Sexy Guy or my hangover. He didn't hand me the drinks or force them down my throat. "I'll take that shower."

"Good. While you're at it, think about what you really want."

I nodded. Just as I was walking out of the room, she stopped me. "The first time I had a one-night stand, I didn't feel good about myself. I had to learn how to separate the physical from the emotional."

One thing I knew for certain was that I never wanted to reach a point where separating the two was easy. Part of my shame with Sexy Guy was I wanted him to call. If he asked to see me again, then our act wouldn't feel as dirty. It would validate we had clicked or had some sort of special connection, which would morally justify my behavior.

Other things I wanted weren't as easy to define. I only had hazy glimpses, shadows really, of what my life could look like a year from now. In high school, pre-Jay, my dreams had been just as nebulous. I'd wanted what my parents dictated I should want: good grades, ace the SATs, go to a top tier school. Beyond those things, I envisioned being a writer—having *a room of one's own* and a sufficient income not to be a starving artist. What kind of writer, what that room looked like, was never defined.

After falling for Jay and having Haley, my life goals took shape. I'd still wanted to be a writer, but more than that I'd wanted a big, happy family overflowing with love. I saw myself driving a minivan, going to little league games and dance recitals, cooking big family dinners, and reading to my children at night. We'd have a nice house—not too big or ostentatious—solidly middle-class. Family movie nights and trips to Disneyland would be our thing.

Jay had shared that vision. Our plan had been to get Jay through law school; then he would support us so I could stay home with our children and squeeze in writing where I could. Jay making partner at a law firm, or establishing his own firm, would provide the financial foundation to support our dream.

As much as we'd wanted more children, my body proved to be a defective baby maker. By the time we'd figured out the problem and attempted a few procedures, Haley was in junior high. We'd considered adopting, but after suffering so many disappointments, we'd agreed that we were content with our little family. Jay had kept up his end of the bargain with his insane drive at the law firm. We bought our dream house. Between Jay, Haley, and I, our home had been full of love for a long time. I had a room of my own to write.

No wonder I'd been a big blob of inertia. I'd had the life I'd wanted, but that life was over. I was young enough to reboot. For the first time, I was free to consider what I wanted for me—not influenced by my parents or Jay or motherhood—just for me

As I undressed and stepped into the shower, I tried to picture what my new life could look like. My current home had clean, modern-lined furniture with carefully selected accents and zero clutter. I visualized a new space with antique mahogany tables, overstuffed shabby chic chairs and mismatched bookcases. For my office, I envisioned my grandmother's old writing desk, a rag rug on the floor, and pictures of Haley with the family she would have sprinkled throughout the room. I could see myself in a comfy chair curled up with my laptop—a new me who drank tea instead of coffee. Next to the chair, I imagined a window with white lace curtains, and outside the window, a big world to explore.

⌒

Val and I spent the rest of the day devising a plan for my new life. We agreed I had to get out of Davis—no more awkward encounters with someone like Billy Peterson. Heaven forbid I bump into Jay somewhere and be forced to witness him canoodling with one of his little girlfriends. Besides, single men my age were in short supply in Davis.

Valerie suggested I move to Los Angeles. She even had some blind dates picked out for me, which was tempting given her professional connections, but after I convinced her San Francisco really did have more straight men than gay, she agreed it would be better. Berkeley was just across the bay. Haley could even live with me and commute to school if she wanted. Besides, Val had a life in LA wholly separate from our friendship. I loved her but couldn't see myself adapting to her lifestyle, and I didn't want her to feel responsible for my social life. Although she didn't admit it, I know she was relieved by my decision.

By the time I dropped Val at the airport Monday morning, I was ready to tackle the world. I vowed to woman up and reinvent myself. My rally song would be *Believe*. Yes, Cher, I believed in life after love. Jay would be the one waking up lonely with regrets, not me. I swore to wake up every day and remind myself that I was strong and believed in life after love. I believed, Cher. I believed. With Cher singing in my head, I called Wendy.

"Kim, I'm glad you called. Did you make a decision?"

"I'm in—provided the terms of my pay are comparable."

"They will be. Have you thought of an angle?"

"I have. I'm the angle."

"Please, enlighten me how *you* are the angle."

"Jay was my first boyfriend, and he took me on my first official date. We didn't have a single break up until the divorce." I bucked up my courage and made the confession I feared would be a deal breaker. "I've only been on one date as an adult. I'm not even sure if it counts. We met at a restaurant, and he requested separate checks before the waiter took our order."

"So you're a Virgin Dater?" she joked.

"Exactly. And I have a name for the column. What do you think of *First Time Single?*"

"Hmm … I like it, but we need something more. One date and your cherry will be popped so to speak. What then?"

"What if I compared my dates to food? Like bologna on white bread slathered with mayonnaise versus a pepper crusted New York steak swimming in brandy cream sauce?"

She barked a laugh. "Now you are on to something."

We struck a deal, and I joined Wendy's writing team as the Virgin Dater. We decided my first article would be about my almost date with the dentist. From there I had plenty of material just from my one night at the club with Valerie. Although I probably wouldn't write about the up close and personal with Sexy Guy, I might write about Billy Peterson. (Names changed to protect the innocent, of course.)

Chapter 8

A FEW DAYS LATER, I went to see Haley, ostensibly to treat her to lunch and a day of shopping in San Francisco, but I really wanted her to see for herself that I was doing better. I didn't want her to dread coming home because she didn't know how deep in a funk hole I'd be. After my night out and Valerie giving me the grown-up girl talk, I also worried about what Haley faced. She and I had discussed dating and sex previously, but back then, I'd preached intimacies in the bedroom should be a consummation of a couple's love for each other. I wanted to believe it still, but my beliefs appeared to be at odds with the current ways of the world.

When I'd left Davis, the sky had been bright blue with sunshine inching the temperature to a scorching 104 degrees. The closer I got to the Bay Area, the darker the sky became. San Francisco was clouded over and gray, and I hoped it wasn't an omen.

We both deserved something extra special, so I took her to Hakkasan, an upscale Asian-fusion restaurant close to Union Square. I still hadn't decided how to broach everything I wanted to discuss. As we sat across from each other, I picked at my grilled seabass.

Never one to hold back, Haley blurted, "Dad called. You're officially divorced."

"We are. Are you okay?"

"Obviously, it upsets me. I mean, I knew the day was getting closer, but I kept thinking Dad would change his mind. Guess not."

Guess not. Haley's eyes brimmed with tears, making my own eyes prick, but I had vowed to woman up. "He's never coming back. I'm sorry."

"I know you didn't want the divorce. How are you holding up?"

"I had a few rough days, but I'm fine. The waiting is over." I shrugged. "I'm getting on with my life. As a matter of fact, I plan to get an apartment in San Francisco. I'm hoping to find something in North Beach." I tried to deliver this news in a cheerful upbeat manner.

Haley brightened. "Awesome. I love North Beach. When you're in Davis, can my friends and I crash there?"

I laughed at her assumption my apartment was going to be a crash pad. "Sorry to disappoint, but I'm not getting a weekend place. I'm moving to San Francisco."

"What about our house in Davis?"

"I'm selling it."

Oh, God. I'd said the wrong thing. Haley's face fell and her tears mixed with her spicy prawns. "You're selling our house?"

"Honey, I can't afford to keep the house and an apartment in San Francisco. Besides, the house is too big for only me and the cats. Don't cry, Sweetie."

The waiter stopped at our table and asked how everything was. I wanted to tell him *"not good,"* but I knew he was referring to the food.

As soon as he walked away, Haley hissed, "But Mom, Dad only has a one-bedroom in Sac. What's going to happen to me?"

"Honey, you'll always have a home with me. I plan on getting a place with two bedrooms. You can help me pick it out if you want."

"But it won't be the same. It won't be our family home where I grew up."

I refrained from pointing out we hadn't bought the house until she was almost ten. "Please try to understand I need to regroup. I need a fresh start."

Haley stopped crying and I handed her a tissue to blow her nose. "I'm sorry, Mom. I know you do. This is all Dad's fault." She looked up with fierce eyes. "I hate him."

It was the first time Haley squarely placed the blame on Jay's shoulders. Part of me wanted to agree and indulge in an all-out bitch fest. My motherly instincts won out. "No, sweetie. That's not true. You don't hate him and neither do I. He and I both are to blame."

"What did you do? He's the one who left."

"In retrospect, I never told him how much I appreciated him. Nobody wants to be taken for granted, and there were other things."

I'd given Haley enough of a shock. The mom-daughter sex and dating chat would have to wait. I took her shopping and bought her a dress at Urban Outfitters and a pair of sandals at Bloomingdale's. A new pair of shoes always made things a little better with Haley.

I drove under gloomy skies out of the Bay Area and back to Davis, ruminating about what I'd told her. After Jay had left, I began to realize just how much I had taken for granted. When my car had needed an oil change or the tires were due to be rotated, Jay had taken care of it. He'd trade me cars for the day and that would be it. If a faucet leaked, it miraculously wouldn't be leaking a few days later. I didn't have to think about the lawn needing a mow or the gutters being cleared of leaves. Even after he moved out, Jay took care of things until he was able to arrange a lawn service and find a handyman for the odd jobs.

After he began practicing law, I took money for granted, too. It had been a relief not to be the one worrying about bills. I'd shouldered the money concerns all during his law school years and had gladly shifted the load to him. At some point, I'd stopped acknowledging everything he did. He didn't thank me when I washed his clothes or cleaned the bathroom. Why should I thank him? We were both simply doing our jobs. Right? In truth, it had annoyed me not getting a thank you now and then. He must have resented it, too.

When I really thought about it, I knew there were times Jay had tried to talk to me about his unhappiness. A few months after his mother died, he'd asked, "What do think if I got a motorcycle again?"

"What? You want to be a Law Dog on a Hog?" I laughed. "I can't see you in a suit flying down the freeway."

"Don't laugh at me. I wouldn't ride it to work. It'd be for weekends."

"Hey, Easy Rider," I joked, "I think your bad boy days are over."

"Glad I gave you a chuckle," he snapped and walked out of the room.

I should have asked why he wanted the bike. At the time, I'd been more concerned about him killing himself out on a joyride. I had laughed it off and refused to take it seriously because I knew it would make him drop the idea faster than a rational discussion. No wonder he had stopped talking to me about certain things.

And I did understand some of his regrets. We both loved Haley and never regretted keeping her, but it meant we had to grow up so fast. We didn't get to have the college dorm or sharing-an-apartment-with-a-group-of-friends experience. I didn't get the Country Club wedding my mother and father had promised since I was a little girl. I didn't go to Bryn Mawr or Smith. I went to Community College and finished my degree at UCD after Jay finished law school. It was not the college experience I had dreamed about. No sorority sisters for me. Jay had planned on joining a fraternity and looked forward to the college parties. He had talked about the possibility of studying abroad for a year or working in Alaska during a summer break. Joining the Peace Corp had interested him, too.

As soon as we made the decision to keep Haley, those possibilities were gone. We had to focus on building a stable life for our beautiful baby girl. She became our priority, and rightly so. Over the years, we repeatedly assured each other that none of our pre-Haley dreams mattered. Our life didn't unfold the way we'd planned in high school, but we were happy.

For me, it wasn't a lie. I was happy with our little family and our life. I grew up in such an emotionally cold house, and in contrast, Jay's family was so warm and loving. Jay was warm and loving. Of course, there were times when I thought about what life would be like if we hadn't had Haley at such a young age. How could I not? Jay must have thought about it more than I realized. He'd said he needed freedom. Well, he was free now, and I sincerely hoped it brought him the happiness he sought.

I tapped on the car stereo, shuffled to *Cher,* and set *Believe* on repeat. *I believe in life after love, Cher. I believe. I believe.*

As soon as I drove over the pass approaching Fairfield and out of the Bay Area, the sun miraculously broke through. A foggy area in my own mind also cleared. I had failed Jay. If I had been more attentive to what he was feeling, I wouldn't have been blindsided. I had willfully shut my eyes to his discontent. It didn't excuse the way he'd abandoned our marriage but accepting my share of the blame left me more peaceful.

I was on an I-am-a-strong-woman roll and drove to Nugget before going home. I hadn't been back since the parking lot incident. Of course, I had no idea if Joshua would even be there.

My confidence ran high as I jauntily swung a black metal basket and clicked down the produce aisle in my going-to-the-city heels. I picked out a red bell pepper, an heirloom tomato, and some fresh basil, and then turned the corner to the meat section. From the chicken case, I had an unencumbered view of the checkout stands. Joshua was checking in the express lane.

My whole body quivered at the sight of his hard, lean body. How ridiculous was that? I was a grown woman. Why did I allow him to unnerve me? I crossed to the bakery and placed a petite sourdough round in my basket. Joshua's lane was closest to me, less than ten feet away. He saw me and smiled sheepishly before turning his attention back to the customer in front of him. A few steps placed me in queue for his services.

He snuck a peek at me each time he greeted a new customer. As the line shortened, my shaking increased, but I had to establish all was forgotten: that seeing him, shopping at the store, was no big deal. I tried not to stare at his mouth or to remember how good his lips had felt. Shame washed over me. He was so young, so sweet.

Only one customer remained in front of me. A hand snatched up my basket and a smiling clerk offered to take me in the next lane. Joshua's face flashed with disappointment, and then he nodded, indicating I should take the offer.

As I followed the clerk, Joshua said, "Hey, Kimberly?"

I turned and our eyes met. "Pineapples are on sale for a buck." He winked. "They're really sweet. Chop 'em up with mango and jalapeno; it's a great salsa with grilled pork chops."

I laughed and then he laughed, his eyes twinkling. We were good. He understood we could only be friends and was fine with it. Interesting how so much meaning could pass between us with a look and a few meaningless words. If he was older, or I was younger, who knew?

I had pulled down all the shades before I left for the Bay Area, but I still came home to a warm house. I flipped on the AC, put my groceries away, and then, checked the blinking light on my telephone. I had two messages. The first was from the veterinarian's office reminding me of my cats' vaccination appointment; next, a deep, gravelly voice played.

"Hi, Kimberly. Uh, this is Kevin. I was hoping you could give me a call." He left his number and finished with, "Okay, thanks."

My heart hiccupped. I replayed the message. It was his voice—Sexy Guy from the bar. I replayed the message a third time and wrote down his number.

Okay, now I knew his name was Kevin. I wanted to call him back, but I didn't want to call him back. In my hazy memory of the night, I'd had fun with him for a while. He'd made me laugh. If we hadn't transgressed the lines of decency, I wouldn't hesitate to call him back. As things stood, the prospect of facing him sober was mortifying. Was he fishing for a booty call? Did he have an itch he wanted me to scratch?

I wouldn't know unless I called him. Why the hell not? He answered on the third ring.

"This is Kevin." Definitely my Sexy Guy.

Amazingly, my palms weren't sweaty, and my voice wasn't shaky. "Hi, Kevin. This is Kimberly. I'm returning your call."

"Oh, hey. Hi. Thanks for calling me back. I tried to text you, but it didn't work."

"No, sorry. This is a landline." Why had I given him this number? I rarely gave out my home number and blamed the alcohol.

"I figured it out. Last landline in California, huh?"

I had the landline because I generally silence the ringer on my cell when I write and invariably forget to turn it back on and then can't remember where I set it. Jay and Haley needed a reliable way to reach me. We both laughed. "Yeah."

"So uh, how have you been?" he asked.

"I've been good. And you?"

"Good. I've been good …" Wow, was this call going anywhere? "Well, I had a hell of a hangover on Sunday, but other than that I've been good."

"I was more than a tad hung over, too." *Good.* We'd both been drunk. For some reason, our behavior didn't seem as unpardonably disgraceful.

He chuckled. "Yeah, I figured. Crazy night, huh?"

I laughed a little, too. "Pretty crazy."

"So I was wondering if you'd like to have dinner Saturday night?"

"Dinner?"

"Well, yeah. Nothing crazy, just dinner."

"Sure, I'd love to have dinner with you," I said bouncing up and down, thankful he couldn't see me. A date, an actual date.

Chapter 9

FIRST TIME SINGLE

"The Virgin Dater"

As disastrous as my foray into the single world had seemed last weekend, turns out the nightclub adventure hadn't been the complete exercise in humiliation I'd thought. Sexy Guy, who I wrote about last week, asked me to dinner. The mere thought of facing him sober felt so mortifying that I considered declining, but Sexy Guy had been fun and from what I remembered, he was ... well, sexy. He promised nothing crazy, just dinner. I agreed and now I don't know if I'm more excited about seeing him again or the whole concept of an honest to goodness, coming-to-my-house-to-pick-me-up-official date.

My last first date was twenty-years ago. My ex-husband and I had been seeing each other for months before he met my parents and took me to Homecoming. Did that even count since we'd already declared our love? I'd been more nervous about him meeting my mother and father than being alone with him.

This round is different. I barely know Sexy Guy, and I'm not ashamed to admit that I am scared as hell that I'll commit some dating faux pas. To prepare, I've been researching the interweb for guidance. There seem to be a lot of "don'ts" on advice lists. Don't talk about your ex or your children. Don't discuss marriage, politics, or religion

Allowable subjects are the weather, his zodiac sign, and sports, but sports are out for me since I have no idea who won the Super Bowl last year and couldn't name a pro baseball player to save my life. Yikes! Luckily, Sexy Guy seems confident, so I plan to let him steer the conversation.

I also read about the pros and cons of ordering dessert. According to the experts, having dessert at the restaurant blows the excuse of inviting your date back to your place for something sweet. It also enhances post-meal lethargy, not advisable if tangling sheets is next on the agenda. On the other hand, if post-meal calisthenics is not on the menu, ordering a chocolate bomb with two forks is a great way to extend getting-to-know-you time. Who knew?

Apparently, shoe choice is critical. Heels are a must. Flats are flat-out lazy. Literally, put your best foot forward!

There seems to be much debate over women reaching for the check. Traditionalists believe if the man did the asking, he should pay for the first date. Some men like the woman to make the reach, even though they'd never allow the woman to touch the check, while others consider it emasculating. Many appreciate splitting the bill. I swear dating was not this complicated when I was in high school.

Wish me luck and stay tuned. Will Sexy Guy be the juicy ribeye I hope for or a Hamburger Helper Sloppy Joe?

———

My doorbell rang at six-thirty-three. Apparently, Kevin was one of those show-up-early guys. I took a last glance in the mirror, heaved a deep breath, and opened the door.

Jay stood on the porch squinting from the sun. His mouth pinched up—the same way Haley's did when she wasn't happy. I wasn't happy. I hoped he wasn't going to make a habit of showing up every Saturday night.

"Kim, I need to talk to you."

"This really isn't a good time. I wish you'd called first."

He scanned me head to toe. "Going somewhere?"

Pretty obvious given I was wearing a body-hugging, aquamarine sundress and heels. I hoped Jay noticed the color matched my eyes and the v-neckline showed just enough cleavage to be provocative without being slutty. "I have a date. Whatever it is, can it wait until tomorrow?"

"What time is your date?"

"Seven."

He glanced at his watch. "You have time." He wasn't leaving until I agreed to talk to him. After being with a man twenty years, you know certain things.

"Ten minutes and next time, call first."

He walked in and followed me to the kitchen. We always had our big talks in the kitchen. I didn't know why. It was just one of those things.

"So what's so important it can't wait?"

He gave me a level stare. "I spent the day with Haley."

"Oh." I knew what this was about. "I was going to call you."

"You're selling the house?" He exploded without giving me a chance to explain. "I God damn can't believe it! I agreed to the fucking alimony so you could keep up with the mortgage and you don't want it? You vindictive bitch!"

Never, ever had he resorted to name calling. It told me exactly where I stood and just how furious he was. "Screw you, Jay! I did want the house, but things have changed."

"What? What has changed so much? Our divorce hasn't been final even two weeks!"

"You want the truth?"

"That's why I'm here," he hissed.

Rage unfurled inside of me. "Every single thing has changed because we aren't fucking married anymore!" I shuddered. Tears stung my eyes and my anger morphed to grief. "I thought you'd wake up and come home, but you didn't, and I can't live here alone."

My confession and tears took the fight out of him. He pulled a blue and white plaid handkerchief out of his pocket and handed it to me. I thought it rather old-fashioned of him to carry a handkerchief. When sorting laundry, it had grossed me out every time I pulled a soiled hanky out of his pocket, but times like these a handkerchief was welcome.

He waited until my crying subsided before he apologized. "I'm sorry. I shouldn't have called you a bitch. You didn't deserve that."

"It's okay," I said. "I understand why you're angry, but I need a fresh start and I can't do it living here."

"I get it, but please, don't sell the house." He used the same low, heart-squeezing tone he'd used when he asked me to marry him.

Our house was not a starter home. A professor of Economics had custom built the place in the late fifties. It was a mid-century modern with built in bookcases and a bright white and yellow tile kitchen with matching yellow appliances. This was supposed to be the Braxton Family home where we would host family gatherings and our grandchildren would visit. We were supposed to leave the house feet first. Those dreams were over. "It's time to sell."

"Please, Kimmy. Please, don't do it," he begged.

He'd fallen in love with the house the first time he saw it. I had attended the open house earlier in the day and couldn't wait for him to get off work so I could show it to him. He'd maintained a poker face during the walkthrough with the realtor, but as soon as she'd left us to wander on our own, his stone face broke out in a dimply smile. We'd stood in this very room when he'd said, "This is it, Baby. This is our house." It had needed a ton of work, and he and his dad had spent countless weekends painting, tiling, refinishing the built-ins, and a long list of other projects. A large part of Jay's self-identity had been vested in this house, but until last week, he hadn't set foot in it for over six months.

"I didn't think you cared about it anymore."

"Well, I do. I'd buy it from you if I could, but you wiped me out."

"You can't be too broke if you can drop fifty-grand on a Camaro."

"Who the hell told you that? I doubt it's even possible to spend fifty-grand on a Camaro. I bought a used Honda Accord."

I shouldn't have believed the gossip and couldn't imagine what was being said about me. "Paige told me. I'm sorry. I shouldn't have believed her, but it doesn't matter. It's time to sell."

"Let me rent it or do a lease-to-own. Give me this much. Come on, what do you say?"

"I need the money to start over in San Francisco."

"Sell the Porsche. I'll help you."

I didn't want to tell him I'd already planned on selling the car. I had never intended to wipe him out. Asking for everything had been a failed, desperate ploy to delay the divorce. I softened. "Okay, we'll work something out."

"Thank you," he said, heaving a sigh of relief.

His eyes drifted away from me and fixated on a collage of family photos on the wall. His tense stance slumped and for a moment, I thought he might cry. He seemed so lost just standing there, not making a move to leave, as if he were off course and didn't know which direction to try next. My heart hurt for him. No matter how well I thought I knew him, Jay could still be a mystery. How could I ever really know what was going on inside of him? How deeply he hurt or regretted or simply felt something essential was missing? I had no idea. All I knew for certain was that Jay was not a shallow person and part of him was adrift.

I reached for him. He wrapped his arms around me and buried his face in my hair. We stood in the middle of our kitchen holding each other, with our bodies twined tightly together, with him clinging to me as if I were a life preserver. He breathed heavily in my ear and just as he pulled back to look at me, just when his lips were a sliver from mine, the doorbell rang.

With dazed eyes, he jumped back and said, "I'm sorry, I wasn't thinking." For a moment, I'd thought he was coming back to me, and then in a crushing blink, his wall had gone back up. But the feeling had been there—that unmistakable feeling, when your hearts beat as one, you are breathing in unison, and warmed to your very core. You come to know what the conclusion will be after twenty years of intimacy. I knew it and so did he.

Before I realized what was happening, Jay was in the front room and answering the door. He blocked the entrance with his body.

I heard Kevin's voice. "Hi. I hope I have the right house. I'm here for Kimberly."

"You have the right house. Come on in," Jay said with his fake nice voice.

He stepped aside and let Kevin take a few steps into the entryway. Kevin was more handsome than I'd remembered. A few inches taller than Jay, he was neatly dressed in a pair of lightweight khakis and a solid sea-green Tommy Bahamas shirt. He was also clean-shaven. I had no reason to be ashamed of my date.

"Hi, Kevin. It's nice to see you again," I greeted with a smile, trying to mask how uncomfortable I was with my ex-husband standing between us.

"Hey. Good to see you, too. You look great."

"Thank you. Kevin, this is Jay. Jay, Kevin."

The two men shook hands, and I expected Jay to make a hasty exit. Instead, he made conversation. "Nice to meet you. I'm Kim's ex-husband. I take it you're her date?"

I could've killed him. He was using the same tone he used when Haley's dates picked her up. I would've kicked his butt out, but I didn't want to make a scene in front of Kevin.

"Yeah, we're going out to dinner."

"Oh, yeah? Where are you taking her?"

"Mustard Seed. I've never been, but a buddy of mine recommended it."

Mustard Seed had been where Jay and I had celebrated our last anniversary. Jay tensed, so I knew this wasn't lost on him.

"It's one of Kim's favorite restaurants. Hope you made a reservation."

"Yeah, we have a reservation."

"Inside or patio?"

"I figured Kimberly would prefer the patio." He checked to see if I caught his reference. My cheeks warmed. He grinned at me, and I stifled a laugh.

I had no idea what Jay thought he was doing, but he asked using his lawyer voice, "So, Kevin, what do you do for a living?"

"Okay, Pops, that's enough," I interjected.

Kevin didn't seem bothered in the least by Jay's questioning. If anything, he was amused. "I'm a firefighter."

"Oh, you're not a med student?"

Kevin looked puzzled. "No," he answered before turning to me. "Ready to go?"

I grabbed my purse and all three of us walked out the door and down the pathway to the sidewalk. I noticed Jay's Honda was parked in my driveway. Jay's attention was focused on the sparkling fire-engine-red Dodge Ram 4x4 parked in front of the house.

Jay asked, "What's under the hood?"

"Hemi," Kevin answered with pride.

I had no idea what it meant, but Jay nodded with grudging approval.

Jay glanced at my narrow dress and then back at the tall truck. "Kim's going to need a ladder to climb up." Exactly my thought.

Kevin gave me a wink—dang, the man knew how to wink. "Won't be a problem."

Right in front of Jay, he put his hand on my lower back, guided me to the passenger side, opened the door, and lifted me onto my seat. Then he stepped onto the floorboard, reached over, and buckled my seat belt. After he shut my door, Kevin exchanged a few words with Jay. I couldn't hear what they said, but Kevin was stifling a laugh when he hopped into the driver's seat. He grinned at me and started the engine with an intentional roar. I peeked over my shoulder at Jay. He stood tight jawed with his arms crossed and glared as we drove away.

Since the restaurant was less than a mile from my house, we didn't have an opportunity for much conversation until we were seated. It really was one of my favorite restaurants. The place was very California with its casual ambiance paired with a sophisticated palate. The warm evening was perfect for outdoor dining. We were given a cozy table next to a small fountain that trickled soothingly and filled the silence while Kevin studied the wine list.

He exuded a raw and purely male energy, which set my hormones on alert, but also made me feel out of my element. Jay was uber masculine too, but education and professional life had polished him. Kevin lacked the refinement. I visualized him with a scantily dressed pin-up girl, washing his red truck and getting them both all soapy. They looked good together. I could see it as a Dodge Ram commercial on ESPN.

Not knowing anything about a Hemi, I couldn't think of a thing to say that might interest him. The more I studied his handsome face, the more thick-tongued I became. His face wrinkled into a frown, and he tossed the list on the table.

I plucked up my courage. "Find something you like?"

"Yeah, Holly's Hills."

"Actually, it's Holly's Hill, singular."

He chuckled and then admitted, "Honestly, I have no idea what to order other than I like the name." He handed me the list. "Why don't you pick something out?"

Jay would sneer if he knew. He liked beer as much as any man, but he'd become a bit of a wine snob. Why was I worried about what Jay would think? I smiled at Kevin's honesty, liking that he didn't try to bluster through. "Actually, Holly's Hill is a great choice, but what do you like to drink?"

"Beer. Occasionally, I'll go for a whiskey or scotch, but mainly I like a good beer."

"We don't need to order a bottle of wine. I'll just order a glass and you can have a beer."

We continued filling pauses with menu questions until the waiter returned to take our order. With choices made, I was keenly aware of Kevin eyeballing me as if he were hungry to touch me. It was unnerving because I was keenly aware of being hungry for his touch.

He snickered for no apparent reason. I asked, "What's so funny?"

"Your ex-husband's face when I lifted you into the truck. I shouldn't have done it, but damn his face was funny. It was like he couldn't believe I did it." He laughed louder.

I laughed too. "I wish I could have seen it. What did he say to you?"

"Oh, nothing really. He just made some comment about driving safe. You know, like I was a teenage kid taking his daughter out."

"What did you say?"

"I told him I'd take especially good care of you." Kevin's eyes twinkled mischievously. "Then I told him, 'I promise to have her in bed by midnight.' That really got him."

I laughed some more. "No wonder he was standing there with his arms crossed."

"I had a hard time keeping a straight face. I'm sorry. Hope I haven't caused a problem."

"No, it's fine. I don't know what his deal was."

"It's obvious—the dude was jealous."

I shook my head. "He left me. Tonight was only the second time I've seen him in six months. He has a girlfriend."

"The way he was acting, I wouldn't have guessed."

Our conversation was interrupted by the waiter bringing us our drinks and appetizer. I watched Kevin take a long drink of his beer. It reminded me of how he had tasted. I shifted in my seat and took a sip of wine.

He set his glass down and asked, "So, how long have you been divorced?"

"We've been separated for over a year, but officially divorced for about two weeks. Last Saturday was sort of my coming out party."

"Explains a few things," he said.

I was afraid of his answer, but asked, "What things?"

His eyes narrowed and he wiggled his finger inviting me closer. We both leaned over the table. "Just how much do you remember?"

"Enough," I said embarrassed, my cheeks flushing. "I remember you were very sweet helping me look for my friend."

"Can I confess something?"

"Sure."

"I knew what she looked like because I saw you come in together. I saw her a few times, but didn't tell you," he admitted a little sheepishly.

"Why wouldn't you tell me?"

He shrugged his broad shoulders. "I was having fun with you. I wanted to keep you a while longer. You're not mad, are you?"

How could I be upset about it? "No. I have my own confession."

He grinned and encouraged in a low whisper, "Let's hear it."

"I couldn't remember your name," I whispered. "But I recognized your voice when you called."

A belly laugh burst from his lips. I laughed with him. It wasn't that funny, and may just have been my nerves, but I laughed so hard a tear ran down my cheek. People at the other tables turned to look at us. Kevin reached over and wiped my tear with his thumb.

"Let me introduce myself. My name is Kevin Savage."

We shared the crab cakes as an appetizer. No surprise, Kevin ordered steak while I ordered scallops. We reached across the table and fed each other a few bites, laughing. We also did a lot of subtle, and not so subtle, knee touching, feet bumping, and hand brushing. Kevin even cleaned a dab of sauce off my chin. It could have been the wine, or Kevin's light-hearted manner, but I had fun. I'd been lonely for what felt like forever and this one night, a few laughs and a handsome face smiling at me were all I needed to be perfectly happy.

The waiter brought the dessert menu and I waited to see what Kevin would do. He barely glimpsed at it before he set it on the table.

"Want to skip dessert and walk around? We can grab an ice cream later."

I wasn't sure what this meant in terms of the dating "signals." Did he want me as dessert? Maybe he didn't care for the frou-frou options on the menu, or he wasn't a dessert guy. In any case, it was a pleasant night and Davis had a lively downtown on summer evenings.

"Sure, sounds great."

Kevin asked for the check, and I geared up for the reach. I figured safer to risk emasculating his ego, which seemed unlikely in Kevin's case, than assume he'd pay.

I'd stressed over nothing. The bill never left the waiter's hand. Kevin dropped two one hundred-dollar bills on the check presenter before the tray hit the table.

As soon as we walked out, Kevin took my hand. I led him down an almost dark path which connected the back of the restaurant to downtown Davis. He stopped me and stepped us into a shadowed corner of the walkway. Pulling me close, he said in his low, gravelly voice that made my skin tingle, "Hey, Luscious."

"Hey," I softly echoed.

"I'm having a good time with you."

Then, he kissed me soundly. It was finally dark enough for the pathway lights to flicker on. He pulled away and his face caught the light. His eyes were especially green and sleepy looking. I had seen the same expression on Jay hundreds of times. I wondered if all men got that heavy lidded, dazed air when they were turned on.

"I've wanted to do that all night," he practically growled.

It was déjà vu. I was reminded of the first time Jay had kissed me. Before I could think better, I whispered in his ear, "I have ice cream at my house."

He grinned. "Then, what are we doing here?"

We walked back to his truck. Once again, Kevin lifted me onto the seat and buckled me in. This time he kissed me before he shut the door. He kissed me again when we stopped at a traffic light. When he pulled up to my house, he told me to hold on a second. He came around to my side and carried me from the truck to my front porch, making me laugh.

Once in the house, Kevin was kissing me before I could get a light on. He cupped my butt and pulled me tightly against him. I was on my tippy toes and his hard thigh muscles were flush against mine. If it weren't for the purr of the air-conditioner, I would have sworn the AC was off. Then, I heard another purr and soft fur rubbed against my legs.

Kevin let go of me with a chuckle and bent down to pick up my cat. "Who's this guy?"

I flipped on the lights. "This guy is Buzz. My other cat is Woody."

"Woody and Buzz, funny. My kids love those movies." His smile slipped and his eyes shifted to Buzz.

Before now, he hadn't mentioned having children. I'd told him about Haley. Why he hadn't he volunteered the information earlier? "I didn't know you have kids."

He scratched Buzz's head. "Guess it didn't come up."

He didn't elaborate. I'd already noticed he didn't wear a ring and hadn't detected any tan line on his finger. He probably had a particularly nasty divorce. The mood had cooled, so I suggested we have the ice cream. He followed me to the kitchen.

"Wow, you have a yellow fridge and stove," Kevin observed.

"Yep, I do," I said with a chuckle. Jay had indulged my whim and had an auto body shop paint my appliances to match the tile. I loved my kitchen.

While I scooped Ben and Jerry's, Kevin studied the collage of photos on the wall. I wondered what he was thinking, seeing images of Jay riddled among the photos. An image of Jay staring at those same pictures flashed in my head, sending pangs zinging through my chest. Kevin's kisses set me on fire, but it was different from the way Jay heated me. I wondered if I would ever meet someone who would give me the warmth and comfort Jay had.

A lump grew in my throat. I swallowed. "Kevin, ice cream?"

He turned around and grinned, apparently having forgotten the awkward moment in the living room. "Phish Food?"

"Yep. I hope you like it."

"My favorite. Although Karmel Sutra runs a close second."

"Ever had Cherry Garcia?"

"Sissy flavor. The guys in the station wouldn't let me live it down if I walked in with it."

"So what's a manly flavor?"

"*Chubby Hubby*," he said with mock seriousness and then chuckled.

I chuckled too. He crossed the short distance between us, lifted his spoon to my lips, and fed me. Then he quickly slipped his tongue into my mouth, and we shared. "Mmmmm. My favorite way to eat ice cream," he said. "Did you like it?"

What was not to like? He pushed up the skirt of my dress and lifted me onto the counter, wedging himself between my legs. We finished eating, sharing cool bites and chocolate kisses.

I knew what was coming. *In bed by midnight*, but what did I actually know about Kevin? Nothing significant. I knew what kind of ice cream he liked; he wasn't a wine drinker; he was proud of the Hemi under his hood.

Joshua's sweet face flashed in my mind. If he and I were on a first date, we probably would be discussing books we had read, classes we had taken, and cities we would like to visit. Most likely, the night would end with a lovely kiss on my doorstep.

I remembered Mitchell Mayer not asking me to the dance because I wouldn't let him cross the panty line. Would Kevin call me again even if I did sleep with him? It felt so good to be close to someone, to have strong arms around me, to have a teasing tongue running down my neck, making me feel desired. I craved the weight and heat of a man's body on top of me. I wanted it. God, how I wanted it, and I would take one night even if that's all it would be.

His hand slid up my thigh, stopping at my panties. For once, he didn't joke. "Just so we're clear, I'm not looking for anything serious."

Kevin's brutal honesty stung. I wanted to pretend we had potential. My heart ached for the love of a man. The pain of it was overwhelming. I heard myself whisper, "Neither am I." Then I kissed him fiercely, hoping the heat of Kevin's body would cauterize my pain.

"Damn, you're a good kisser," he murmured. "Do you have a bed around here?"

I led him down the hallway past Haley's room and my home office, stopping just short of my room, and walked him into the guestroom. If it was just sex, I didn't want to have it in a bed where I'd known love.

Chapter 10

*K*EVIN RUBBED AGAINST me while his tongue explored my mouth with slow licks. He was bigger and heavier than Jay, his weight unfamiliar, but he still felt good. I unbuttoned his shirt, eager to feel his bare chest pressed against me. This was about the time when Jay would brace his body on his left side and start running his right thumb over my left nipple. Kevin didn't. He rolled over and positioned me on top. I wasn't used to this position—at least not at this stage. I sat up straddling his hips, intending to stall him by pushing off his shirt.

Why did I feel like I didn't know what to do? I knew what I was doing. Kevin wasn't Jay. Of course, sex would be different.

He reached behind me, unzipped my dress and tugged the straps off my shoulders and down my arms. Then he murmured, "I wanna see you," and flipped on the bedside lamp.

Without thinking, I yanked my dress up, covering my exposed flesh and slid off him.

His eyes blinked as they adjusted to the light. "Hey, you okay?"

"I'm sorry. I haven't …." Embarrassed, I scooted away from him.

It seemed an eternity before he spoke. "You haven't been with anyone since your ex?"

"No," I whispered.

"It's okay. I get it." He wrapped his arm around my waist, pressed his bare chest against my unzipped back and nestled his khaki covered leg between my thighs. Unsure what to do, but at the same time craving the closeness, I rested against him and watched ten minutes tick by on the bedside clock. I thought he'd fallen asleep, but then he shifted and rested on his elbow so I could look up at him. Kindness shone in his eyes, and he kissed me softly. "Hey, starting over is tough. I understand you not being ready for this. I'm going to take off and let you sleep."

Slightly panicked, I realized just how much I didn't want to be alone. "*Please*, don't go. I want to be with you."

"You sure?"

"Yeah. It's been a long time and I'm just nervous."

"Don't be. It's like riding a bike. I won't let you fall and skin your knees."

"Do you mind turning off the light?"

He switched off the bedside lamp and kissed me gently for a while before undressing me. Taking his time, he caressed my body and gave considerable attention to each of my breasts before easing into me, careful not to go too fast or rough, and made love to me with long, steady strokes. True to his word, he was a generous and considerate lover. His tenderness surprised me, just as it had the other night when he cleaned my hand after our drunken indiscretion.

Afterwards we whispered in the dark for a while. Ironically, Kevin was more illuminating, more real with the lights out. He let go of his joking manner, and I learned a few more things about him. He was thirty-eight, had an eleven-year-old daughter and a son who would be nine in September. He had a tattoo on his left shoulder that he'd gotten when he was in the Marines. He had enlisted when he was nineteen and had considered being a lifer, but his wife had talked him out of it after his second enlistment. Instead, Kevin had gone back to school, gotten his degree in Fire Science, and accepted a job with the Sacramento Fire Department. It had been a turning point in his life, and he'd never regretted the decision.

Before too long, he fell asleep. I was wide-awake. Funny how different some things were between Kevin and Jay while others were practically the same: the heavy-lidded-turned-on expression, the post-sex need to pee, and me lying energized while he slept like a beached whale. I did the same thing I often had done after Jay and I'd had sex. I cleaned myself up; then, I went to the kitchen, spread some peanut butter on Wheat Thins, and washed them down with a glass of wine. Afterwards, I crawled back in bed and lay down next to him.

I didn't know what to make of Kevin. He'd been abundantly clear that he didn't want a relationship. On the other hand, how could I stop the emotions swirling in my stomach and piercing my heart when I'd been treated with tenderness and kindness? He had taken away my pain. It would probably be back, but for now, it was gone.

Listening to his light snores, I ran my hand over his broad, smooth, and almost hairless chest. I knew every nuance of Jay's chest: the crescent scar he had from a bicycle accident when he was ten, the birthmark just to the right of his left nipple, his right side was slightly hairier than his left. I wondered if I would get to know Kevin's chest just as well.

His eyes flickered open, and he asked groggily, "What are you doing?"

"Admiring your chest."

He smiled. "Glad you like it. How you doing?"

"I'm good."

"Told you it was just like riding a bike."

"Thanks for not letting me fall and skin my knees."

"Well, I did promise your ex-husband I'd take especially good care of you." He took my hand and kissed it. "You have the softest hands." He sat up and ran his hand through his hair. "Sorry I fell asleep. What time is it?"

"Around one."

"It's late. I should take off. I have to be at work at eight."

I thought about asking him to stay, but I sensed he'd say no. He already was rummaging around for his clothes. Disappointing, but at the same time, I was relieved he was going. My affection for him had increased exponentially in the last few hours. It was best if he left before he fully engaged my emotions.

Kevin dressed with fire-drill speed and a minute later, kissed me goodbye. It wasn't a big romantic kiss with warring emotions wanting to stay. There was very little passion in it, not even close to the way he had kissed me earlier. Shooting for a quick exit, he didn't even want me to get out of bed and walk him to the door.

"I'll call you," was the last thing he said before walking out. I listened to the front door open and close. A few seconds later, the roar of his Hemi broke the silence and then faded away. He took all the warm fuzzy feelings I'd enjoyed, leaving me cold with his indifferent exit.

I got up to check the lock on the door. He'd locked it—at least it was something. Feeling deflated, I went to my own bed and hugged Jay's pillow. It was official. I'd had sex with someone besides Jay, with someone I barely knew and didn't love. But Kevin had been a lot of fun and the sex was nice. I'd had an orgasm, which I couldn't complain about. I'd enjoyed the warmth of his skin and whispering in the dark. All in all, it had been an enjoyable evening, so why was I allowing myself to feel so bummed and to be honest, guilty?

I was a divorced woman. Kevin was a grown man and had been candid about what he wanted. Neither of us had been drunk. The sex had been consensual—what was there to feel guilty about? The answer was simple: Jay. As much as I didn't want to be, I was still in love with him. I began to wonder if I would ever stop loving that man.

Maybe more sex was what I needed to numb the pain and push Jay out of my heart. While Kevin had been making love to me, I'd felt wonderful. He had wiped thoughts of Jay out of my head for a few hours. I had a title for an article. *Can Physical Love Supplant Emotional Love?* I'd have to ponder that one.

The next morning, I was up and moving by seven, but most thoughtfully waited to call Val until mid-morning. I sat at my kitchen table and doodled on the Sunday paper while we talked. After I had given her the pertinent details, came the fun part—dissecting what it all meant.

"Kevin thought Jay was jealous. Do you think he was?"

"It's only natural. He's never seen you with someone else. Knowing Jay, he doesn't want you, but he doesn't want anyone else to have you either."

"Why do you say that?"

"You're like his old Kawasaki. Remember how he loved that bike and would wash it and take it for a ride every weekend?"

"Of course I remember. It drove me batty how he used to obsess over it."

"Right. He loved it, but decided riding was too dangerous of a hobby for a father."

"Your point being?"

"My point is even though you guys needed the money, he wouldn't sell the bike. It sat in his parents' garage for a year. He didn't want it, but he couldn't stand anyone else riding it."

"So, I'm the Kawasaki?"

"Yeah." Valerie giggled. "Did Kevin really tell Jay he'd have you in bed by midnight?"

I laughed. "He did and *he did.*"

"Yes!" I visualized her doing a happy dance. "So is he a ribeye or a Sloppy Joe?"

Neither description fit. "More like barbequed ribs with sweet heat sauce."

"Made you want to suck his bone clean?"

I hooted, and when we stopped laughing, she asked, "Are you going to see him again?"

"I don't know. He said he'd call, but he also said he wasn't looking for anything serious. What do you think he meant?"

"I'd say he wants a playmate, not a girlfriend. You okay with that?"

"I guess. There's something about his green eyes and maleness oozing from him that's so fricken sexy. He's a fireman! Every woman's fantasy, right? But I don't know ...." I hesitated to tell Valerie my reservations. I sounded snooty even in my own head.

"What don't you know? The guy's hot, and it sounds like he was nice enough."

"I guess it bothers me he's not an educated man. Well, that's not true. He has a degree in Fire Science."

"He's not a *cultured* man."

"Exactly. Don't get me wrong—he's plenty intelligent, just rough around the edges if you know what I mean."

"I get you. Lady Chatterley feels like she's slumming it with the sexy gamekeeper."

We both giggled. "No! It's just I see myself with someone who wears a suit to work, someone who would know the exact wine to order. I know it's snobby and stupid."

"You elitist bitch," she joked.

"I know, I sound like my mother. He's fun. He's nice ...."

"So what if he's not your Mr. Perfect. There's nothing wrong with having a summer fling. He doesn't want more. I say no harm, no foul. Have fun. You don't have to marry him."

That was just it. In the depth of my puritanical soul, I couldn't shake feeling depraved for having sex with someone I wasn't serious about. I couldn't admit to Valerie that if I were going to sleep with Kevin again, I would want a little bit of love from him. I wanted to win his affection even though I didn't know what I would do with it if I had it.

I set the phone back in the cradle and went to the front room. The sun had shifted enough to let in the light without baking the house. When I opened the curtains, I swear I caught a glimpse of Jay's car rounding the corner. Damn, him. He was checking on me, doing a drive by to see if Kevin's truck was still here.

Less than two minutes later, my home phone rang. I raced back to the kitchen to grab it. Sure enough, *Jay Braxton* and his cell number lit up the screen.

"What do you want?" I asked.

"Good morning to you too, Sunshine. Someone's grouchy. Didn't sleep well?"

"Extremely well, thank you very much." I smiled and added, "I was in bed by midnight."

Jay grunted and asked edgily, "How was your date?"

"Fantastic. Kevin was very attentive."

"Does Kevin have a last name?"

"Savage. Why do you ask?"

"I don't trust the guy. You shouldn't either."

Jay could be such an ass. "What's wrong? Jealous?"

"No, but I still worry about you. I swear, firemen and cops are the most randy bunch of guys. I don't want to see you hurt, that's all."

"No, I think you don't want me, but you don't want anyone else to have me either. I'm like your old Kawasaki gathering dust in your parents' garage."

He laughed at the metaphor. "You and Valerie come up with the craziest theories."

"Do you have my phone tapped?"

"Come on, would I really tap your phone? After listening to you two yap, yap, yap for years, I know the way you gals think." He was smug, but there was fond teasing in his voice.

"You think you're soooo clever," I teased back.

"I know I'm clever." His voice lowered. "Are you busy today?"

My heart thumped faster. Maybe seeing me with someone else was all it took to make him come to his senses and realize he still loved me. "Why do you ask?"

"I talked to a guy who's interested in the Panamera. I'd like to show him the car and then maybe we can have lunch and review a plan I worked out for taking over the house." The fond familiarity disappeared. Jay was all business, and I was an idiot. He didn't want me back. He wanted his house back. The tender moment we'd shared in our kitchen the night before had been an aberration—a moment of weakness brought on by a wave of nostalgia. I sunk down on the floor and leaned against the cupboard while Jay talked. "I figured you'd be anxious to get things settled. When are you planning to move?"

My voice squeaked out, "I'm shooting for beginning of September."

"Works for me. Will you be home around noon today?"

"You can show the car, but I won't be here. I have plans." I didn't have plans, but I wasn't up for seeing him. He had no idea how much he jerked my heart around; no idea how he ignited my emotions and had me ricocheting between dejection, hopefulness, and fury.

"Can I come over now? I'm not far away."

"I know. I saw you drive past the house."

"Oh." He obviously didn't know what else to say.

There I was again with an apple-sized lump in my throat, a weight on my chest, and tears pooling on the edges of my eyes. He didn't drive by to check on me. He drove by to see his house, just as he had done while we waited for escrow to close all those years ago. He couldn't wait to have me out so he could move in. I couldn't say anything without crying.

"Kimmy? You still there?"

"Yeah, I'm here."

"Are you crying?"

"No."

"I know you're crying," he said as if he gave a shit. "I'm coming over."

My pain gave way to anger. "DON'T. I don't want you hovering around here like some vulture waiting for my carcass to be out the door!"

"What the hell are you talking about?"

I steadied my voice and clamped down my emotions as much as possible. "Put your plan for the house in writing. I'll have my attorney review it."

I hung up and went to the guest room. The bed was a heap of jumbled sheets. I fell on it and pushed the memory of Kevin's cool exit out of my mind as I hugged the pillow he had slept on and inhaled faint hints of sandalwood and spice. I wished he were next me, numbing my pain. I wanted his strong, warm body pushing the love I had for Jay out of my heart.

Tempting as it was to wallow in self-pity, I pulled myself up, found my iPod, and queued up Cher. I had no control over Jay, but I had control over my reactions to him. I could let heartache consume me, or I could do something positive. No more pity parties. As a woman of action, I planned to go shopping for a new bed and all new bedding. The next time Kevin was over, I'd have him in *my* bedroom.

Chapter 11

I WAS BEGINNING TO wonder if there would be a next time with Kevin. Urban wisdom dictates, and Valerie concurred, if a man likes a woman, he'd call or text within three days of their last encounter. I didn't think about it Sunday—at least not too much; I'd been busy shopping and washing sheets. Every time my phone rang on Monday, I'd jumped. By Tuesday evening, I was convinced I'd never hear from Kevin again.

Weary of pathetically checking my phone for a text and waiting for a nonexistent call, I changed my clothes and was about to head to the gym when my home phone made a teasing sound. Dreading and anticipating disappointment, I peaked at the caller id.

My heart did a little zippidy-doo. "Hey, Kevin," I answered much less coolly than I'd intended.

"Hey, Luscious. How'd you know it was me?"

"I'm psychic."

"Or you have caller id."

"Damn. I'm defrauded."

He laughed. "I had fun the other night."

"Me, too."

"I was hoping we could have some more fun. What are you doing?"

"Getting ready to go to the gym. What are *you* doing?"

"Thinking about you," he declared with his low gravelly voice sounding extra sexy.

"Oh, really?"

"Uh-huh. I've been thinking about you all day."

"Then why didn't you call earlier?"

"My kids were with me, but now they're with their mother. I thought I'd have them all night, but now I'm free. You up for company?"

Booty Call. He didn't ask me out. He wanted to see me now, at night, no date. This was a booty call. Did I care? No, I did not. I said, "Come on over."

"I'm already halfway to your house," he answered with a chuckle.

I bemoaned my new bed hadn't been delivered yet, and quickly brushed my teeth, shaved my legs and pits, and put on a clean pair of khaki shorts and a polo shirt. I checked myself out in the mirror. What was I thinking? I looked like I was heading to a PTA end of year barbeque. I yanked off the mom khakis and conservative polo and wiggled into a pair of butt hugging cut offs and a snug tank top. A minute later, Kevin's Hemi announced his arrival.

Grinning, he sauntered sexy as sin up the pathway to my door. Faded jeans hung from his hips and a Sacramento River Cats t-shirt stretched over his broad chest and biceps. He wasn't clean-shaven, but dang, was he mouth-watering with a sprinkling of dark stubble. I checked my desire to lead him straight to the bedroom. Even though I knew why he was here, I wanted to be civilized about it.

I greeted him with a smile.

He dipped his head and greeted me with a toe-tingling kiss, his eyes already heavy lidded. "How you doing, Luscious?"

"Alright. Would you like a beer?"

"Sure, I'll take a beer."

Luckily, I'd stocked up the day before, just in case. He'd ordered an Anchor Steam at the restaurant, but I thought he'd been drinking Sierra Nevada at the club. I had a six-pack of both chilling in my refrigerator. He took a Sierra Nevada, no glass.

Five minutes later, we were making-out on the family room couch. Ten minutes after that, we were in the guest room ripping off clothes, where we stayed undressed for the next couple hours. This time I wasn't nervous. This time Kevin wasn't slow and gentle. This time I got a taste of how good it felt to have mama-needs-to-get-laid-wild-monkey sex. The kind of sex where you're not worried about anyone's emotional state or getting lost in someone's eyes. Just sex for pure physical pleasure. It was freeing. I sensed Kevin was freer. He didn't have to worry about me the way he had the first time, and the sex was great. He made me feel great.

Kevin had no hang-ups with his nudity. He walked buck-naked back into the bedroom after disposing his condom in the bathroom. He slid back in bed and spooned me.

"I like spooning you. It's like a two-for-one. I get to press against your beautiful round ass and cup your soft cans at the same time." His muscular, hairy leg resting between my thighs and his bare chest warming my back sustained my arousal. I had no complaints with spooning.

We'd had to burn some of the lust out of our systems before either one of us could focus on conversation. With our bodies temporarily satiated, he asked, "So what've you been up?"

"Mmmm … writing … and I've been cleaning out cupboards. I'm not sure if I told you, but I'm moving to San Francisco in September."

"No, you didn't." His voice caught and he sounded disappointed. I liked that. "Need to get away from your ex, huh?"

"Yeah."

"I can relate."

He didn't elaborate, and once again, I had to stop myself from asking about his ex-wife. He propped himself up and studied my face with the little bit of light provided by a candle I had lit. He brushed a strand of hair off my face and grinned.

"Did you really not have sex from the time your husband left until me? I mean, that had to be at least a whole year."

"Yep, a little over a year."

It still boggled me why Jay made love to me the night before he left. I wouldn't have thought too much about it if he hadn't. All he would have had to say was *I'm too wiped,* but he hadn't, making it easy to remember the last time I'd had sex.

Kevin kept grinning and asked playfully, "So what did you do for a whole year?"

"Kevin! I can't believe what you're asking."

He laughed at me. "What? We just had some smoking hot *sex*. You about blew out my eardrum, so I know it was good for you, too. You embarrassed to talk about it?"

"You're making me blush." Jay and I had rarely discussed sex. It was just something we did. I guess I'd been more fervent than I'd thought and hadn't realized I'd been so vocal. At least Kevin appreciated my enthusiasm.

"Don't be embarrassed with me. I love sex. It's the most natural thing in the world between two people. You don't have to be shy about telling me what you like." He lowered his head close to my ear and whispered. "You can tell me. Did you buy a vibrator?"

I snorted with laughter and couldn't answer.

"Knew it! Luscious has a play toy," he continued to tease. "Can I see it?"

"No!"

"How are you going to write about sex if you're too embarrassed to talk about it?"

"I'm not going to write explicit blow-by-blows."

Kevin snorted with laughter. "What? You gonna call it a mouth mambo?"

I blushed again. "I didn't mean it that way. I write more about relationships and emotions. I throw in humorous anecdotes but leave out names."

I could feel him tense. He edged away from me and rolled me on my back so we could face each other. He stopped grinning. "We're just having fun, right?"

"Yeah, just fun. You make me feel good." I answered honestly. Physically, I was extremely attracted to him, but he wasn't my Mr. Perfect. Kevin had two school-aged children. I was finding my balance and getting over Jay. Kevin was fun and *fun* was perfect.

My answer must have satisfied him because he smiled happily and cuddled next to me again. "Aren't you going to ask me what I've been up to the last couple of days?"

"What've you been doing?"

"I spent yesterday and today with my kids. I took them on a fishing trip."

"Sounds like a nice time. You're off a lot, aren't you?"

"Sort of. We work twenty-four-hour shifts starting at 8 a.m., and then have two days off. In an emergency, we work more, but mostly that's how it works."

"Oh, so you really did have to work Sunday."

"Uh-huh and I was a real-live hero. Do you want to hear about it?"

"Yeah, tell me."

"It was about six o'clock at night and we got sent out because some toddler had locked her parents out of their house."

"Where was the toddler?"

"In the house. Apparently, they were eating dinner on their deck and their two-year old slipped inside. When she shut the sliding door, it locked."

"I take it all the other doors were locked the windows were closed up because of the air conditioning?"

"You got it. Anyway, when we got there, the dad was calm, but the mom was losing it."

"I don't blame her. I'd be freaking out too if it were my daughter."

"Sure and we didn't know if the little girl was in any kind of real danger. If she wasn't, we'd pick the front door lock. If she was, my job was to boot it open. So I'm walking around to the front with the dad, while the other guys spread out to peek in windows to try to find her and I get the call. Boot the door. I ran to the front. One good kick and I'm in."

"You can do that?"

"There's a technique to it, but yeah, it's part of our training."

I envisioned his strong leg in motion. "If you're trying to impress me, it's working." He chuckled and flexed his muscles against me. I giggled and urged, "Okay, what happened next?"

His voice lowered dramatically. "I found her in the kitchen."

I imagined the toddler bleeding from a knife wound or knocked out after falling off a counter. "What happened to her?"

"She was standing on the counter with her face covered with cookie crumbs and an Oreo in each hand. She looked at me with her big brown eyes and said, 'Cookie?'"

"What'd you do?"

"Ate it."

I laughed. "You ate it?"

"Actually, I picked her up first. She was barefoot and standing on a cutting board with a knife still on it. She could've easily been hurt. We figured the little rugrat probably locked her parents out on purpose just so she could eat cookies."

That night was the real beginning of our non-relationship. I saw him a couple nights a week, and the first thing we always did was rip off each other's clothes off. It reminded me of Jay and me when we were in the first throes of discovering each other's bodies. The difference was Jay and I had had more enthusiasm than skill. Kevin knew exactly what he was doing. He eased me out of my comfort zone and had me in positions I would never have imagined. Nothing kinky, *uninhibited* described it best. Kevin had no inhibitions. He didn't understand why I preferred the dark, but he respected my request to keep the light off.

Sometimes we went out for dinner. Sometimes I cooked. We never met each other's friends. He never stayed the night. We never discussed anything significant. He recounted things that happened at work, never bad things, just anecdotes he thought I'd find amusing. Occasionally, he brought me flowers, and I stocked beer in the refrigerator for him.

Every now and then, Kevin took my breath away with a tender kiss or unusually gentle touch or a soft look in his beguiling green eyes, but ninety percent of the time, he kept things light. I welcomed him like a delta breeze whenever he blew into town, knowing he wouldn't stay long. We were two people seizing the pleasure of the moment, and I was surprisingly satisfied with this arrangement. Sleeping with Kevin was different than it had been with Jay. It just was. I liked Kevin, lusted for him, but my heart wasn't engaged. Kevin either didn't notice or didn't care, and my puritanical guilt eased with each visit.

I worried this made me a bad person. I didn't like the idea Kevin was using me, but maybe I was using him. Maybe we were using each other?

Despite renewing somewhat regular communication with Jay and seeing him more frequently, the more time I spent with Kevin, the less I thought about Jay. Interestingly, my fascination with Joshua held strong. I stopped feeling nervous around him and looked forward to our chance meetings. The last time I'd seen him, I'd been cruising down the dairy aisle when I'd heard his voice coming from behind.

"Oh hey, Kimberly, how's it going?" I turned to face him, and his body brushed mine. He grinned down at me and peeked in my cart. "Looks like you're grilling tonight. Don't forget your cheese."

"Cheese?"

"Yeah, Tillamook extra sharp cheddar two-pound blocks are our featured Secret Saver."

"That's a lot of cheese for one person." We both laughed, and he walked me to the deli section and had me buy a couple slices of fontina.

Joshua was my guilty pleasure—my secret friend who had a way of making me smile.

I didn't know how long things would last with Kevin, but for now, I simply enjoyed the ride. Valerie and I agreed, it was a perfect summer affair.

Physical love was displacing emotional love. It was possible.

Chapter 12

KEVIN HAD SHIFTED gears on me the night before. He hadn't said anything specific, but when he'd left, it'd been the first time in the seven or so weeks we'd been seeing each other that I'd sensed hesitancy at his departure. He hadn't given me a perfunctory peck and gruffly said, "I'll call you," in a manner which always made me doubt he actually would. Instead, he'd taken my face in his hands and given me a long, lingering kiss. I had opened my mouth to ask him not to go but the words froze in my throat. I wasn't sure if I hesitated because I was afraid of wanting more than he was willing to give, or because I didn't want to give more.

When my phone rang the next morning, I was surprised—but not astonished—to see Kevin's name on the screen. He typically didn't call when he was at work. He just had learned his kids were going out of town with their mother for a few days, which meant after his shift ended, he'd be completely free for two days. His voice was playful, and I visualized him grinning like crazy.

"So hey, Luscious, how does a quick trip up to Tahoe sound? I can get us a room with a hot tub at one of the casinos. We can do a little gambling, maybe catch a show."

I snickered. He wasn't thinking about a show. He was thinking about being naked in a hot tub. "Sounds like fun, but I already made plans to be in San Francisco. I'm sorry."

"That's a bummer," he answered as if it wasn't a big deal, and he wasn't too bummed.

I didn't want him to think I expected him not to go just because I couldn't. "I'm sure you can find someone else to go with you."

"What the hell is that supposed to mean?"

I'd never heard him cross, and it shook me. "It means I don't mind if you go with someone else."

A couple beats passed before he said, "I don't want to go with *some-one else*."

I hadn't intended to hurt his feelings and backpedaled. "I didn't mean it like that. I meant one of your buddies from work."

He chuckled. "I'm not sharing a hot tub with any of those guys." His voice lowered. "I wanted to spend a whole night with you."

The phone warmed against my ear and the armor protecting my heart cracked, allowing a little love to seep in. It was dangerous; I was asking for heartache but couldn't stop. "We don't have to go to Tahoe for you to spend the night with me."

"I didn't think you wanted me to stay."

"Why would you think that?"

"You've never asked."

He was right—I hadn't. I justified it because I was almost certain he would say no. After all, he was the one who had proposed a no-strings affair. Obviously, he hadn't wanted to leave the night before. He had been angling for an invitation to stay.

"Why don't you come with me to San Francisco and then stay the night?"

"What are you doing in the city?"

"Taking my daughter to lunch and then touring apartments."

"I don't think that's a good idea."

"Why?"

I could hear him taking a deep breath. He exhaled into the phone, "You seriously want me to meet your daughter?"

Apparently, nothing I said was going to be the right answer. I backpedaled again. "She's not a little girl. She can handle my *friend* coming with us to lunch. It's not a big deal."

"Is that what I am?"

"Kevin, I seriously don't know what you're asking me."

"Forget it. Look, how about if I just come by when you get back? We can go to that burger place you keep telling me about."

"Will you bring your toothbrush?"

He chuckled. "Yeah, I'll bring my toothbrush."

Baffled, I hung up the phone. Kevin had been abundantly clear he wasn't interested in a girlfriend, but now he was upset because I wasn't possessive enough? Then, he recoiled when I tried to include him in my life. He should come with a decoder.

So frustrating. I picked up the phone to call him back and then set it back down. When Jay used to say forget it, I'd bug him until he told me what his problem was. Half the time I'd regretted knowing. I decided to let it go. I wasn't Kevin's wife or even his girlfriend. I was just someone with whom he was *hanging out.*

⸻

It turned out to be a good thing Kevin wasn't with me in San Francisco. Haley and I needed time alone. She ended up spending the whole day with me. It didn't take long after I'd picked her up for her to spill her troubles.

Without warning, and just as we crossed the control lights entering the Bay Bridge, she blurted, "I don't want to go back to school."

I tapped the breaks in order not to hit the car in front of me and forced myself to keep my eyes on the road. Her announcement wasn't something any mother wants to hear, let alone while driving sixty miles an hour in heavy merging traffic. My gut reaction was no way—just wait until Jay heard about it.

As calmly as possible I asked, "How long have you been thinking about it?"

"Ever since I found out you were planning to move to San Francisco."

"What does my moving have to do with you dropping out?"

"I wouldn't drop out. I'd take a leave of absence."

"Do you know how hard it is to get into the groove of school after taking time off? If your father hadn't kept me motivated, I don't know if I could've done it."

"It's not like I have a baby to worry about. Come on Mom, you're regrouping. You know, figuring out what you really want to do. I can use some regrouping, too. Honestly, I don't want to be a lawyer and Political Science is boring. I like talking politics with Dad, but it's nothing like all the classes. I just can't get into it, and I'm dreading next semester."

Haley dribbled tears, making it hard to stay stern. "There's tissue in my purse."

"Thanks," she sniffed and dug through my purse. After she blew her nose, she pleaded her case. "I don't know what I want to do, and it seems like a waste of time and money to keep going to school. I'll go back. I just want a little time to chill, think ... and have some fun. Plus, I'm burned out. I shouldn't have taken classes this summer. I'm tired. I'm just so tired."

She had a point. Just because Jay and I had rushed through life, didn't mean Haley had to move at our pace. She was young and had time. What did it matter if she took a break to clear her head and find a new direction? Jay wouldn't be happy, but not having to pay her fall tuition would be a welcome break. Besides, she looked exhausted. She'd pushed herself with too many classes. Like Jay, she was a type A. It would be good for her to learn to relax.

"I suppose a break might be a good thing. You won't be able to live in the dorm though."

"I know. I figured I'd live with you."

"Me?" *Kevin.* What would happen to my new sex life? Not just sex, what would happen with Kevin? It hit me he meant much more to me than I had dared admit.

"Sure. You said you were getting a two bedroom so I could have my own room. You said I would always have a home with you."

"Honey, I know, but wouldn't you be happier rooming with girls your own age?"

"No. I'll still have my friends. I can hang with them, but I don't like having a roommate. I like having my own space."

"You'd have to share space with me."

"That's different. You're my mom."

"But what about ... boys?"

Haley snorted. "I don't have a boyfriend. I haven't had time for one, but I wouldn't mind finding one." Through the corner of my eye, I saw her smile at the thought. "Don't worry; I won't have sleepovers with you in the apartment. Jeesh, how embarrassing would that be?"

Yeah, jeesh—how embarrassing. "Have you thought about living with your father? He'll be back in the house, and you can have your old room. You still have friends in Davis."

"Not good friends. There's no way I'm living with dad," she stated firmly. "He's dating. It'd be just too weird. Besides, he treats me like I'm still in high school, and I don't want to live in Davis. I want to live in San Francisco."

Did she assume I wasn't dating? That I was too old to date? Before I could articulate my next argument, my phone rang and lit up the car Bluetooth screen. I was changing lanes and asked Haley, "Who is it?"

"916—pretty sure it's Dad's office. Should I answer?"

"Sure, go ahead."

Haley tapped the screen and said, "Hey there."

"Hey, Luscious. When are you going to have your beautiful ass home?"

I cringed hearing Kevin's gravelly voice all intimate and playful. He liked a little phone foreplay before he saw me. In truth, I liked it too.

"Uh, Kevin. You're on speaker and my daughter is in the car."

"Oh, sorry. Hi, Haley."

"Hi," she squeaked.

"Kimberly, can you call me later when you get a chance?" He'd had a buzz kill; his playfulness and intimate tone were gone.

"Sure. I'll call you back after I park."

As soon as the phone disconnected Haley exclaimed, "Who was that?"

"My friend, Kevin Savage." I did my best to sound casual, which was nearly impossible with Haley practically jumping out of her seat. "I told you about him."

"*Luscious*? Your *beautiful ass*? He calls you *Luscious*?"

"Apparently."

"Mom, wow. I mean, you said you had a new friend, not that you were like, you know …. Is he your boyfriend?"

Being a mother, I was supposed to set an example. I couldn't tell her Kevin wasn't exactly my boyfriend, just someone I had sex with a couple times a week, no strings. I really didn't know what he was. "I'm too old for boyfriends. He's my *friend*."

"What does he do for a living?"

"He's a fireman."

Haley snorted with laughter. "Jeeze—well, good for you. Didn't know you had it in you. I imagined you dating some widowed old geezer, but you're dating a fireman who calls you *Luscious*." She snickered again.

"Haley Braxton, enough. I'm not that old."

"I know, but you're my mom. It just didn't occur to me. Do you have a picture of him?"

I sighed. "There's a picture of him on my phone. I'll show you after I park." There were a few text messages I'd rather Haley not see and didn't want her cruising around my phone.

After I'd maneuvered off the freeway and pulled into a parking space, I flipped through my phone until I found my favorite photo of Kevin, grinning with a day's worth of whiskers covering his strong jaw. The photo captured his playful nature and his twinkling green eyes. I couldn't help smiling when I handed my cell to Haley.

"Wow, he's definitely not an old geezer."

"Nope, he isn't."

"Not that I'm crushing on your guy, but he's like hot. Hope you're using condoms."

"Haley!"

"Just saying."

"And I'm not discussing this with you. *Jeesh.*" I took my phone back and looked at him one more time before I closed the application. "He makes me laugh. I have fun with him. Now can you please give me a minute? I need to call him back."

Haley waited outside the car while I called Kevin and arranged to meet him when I got back. He was back to his easygoing self, but with a small difference. There was more affection in his voice, and I responded in kind. I couldn't deny something real was growing between us. It couldn't be "just for fun" anymore. Kevin had never been explicit as to why he didn't want anything serious. I assumed it had to do with his children. My only certainty was things had changed, and we couldn't continue as we had.

When I got out of the car, Haley asked pointblank, "So are we going to be roomies or what?"

I felt like a bad mother for not welcoming her with open arms. A few months ago, I would've been thrilled. Since then, I had grown accustomed to having *my own space.*

"You need to talk to your dad first. He's the one paying for college."

Haley made her eyes big and batted her lashes. "I was sort of hoping since you and Dad are getting along these days that you'd talk to him first?"

"Oh no, little miss. Your please-mommy-please eyes won't work. If you want to be treated like an adult, you have to do the grownup thing and talk to him yourself." Knowing Jay, there was a good chance he'd talk her into continuing with school. If he did, I'd be off the hook.

⸺

When I pulled into my driveway, Kevin's truck was already parked in front of the house. He sat reclined on the front porch with his long legs stretched out. A small duffle bag and a bouquet of flowers rested next to him. He stood when he saw me and met me halfway.

"Hi, Handsome," I said and smiled up at him.

"Hey, Gorgeous. You've never called me that before."

"I know but I've thought it. You are handsome. Uhhmph," I gasped when he scooped me up around the waist and carried me to the porch.

"What took you so long?" he asked.

"Traffic. I'm sorry."

"It's okay." He set me down and handed me the flowers. "These are for you."

"Thank you. They're beautiful." I reached up and gave him a quick kiss before unlocking the door.

He picked up his duffle bag, followed me into the house, and asked, "Should I put this in the guest room?"

His question stopped me dead in my tracks. Although my new bed had been delivered weeks ago, we'd stuck to the guestroom. I had deluded myself into believing he hadn't noticed and was afraid of giving the wrong answer.

"Please, put it in my room."

Kevin's smile widened. He went straight to my room. When he was here, I always kept doors shut. I wasn't sure how he knew which door led to my room. After being in so many houses, he must have had a sense of where the master bedroom would be.

He walked in the kitchen as I placed the flowers, which were now in a vase, on the table. I turned around and hugged him around the waist, and he wrapped his arms around me. Our embrace wasn't charged with sexual energy the way it had been only a few nights ago. It was more as if we were simply happy to be close again.

He nuzzled my hair and murmured, "Did you miss me?"

"I did. I missed you a lot," I murmured back. "I'm glad you're staying the night."

We were inching closer, like dipping our toes to test the temperature of the water. I was afraid he would pull back any second and remind me we're just having fun. I gazed up and our eyes met. He gave me a tender kiss, taking my breath away, and then the moment was over. He pulled back and a coolness zinged me. I wanted more and couldn't pretend otherwise.

"I'm starving," he said. "Let's go eat."

We left without having sex first. It made me feel like a real couple. We didn't have to be naked to get pleasure out of each other's company. Since it wasn't too hot, we decided to walk, and Kevin held my hand.

"Did you see an apartment you liked?" he asked nonchalantly.

"I did. It has hardwood floors, two-bedrooms, and an actual dining room. The kitchen is smaller than I'd like; otherwise, it's perfect."

"Is it in a safe neighborhood?"

"Yes."

"How secure is the building?"

I smiled up at him. "Are you worried about me?"

He glanced down at me and frowned. "Well, yeah. How long does it take to get there?"

"About an hour and half depending on traffic."

"That's not too bad," he said more to himself than me. He didn't elaborate, and we walked in comfortable silence for the next couple blocks.

"So what did you do today?" I asked, breaking the quiet between us.

"I checked out a couple townhouses and condos."

"I didn't know you were planning to move too."

"My place feels more cramped every day. I should have moved a long time ago."

I'd never seen his place, but suspected he lived in some man cave. I hoped it meant he planned to have me visit and wanted a decent home in which to entertain me.

"What's stopped you?"

"Kids, timing." He paused and shrugged. "Just things."

Our conversation was halted by the crowd spilling onto the sidewalk and grassy area in front of the restaurant. I wasn't surprised by the line. It was Farmer's Market night and downtown crawled with people out enjoying the evening.

The first person I recognized was Carol and then her husband, Richard. Carol did a double-take and elbowed Richard. He appeared equally alarmed. I hadn't spoken to her since the night she hosted my divorce party. I smiled and did a sort of I-come-in-peace wave.

She forced a smile as I approached her and gave me a half-hug. "How've you been?"

"I've been great. Carol, this is my good friend, Kevin. Kevin, these are my friends, Carol and her husband, Richard."

They all said hello and shook hands politely. Kevin slipped his arm around my waist and kept it there, squelching any doubt as to the nature of our friendship. I was deeply grateful for his gesture; his possessiveness didn't escape their notice.

"It really is good to see you," Carol said leaning toward me. "I've been meaning to call you. Can I steal you for a minute?"

"Sure." She and I walked a few feet away. "I hope you got my thank you card."

"I did. It was lovely." She glanced over my shoulder and said in a rush, "Please, don't think I'm choosing Jay over you. I would've much rather had you wine tasting with us than that Amber girl. Honestly, it was uncomfortable for everyone."

"Thank you for telling me."

The initial uneasiness between us dissipated. I was about to suggest we share a table when she said, "I hate this, but Jay is meeting us with a date any minute."

So much for not choosing Jay over me. "Thanks for the warning."

I went back to Kevin and was about to recommend another restaurant when Jay just had to show up. "Hi guys, sorry we're late. Parking was a bitch."

Kevin and I turned in unison to face Jay. The smile on Jay's face froze. The girl with him couldn't have been older than twenty-five. Kevin stood directly behind me and placed his hands on either side of my waist while Jay glared at Kevin with open dislike.

Richard broke the tension. "No worries. We were just catching up with Kimberly." Clearly not wanting to be caught between Jay and me, he turned to his wife and said, "Let's go check on the wait."

Before we had a chance to leave, Jay thrust his hand at Kevin and said with his phony nice voice, "Hey, man. Good to see you again." The men shook hands; their knuckles whitened, and veins popped up from both their hands. Then, Jay introduced his date. "Kimberly, Kevin, this is Brittany."

It was a surreal meeting, but I tried to play it cool. "Nice to meet you, Britney."

"No, not Britney, like Britney Spears. I'm Britt*any*."

"Ah," Britt*any*, a young name for a young girl. I was determined to be polite and asked Britt*any*, "As in the French region?"

She wrinkled her brow. "I don't think so."

I let it go. "So, do you live in Davis?"

"No. I live in Natomas with my girlfriends, but I work for an attorney in Davis. I'm an administrative assistant." She eyed Kevin and giggled for no apparent reason. Red blotches colored her face. I wasn't sure if she was intimidated by my presence or Kevin's.

Ignoring her, Jay smiled at me the way he used to when we'd been apart for a bit. His smile said *just looking at you makes me happy.* "You look really nice tonight, Kimmy."

I couldn't help smiling back. "Thank you."

Kevin wrapped his arm around me again.

As if not wanting to give the wrong impression, Jay draped his arm on Brittany's shoulder and said to her, "You look beautiful tonight, too."

She let loose another giggle. I decided only her youth saved her from being plain. As far as I could tell, she didn't have a sparkling personality or the intelligence to compensate for her shortfalls. The whole situation was wrong, and everyone except Brittany knew it. Jay should not have had his arm around that girl, and I should not have been leaning against Kevin. Jay and I should have been together, but as things stood, Jay would rather be with unspectacular Britt*any* than with me. It would have hurt a lot less if she looked like Scarlett Johansson or had a P.H.D. in nuclear physics.

Moreover, Brittany was staring lustfully at Kevin. She already had Jay. Why was she batting her eyes at Kevin? I began to worry Brittany knew some secret voodoo-he-doo to captivate men and was trying to work her magic on Kevin.

She blurted, "You're March, aren't you?"

Kevin chuckled. "Yeah, it's me."

"I knew it," she squealed.

Kevin explained, "I'm in one of those firemen calendars—you know, for charity."

"My roommates think you have the best abs. Our calendar is still on March," she said with another giggle.

Jay's jaw twitched, and I knew he was grinding his teeth. So was I. Part of me was fuming over the way the twit was blatantly flirting with my guy and part of me, stupid me, hurt for Jay. He was a handsome, sexy man. What was that little fool doing?

I opened my mouth to shut her down, but Jay said, "I hear they airbrush those calendars."

Kevin laughed and tightened his grip on me. "Kimberly is the only one who could tell you for sure." Then he said for my ears only, "Let's go. It's a little crowded here."

We made our excuses and moved on to a pub not too far away but far enough to be removed from them. With our spirits a little lower, we drank our beer, ate our bar food, and pretended nothing had happened until a droplet slid down my cheek.

Kevin took my hand and brought it to his lips. "Don't cry, Baby. He's not worth it."

"I know. It's just … why Brittany—not that I care he's with someone else …" I did care, but I wasn't going to tell Kevin. "… but *her*?"

"Want to know what I was thinking?"

I shrugged. "What?"

He set his burger down and leaned closer to me. "He's standing there with that giggly girl who's not even close to being in your league, and all I could think was the guy's an idiot. You're beautiful. You're smart and fun. You're great in the kitchen and great other places, too. Did he honestly think he'd find someone out there better? The guy's a fucking idiot."

I had to smile at his assessment. I wasn't sure how much he said just to make me feel better, but I hoped he was sincere about at least half of it. I also hoped it meant he wouldn't be kicking me to the curb as Jay had done.

"Thank you for saying it, but Jay and I had our problems."

"Most couples do." Kevin looked at me with kindness. "I wish he didn't bum you out. I wish I could burn him out of you."

"When I'm with you, you do."

A small smile curved his lips. "Maybe I should spend more time with you."

I grinned, liking his suggestion. "Maybe you should."

Chapter 13

KEVIN SURVEYED MY collection of A&E dramatizations of classics, which included my favorite version of *Pride and Prejudice* starring Colin Firth, and immediately vetoed any "chick" movie. *Bridget Jones Diary*, also starring Colin Firth, was probably out, but I suggested it anyway.

He frowned. "Come on, don't you have something with a little action."

"There's a fight scene between Colin Firth and Hugh Grant in *Bridget Jones*." The smirk on his face told me he wasn't buying it. "Check the bottom drawer of the TV cabinet; there should be something with a few explosions and blood. Pick out anything you like. I'll make us some popcorn." Walking away, I chuckled. Jay and I'd had similar conversations.

When I returned with the popcorn, Kevin had *Men In Black* on the screen. Like ghosts lurking about, every now and then something would jolt a memory of Jay.

Men In Black and *Titanic*, starring a young Leonardo DiCaprio, had been playing the summer we had started dating. I, of course, had been dying to see *Titanic*; Jay had wanted to see *Men In Black*. After a little debate, Jay took me to see Leo.

We'd walked hand-in-hand out of the movie theater.

"I can't believe I sat through that movie," Jay said with an exaggerated groan.

"I loved it," I said grinning and laughing at him.

Jay laughed, too. "Since it made you happy, I guess it was worth mowing a few lawns. You know what this means, don't you?"

"You're a really good boyfriend?"

"Well, that too." He stopped walking, pulled me around to face him, and held both my hands with our fingers entwined. People had to step around us to get into the theater, but no one else existed for me except Jay. He smiled and said, "I must be in love."

Looking into his eyes with my heart swelling, I knew I would love Jay Braxton until the day I died, maybe even longer, and said, "Me, too."

It had been the happiest day of my young life. To prove I loved him as much as he loved me, I'd spent my babysitting money treating him to see *Men In Black* the next night. I had assumed Jay forgot all about it, but for our tenth wedding anniversary, he gave me a copy of *Titanic*. Coincidentally, I gave him a copy of *Men In Black* the same night. We had arranged for Haley to stay the night with a friend and spent our anniversary watching the movies and making love on the couch and family room floor.

Not wanting Kevin to know any of this, I said, "Sorry, I've seen that movie a few times too many. What do you say to *The Wedding Crashers?*"

The comedy was a good compromise, and we both thought it was a funny flick. By the time the credits rolled, Jay was out of my head. It occurred to me this was the longest Kevin and I had been together without ripping off our clothes. I hit the remote and grinned up at him.

"What?" he asked.

"We've been together for over four hours and our clothes are still on."

He reached his hand under my shirt and fondled my breasts. "We should do something about that." He kissed me and then picked me up and started carrying me to my bedroom.

I lightly protested, "You do know I can walk, right?"

"I'm aware, but I like carrying you."

"Why's that?"

"Because it turns you on."

I laughed. "What woman wouldn't like a big strong man carrying her?"

He dropped me on the bed, crawled on top of me, and asked, "Is that all I am to you?"

His tone was light, but underneath he was testing the waters again. I wanted to tell him he had come to mean much more to me, but worried about coming on too strong.

"No." I smiled and rubbed my hands up his chest, over his shoulders, and down his bulging biceps. "You're my big strong *lover*."

He smirked and chuckled. "Guess it's better than being your *good friend*. So next time are you going to introduce me as your big, strong *lover*?"

I laughed again. "I think I will."

He laughed too, before he asked more seriously, "Tell me something. Why haven't you invited me into your bedroom before?"

How could I tell him that the first time we were together, I didn't want to have sex with him in a bed I had shared with Jay? Jay's side of the bed had still smelled like him, and I had gone a whole year without wanting a new mattress because there had been an indent from Jay's body on the left side of the bed? Later, I didn't know how to explain.

"I didn't think you'd noticed."

"You must really think I'm stupid. None of your things are in the guestroom. There's no make-up or perfume, no bracelet sitting on a dresser."

"I know you're not stupid. I'd hoped you hadn't noticed."

"Kimberly, you can tell me." He looked into my eyes. "Are you uncomfortable with me being here now?"

"No. I like you here."

"Then tell me," he whispered close to my ear and then nuzzled my neck.

His kisses tickled, and I wiggled underneath him. "If I tell you, will you tell me something?"

His eyes sparked and twinkled playfully. "What, like Truth or Dare?"

I giggled. "You're on—truth or dare?"

"Dare."

"I dare you to tell the truth."

"Ah, that's cheating." He rolled off me and flopped on his back.

"Nope, it's a loophole in the rules."

"Shit ... alright, lay it on me."

Did I really want to know? I had been curious. I sat up a bit, leaning on my elbow. "The night we met, you said you'd call me, I didn't believe you. Why did you?"

He groaned and covered his eyes with his hand. "Ah hell, you're going to hate me ...."

"Did you think you were calling someone else and got me?"

"No. Trust me, I knew exactly who I was calling."

"Then why would I hate you? Tell me," I insisted, pulling his hand down from his eyes.

He sighed. "Shit. You're right, I wasn't going to call, but you gave me a handjob. No one's done that since high school. I couldn't stop thinking about how soft your hands were."

A belly laugh burst from my lips. I jumped on top of him, straddling his hips, and wiggled against him. "So my high school moves won you over?"

"That's about it, but I also liked that you were easy to make laugh. Ah, hell. Okay, my turn—truth or dare?"

I knew what he was going to ask and slid off him. "Truth."

"Why were we in the guest room this whole time?"

I didn't lie, but I only told him part of the truth. "I still had the bed Jay and I'd shared."

"Oh." He paused, his brows furrowed together, and he asked, "Is this a new bed?"

"Brand spanking new." He smiled at that. "My turn. Truth or dare?"

He now knew the loophole and groaned like a defeated man, "Truth."

I asked quietly, "Do you like me?"

He took my face in his hands and stared into my eyes. His eyes softened and turned a darker shade of green. He answered just above a whisper, "Yeah, I like you. I like you a lot." His expression, tone, and touch were so far away from "just for fun" and so close to love, it made my stomach hurt in a good way. He gave me a tender kiss and murmured, "Truth or dare?"

I wanted to throw him and boldly answered, "Dare."

"I dare you to make love to me with the light on." His voice was thick and intimate, a lover's voice. "I want to see you … all of you. Come on, love me, love me with the light on."

My heart pounded. It raced not only because he wanted the light on, but also because I wasn't sure if he asked me to love him or simply to make love to him. I didn't want to over-interpret his meaning, and I didn't want to repulse him as I had Jay. Water pooled in my eyes.

"Baby, I don't know what you're afraid of, and you don't have to tell me, but trust me, I won't let you skin your knees."

I nodded my assent, and knowing I was nervous, he undressed me slowly. He gazed at me with appreciation and kissed each body part as it was exposed. He kissed the arch of my foot and the back of my knees. He ran his hands lovingly between my thighs and over my waist. With each piece of clothing peeled off, my anxiety lessened. Kevin wasn't repulsed. He was turned on by what he saw. His touches, his kisses, and his licks were a balm soothing the wound Jay had inflicted. He massaged my back and then kissed and pleasured me unselfishly.

I was equally delighted by seeing him. I loved seeing the gratification on his face when he joined his body with mine. I relished the sight of his wide bare chest braced above me. I liked catching glimpses of his hairy legs, his arms corded with muscles, and his strong back. However, when Kevin braced himself over me to take us home, I couldn't look at him.

"Open your eyes," he urged with a heavy voice.

I did and focused on his chest.

"Look at me. Come on, Baby, look at *me*."

My gaze traveled up his body and his eyes were waiting for me. It was as if he wanted assurance that I was with him physically, mentally, and emotionally—that I wasn't fantasizing about someone else, that I was totally with him.

"Say my name."

"Kevin."

His eyes held me and sent me careening over the edge.

—

The next morning, I woke to Kevin's hand between my legs and his mouth nibbling my neck. I rolled over and grinned up at him. "What are you doing?"

"Waking you up. I'm an early riser."

Kevin was up and ready to go—what a nice way to start the day. I couldn't remember the last time I'd had morning sex. Jay and I hadn't even had it on our fifteenth wedding anniversary trip we'd taken sans Haley.

While Kevin showered, I cooked breakfast. The sun shined through my windows, and I caught myself being happy. Even the memory of Jay with Brittany didn't dampen my mood.

Kevin walked in with a sunny smile and my day got a little brighter. He caught me around the waist and asked, "So hey, Luscious, got any plans for the day?"

"My usual. I didn't write yesterday. I should get some work done today."

"Blow it off. Spend the day with me."

"I hate going two days in a row without getting something written."

"You can write all day tomorrow. Spend the day with me, please." He kissed my neck, knowing how it drove me wild. "Please …."

That was all it took. "What do you want to do?" I pictured us driving to Napa for the day or maybe over to the coast.

He said, "I wanna take you fishing."

I scrunched my nose at him. "Fishing?"

"Uh-huh. It'll be fun. Just the two of us. I know this little creek in the foothills. It's pretty. You'll like it. We can pack a lunch and make a day of it."

"Oh, you mean a picnic."

"I don't picnic. I fish."

We finally agreed he would fish, and I would picnic.

⎯⎯

Flying down the highway in his big truck with Nickelback blaring from the stereo and Kevin singing along with his gravelly voice was more fun than I ever would have imagined. I liked the view from riding high up, and Kevin groping me while he drove made me feel like a teenager. I caught myself being happy again—no hurt, no anxiety, just happy.

My only qualm was when we left the highway and bounced along a backcountry dirt road. He told me to hold onto my seat, shifted the truck into four-wheel drive, and left the path. About a mile later, he pulled to a stop and asked, "What do you think?"

He hadn't exaggerated about the beauty of our destination. Wildflowers sprinkled the banks with vivid colors, and the creek bed, covered with speckled rocks, dappled in the sun. "It's beautiful." I took a couple pictures with my phone. "I wish I'd brought my good camera."

"It's my secret spot. I stumbled on it a couple years ago and come here when I want to be alone, so don't tell anyone."

My heart swelled knowing he was sharing something so personal and special. "Your secret is safe." I chuckled. "I couldn't tell anyone how to get here even if I wanted to."

The weather was perfect—not so hot as to be uncomfortable but warm enough for a lazy summer day. We did a little fishing, a little picnicking, and a little old-fashioned necking. I did a little napping next to him while he fished. What we did more than anything was talk.

I learned he had played football in high school, but his big sport had been baseball. He'd started college on a baseball scholarship but dropped out after his freshman year. College wasn't his thing, so when he met a Marine recruiter on campus, it'd seemed like a good idea to enlist.

"How long were you married?" I asked.

He turned away and mumbled, "Nine years."

By my estimation, given his daughter's age, his marriage had to have been over for several years. "What happened?"

He kept his gaze on his line as it bobbed in the creek. "She cheated. End of story."

His reply left me more curious than ever. Kevin must have been really in love to be so unwilling to talk about it this many years later. I wondered whether a fear of getting hurt or an inability to trust again was the real reason he was hesitant about a serious relationship.

I tried to be as open as possible when he wanted more details about Jay and me. He asked, "If you two were so smart, how did you end up pregnant?"

"We had academic smarts but were completely clueless about the proper use of a condom. Jay left too much room for the tip and didn't have it on all way. It just slipped off."

Kevin laughed until tears ran down his face. "I'm sorry. I know it's not funny, but damn how could he have not known it was slipping? I can just imagine the look on your ex's face. He must have been like 'Oh, shit!' What did he say?"

"Oh, shit!"

"No shit?"

"No shit. He was so excited we were finally doing it that he didn't notice until it was too late. His face had been pretty comical. I knew I was pregnant immediately. Jay told me not to panic. He said it was highly unlikely I'd get pregnant our first time, but I did."

Kevin stopped laughing and asked, "Weren't you a little rich girl growing up?"

"Not crazy rich, but yeah, my parents are the country club types."

"So how did they handle it? Did they support you guys?"

An image of my father standing in our den, red faced and his body shaking with fury, popped into my head. "No. My father gave me an ultimatum: either get an abortion and never see Jay again, or I was no longer his daughter. My mother had sided with him." I had been my father's angel, a good girl who never caused problems. He'd always controlled our home—and he had controlled it—with a cool, even temper; it had scared the hell out of me to see him explode with so much rage. He had been convinced that I was throwing my life away; thus he forced a choice, never considering I would choose Jay and our unborn baby over him. He saw it as an act of unforgivable betrayal. My chest tightened and ached just thinking about it.

Kevin's eyes bugged and he shook his head. "Whoa, that's some heavy shit at any age, and you were only seventeen."

"It had been pretty intense. Luckily, Jay's parents were more understanding. They let me live with them until Jay and I were able to get our own apartment."

"Did you ever reconcile with your folks?"

"Not really. They love and accept Haley, but my father has never forgiven me and never will. The kicker to the whole story is that my getting pregnant was practically a miracle."

"How so?"

"Apparently, the quantity and quality of my eggs is low. I had no idea until I tried to get pregnant again and couldn't." We'd tried to have another baby as soon as Jay had finished law school. Since I got pregnant so easily the first time, we'd thought I was so fertile that all Jay had to do was look at me without a condom and I'd be pregnant. Five years, buckets of tears, and a couple medical procedures later, we gave up. "I think it adds to my father's guilt and makes it even harder for him to get past everything."

"I'm sorry, that sucks." Kevin squeezed my hand and then adjusted his fishing line.

"It did, but life goes on and for the most part, I've had a pretty good life."

"That's good." I could see Kevin taking in my whole sad story. He nodded his head, answering some internal dialogue. "You know I don't like Jay, but I have to give him some props for sticking by you. Most seventeen-year-old guys would have dumped you and told you to get an abortion."

What Kevin didn't know was that Jay hadn't been a typical teenager. He hadn't been the smartest guy in class or the most talented athlete; he'd excelled by sheer will. He still excelled. He worked harder than anyone else I knew, but that wasn't the only reason for his success, or why he was so well-liked. Jay never shirked his responsibilities. Once he had committed to something—whether a goal, a job, or a relationship—he gave it his all and then some, which was another reason why I never thought he would leave me.

Kevin and I sat quietly for a while. My mind had already wandered to other things when he observed, "If Jay was the first guy you slept with and I was the first after Jay, that means Jay and I've been it for you."

"That would be the logical conclusion."

"I guess I'm assuming you haven't been with anyone else since we met."

"I haven't. Just you."

Kevin nodded. I couldn't tell if he was pleased with my answer. He turned away from me, reeled in his line, and recast it. He likely was a bit uneasy with the shortness of my list. After all, I had married the first guy.

I thought the subject was forgotten, but when we were in bed that night and things started heating up, Kevin asked, "You seriously can't get pregnant?"

"No. I haven't used birth control in over twelve years. Why?"

"I was just thinking. I haven't been with anyone else since I was tested last. I'm disease free. You haven't been with anyone, so I know you're disease free. Can we skip the condom? It would feel so good for me."

I felt exceptionally close to him after being with him non-stop since the night before. We hadn't talked about our relationship becoming serious, but I was sure we had turned a corner. I wanted to make him happy.

It's funny how the removal of a thin layer of latex brought us even closer together. We didn't have sex. We made love, and it was even better than the night before. He didn't toss me around in six different positions. He held me close and was slow and tender, as if he savored every moment. When he held me, for the first time in a long time, I felt like someone cherished me—might even love me.

With the glow of our lovemaking fading, Kevin whispered, "Truth or dare?"

"Dare."

"I dare you to tell the truth."

"Okay."

"Do you still love Jay?"

I took a minute to think about it. The question was too important to gloss over with a flip answer. "In a way, yes. I do." Kevin's body tensed. I turned to face him. "Let me explain. I spent every day for over half of my life loving him and being his partner. I can't help loving him, but I don't love him the way I used to."

He sighed. "I guess I get it."

I was happy to leave things where they were for the time being. Words of love and the future could wait. I grabbed Kevin's arm, pulled him close to me, and went to sleep quite content with Kevin's chest pressing against my back, his arm draped over my waist, and his muscular, hairy leg resting close to my thigh.

I woke up to Kevin fully dressed and sitting next to me with a long face. He was going to miss me—*how sweet.* I sat up and glanced at the clock. It was only six. "Your shift doesn't start until eight. Let me fix you some breakfast."

He gently pushed me back on my pillow. "No. You stay in bed."

His manner was so serious. "Something wrong?"

"No. The last two days have been … well, special. You're a special lady—don't ever forget it. Take care of yourself, okay?"

He stood and walked toward the door with his duffle bag hanging from his broad shoulder. No kiss. No hug. No, I'll call you.

"Hey, Kevin? Truth or dare?"

He stopped but didn't turn around. "Truth."

"Are you going to call me?"

"Told you upfront I wasn't looking for anything serious."

Ka-Pow! Blind-sided, again. Breathe, damn it! Get some air in those lungs!

No! Damn it! I was not going to let him walk out the door as if I was nothing more than a discarded condom. He owed me an explanation. I quickly rummaged around, pulled on my bathrobe, and raced after him. He was already in his truck and igniting the Hemi. As I ran toward him, my toe jammed into a raised crack in the concrete. *Ouch!* Jay was supposed to have fixed that crack. Damn him! I fell hard, my body bouncing on the pavement, and my knees screamed with pain. By the time I lifted my head, Kevin's truck was halfway down the street.

After a few tears and a few deep breaths, I picked myself up and stared down at my knees. Both were bleeding profusely.

Chapter 14

ALL MY NEIGHBORS knew Jay had left me. The thought that one of them now had witnessed me taking a fall in pursuit of a man was too embarrassing to contemplate. I scanned the house across the street and the houses to my left and right. No one came to my aid; my shame was safe. I limped into the house and sat on the edge of the bathtub to clean my knees while tears streamed down my face. Kevin had been a fling. Why was I crying over him? It wasn't logical, and for some reason I blamed Jay, which wasn't logical either.

After an extra-long shower, I called Valerie. "Can you believe I actually thought we might be falling in love? I let him stay the night two nights in a row, and he just … Urrgh."

"He did say he didn't want anything serious."

"Yeah, but he didn't act that way, especially the last two days. He asked if I still loved Jay, for heaven's sake. What was I supposed to think?"

"What exactly did you tell him?"

"I told him I loved Jay platonically."

"Did you use those exact words?"

I had to think. "No, but it's what I meant."

"Hmmm … he probably got spooked. Must be a commitment-phobe, or he's married."

"He's spent too much time with me to be married," I said shuddering at the thought.

"Did you Google him? Check Facebook?"

"Of course, but he's not on Facebook and all I could confirm is that he works for Sac Fire Department and lives in Elk Grove, just like he said."

"Hmmm … his wife could travel or work nights. You've never met his friends or been to his house. He didn't spend the night until his kids were out of town with their mother."

I refused to consider the possibility. "No, he's not that kind of guy. Should I call him?"

"No. You should sneak into his house and boil a bunny," she said evilly.

"Very funny. Seriously, should I?"

"Don't," she ordered. "The guy clearly has issues. Forget about him as quickly as possible. I read an article that said it takes approximately one month for every year together for your heart to heal, so you should be over him in about four or five days."

"Great. By that math, I have another six months to go before Jay's out of my system." Although my gut told me Jay would always have a part of my heart.

"So get yourself a new lover as quickly as possible and forget them both."

"Sure, easy. I'll just trot on down to the meat market and pick up the hunk of the day."

Valerie and I both giggled and she suggested, "Why not trot down to Nugget Market and see what your little friend is up to? At least with him, you'll know it could never be serious."

Joshua was a sweetie. He had a habit of peeking in my cart whenever I passed him in an aisle. I wasn't sure why, but he always scanned my selections with interest. The last time I saw him, he'd persuaded me to try a new brand of juice infused organic tea. He'd been quite insistent and escorted me to the refrigerated drink section. After handing me the bottle, he'd stood so close the slightest forward movement would have had us touching. He had gazed down at me with his mesmerizing eyes and let slip his girlfriend was addicted to the drink. I almost laughed. His expression had said, "Shit! I shouldn't have said that." The tea had been quite delicious.

"True, but my little friend and I are just that, friends. Give me a day to lick my wounds."

"Fair enough, but no pity parties. You are a woman of action."

Damn straight. I hung up and wrote a seven-hundred-and-fifty-word rant on how easy it was to get burned by a fireman.

> The myth is firemen are good and honorable, like Joaquin Phoenix in Ladder 49. My guy looks even hotter than Joaquin. Firemen have heroic jobs and naturally act the hero when they're off the clock, too. They talk a good game. They may be the alpha males of the world, but watch out ladies, they know it! They'll leave your heart in ashes if you're not careful.

I was well aware my beef was with one particular fireman and that there were multitudes of firefighters who were all-around great guys. I'd never post the piece, but it sure felt good to write. Afterwards, I scrubbed down my kitchen, which made me feel a little better, but I still couldn't stop thinking about what had happened. I changed into yoga pants and teed up Charlene Johnson on my DVD player, planning to pretend I was punch, jab, and kicking Kevin. Then I remembered the Chubby Hubby I'd bought for Kevin sitting in my freezer, so I scarfed it down while I watched Charlene and imagined I was punching and kicking. It was the perfect two-for-one release. Besides, I'd read if you seriously visualize physical action, it's almost as good as actually doing it. (I'll remind my derriere of that the next time I look in the mirror.)

The next day, I called the lease company in San Francisco and negotiated a pro-rated, mid-August move-in date. I'd learned some things from having had a lawyer as a husband and wanted a couple weeks for painting and sprucing before completely moving in. Then I packed a few boxes and drove a load of donations to the SPCA thrift store. No pity parties. I kept moving, but the motion didn't stop me from thinking.

In my fantasy, Kevin sends me a dozen red long-stemmed roses, the expensive kind that cost more than five dollars a stem. I don't respond. The next day, he sends me two dozen. I agree to see him. He confesses the depth of his feelings have frightened him. He misses and wants me. Will I please, please, *please* give him another chance? I'll think about it.

I couldn't help checking Kevin's schedule off the calendar. Off today. Off today. Working today. Off today. Off today. After he'd had two shifts and two sets of days off, my hope ran out. He really wasn't going to call begging my forgiveness, and I was not over him, even though it had been more than five days.

I wrote another piece—this time about myself.

> Was I inherently repulsive, like a Twinkie? Everyone loves a Twinkie at first, delicious spongy cake and inside, a surprise of creamy goodness, but after you've had two, three at the most, your stomach churns and you question why you took the first bite. How could I have been blindsided, not once, but twice? Was I seriously so obtuse?

I wasn't sure if I would submit that one either.

In retrospect, I could see the signs I had ignored with Jay: coming home late, always tired, but somehow found energy for the gym, growly with me but not with anyone else. I made excuses for Jay: he was overworked, had a lot of pressure, just hungry and needed a good meal.

When I reflected on my time with Kevin, he'd been moving toward me, not away. His rude exit didn't negate that he had held me and gazed at me as if I'd mattered to him.

On Kevin's third workday after his abrupt departure, he still hadn't called, but Jay did. He asked if he could come over after work. He made a case that we had too much to discuss over the phone, and we had to make some decisions about what I would be taking with me, leaving for him, or donating. I reminded Jay, per our divorce settlement, everything in the house belonged to me. He asked me to be reasonable. Did I really want to empty the house completely? Couldn't we be civilized? He would bring an extra good bottle of wine.

Nothing good could come from us being alone together, but I agreed. As I prepared for my evening with Jay, I couldn't stop thinking about Kevin and his pained expression when he'd left. What the hell had happened? About mid-afternoon, I couldn't stand it any longer. Knowing he was working, I still chucked Valerie's advice, sucked it up, and called him.

"I only have a minute," he said, not even saying hello.

His curtness made me want to hang up, but after coming this far I plunged forward. "I want know what happened the other morning. Did I do something?"

He grunted and I took it as a yes. "Kim, I really like spending time with you, but ...."

"But, what? Did I kick you in my sleep? Did I drool on you? Do I snore?"

I'd hoped to get a chuckle out of him, but he remained stone cold. "No, you don't snore."

My throat ached and tears stung my eyes. "Then, what? I thought ... I don't know." A bell rang from Kevin's end of the phone. "Sorry I called."

"Hey, hey, don't cry. I have to go, but how about if we talk tomorrow?"

I didn't want to wait for tomorrow to find out what I did that was so horrible it had caused him to walk out the way he did. It made me want to throw something at him. Since I couldn't, I settled for a less than biting, "Sure, whatever."

I started to hang up, but Kevin stopped me. "Hey." His voice dropped low and intimate. "I'll be over as soon as I can, as soon as my shift ends. I've uh, I've missed you."

Not a dozen roses, or a declaration of love, but I melted anyway. We had hit a speed bump in our relationship—that was all. *Kevin missed me.* Everything would be okay.

⌒

Since Jay was making an effort with the wine, I put together a nice spread of finger food, including Jay's favorite bruschetta. Originally, I had planned to serve him Cheez Whiz on Ritz crackers topped with a pimento, but then I'd have to eat it, too.

Jay came straight from work. He walked in the door with a huge smile, pecked my cheek, and set his briefcase by the entrance table. It had been the spot for his briefcase since the day we moved in. He followed me to the kitchen, took off his jacket and tie, and rolled up his sleeves just as if he lived here and had never left. A small tickle of desire stirred in my stomach. I couldn't help it. Something about seeing his bare forearms and neck, which had been hidden from public view all day, used to make me want to crawl all over him, and apparently, still did. I quickly clamped down on the impulse.

He washed his hands and stuffed a bruschetta in his mouth. "Mmmm. That's good. I swear, when we first got married, I never thought you'd be a good cook. But you've developed serious chops."

The first meal I prepared for us had been spaghetti, made with hamburger meat and a package of Lawry's seasoning. I had served it with a green cardboard cylinder of cheese and a salad of iceberg lettuce tossed with Wishbone Italian. Over the years, I worked to improve my culinary skills, and Jay's rapture over a good meal had spurred me to try new things. He always had been especially sweet after I cooked him something special.

"Not exactly the tuna-macaroni we used to have."

He made a face. "I can't believe we actually ate that stuff."

I shrugged. "We were broke; we ate cheap."

"Yeah, but those were some good times, weren't they?"

"I guess so." He hummed with a frisky vibe and eyed me quite fondly. He must have won a big case earlier in the day. Jay was typically juiced after a big win, but it had nothing to do with me. I turned to get down the wine glasses. "Hey, where's the wine you promised?"

"Sorry, no time. Do you mind if I grab something from the fridge?"

I followed him to the garage where we kept an indoor wine cellar. On the top shelf was a bottle of 2012 Luna Howell Mountain Cabernet which we had picked up on one of our wine tasting expeditions. Jay bought it for one particular occasion. He pulled it out and turned to me with his toothpaste ad smile, dimples and all.

That explained his mood. "Congratulations, you won the Conway case."

"Yep, and they're out of appeals. Know what this means?"

Oh, I knew. The Conway case was a multi-million-dollar intellectual property lawsuit he had been litigating for over three years. The firm specialized in construction and commercial real estate and a small amount of personal injury as it related to construction; intellectual property was not in their wheelhouse. A friend from law school had referred Stephen Conway to Jay because Jay had been the top student in their intellectual property class. The firm's partners had thought a win was a long shot, so they let Jay run with it even though he wasn't a partner. The firm would collect thirty percent of the settlement, and Jay's take would be close to seven figures. "Monster pay day for Jay Braxton?"

"Not just that, but I'm being made a name partner."

I tried to say cheerfully, "That's wonderful, good for you." He'd spent hundreds of hours on the case and making name-partner was a goal I had shared with him. I was a terrible person for not being ecstatic for him, but I felt cheated *his* success wasn't really *ours* to celebrate.

His smile slipped. "I thought you'd be more excited. You're the first person I've told."

"I'm very happy for you." I rallied a full-on smile. "Come on, let's open the wine."

Jay followed me back to the kitchen and chatted as he opened the bottle. "I know it's a little weird, us sharing the bottle, given everything, but I really wanted to celebrate with you. You always believed in me, and now that I'm on my own, I realize how much you supported me. Well, anyway, thank you."

"You're welcome and thank you for saying it." This was more than a little weird. If I didn't know better, I'd think Jay was angling to share more than a bottle of wine.

He handed me a glass and his fingers unnecessarily brushed my hand. I felt obligated to offer a toast. "Here's to Johnson, Silverstein, McDonough, and *Braxton*. Cheers." We both took a sip. I held the wine in my mouth and enjoyed the satin texture and hints of blackberry, plum, coco, and a hit of nutmeg dancing in perfect harmony on my tongue. Our eyes met, and held a beat before we swallowed, sighing in blissful unison ... bringing a smile to both our faces.

My eyes broke away first, and I focused on swirling the wine in my glass. Jay did the same. "Damn it's good. Remember the day we bought it?"

"Of course." My chest ached more than a little, remembering how happy we'd been that day. I forced a smile. "I always knew you'd win."

"I wasn't so sure, but when you insisted that we buy the bottle, I couldn't let you down." Jay's eyes softened. "The weather had been perfect, and we stayed at that bed and breakfast in Yountville, remember?"

"Yeah, it'd been a good day." We had left Haley with Jay's parents and then bickered for most of the drive to Napa about something insignificant, but after our first winery, all had been forgiven. We'd held hands and eyed each other all day like a couple of horny teenagers.

Jay took another sip of wine and glanced around the kitchen.

I asked, "Should we start with the kitchen?"

"No. How about we sit in the living room and enjoy the wine first? It's been ages since we talked. What do you say?"

"I say you're freaking me out. Your frisky vibe is going. Now you want to sit and share some wine." I narrowed my eyes. "What's going on? What do you want?"

He laughed and took a step toward me. "Nothing, Kimmy."

I took a step back. "Nothing? Really? Don't forget how well I know you."

"Ah, come on. I'm just in a good mood. Relax … sit with me. I promise I'm not trying to seduce you." He flashed his most winning smile. "Please?"

I still thought he was up to something, but acquiesced. "Fine."

I grabbed the wine and Jay snatched up the plate of bruschetta. We went to the living room, and I sat on the couch, assuming Jay would sit in the leather club chair—it had been his favorite reading spot—but he plopped down next me. He ate another bruschetta and sipped his wine with satisfaction. Then he leaned back with his legs spread, relaxed and open.

"I love this room," he said as much to himself as to me. "I always liked the way you decorated it. It's comfortable. Feels like home."

Yeah, a home I was leaving, and he was taking. Growing up, my mother's living room had been a showcase reserved for guests. I'd grown to hate cold, formal rooms that no one used. Consequently, when decorating my own home, I had taken great pains to hunt down classic furniture pieces that were both attractive and comfortable.

"Well, you can decorate it however you want," I said. "I'm taking the furniture in this room. Maybe Brittany can help you pick out new stuff."

Jay shook his head and frowned. "I don't think so. I only went out with her a couple times. She's not really my type. She's too …"

Young? Giggly? Airheaded? "Unsophisticated?" I asked.

"I was going to say *vacuous*, but unsophisticated works." We both laughed. "It was so awkward the other night. I'm sorry about Brittany and everything. I know it shouldn't bother me to see you with someone else, but it sets me on edge."

The feeling was mutual, but I wasn't going to admit it. "Someday you'll get used to it."

Jay shrugged and refilled our glasses. "So I talked to Haley about the leave of absence."

"What did you tell her?"

"It's a great idea, especially after she told me she planned to live with you."

I'd prepared for the possibility of Haley moving in with me and was starting to look forward to it, but I swear Jay enjoyed putting a damper on my love life and that irked me. "Really, Jay?" I started to stand, but he grabbed my arm and my wine glass before it spilled.

"Whoa—joking," he said laughing. He set my glass on the table and angled toward me. "Don't worry. I told her she could take the leave, but she should live at home with me."

"Oh, that's not what I expected."

"I didn't think so." He smiled. "God knows, I've got the space."

"What about your little girlfriends?" It was a cheap shot, but Haley would be upset by a Brittany or Amber staying the night. They were closer to her age than Jay's.

He cringed and didn't attempt to defend them. "I'm taking a hiatus from dating. Now that I'm a name partner, I plan to focus on work and regroup too. Besides, I miss Haley and want to help her find some direction again. I can get her a job at the firm."

"What kind of job?"

"Nothing glamorous, mainly admin stuff, but she can help me with some research and get a better sense of what it's like to be an attorney before she gives up on the idea."

"Oh. I guess that all makes sense. It'd be good for her. Thank you."

"Did I surprise you again?"

"Well, yes."

Jay smiled smugly, but he'd won this round. "I don't know why. I've always been more of a homebody than most of my friends." It was true, which was another reason his leaving me had been so unexpected. He handed my glass back to me and leaned into the couch. "Haley told me you're moving to North Beach?"

"Yeah, I found a little place with two bedrooms."

"Can you afford it?"

"As long as you don't skip out on alimony."

He blanched, as if offended, and shook his head. "I'd never do that to you. I told you before, I'll never stop caring about you." He continued with his voice low and sincere, "I know you and Val are besties, but you and I were best friends for a long time, too. I don't want you stressed about money. Whatever you need, just ask. With the Conway win and making partner, I'm flush again. I couldn't have done it without you, and I owe you."

"I'll be fine, but thanks for the offer." His sincerity reminded me of my old Jay, the pre-divorce Jay—the man who was generous, the man who enjoyed taking care of me and being home. I drained my glass and my tension eased. I liked him when he wasn't being an asshole. "Ready to do this?"

"Not yet. Let's finish the bottle first." He poured more into my glass. "I love this house exactly as it is. I'll make it easy. Leave anything you don't want."

"Even the flowered print chairs in the family room?"

"Even those."

"I distinctly remember you saying they were girlie."

"They are, but I'll keep them."

I chuckled. Jay had never been a fan of the chairs, but I'd convinced him the flower print brightened the room, making them a perfect choice.

He grinned at me. "What's funny?"

"I pictured the house turning into a man cave, but you're keeping my flower chairs."

"I'm a man of surprises." We both laughed and he took my hand. His hand was warm and the weight familiar. "This is nice, isn't it?"

"I guess."

He inched closer, still holding my hand. "I've really missed my friend."

I pulled my hand away. "Jay, please don't."

"Other divorced couples stay friends. Can't we try?"

"It's awkward. Even in high school, we were never just pals."

"So what?" He took my hand again and squeezed it. "Don't you miss how we used to linger over dinner and talk? I know I do."

One of my emotional scabs broke open, and I swallowed against the pain. I was never one to have a gaggle of girlfriends. I'd had Jay, Haley, and Val, and they had been enough. Of course, I'd had other friends, but none that I'd confided with the way I did with Val and Jay. In losing Jay, I'd lost my husband, my lover, and the person whom I told my deepest, darkest secrets. I'd shared things with him that I hadn't even told Val. Did I miss him? Yes, to the very depths of my soul. The vacancy in my heart had been filled with a loneliness that could swallow me up and consume me if I let it. I couldn't risk opening myself up, only to have him shut me out when he found his next girlfriend.

"I'm sorry, but it's not possible."

He dropped my hand. "Are you saying no because of that fireman? You're not planning to keep seeing him after you move, are you?"

I didn't want to talk to him about Kevin, but Kevin was an easy out. It was better for Jay to know. "I know you don't like him, but—"

"Kimmy." Jay grimaced and sat up straight. "He's married."

My stomach rolled, and I set my glass down. "Oh come on, I think I would know."

"It's true." He set his glass down, too. "I wasn't going to say anything because I thought you'd stop seeing the fucker when you moved."

"How do you know?"

"The calendar he's in has his bio in the back. It says he's a Sacramento firefighter who lives in Elk Grove with his wife and two children. I'm sorry."

"It doesn't mean he's still married. Those calendars are done way in advance."

"Which is why I asked the P.I. who works for the firm to run a routine check. That lowlife lives with his wife and kids." Jay looked me straight in the eyes. He wasn't lying. He put his hand on my shoulder. "I could kick his ass for hurting you."

I stood to get away from him, not wanting him to see me cry. He got up too and pulled me against me. "Hey, you're better off without him."

Letting him soothe me kicked in like muscle memory. I leaned into him, sucked in his citrusy, ocean breeze scent, and cried into his chest while he ran his hand up and down my back. My tears eased, but we stayed glued together. He kissed the side of my head once, twice, a third time, with his mouth inching south and his embrace tightening. Thoughts of Kevin's betrayal faded away as warmth pooled in my center and Jay hardened against me. A voice in my head whispered a warning. When Jay's lips reached my neck and then my mouth, the voice was silenced by mind-numbing, unstoppable wanting. My hands tangled into his thick hair, and I pushed against his erection as we kissed with a fevered urgency. His hands slid up my shirt, and he pulled away just enough to murmur, "You feel so fucking good."

Everything about him made me crave more—his touch on my bare skin, the way he smelled, his hard body pressing into me—feeling how much he wanted me, too. I supposed this was the way addicts felt after drying out and then getting a taste of the forbidden. I succumbed to a psychedelic, Jay Braxton high, and kissing wasn't nearly enough. I needed to feel his weight on top of me. Needing him inside me, I tugged his shirt out of his pants. He maneuvered us to the couch, eased me onto the cushions; then said with a husky voice, "We should shut the curtains or go to our bedroom."

Our bedroom? Our Bedroom. "Stop, wait … stop," I said, slowly snapping out of the lust filled haze and pushed him back. "I won't be your one-night stand." Breathing hard, I stared at him with my heart pounding, willing him to tell me I would not be a one-nighter, that he wanted more from me … that he wanted us to have a bedroom together again.

Jay stood, held up his hands, and backed away. "I'm sorry. You're right."

My turned on, crazy desire high crashed with a thud in my stomach. "Please leave," I managed to choke out, holding back a sob.

He dropped his hands and his expression hardened. "He's a fucking asshole. He's not worth crying over."

Jay was the asshole. How could he not see he was the cause of my current torrent? How could he not know he'd crushed my heart yet again? "Funny, that's what he said about you."

"Kim … just ask him if it's true."

"I intend to. Right now, I'd like to be alone."

Jay left without argument.

As soon as the door shut, I let out a scream and hurled a throw pillow across the room. Once was not enough. I picked up another pillow and sent it flying with an f-bomb. Only then did my pulse begin to slow. I slumped onto the couch and emptied the rest of Jay's glass of Luna into my own and took a gulp. God damn, Jay. God damn him. This was exactly why we couldn't be friends. Did he really think he could waltz in, turn on the old Braxton charm, and sleep with me? Apparently, he had, and it had almost worked. *You're not a one-night stand.* That's all he would have had to say. It was a close call. He'd hurt me, but how much more wounded would I be if we'd made love? Screw Jay. I was done, done, done with him.

And screw him for interfering with my love life. Kevin couldn't be married, no way.

Of course, he could be.

We only saw each other in Davis ... I'd never met his friends or children ... he always paid for dinner with cash. Damn, it was true.

I thought I had been so cool and sophisticated about our affair: no strings, a few laughs and great sex—how adult of me. God, I was an idiot. I didn't know how to stay detached.

The awful, chest-crushing sensation wasn't the same as when Jay had left me, but heartache was heartache. It hurt. How could Kevin have done this to me, knowing everything I'd been through? How could he have gazed at me and touched me with so much affection, making me care about him, with a wife at home? Moreover, what about his wife? Did Kevin's wife love him the same as I had loved Jay?

I picked up the pillows I had tossed and arranged them back on the sofa and then took the wine bottle, glasses, and plate with one remaining bruschetta to the kitchen. When I finished cleaning up, I leaned against the counter, staring at the collage of family photos chronicling the life I had shared with Jay.

I visualized a similar wall of photos in Kevin's house—pictures of him with his wife and children picnicking and fishing at his secret spot. Vomit rose to my throat, and I choked it back. God, I hoped they never learned about me. What if his wife called to confront me, or worse, showed up on my doorstep with a gun? I was the *other woman*. How was it possible I, Kimberly Kirby, had become *that woman*?

When I'd equated him to barbequed ribs, I'd overvalued him. He was a swine—only tasty ribs were too good for him. A pork butt was more fitting, and the ass would be at my doorstep in less than twelve hours. I took a swig of wine straight from the bottle, picked up my cell, and scrolled to Kevin's number. My finger hesitated over the dial icon. I was buzzed—not so drunk to be numb all over, but enough to say things I'd regret. I set the phone down.

My experience with Jay had taught me a calm discussion got me further than a hissy fit. I didn't want to be drunk or hungover and all crazy when I confronted Kevin. Ditching my plan to drink until I passed out, I corked the wine and opened a bottle of water.

Chapter 15

I FOUND IT EASIER to focus on my anger with Kevin than think about what went down with Jay and how good it had felt to touch and be touched by him. Once asleep though, Jay took over my dreams. I woke up hot and bothered twice and hoped Jay was having an equally miserable night. I had been more turned on, less conscious—more in the moment, than I ever had been with Kevin. Something about Jay lit me up. There was an electricity between us. I know he felt it, too. Why couldn't he just admit it? More troublesome than the physical longing, the year-long ache of missing him was on the verge of splitting open and that I could not live through again. After waking a third time, I couldn't get back to sleep. Hence, I was dressed, and ready when my doorbell rang the next morning. I had planned to stay cool and collected, but my stomach bunched, and my hands shook when I opened the door.

Puffy eyed and shoulders slouching, Kevin looked dog-tired, but he grinned and appeared happy to see me. He leaned toward me, ready for a kiss. I jerked back as pain and anger flashed through my chest.

His grin inverted. "I get it. I'm in the doghouse, but you gonna let me in?"

I swallowed and opened the door wider. "Would you like some coffee?"

"Love some."

He stepped inside to follow me to the kitchen. I told myself to stay calm, but before we were out of the entryway, I turned on him. "You're married!"

"Who told you I was married?"

"Jay."

"What the hell would Jay know about me?"

"He didn't trust you. He told me not to trust you and like an idiot, I thought he was just being an ass. He had a P.I. run a routine check. You're married, your family lives in Elk Grove, and you live with them."

"He had a P.I. check me out?"

"YES."

Kevin shook his head in disbelief and clenched his fists "Unfucking believable." I worried he might punch a hole my entryway wall.

"Don't deny it. I know it's true."

"You don't know shit about it, and neither does your asshole ex-husband! Did the P.I. fuck tell you we're separated? Huh? Did he tell you we don't sleep in the same bed? Huh? Did he tell you that?"

"No, but if you're separated, why do you live there?"

"Why do you think? For my kids! Did he tell you my so-called wife is a nurse who works nights? If he really did his job, that dick would know I'm only there when she goes to work, and the bitch has been screwing an emergency room doctor for the last year. I loved her, and she ripped my heart out and stomped on it. Bet no one told you that, did they?"

He had me there, but I wasn't ready to back down. "Why aren't you divorcing her then?"

"I *am*, but with kids at home it's harder to work things out. I won't abandon my kids. I won't walk out on them, but believe me, I'm divorcing her."

"I just find all of this hard to believe." I turned away from him and walked into the living room. He followed me. The movement helped me regain some control of my voice. "Moving out of your house doesn't mean you would be abandoning your children."

"It's complicated."

"Not really, Kevin. Ever hear of joint custody?"

"Hey, I don't make Jay's money. I can't afford to cover a mortgage and a place of my own; neither can Cathy. I can't let my kids be evicted. I've been stuck the last six months while we've been trying to sell the house." He walked up to me, tentatively took my hands in his, and said in a conciliatory voice, "Baby, it finally sold. I'm moving out next week."

It seemed plausible, but there had to be more to the situation. I dropped his hands and my voice raised again. "If everything is so explainable, then why not be honest?"

"You don't believe me?" He took his phone out of his pocket and held it out to me. "Take it. Hit 'home' and ask for Cathy. I don't give a shit. She already knows about you."

Kevin stared at me, his eyes not blinking. As a child, I had never been good at playing chicken. I blinked. "I don't want to talk to your wife!"

"Then what the hell do you want, Kimberly? What do you want from me?"

"The truth. I want to know why you lied to me."

"I know I should have told you, but I didn't lie," he insisted. "I never said I was divorced. You assumed I was, but I didn't lie about it."

It was my turn to shake my head in disbelief. I turned my back to him and stared out my front window, watching a guy jog by with his dog. Kevin was right. He never actually said he was divorced. Given his daughter's age, and how long he'd been married, I had assumed. Why did I keep doing this to myself? Why did I keep turning a blind eye to the obvious?

Kevin sighed behind me and muttered, "Shit." When he spoke again, his voice was low and contrite. "I'm sorry. I'm really sorry I wasn't upfront about everything. The last thing I wanted was to hurt you."

I turned to face him. He had the decency to look ashamed. "I feel so stupid and used." I couldn't stop the tears. I didn't know if I was more hurt or humiliated. It was an awful combination of both.

"Don't, please don't. I care about you. You know I do." He tried to put his arms around me, but I pushed him away. He took a step back. I could see in his eyes he was hurting, too.

"Why didn't you just tell me?" I thought back to the day we had gone fishing, and he'd told me his wife had cheated on him. He could have told me everything that day.

"If I ever thought things would go this far, I would've told you before we slept together. At first, I loved coming here just to have a few hours when I didn't have to deal with all the bullshit at home. Later, I didn't know how to tell you. You've been the best thing in my life for a long time, and I didn't want to lose you. I swear, Kim, I really thought we would just have a few laughs. I knew you weren't over your ex-husband and I wasn't your type, but we had fun together. Admit it. You were using me at first, too."

I tried to think of what I had done to make him think I had been using him. I'd always taken his calls. I'd never put him off when he wanted to see me. "How can you say that?"

"I may not have a law degree, but I'm not stupid. I know I walked in on something between you and Jay the first night I picked you up. I could feel it between you. I've noticed the paintings on your walls, and the books in the family room, and the special fridge just for wine. Hell, a Panamera was sitting in your driveway the first night we went out. I knew you were nervous we wouldn't have anything to say to each other, but you sure loved the way I made you feel, didn't you? You loved the way I loved your body and made you laugh. So, don't make me out to be the bad guy, especially when you're still not over Jay."

"Is that why you walked out last week?"

He glared at me. "You said you still love him."

"*Platonically.* I meant *platonically.* Sorry I didn't make that clear."

"Well, you didn't. I've hated watching Jay jerk you around, making you cry. I could have kicked his ass the other night. How do you think it made me feel, after we'd spent all that time together, to hear you still loved him?"

If the situation were reversed, I'd be hurt too. "Not so good?"

He heaved a sigh and his shoulders slumped. "Like shit. Honestly, you've confused the hell out of me. Every time I thought we were getting closer, you'd do something like call me your *friend.* Here I was getting all crazy about you, and you made me feel like you just wanted someone to warm your bed and make you laugh. I couldn't do it anymore."

The game playing was ridiculous. I took his hands in mine. "I was trying to keep things casual because you said that's what you wanted."

He entwined his fingers with mine and pulled me closer, until our bodies were almost touching. "But that was before—"

"It's okay. You don't have to explain. I won't lie to you; at first, it was much more of a physical attraction for me. You're incredibly sexy. I'm sorry, but it's the truth."

He chuckled. "You don't need to apologize for thinking I'm sexy." He winked, making me smile. "After you called and started crying, I knew you weren't just using me for my body."

I chuckled, too. "No, I wasn't." I reached up and touched his cheek. "Are you really getting a divorce and moving out?"

"Yeah, call my attorney if you don't believe me."

Despite everything, my gut told me Kevin was telling the truth. "I believe you."

He pulled me all the way against him and wrapped me up in his strong arms. It was comforting and nice. He murmured in my ear, "I've missed you."

"Missed you, too." I peered up at him and ran my hand over his wrinkled brow. "You look exhausted. Rough night?"

"We went out on a call for a car fire at three this morning. I've been up ever since."

"Do you want to skip the coffee and lay down? That is, if you don't have to get home."

"I'm free for the day." He bent down and kissed me lightly on the lips, relieved our fight was over. "Lay down with me?"

I let him carry me to my bedroom. Maybe I shouldn't have been so quick to forgive, but like me, Kevin had had his share of heartache. His life was messy and complicated, leaving me uncertain if we had any kind of future. He'd made a mistake, but he'd brought some joy back into my life. He deserved a second chance.

Chapter 16

WE LAY TOGETHER with my head on Kevin's bare chest and him running his hand over my bottom and lower back. His hands were callused and rougher than Jay's, but he had a light, soothing touch. The house was quiet, and I could hear Kevin's heart pumping. I liked being close again, but a nagging voice in my head denied me peace. I tried to drown it out by focusing on the rhythm of his heartbeat, but the voice kept asking what the hell I was doing with a man whose life was bound to get messier before it got better. The voice questioned if Kevin still, deep down, loved his wife and whether we were two random balls rebounding against each other.

He must have been doing his own thinking because he said, "I can't start things over, but I'll tell you anything you want to know."

There was so much I wanted to know. "When did you find out she was cheating?"

"About nine months ago. Things were strained and my gut told me something was going on, so I called her at work one night. The nurse on duty said she'd gone on break, but she wasn't in the break room. Where do you go at two in the morning?"

"I don't know."

"Yeah, so I waited up for her. She straight-out told me she'd been with the ER doc. She said she was sorry and begged for forgiveness. It was hard, but because of my kids, I gave her another chance. About two months later, I found out she was still sleeping with the guy. I tried to kick her out. She refused to leave, and next thing I knew my kids were standing there crying, begging me to let her stay. It's been a shit show ever since."

"Am I the first woman you've been with since everything happened?"

"Yeah. My buddies got me drunk and dragged me out with them the night we met."

I never thought, well not too much, about what Kevin's wife looked like. Now I couldn't help wondering if she was more attractive than me, and if sleeping with me was his way of saying f-you to her. "Do you still love her?"

He answered with certainty, no hesitation whatsoever. "No, no I don't. She could be hit by a car and die tomorrow, and I swear I wouldn't care. It'd make my life so much easier. I know it sounds cold, but sometimes I wish for it." He paused before continuing, "It's crazy, you know, I don't know why, but it still …." Kevin swallowed. His lids blinked fast, but not in time to stop a leak from the corner of his eye.

I knew what he was feeling—that hollow emptiness, the feeling of being one-half of a whole with the other half missing. For the last year, I seriously doubted I would ever feel whole again. I saw myself as a four-legged table missing two legs cattycorner from each other; technically, I could stand, but the slightest movement sent me crashing. I never wished for Jay to die, but sometimes I wondered if it would hurt less if he had. I was better, feeling whole again, and eventually Kevin would as well. In the meantime, damn, it hurt.

He rolled away from me with his shoulders shaking. I wrapped my arm around his waist and hugged his back. His muffled sobs vibrated against me, and I held closely against him until his shuddering subsided. God only knew how much more he had bottled up inside. I reached over and kissed his wet cheek.

He turned his face toward me. I kissed him again and made love to him. I wasn't sure if we were having make-up sex or comfort sex. I wanted him to feel wanted, to feel close to someone. Afterwards, we held each other tightly with our arms and legs tangled together. Eventually, his grip eased, and light snores vibrated out of him.

I stayed next to him for a while longer, listening to him breathe, and thinking, thinking, thinking. The voice in my head questioned what we were doing with each other. Not hiding his personal issues anymore, he would be turning to me for support. Could I be that person at this stage of my life?

Did I want to be? We had to have a candid conversation about what we both wanted before making any decisions.

Kevin showed no signs of waking, so I left him sleeping and went to take a shower. The water washed away some of my unease and helped clear my mind. I turned the tap up to full blast, finally drowning out the nagging voice inside my head.

At first, I thought there was a group of college kids walking by my house being loud and obnoxious; then I realized the noise was coming from inside my home. Not bothering to turn off the faucet, I grabbed a towel and opened the door from my bathroom to the bedroom. Kevin wasn't on the bed.

Jay's voice boomed from the hall. "You heard me, asshole! Stay away from Kimberly!"

"Fuck you! You're the one who needs to stay away," Kevin growled.

"This is my house, and I want you the fuck out now!"

I shot down the hallway and found them in each other's face. Jay wore his lawyer suit and his lucky Hickey Freeman red power tie I'd helped Haley pick out for Father's Day a couple years ago. Kevin stood barefoot wearing only his jeans with his bare chest puffed and flexed. Their fists clenched and the room vibrated with angry testosterone.

"Hey, hey, guys. Let's take a breath." It was a futile attempt to defuse the situation.

Kevin kept his eyes on Jay. "Baby, please, go back to the bedroom. Jay and I have a few things to settle."

Jay sneered. "Yes, we do. Why don't we step outside?"

This could not be happening. It was like the scene from *Bridget Jones* when Hugh Grant showed up and Colin Firth asked him to step outside. Only, this was not a movie. Kevin and Jay wouldn't have a wussy fight. It would be bloody. Kevin was bigger than Jay, but Jay had boxed as a youth and knew how to take care of himself—as did Kevin, for that matter.

Images of police sirens and the two of them going off in handcuffs raced through my head. Jay would be disbarred, and Kevin would lose his job. My neighbors! Oh my God, I had respectable neighbors who were college professors and professionals.

Adrenaline pounded through me. I pushed between them and shouted at Jay, "Outside now!" With a growing sense of power, I turned to Kevin. "And you, put your shirt on!" I spread my arms apart, determined not to let them get any closer.

Kevin had the audacity to laugh at me, and Jay cracked up, too. I glared from one to the other. "What are you two laughing at?"

Kevin reached down, handed me my towel, and walked back down the hallway.

I quickly wrapped the towel around my body. At least neither one had seen anything they hadn't seen before. Jay took off his jacket, draped it over my shoulders, and hissed in my ear, "My car, now." Then he ushered me out the door and into the passenger seat of his car.

Once in the driver's seat, he asked, "What were you thinking? You could've been hurt."

"I might ask you the same question. Fighting? Really?"

"What? You think he would've won?"

Jay would have put up a good fight, but Kevin was bigger and really wanted a piece of Jay. On the other hand, Jay really wanted a piece of Kevin. "No, it's not what I'm saying."

He grunted. "I would've taken him."

"Jay!"

"I don't want that guy in our house!"

"It's still *my* house!" Not answering, he stared straight ahead. I mentally tucked away his slip of the tongue for future deconstruction. "What are you doing here anyway?"

Jay released a heavy sigh. "I came to talk to you about last night."

Oh God, I did not want to hear about how he hadn't been thinking and wanted to be *just friends*. Besides, Kevin was waiting for me. "I've moved on and don't want to talk about it."

Shaking his head, Jay looked down at his lap. "Can I at least say I'm sorry? I hadn't been looking for a quick lay."

"Okay, is that it?"

"I was going to invite you to lunch."

"Is that why you're wearing your lucky tie?"

He shrugged and shot me an accusatory look. "I sure as hell didn't expect that fucker to be here. What are you doing? You know he's married."

"You don't know the whole story. Kevin's wife cheated, and he's getting a divorce."

"You're buying that bullshit?"

"Yes, I believe him. Here's the deal, Jay. You have to stay out of my life. Who I see and what I do doesn't concern you."

"Not true, it *concerns* me."

"It shouldn't. The day our divorce finalized you lost all rights."

"That's bullshit and you know it. I've known you since the seventh grade. Nothing important in your life has happened that didn't involve me. We grew up together and raised a daughter together. Like it or not, you can't erase twenty years with a piece of paper." Nope, you couldn't erase twenty years with a piece of paper. Jay was a damn good litigator.

When we'd exchanged our wedding vows, we'd meant what we said. We both swore our souls fused together that day. I had a mental flash of the day Jay took Haley and me home from the hospital to our one-bedroom apartment with orange shag carpeting and popcorn ceilings. Our only furniture had been a stained beige couch we'd picked up at a garage sale, a card table with folding chairs Jay's parents had leant us, a bed for us, and a bassinette for Haley. She had been beautiful and perfect, but so tiny and helpless. A tsunami of fear and doubt had washed over me. Sensing what I'd been feeling, Jay had draped his arm around me and said with all the cocky confidence of youth, *"She's a miracle, and we'll always be a family. Nothing will ever change that. You're going to be a great mom, and I promise someday we'll have a real home."*

I'd always be tied to Jay, but he lost some rights when he signed those divorce papers. Like it or not. "That doesn't mean you get to butt into my love life."

He took a breath. Whenever Jay stopped to take a breath, I knew I was winning. I waited, the silence growing, but held my ground. Finally, he said, "Come on, Kimmy, don't be mad at me; I was just watching out for you. He's not good enough for you."

"Oh, yeah? Who in your opinion is?"

"I don't know," he said, shaking his head.

He wanted to be my friend, I'd felt *so fucking good* to him, and he didn't want me with Kevin. Enough was enough. "Do you want me back?"

He didn't immediately reply. When he did, his words came out croaky. "Sometimes I really, really miss you, but things are better this way."

Why? Why were things better? I didn't dare ask. "Then, why are you doing this?"

His jaw clenched, and he looked like he was on the verge of tears. "I can't help feeling protective of you; seeing you with that guy makes me crazy. I guess …." Jay shook his head again and stared out the window. "Forget it."

I couldn't deal with him anymore. "You have to leave me alone to live my life." I shrugged his jacket off, adjusted my towel, and began to step out.

He grabbed my arm. "Hey, I'm sorry. I'll butt out, but I'm not wrong about that guy."

I got out and slammed the door. Walking toward the house, I listened for Jay to start the engine of his Honda and drive away. I didn't hear anything and looked back when I reached the step. Because the glare in my eyes, I couldn't tell what Jay may have been thinking, but he started his car and left.

Kevin leaned against the doorframe, waiting for me with his hands shoved in his pockets, still barefoot and bare-chested. No denying the man was sexy. Hard to stay mad at him when he had a body that begged to be licked, but I managed. He draped his arm over my shoulder. I slipped out from under him and went back to my shower to finish rinsing shampoo out of my hair. The hot water was almost out, but the cool water didn't bother me.

Kevin walked into the bathroom, unbuttoned his fly, yanked off his jeans, and opened the shower door. His eyes were droopy, but nothing else about him drooped.

"Kevin! I'm super mad at you."

"I know," he said, but stepped in with me anyway. "I had a rough night and a rough morning. I need a shower." He picked up my shower gel and squeezed some in his hand. "You don't want to stay mad at me."

"Yes, I do."

He smirked and lathered me up with his big hands slipping and sliding in just the right spots. "Feel good?"

It did, but I wasn't ready to give up my anger. Plus, my head was too full of Jay. "I can't believe you're in the mood after everything that just happened."

"Weird, huh?" He kissed my neck and teased my nipples while he rubbed against my soaped-up body. "Watching you play the hero in your birthday suit really turned me on."

Despite being mad at him and gnawing guilt for allowing him to pleasure my body while my mind replayed everything Jay had said, Kevin's naked body gliding against me turned *me* on. My traitor body responded, but his body pumping into me could not push Jay out of my head.

After having his way in the shower, Kevin was not getting off the hook for a serious conversation. With both of us wrapped in towels and lying on my bed, I said, "I know you don't like Jay, but you shouldn't have gotten in his face."

He snickered, as if the whole incident were a joke. "I didn't plan on beating the crap out of him, just enough to make him back off." Kevin flexed his muscles, trying to tease a smile out of me. "I would've taken him."

"Kevin!" I was in no mood for jokes. "Why isn't this bothering you more?"

"Because I'm the one you wanted to stay." He grinned and kissed my cheek. "Hey, Luscious, nothing happened, so let it go."

"I can't 'let it go'. It can't happen again."

"What? You don't like two guys fighting over you?"

Why would he possibly think it would make me happy to see two men I cared about bloody each other? I didn't like it. I was beginning to see Kevin in a different light, and I didn't like that either. "I don't want you fighting with Jay or doing things to antagonize him."

Kevin sat up, all lightheartedness gone. "Hold on, I was just trying to take care of him for you. Why are you taking his side?"

I sat up too and pulled the towel closer around me. "I'm not, and I don't need you to 'take care' of Jay. He's a part of my life. I'm perfectly capable of dealing with him."

"I don't like it, Kim. I don't like the games he plays with you. I'm telling you there is no god damn way I'd get into a fight over Cathy. I don't give a rat's hairy ass what she does or who she sees. If it weren't for my kids, she wouldn't exist for me."

"You could amputate her out of your life just like that?"

Kevin snapped his fingers. "Just like that." He put it out there like a challenge, as if he expected me to snap my fingers and *POOF!* Jay wouldn't exist for me.

"Your situation is completely different. Cathy cheated on you; Jay didn't cheat on me."

Kevin's voice was cool, but his eyes snapped louder than his fingers had. "He dumped you so he could fuck girls like Brittany. I don't see much difference."

Wow, just wow. Tears stung my eyes, and I hated it. He reached for me, but I pushed him away.

He grimaced and closed his eyes. "I'm sorry. I'm so sorry. I shouldn't have said that."

"I'm sorry, too," I said once my tears slowed. "I told Jay to butt out."

"What a pair, huh?" I nodded and managed a smile. He tucked a strand of hair behind my ear and tilted my chin up at him. "Hey, I'm crazy about you. I want to be your guy, your boyfriend, significant other—whatever name you want."

I thought this was what I'd wanted, but now that Kevin granted me my wish, my stomach felt sick. I knew Kevin. I knew his sense of humor, his kindness and tenderness, but he had another side, too. He'd hidden a lot from me. Now that I had a fuller picture, I wasn't so sure about him. Without thinking, I asked, "Did you ever cheat on your wife?"

He dropped his hand from my face and nodded his assent. "It was years ago. I thought she'd forgiven me."

"I wasn't your first since you separated from Cathy, was I?"

"No, but I haven't been with anyone else since we met." His answer was the final deathblow. I didn't know how to respond.

He turned away from me and went to the bathroom. When he returned, he had his jeans on. He plopped heavily on the bed, and staring straight ahead, asked, "Truth or dare?"

"Just ask. I don't want to play any more games."

He turned to me, and his eyes locked on mine. "How do you feel about me now?"

I wished a telemarketer would call or a couple Mormon boys would knock on my door, anything that would buy me a fraction of time to think. No such luck. "I don't know."

He took my hands and refocused those beguiling green eyes of his on mine. "I know you're scared, but I learned my lesson a long time ago. No more lies. I want you to be a real part of my life, meet my friends and my kids. Don't move to San Francisco. Give us a chance."

Kevin had cajoled and coaxed me into doing so many things that previously I'd only done with Jay. The specialness Jay and I had shared was gone except for one thing: I had yet to have a serious relationship with another man. I cared about Kevin, but I didn't love him and no longer trusted him. I couldn't shape my life around a man I didn't love or trust.

"I'm sorry," I said, not wanting to cause him more pain. "I can't stay."

Kevin stood, retrieved his t-shirt from the side of the bed and yanked it on with an angry jerk. "Platonic bullshit—you're still hung up on Jay."

I'd now seen it enough times to know Kevin's defense mechanism was to lash out when he was hurt. I didn't like it, but at least I recognized his anger for what it was. "This is about you and me," I said, taking his hand and pulling him back next to me. "I've just started feeling stable again, and you … you're not even divorced yet. You live in the same house with your wife." He stared at me, not responding. "You're not ready either."

He nodded. "I still don't want you to go."

"Kevin …." He hugged me close, as if he could physically keep me from going, but no matter how tightly he held me, I was already gone. Like a light switch coming on in the gym when the dance is over, and you can see the boy you thought was so cute is just average and the starry sky is nothing more than Christmas string lights, a moment of clarity hit me. Even if Kevin hadn't lied, I would never be in love with him, and whether Kevin admitted it or not, he was still emotionally entangled with his wife.

I had wanted love so badly I'd fooled myself into believing Kevin might be the one. I had done the same thing with Jay. I had wanted to believe we had a perfect marriage so desperately that I willfully had refused to see the cracks and fissures in our marriage. When he had tried to talk to me, I had practically stuck my fingers in my ears and sang, *"La la la la la."*

"San Francisco isn't that far away. Come visit any time you need a quick getaway."

He forced a smile, gave me a squeeze, and got up to finish dressing. I almost offered him lunch but didn't want to prolong our goodbye. For the first time in a long time, I craved solitude.

When he was ready, I saw him to the door. He gave me one last kiss. "Bye, Luscious. Take care of yourself."

Whatever infatuation I'd had for him was over, but I still admired his backside and masculine gait. When he reached his truck, I yelled, "Hey, Kevin! I'll call you!"

He chuckled and gave me a wave before stepping into the cab and firing up the Hemi. I stood on my porch and watched him until he rounded the corner.

———

I decided to speed up my move date, and a few days later, went to Nugget with the intent of telling Joshua I was leaving. I didn't want him to wonder what happened to me. I wanted to see his great smile one last time and thought maybe we could have a drink together before I left.

I went to the store two days in a row, but he wasn't there. Over the next few days, I created three excuses to go back. No Joshua. Disappointment weighed me down after each expectant jaunt. I finally wrote a note and asked a clerk to give it to him. He told me Joshua had quit. His last day had been about two weeks prior. I was the one left wondering, whatever happened to him? Where did he go?

Most likely, he had left town and graduated to the next stage of his life. I was ready to move, too. There was nothing holding me here except memories of a life that no longer existed.

Chapter 17

Late September

FIRST TIME SINGLE

"Theory Testing"

The other day, I read on the internet that according to a recent poll, men think about sex every seven seconds. I find this hard to believe and consider the anonymous poll scientifically dubious. If it were true, how would any serious work get done? How would bridges be built? Books written? I can't imagine Tom Brady in the middle of a play, searching for an open receiver, then pausing to consider whether he would get lucky after the game. I simply can't imagine it. Of course, Tom would get lucky; Gisele adores him.

    The article got me thinking about a human sexuality class I had taken in college. My professor had taught a more plausible theory that teenage boys think about sex literally all the time, whereas a grown man thinks about it at the most every four minutes, but more likely, whenever he has mental downtime. He claimed most men perform an automatic sexual evaluation of almost every female they meet, a quick yes or no of potential.

At the time, I was married and insanely in love with my husband. Disturbed by my new knowledge, I asked if he agreed with the theory. At first, he dodged answering, but eventually concurred. He claimed for him the phenomenon was fast, and most of the time he was only semi-conscious of it. For a while after his confession, I had scrutinized my ex-husband's interaction with other women. His eyes would scan them over and his expression would say, *"Yes,"* because she had nicely shaped breasts or some other attractive feature. *Then, it would say, "No,"* because he was married. Once the "no" was established, he wouldn't give the woman a second thought. At some point, I tuned it out because I stopped viewing his behavior as a threat. Of course, he must have started thinking, "Yes, yes, yes," because he did leave me, the rat bastard.

Being single, I had to rethink the theory, and not because I sought an explanation for why my ex walked. No, if knowledge was power, then ladies, I was convinced this bit of information gave me an advantage. I went with two basic assumptions: one, men think about sex frequently, and two, single men are constantly evaluating the sexual possibilities of every new woman they meet.

Why should a fear of rejection stop me from walking into a bar or striking up a conversation while waiting in line at a coffee house? I am not a perfect ten by any stretch of the imagination, but I'm not unattractive either. After all, my ex-husband is handsome, and my first post-divorce guy was featured in a calendar without his shirt.

Surely, all I would have to do is smile, or give some other small indication I was open to conversation and social interaction, and men would want to talk to me to explore the possibilities. I had power over the traffic light.

A frown indicates stop, a smile proceed with caution, and a wink a clear indication of go, dog go.

Bolstered by my theory, I went to check out a South of Market sports bar. Ladies in my divorcee support group swore it was *the* place in San Francisco to meet eligible straight men. The entrance was in an alleyway, but once inside it was supposed to be a class operation and frequented by well-dressed bachelors who worked in the financial district.

I considered inviting a friend from my group to join me but remembered the advice we'd been given by our group's dating guru: do not travel in packs if you want to be approached. A confident woman by herself is sexy. According to her, what men find even hotter is a confident woman who shows a hint of cleavage, a lot of leg, and smears her mouth with red lipstick.

Therefore, I did just that. I put on my fitted white blouse with a top button just above the decency point, my black pencil skirt, and wide black patent leather belt. A pair of red pumps and cherry red lip plumper completed the look.

I arrived early and wasn't disappointed by the service or ambiance. Although a sports bar with standard big screens and pre-game commentary blaring, they served tapas and offered an extensive selection of wine by the glass. I ordered a glass of Malbec and nabbed a table in a perfect spot to survey men as they came in and to be sure I was seen as well. Three chairs surrounded the high-top table. I pushed one to another table, dropped my purse in the other, and hopped onto the third.

It didn't take long before a stream of suits rolled in, and the place became standing room only. The first half hour, I received my share of glances, but no promising smile exchange and no temptation to wink. Admittedly, I was nervous, so I ordered a second glass of wine, just to help me relax and get in a bolder mood.

About halfway through my second glass, he walked in. Tall, squared-jawed, and broad-shouldered, with just enough grey in his temples to be sexy. I used to buy my ex's suits, so I know an expensive suit when I see it. His was expensive, at least two thousand or more, and his shoes were Ferragamo.

His eyes scanned the crowd before settling on me. I smiled, crossed my legs, and let my shoe dangle flirtatiously from my foot. He smiled back, but then his attention was caught by a man who was waving at him from another table, which appeared to be the hub of some office party.

My guy gave him a wave, and then glanced at the vacant chair across from me. He smiled at me again. Before I even had a chance to test the power of the wink, he began crossing my direction. He walked with purpose and confidence, a modern personification of Don Draper. I immediately thought of a New York Prime steak and could only hope he wasn't an ass like the television character. He stopped next to the chair I had waiting, and his smile widened.

"Excuse me," he said. "I was wondering if you are saving this seat for anyone."

Only you, you dreamy man. "No, I'm here by myself."

"In that case, you mind?" He tilted his head to the chair.

I met his gaze, cool and nonchalant. "Not at all."

He pulled the chair out and picked up my purse. "Where would you like this?"

"Oh, I'll take it."

He handed me my purse, but instead of sitting down, he picked up the chair. He gave me a quick wink and a "Thanks" before turning away. He reminded me of my

cat, Buzz, prancing off with a dead mouse in his mouth.
He puffed his chest and strutted with the chair to the
waiting group where it was presented to a tall brunette
who could have been a model.

I plan to try on-line dating next.

The real story was much less dramatic. I'd been wearing jeans and a Gap
sweater. Sadly, the red stilettos only existed in my fantasy closet. Not on the
prowl either. I'd been waiting for a new friend, Gina Del Toro, to meet me.

I hit send, and my post whizzed its way through cyberspace to Wendy.
Writing stories about married life—what it meant to be in it for the long haul,
sticking together through thick and thin, weathering all storms hand-in-hand—
had been easy because I had written from my heart. The blog was more of a
struggle because I wasn't in a mindset for dating, but so far, Wendy had been
pleased with my submissions. Apparently, my stories "rang true" enough to
pass her scrutiny, and my fan base was growing. Woo Hoo!

I may have stretched the truth with my readers, but after Kevin, I vowed
to be honest with myself. Not dealing with a problem, not liking a new reality, didn't make it go away. All denial did was impair my judgement. Kevin
had called it when he'd accused me of being hung up on Jay. I had been, but
since moving to San Francisco, days passed without me thinking about Jay.
However, flashes of Jay's arms around me and running my hands through
his thick hair still haunted me from time to time. Sometimes I wished I had
made love with him the night he'd kissed me senseless. If we'd slept together,
maybe we'd be together now. The more likely narrative would have been that
I still would be living on my own in San Francisco, only with a little less
dignity. I'd given Jay an opening for getting back together. He didn't take it
and that was that. I purposely haven't seen or spoken to him since the day I
broke up with Kevin. It was a good decision and one I planned to stick with
as long as possible.

On reflection, living in Davis had been like being caught in a riptide. Every
time I thought I was emotionally disentangling from Jay, something would
yank me back to him—seeing him, bumping into old friends, or a memory
triggered by mementos that had filled our home. Getting out of our house,

not seeing him, and not having constant reminders of him surrounding me made it possible to move on. I'd needed a new beach so to speak.

Singlehood stopped being as lonely as it used to be, and somewhere along the line, I came to enjoy long periods of solitude. Moving to a thousand-square-foot apartment helped—the space didn't feel too big for one person. After enduring city crowds, I loved retreating to my cozy, quiet apartment. I didn't even have to worry about the cats. They stayed with the house. If it weren't for *First Time Single,* I would be perfectly content taking a vacation from dating.

Since moving, I'd kept a strict writing schedule and hadn't failed to write less than two articles a week. I'd even managed to complete an outline for a novel that had been bouncing around my head. Just this morning, I'd clicked away as the sun came up. By two o'clock, I'd earned a break and powered down my laptop.

In Davis, I ran into people I knew all the time and still left the house without make-up. Funny, I only knew Wendy, who was becoming more of a friend than a boss, her husband and a couple of other writers in San Francisco, but I couldn't bring myself to venture out without my hair in place and being properly dressed. Thus, I pulled on my black boots and changed out of my UC Berkeley sweatshirt and into a black cashmere sweater. Black was my new color. More sophisticated. I'd learned no matter how sunny and blue the sky appeared, one should never leave without a jacket, so I grabbed my trench, also black, on the way out.

A few minutes later, I breezed down Columbus Avenue and into City Lights Books, my new favorite place. Open since the early fifties, the store was cramped with narrow aisles, but had loads of character and a fabulous selection. I loved the intimate vibe and that the store was open until midnight. One or two nights a week, I'd browse through shelves and rarely walked out without making a purchase.

For some reason, I was in the mood for weightier reading and wound my way to the Virginia Woolf section. I glanced through a couple possibilities when big hazel eyes rounded the corner. "Joshua?"

For a second, I thought he didn't recognize me, or maybe I'd been mistaken. Then his face broke out with his great hey-it's-you smile. "Kimberly, hey, hi. Wow," he said while simultaneously hugging me. "What are you doing here?"

"I moved to San Francisco mid-August. I only live a few blocks from here."

"Me too. I mean I live in the city, not in North Beach. I have a place in the Sunset."

"With your girlfriend?"

"Girlfriend?" He cocked his head and connected the dots. "Oh, no. No, it was a casual thing. We split when I moved." Hearing he was single made me happier than it should have. He glanced down and pointed to the copy of *The Voyage* in my hand. "Whatcha got there?"

I held it up and shrugged. "Virginia Woolf. In the mood."

"Interesting read. Have you ever read *Orlando?*"

"No, but I've read some of her short stories and essays."

"Right on. I always knew you were a smart lady."

I laughed and received a giddy smile from Joshua and a hostile glare from a woman who was browsing through Evelyn Waugh.

Joshua whispered, "Are you busy? Wanna catch up over a cup of coffee? My treat."

I hadn't made very many friends since moving to the city, so sitting across from Joshua's adorable, familiar face sounded delightful. "I'd love to."

Joshua waited for me outside while I made my purchase. He seemed different, older, since I'd seen him last. It could have been he wasn't wearing fluorescent sneakers or surrounded by college students, but he exuded a more mature aura. I glanced out the window at him. He was still slim compared to Jay and Kevin, but he'd bulked a bit. The transformation must have started before he'd left Davis, but I hadn't noticed. If I were meeting him for the first time, I would guess him to be closer to thirty than twenty.

I walked out of the store and Joshua pointed to a bar. "How about a drink instead?"

"Isn't it a little early for happy hour?"

He grinned. "It's five o'clock somewhere."

I couldn't remember the last time I'd had a drink in the middle of the afternoon, especially on a weekday. Jay used to drink beer now and then on Saturday afternoons while he worked around the house, but outside of wine tasting trips, I rarely did. What was stopping me? I had no obligations the rest of the day, and no one would be expecting dinner in a few hours.

He led me to Vesuvio, a bar close to the bookstore, and explained, "This place used to be a Beat poet hangout. Jack Kerouac supposedly hung out here when he made his way to SF."

The décor seemed unchanged since its heyday. Small and informal, Beat art decorated the walls and most of the light filtered through stained glass windows. I could imagine it filled with black-beret-wearing artistes smoking hand-rolled herb cigarettes. The bar didn't look like the kind of place that had ever stocked pineapple slices or rainbow-colored drink-umbrellas. Joshua ordered two Stellas from the bartender, and we took our beers to the second-floor balcony where we had a great view of Columbus and Broadway.

Joshua scooted his chair a little closer. "So, tell me what you're doing here?"

"Same thing I was doing in Davis—living and writing. You?"

He raised an eyebrow. "That's kind of vague, but okay. Believe it or not, but I got a job as a sous chef."

"Sous chef? Where did that come from? Didn't you tell me you were a history major and were applying for management training programs?"

He chuckled and took a drink of his beer. "I was. Pretty wild, huh?"

"Don't you have to go to culinary school for that kind of work?"

"I went to culinary school. I have a certificate from the American Culinary Institute and worked as a cook for a couple years."

When was all this? "How old are you?"

He laughed. "Twenty-seven. I took a few detours before I got my degree. I think going back to college made me regress."

"Sounds like it." His face fell. "I mean the detour part. So what's your story?"

"I'll tell you mine if you tell me yours."

"Fair enough. You first."

He narrowed his brows at me, and then grinned, shaking his head. "Alright, here goes. My father is a professor and being the professor's son, I graduated high school when I was sixteen. At the time, I planned to be a veterinarian, which is why I applied to UCD, but after my junior year, I knew it wasn't for me."

"What made you change your mind?"

"I don't like animals."

I snorted beer, and Joshua laughed too. He handed me his drink napkin, and I wiped up the sprayed beer. "That would be a good reason."

"Yep, I thought so. Anyway, I'd always liked to cook, so I decided to give culinary school a try. After I finished, I worked here in the city until my dad convinced me to finish my degree. Dropping out hadn't thrilled him."

"That's understandable, but do you like restaurant work?"

"Oh yeah, I love it. Being in a kitchen again feels like home. My parents thought I'd hate the long hours and working on my feet. I actually prefer it, which is probably one of the reasons I liked working at Nugget. Somewhere along the line I got kinda hung up on the idea I had to do something more corporate or academic. None of those things really appealed to me though, so I got stuck in Davis a little too long."

"What made you decide to go back to cooking?"

"An old buddy from culinary school called me out of the blue. He was opening a Latin-fusion restaurant in the Mission and asked me to work for him."

"How's the restaurant doing?"

"Really great. We got a couple awesome reviews. It's called De Noche."

"De Noche? As in the night?"

"Yeah, we're only open at night, but we close late. Come check us out. I'll make sure you're comped."

"I just might take you up on that offer." I took another drink. I still couldn't reconcile the Davis Joshua with this man sitting in front of me. "*Sous chef,* very impressive."

He chuckled. "Sounds more impressive than it is. The staff is small."

"I'm still impressed."

Joshua's cheeks flushed. "You make me feel really good sometimes." We both laughed, and then took a sip of our Stellas. Some of the youthful, sweet Joshua I'd known was still around. We watched a transvestite with a red wig sashay down the street. "We're definitely not in Davis anymore."

"Nope. Little different here, and I love it," I replied.

"Me, too," he agreed and asked, "So why are you here?"

Hmmm. It was a good question. Joshua and I had chatted it up all summer at Nugget, but I never revealed too much personal history. Being out of Davis and no longer his customer, I saw no reason why I shouldn't treat him as a friend.

"My husband and I divorced. I didn't have a reason to stay."

"Huh. Makes sense."

"I thought so."

He nodded his agreement and chugged the remainder of his beer. "Want another?"

"I probably shouldn't."

"Why? Do you have to be somewhere?"

That wasn't it. Joshua was older than I'd thought, but he was still too young for me. If I bought, however, it would keep things in the friend zone. "Only if the next round is on me."

He gave no argument and waited while I went back down the stairs to order. Seeing him so out of context threw me. I kept having to adjust my perception of the Joshua I'd thought I knew. The smile was the same, and the eyes, but he wasn't the fresh-faced kid I'd thought.

When I came back, he was staring out the window. I asked, "See something good?"

His gaze focused my face and held a couple beats. "Always." He grinned and peered back out the window. "One of my favorite things to do in San Francisco is people watch." Which was exactly what we did as we downed our second round. I liked people watching, too.

After a while, he observed, "You've never told me what you write about."

Oh boy, here we go. "I write a sex and dating column for divorced women."

This time *he* snorted the beer. "Holy shit! Seriously?"

His reaction wasn't much different than that of other men I'd told. One guy told me if I ever needed someone to write about, he'd be happy to volunteer and let me use his real name. "Seriously, but I do other freelance writing, too."

"That's cool. Where can I read your stuff?"

"Online." I thought it was a perfect exit line and stood. "I have to go. It was really great seeing you again."

"How about giving me your number? I'm off on Wednesdays. Maybe we can hang out again soon?"

Joshua was easy company. Why couldn't we be friends? I wrote my number on a napkin, and he put it in his wallet. I said goodbye and made it to the bottom step of the stairwell when he stopped me. "Hey, what's your last name?"

I forgot I'd never told him. I didn't know his either. "Braxton. What's yours?"

"Stone." Joshua Stone. Good name. "Is Braxton your maiden name?"

"Nope." I waved over my shoulder and left.

On my way home, the sky glowed an incredible blue, so impeccably clear. More often than not, San Francisco sat shrouded in clouds, but when the sun broke through, the city was glorious. I took it as a good omen; bumping into Joshua meant we were destined to be friends.

Not long after I got home, my phone beeped with a text: *What's your pen name?*

I laughed and answered: *Not telling.*

He responded: *That a challenge?*

I hesitated. If I said yes, would he think I was flirting? On the other hand, the whole reason for the pen name was to have freedom from embarrassment with friends and family. Of course, if he really wanted to, he could probably figure it out. Thank goodness, I hadn't posted the piece about our parking lot kiss. Holy guacamole, that would be embarrassing.

My phone beeped again, and I read: *Free Saturday?*

My heart skipped a beat, and I did a double take before realizing the text was from Haley. Couldn't she hit my number and actually talk to me? Kids today, jeesh. I went with her preferred mode of communication and answered: *Yes, why?*

Should have known. She wanted to go shopping, her favorite pastime. I agreed to meet her in Union Square at ten on Saturday.

Then I answered Joshua: *Good luck.* :-)

Chapter 18

SATURDAY MORNING, I hustled up the steps of the Union Square piazza to meet Haley at Emporio Rulli-il Caffe. She was nowhere in sight, but Jay fidgeted at a table by himself with two cups in front of him. *Haley.* What had that girl of mine been thinking? I was about to turn around and trot back down when Jay's expression stopped me. Something about his eyes and slack mouth gave the impression of a man who was adrift. If I were a fine art photographer, I'd snap his photo in black and white and call it *Lost Man*. I remembered catching glimpses of that expression not long before he'd left me. It saddened me to see then, and it saddened me to see now. Previously, I'd attributed it to his mother's death, but now I wasn't so sure.

Jay spied me and stood. His face lighted with an uncharacteristic shy smile, both nervous and hopeful. I wished I could say I felt the same, but I didn't. I didn't want to see him or deal with him. I was doing great and feeling good. I didn't want him pulling me back into a sea of heartache, but I couldn't walk away either.

"Hi, Jay. What's going on? Where's Haley?"

Jay's smile dropped. "In Davis, why? What'd she tell you?"

"That I was meeting her to go shopping. What did you think?"

"Sorry, Kimmy. We've been duped. I asked her if she'd help me pick out some new suits. You know I hate clothes shopping. Last night she told me she talked to you, and you said you would go with me. I thought …."

"You thought what?"

"I thought it meant you were willing to be friends."

He had the lost look again, and I felt sorry for him. "Oh."

"Don't worry. I understand if you don't want to shop with me."

I glanced at the two cups sitting on the table. "One of those for me?"

He slid the frothy one toward me. "Double cappuccino, non-fat with a dash of cinnamon." It was thoughtful of him to remember and to have it waiting for me. I sat down and dropped my purse on my lap. He sat down, too and smiled. "Thank you."

"Thank you, too." I stirred the foam and licked the small spoon. "So how've you been?"

"Not bad."

"Really?" His cheeks were slightly sunken, and his skin stretched tightly over his cheekbones. "You look kind of thin."

He shrugged. "I haven't had much of an appetite lately. Guess I've dropped a few pounds. Anyway, instead of having my suits taken in, I figured I'd buy new ones."

"So why didn't you just go see your guy at Nordstrom's?"

Jay peered down at his coffee. "Would you have driven to Sacramento to go shopping with me?"

It was a rhetorical question. "Ah, Haley."

"She wants us back together."

I chuckled. "Yuh think?"

He nodded and studied my face as if he were searching for something.

I picked up my cup and turned to face the piazza. An art fair, with at least a dozen artists displaying their wares, splashed the middle of the square with color. The air was crisp, but the sun shone brilliantly, making the whole scene lovely. "Beautiful, isn't it?"

"Yeah, it's great. Want to check it out?"

Every Friday night for years, Jay and I had walked to downtown Davis for dinner. Afterwards we would wander through Natsoulas Gallery, The Artery, The Pence, and other local shops picking out paintings and prints to cover our bare walls. We only bought works that moved us in a personal way. Eventually, our walls were filled, and the outings stopped. Some pieces stayed in Davis, and some moved with me.

I shook my head. "No, that's okay."

"Come on. If you see something you like, my treat. I've been meaning to get you a housewarming gift."

Jay meant well but was a new painting supposed to be a consolation prize? Here, Kimmy, let me throw some money at you to ease my guilt? "Thank you, but no."

"Please, don't be that way."

"What way?"

"Unforgiving."

I supposed I was unforgiving about certain things. I wished I could tell him I forgave him for breaking my heart, for making me feel like crap about myself, and for pulling me back just when I was ready to let go, but I couldn't. I drained my cup. "I don't think this whole shopping thing is a good idea. Thank you for the coffee."

I stood and made it to the steps heading down to Geary Street before I realized he was following me. He grabbed my arm. "Hey, I'm sorry, please, don't go. Please, Kimmy."

"I don't want to fight with you."

"I don't want you fighting with me either." He dropped my arm. "I really do need new clothes. Come on, what do you say? Will a couple hours in my company be so bad?"

He hadn't seemed so despondent since his mother had died. For the first time I noticed the dark shadows smudged under his eyes. Being a softy meant I cried easily at movies, gave money to the homeless, and apparently, went shopping with my ex-husband. I hated being such a softy. I let him guide me by the elbow as we waded through the crowd of shoppers, down the hill to Market Street.

An hour and a half later, we had finished buying him a couple pair of jeans at the Levi's store, where Jay had insisted on buying me a few things too and had made our way to Saks Men's Store. I riffled through racks of outrageously priced suits, while Jay changed into the salesman's recommendation. Saks was out of my price range but dropping the equivalent of half-a-month's rent on a suit wouldn't cramp Jay's budget. It used to bother me how much he'd spend on his work wardrobe, but now I didn't care. It was his money.

He walked out of the fitting room with Bryan, our stylish young salesman, tailing him. Jay stopped in front of me, waiting for my approval. The pants tapered narrowly down Jay's legs and the slim-fit three-button jacket was not a good cut for him.

Jay pulled on the jacket cuffs. "What do you think?"

His belt kept the trousers from falling, and the jacket hung too loose for the style. I walked up to him and checked just how much room he had in the waist. How odd doing something so intimate; at the same time, it seemed natural and comfortable. Weird.

I kept my voice low so only Jay could hear. "How much weight have you lost?"

"I don't know, maybe twenty pounds."

"In two months?"

He shrugged. "I'm tired of eating out, and I haven't gotten the knack of cooking yet."

I refused to feel sorry for him and turned to Bryan. "Let's try forty-two long, and this suit is a little trendy for him. He likes a fuller leg and two-button jackets with a single vent."

Jay smiled down at me and mouthed, "Thank you."

Bryan was quick with an alternative. "We just got in an uber sharp Canali with a traditional leg, cuff optional. Would you like to see it?"

Jay checked with me, and I nodded. "You can show her," he said. "She knows my taste better than me."

Jay went back to the dressing room and Bryan asked, "What does your husband do for a living?"

"He's an attorney." I didn't think it worth explaining I was his ex-wife. "But it doesn't mean he likes pin-stripe."

"Understood. Nothing too fashion forward, but nothing too stodgy either."

It was a good summary of Jay. "You nailed it."

We made small talk while we picked out things for Jay. At some point Bryan asked, "Do you live in the City?"

"Yep, North Beach."

"My boyfriend and I love, love, just love that neighborhood."

"Mmmm, I love it, too."

Together, Bryan and I suited Jay in a classic charcoal grey, a serious black, and a handsome navy suit with new dress shirts and coordinating ties. While he rang up Jay's purchase, Bryan said, "It's been fun working with you. You're such a great couple."

Jay glanced at me, and I shrugged. He said, "Thank you. You've been very helpful."

Bryan beamed. "Well, Mrs. Braxton has great taste."

Jay snickered and draped his arm on my shoulder. "Yes, she does."

Bryan's disposition got even cheerier when he hit the total key. He handed back Jay's American Express card. "May I add you to my client book and let you know when things come in that you may like?"

Jay took the card and shoved it back in his wallet. "Thanks, but I don't live around here."

"Oh, I'm sorry. I thought your wife said you live in North Beach."

Jay grinned ear-to-ear. "It's just a weekend place. Babe, you don't mind if I give Bryan our contact information, do you?"

Great, just great. Do I own up, or play along? I gave him my address but stipulated the suits should be delivered to *our Davis address* when they were done being tailored.

Bryan hugged me and shook Jay's hand before handing him the shopping bag with his shirts and ties. "It was a pleasure meeting you, and you too, Mrs. Braxton."

I hadn't realized how much I no longer saw myself as "Mrs. Braxton." When had that happened? The *Mrs.* was now an alien appendage I had no problem lopping off. Maybe the time had come to drop Braxton and legally go back to Kirby—except Kimberly Kirby sounded awfully cutesy for a grown woman.

We walked out the front doors of Saks and onto Post Street. Jay usually parked at the Fifth and Mission garage whenever he came into the city, and home for me was the other direction. I stopped and so did he.

"That wasn't so bad, was it, *Mrs. Braxton*?"

I punched Jay playfully on the arm. Laughing, he snatched my hand and held my fist against him. "Are you in a hurry? Can I buy you lunch?"

He knew I wasn't in a hurry. If I were with Haley as planned, lunch and dinner would be a given. "Oh, we've probably had enough togetherness for one day. Let's not push our luck."

The playfulness drained from his face. "Can I at least give you a ride somewhere?"

"No, thanks. It's such a beautiful day, think I'll walk." I smiled, wanting to leave on good terms.

"So is that how you've kept it up?"

"What?"

"Keeping the weight off, looking so good."

A compliment shouldn't hurt, but it brought back echoes of pain from the day Jay left. Logically, I knew our problems ran deeper than me packing on a few pounds, but it didn't stop his words from replaying in my head. *The only way I can stand having sex with you is with the lights out for Christ's sake.*

"I wouldn't want my naked body to blind anyone, now would I?" I'd meant it as a joke, but my voice came out sharp.

Jay cringed. He grabbed my elbow and steered me off the sidewalk and into the recess of a closed building. He dropped the bags, took hold of my arms, and bent his head so we were eye level. "I am so sorry about what I said that day. I swear, if there was one thing I could do over in my life, it would be that moment. You have no idea how much I wish I could erase that day."

"It doesn't change the fact that you meant it."

"It wasn't because of your body. I loved your shape. I didn't mind you being heavier either; I liked what it did to your breasts."

"Then, why the whole lights off thing?"

"Because …." He diverted his eyes.

I watched him weigh whether he should tell me. My heart sped up fearing his answer would be worse than what I'd previously believed. I had to know. "Because *why*, Jay?"

He dropped his hands from my arms and his words came out slowly, with him watching me closely, gauging my reaction as he went. "Because … because when we used to make love, you'd stare at me with so much love in your eyes … it was overwhelming. I didn't think I loved you the same way anymore, and I knew you'd see it. I couldn't take it. I felt like such a fraud."

Better and worse than I'd anticipated. He hadn't thought I was physically repulsive. He couldn't take seeing my love for him. Fresh pain sliced me. Only God knew how long it would take to sort out the twist of anger, resentment, and pity I had for him. Yes, pity. How sad for Jay to shun love. I swiped at a tear before it slid down my cheek.

"From the depths of my soul, I'm sorry," he said. "I hope you can forgive me someday."

He meant it. I heard the sincerity in his voice and saw it in his eyes. I couldn't say what he needed to hear, and I didn't know if the day would ever come when I could. His confession hurt more than knowing he'd slept with other women.

"I hope I can, too. Go get yourself a steak. You're too thin."

With that, he let me go.

As soon as I walked in the door of my apartment, I called Haley. She didn't pick up. I sent her a text: *You can't avoid me forever. Call me.*

She called back immediately. "What's up? I was in the shower," she said all innocent.

"You know what's up. *You* were supposed to meet me to go shopping. You lied to me."

"No I didn't. I never said *I* would be there. I asked if you were free, and you said yes."

"Don't split hairs with me, Haley Braxton. You set me up. That wasn't fair to me, or your dad. Did you think we'd spend a day together and magically get back together?"

"Of course not. I'm not a child. I know it doesn't work that way."

"Then, what were you thinking?" That *child* of mine had me seething.

"I'm sorry, okay? I'm sorry, it's just Dad mopes around all the time, and he keeps losing weight. He seems so unhappy. I know he misses you, but he won't admit it. I thought he just needed nudging in the right direction."

"Maybe those things are true, but I can't help him, Haley." If I were the answer to his happiness, he would tell me. "Please, accept your father and I will never get back together. Even if he wanted me back, I don't want him anymore."

How could I ever let go and love him unconditionally the way I had after everything we'd lived through? I would never know if I gave him too much love, if my love was suffocating him. There had been a time when we had been wild for each other. The more I'd loved him, the more he loved me back. About halfway through our marriage, there had been a shift.

I could see it so clearly now, the elusive thing that happened to us. Yes, I should have appreciated him more and nagged him less. I should have taken better care of myself, more for my sake than for him. I should have let him buy a damn motorcycle if it made him happy. Plenty of little things to point to as the cause of our demise, but it hadn't been the little things. There was one big thing, and I finally figured it out. I wondered if Jay had any clue.

Sometime between Jay getting on the fast track at work and Haley's graduation, the balance of our love shifted. The less he gave me, the more I gave him. And the more I gave him, the less he gave me. Deep down, I was convinced if the sum total remained the same, we were good. Because he worked so much, I had to take on the extra burden.

Love didn't work that way, and I could never live that way again. Nor could I live measuring and doling out my affection in bits and pieces, always careful to be in equal portion with his moods. I pitied him. I pitied Jay. Somewhere in this world there had to be a man who could handle all the love I was willing to give and who would be willing to love me the same. I shouldn't ever have to worry about loving my husband too much.

"Mom, are you there?"

"Yeah, I'm here. Haley, you have to promise you'll never pull a stunt like that again."

"I promise, and I am sorry. It was a stupid idea."

"I love you and I forgive you."

"Thanks, Mom. Love you, too."

I hung up with Haley feeling very alone. I hadn't had such a lonesome feeling since the early days of our separation, and I didn't think a solo trip to City Lights would be my fix. I needed to be around people, and I needed to have fun.

Serendipitously, I received a text from Joshua: *De Noche seats until eleven tonight. Amazing special on the menu.* :-)

I called my new friend, Gina Del Toro. She loved to go out and she loved to eat. "Hey, would you be up for checking out a new Latin Fusion restaurant tonight? It's called De Noche."

"Sure but let me check Yelp."

"Don't bother. I know the sous chef."

"Ahh," she teased, "Is he cute?"

I laughed. "He's just a friend, but yeah, he's cute."

"I'm in."

Chapter 19

I'D MET GINA Del Toro in the basement laundry room a week after moving to San Francisco. She had come bustling in with a basket of her dainty dirties. Petite, full-breasted, and full of juice, she exuded sex appeal without trying. Not that I check out women, but I couldn't help noticing how naturally beautiful she was without make-up. She had a personality equally intimidating and had asked very bold questions regarding my single status during our first conversation: *Was he abusive? Did you get a good settlement? Have you had sex with anyone else yet?*

While a bit forward for my sensibilities, she seemed kindhearted, and her vivaciousness was hard to resist. Her apartment was two doors down from mine, and although Gina was a few years younger and didn't have children, we had the shared experience of being recently divorced. Unofficially, Gina was my divorce support group and dating guru.

"So tell me again how you know the chef?" she asked as we walked into De Noche.

"He's the *sous* chef, and I met him in Davis. He worked at my favorite grocery store. I'm sure the food will be good."

The restaurant was bigger and more upscale than I'd anticipated based on Joshua's understated description. We stopped at the hostess desk, and I glanced around while we waited to be seated. The side walls had an ombre paint treatment, moving from twilight purple to midnight blue, which drew the eye to a full moon with *De Noche* slashed across its middle in fiery orangish-yellow on the back wall. Very urban with a lively Salsa beat playing in the background and exuding a vibrant energy, it was quite the hip-happening place and crawled with hipsters—not that I was an expert on what hipsters looked like. Haley would know.

Since Joshua said the last seating was at eleven, we purposely arrived a little after ten, hoping it wouldn't be too crowded. We still had to wait for a table, but once we were seated in a booth, the crowd began to thin and most of the tables remained vacant.

I decided to wait to ask for Joshua until after ordering and perused the menu enchanted by the witty anecdotes explaining the inspiration of each dish, which included selections such as slider-sized *cubanos* made with medianoche, bacon-wrapped plantains with fresh pineapple-jalapeno salsa, and *aguachiles de camaron* tostadas with cilantro-lime sauce.

Scanning the menu, Gina said, "Everything sounds so mouthwatering, it's hard to decide. Did your friend mention any favorites?"

Just then a waiter walked up with two drinks and a plate of appetizers on a tray. "Compliments of Mr. Stone. Watermelon margaritas and bacon wrapped plantains."

Gina met my grin. "Guess your little buddy knows we're here."

"Guess so." I said to the waiter, "Please, thank him for me."

"Will do. Josh said to tell you he'll be able to say hello in a few minutes."

About the time we finished the appetizer, practically licking the plate clean, Joshua walked out wearing a white, grease-stained chef's jacket and checked pants. His face was shiny, and a ring dented his hair from the chef's hat in his hand.

He greeted me with a huge smile. "Hey, I'm so glad you decided to check us out."

"Me, too. So far everything has been delicious."

"Thanks." Joshua glanced at Gina and did a double take.

She had that effect on men. It hadn't bothered me before, but this time, jealousy bit hard, making me question the wisdom of making her my wingwoman.

After introducing them, Joshua turned his attention back to me, still grinning. "Everything is on the house tonight. I'll send out my favorites."

"It's very generous, but I can't let you do that."

"Sure you can." He winked at me and the grind of jealousy I'd felt eased. "Give me about half-an-hour and me and my buddy, Paul, can join you. Sound good?"

"Sounds great. I'd love to meet Paul."

As soon as he turned away, Gina asked, "Are you sure that hottie is just a friend?"

I cringed and hoped Joshua was out of hearing range. "Yes … just friends."

"Well okay, then," she said with a coquettish lilt.

I wasn't sure what she meant by that, and I didn't know what I'd do if she decided to flirt with him—kick her shin under the table? I wished I'd said, *"That's what I'm here to figure out."* I held my tongue. If Joshua preferred Gina, who was I to object?

As promised, he kept dishes flowing to our table and provided another round of margaritas. When the restaurant was almost empty, I spotted Joshua, who had cleaned up and changed into street clothes, making his way to our booth with who I assumed to be Paul. I'd expected Paul to be Joshua's age, but he was closer to my age, possibly older, and quite handsome with his bronzed skin and prominent cheekbones.

Gina's face lit up when she saw them, and she beamed a glittering smile their way. After introductions, and to my relief, Joshua slid in next to me, leaving Paul to sit next to Gina.

"So Paul," Gina said, "Kimberly tells me you own this place?"

"That's right. I grew up in the Mission. Back then Valencia Street wasn't so hip, and my parents owned a small *pupuseria*. A place like this has always been my dream."

Gina asked, "Where are your parents from?"

"El Salvador."

"Really? I'm an immigration attorney, and I work with Salvadorians all the time. How long have you been here?"

"We moved to San Francisco when I was a toddler. I grew up on Peruvian, Salvadorian, Mexican, and all the other great flavors in this neighborhood."

"The food is crazy good, and I love the vibe. I have no doubt you'll do great," I said.

"So far, so good, but I couldn't have done it without Josh. For a white boy, he makes some mean Latin food. He came up with the pineapple-jalapeno salsa and makes carnitas better than me."

I smiled at Joshua. "I had no idea you were so talented. Good thing you left Nugget."

He glowed with a shy smile and shrugged. "You know, Kimberly is a great cook, too."

"How would you know? You've never eaten my cooking."

"No, but I've bagged your groceries and seen what kind of ingredients you buy. Only serious cooks shop the way you do."

"I hadn't realized you'd paid so much attention."

A blush flashed on his cheeks. "Well, I did."

Our eyes met and my stomach warmed, then we all laughed, including Paul and Gina.

We went on chatting while the restaurant closed, and busboys cleaned up around us. After the last of the staff left and the lights dimmed, I signaled to Gina that it was time to leave, but Paul insisted we stay and brought out a bottle of Patron Anejo.

"Sorry," I said, "Unless it's hidden in something fruity, I can't drink tequila."

Paul and Joshua exchanged disbelieving grins, and Paul said, "Then no one has taught you how to drink tequila properly. Josh, give the lady a lesson." Paul poured two shots and set them in front of us.

"I'll need your wrist," Joshua said, locking his eyes on mine. He licked the underside of his wrist, had me do the same, and quickly salted our moistened skin. He lifted his wrist to my mouth and mine to his. "On 'three' lick and then take the shot," he instructed. "Ready?"

Keeping my eyes on his, I picked up my glass. "Ready."

"One, two, three." I licked his salty skin at the same time he licked mine and gulped the shot. As soon as the glass left my lips, Joshua pushed a slice of lime into my mouth. "Suck."

I sucked until he pulled it out of my mouth. "Oh, my," I said, warmed and thrilled by the layered sensations of my wrist tingling from his tongue and the tequila. After that, the Patron was easy sipping and put us all in a lively mood.

Gina and Paul went into full-on flirt mode. He turned up the stereo, pushed a couple tables aside and said to Gina, "You look like a lady who needs to Salsa."

"I do! Besides, I think these two would like to be alone." She laughed and winked at Joshua. Paul pulled her out of the booth and onto her feet while I wanted to crawl under the table. Where had her filter gone?

Gina had more enthusiasm than skill, but Paul had the moves and guided her with a sure hand. They laughed while he tried to teach her some steps.

Joshua leaned over and said, "I'd ask you to dance, but I don't know how to Salsa."

"It's okay, neither do I."

"She's right you know."

"About what?"

"I do want to be alone with you."

"Oh?"

He whispered into my ear, "I read some of your stuff, *First Time.*"

"You found me already?" I buried my face in my hands. "Oh jeesh, now I am embarrassed."

Laughing, he gently pulled my hands away from my face. "Hey, your posts are great and funnier than I'd expected. Did the episode in the sports bar really happen?"

"I took liberties with some of the details, but for the most part, it did."

"What about the dentist who asked for separate checks?"

"True."

"And the guy who said he forgot his wallet after ordering a fifty-dollar meal and still tried to get you in the sack?"

"All true. Until recently, I hadn't realized there were so many jerky jugheads out there."

He snorted a laugh. "*Jerky jugheads?* You mean assholes?"

"Yes," I said chuckling. I have no idea why *jerky jugheads* popped out of my mouth.

"You know, there are plenty of nice guys around."

I cocked my head at him. "Oh, yeah?"

"Yeah." Joshua took my hand under the table and squeezed it. "I'm a nice guy." He leaned in a little closer, close enough to be within kissing distance. "Do you remember when I kissed you in the parking lot?"

I snickered. "Kinda hard to forget."

"It wasn't one sided. You kissed me back."

"You're right. I did."

With his deep eyes fixated on me and buzzing from tequila, I wanted to kiss him again, but it wouldn't be fair to Joshua unless he knew more about me. I didn't want to hide things from him the way Kevin had hid his past from me, and I mentally wrestled with our age gap.

I shook my head. "I'm a lot older than you."

"Not more than a few years."

"Try ten." His eyes bugged. "And I have a nineteen-year-old daughter."

Joshua dropped my hand, sat up straight, and said with mocked shock, "Whoa, blow me over with a feather. You sure are full of surprises." Then he laughed. "Kimberly, I know how old you are and that your daughter's name is Haley."

"How do you know all this?"

"Her ex-boyfriend used to work at Nugget. He pointed you out one day and told me. He thought you were hot, but that was back when you were married."

I'd forgotten what a small-town Davis could be. Haley's boyfriend had thought I was hot? *Blow me over with a feather.* That was too weird for me. I wondered how much more he knew about me. "So you knew I was divorced before I told you?"

"Not so hard to figure out. You used to wear a wedding ring and then you stopped." He laughed and rolled his eyes. "Honestly, other than the little bit you told me, that's all I knew about you. I didn't even know your last name."

The Salsa ended, and a slow, sensual Latin rhythm filled the air. Paul and Gina glided closer together and moved in unison with the music. They looked good together.

Joshua said, "Now, this is more my speed."

He stood and helped me to my feet. I had wanted to touch him all summer. Now my hands were on his shoulders, and his body brushed tantalizingly against me while we swayed in a small circle. He smelled like the restaurant and was very tempting. I relaxed into him and couldn't deny how naturally we moved together.

"I'm really glad you showed up tonight," he said close to my ear. "If you hadn't, I'd planned to call you tomorrow and see if you wanted to hang out with me on my next day off."

"Did you now?"

"Uh-huh." He whispered, "So how about taking a chance on me?"

"Have you ever been married?"

"Nope, can't say I have."

"Any children?"

"That would be negative."

"Criminal record?"

He chuckled. "Clean past, disease free, and I just say no to drugs, including pot."

Honestly, what was stopping me? He knew my story and didn't care I came with baggage. So what if he was a little young? I wasn't in the market for a husband. He was a nice guy and I liked him. "In that case, sure—as long as we go slowly."

He tugged me a little closer and murmured seductively in my ear, "*Slowly* is my specialty."

It started as a giggle in my chest, then his chest rumbled against me, and we both cracked up. "You did not just say that."

He shrugged. "Figured it would make a good line for your column."

On the way home in the Uber, Gina teased, "You and Joshua were awfully cozy for being *just* friends. You know he couldn't take his eyes off you."

"Yeah, I'm pretty sure he likes me." I laughed and teased her back. "You and Paul seemed to hit it off. He couldn't keep *his eyes off you*."

"Or his hands." She giggled. "While we were dancing, he suggested he give me a tour of the back rooms. I think he wanted a tour inside my pants."

"Oh my, but I noticed you gave him your number."

"Why not? He's fun, straight, owns his own business, and looks like a Latin god. Just because I gave him my number doesn't mean I have to sleep with him."

True and just because I'd agreed to see Joshua again didn't mean I committed to anything either. He said he'd text me about doing something on Wednesday. I still wasn't clear if *hanging out* meant going on a date. The whole texting and casual thing were beyond my experience. I'd have to ask Haley. Maybe I should text her?

Chapter 20

I HADN'T OVERINDULGED SINCE the night I met Kevin. Thinking things over as I lazed in bed semi-hungover, all my excessive drinking and questionable romantic encounters happened while under the influence, and all three episodes had been triggered by something happening with Jay. I'd kissed Joshua after downing a couple margaritas at my divorce party. The night at Club Violet and subsequent orgy-bed interlude had been prompted by an unexpected visit from Jay. Now here I was again, foggy headed after a night out attempting to dilute feelings Jay had stirred.

Thank God, I hadn't slept with Joshua, or even kissed him for that matter, so I don't know why a guilty sensation gnawed my stomach. I had agreed to test the waters, but that was all. I hadn't done anything embarrassing or immoral. There was no reason to feel guilty, and maybe the fact that I maintained control meant Jay's power over me had lessened. But I couldn't help analyzing something Jay had said. *I didn't think I loved you the same way anymore.* The key being *didn't think.* He could have said *I didn't love you the same,* but he'd added an indefinable, doubtful *think,* which really could go either way: now he knows he still had loved me, or now he knows for certain he'd stopped loving me.

Ruminating about Jay's cryptic slip was a quick slide to a depressing day, and I'd had enough downer days for a lifetime. Determined to block Jay out of my thoughts, I showered, dressed, and headed out to walk off my hangover. The air was fresh with a sea breeze blowing from the west. The crispness cut through my sweatshirt, encouraging me to move faster.

Before I knew it, I'd trudged to Telegraph Hill, which was capped by Coit Tower. The historic site was built with funds bequeathed by Lillie Hitchcock Coit in the 1930s. She had been quite a character and was made an honorary firefighter in her youth due to her love of chasing fires. The tower itself was supposedly symbolic of a fire hose, but to me, the erection was more phallic than polite society admitted. It was a very touristy thing to do, but I'd never been to the top and had an unexplainable urge to conquer it.

The hike would have been a workout even if my body hadn't been sluggy from too much tequila. I told myself to keep going: one more step, one more step … one more step. Three-quarters up, my butt and thigh muscles burned, and I almost turned around. Who would know if I didn't make it to the top? The answer, of course, was I would know. I had to do it for me.

Once there, my efforts were rewarded by spectacular views. I gazed at Alcatraz and the Golden Gate Bridge in the distance through clear skies. I walked all the way around and enjoyed various panoramas of the city. San Francisco was my new home, and I wanted to embrace her. My lungs stretched and took in the brisk air, and I noticed my headache was gone.

I went home feeling better about myself but with my head still full of Jay. My hurt and anger about what he'd said hadn't diminished, but after seeing him not looking his best and hearing what Haley had to say, I was concerned and dialed Haley. If anything major had happened, she would tell me.

"Hey, Mom, what's up?" she answered.

"I'm mulling over a new piece for my column and hoping you can help me."

"Sure, what do you want to know?"

"If a guy invites you to 'hang out' is that a date or only a friend thing?"

She giggled. "Did some guy ask you?"

"No, strictly hypothetical."

"Yeah, right."

"It *is*."

"Whatever. *Hypothetically*, if it's just two of you, it's a date—unless it's super clear you really are just friends. If it's a group thing, I'd say only friends unless you're already a couple."

"Got it. Good to know." I paused, contemplating how to bridge the gap to Jay. "I know Thanksgiving is almost two months away, but I was thinking—"

"I was going to call you about that. I need to make a slight change in plans."

Disappointment speared my chest. We'd had such a sad, little holiday the year before, I wanted to make up for it. "What are you planning?"

"Dad came home really bummed yesterday, and I wanted to cheer him up. We started talking about how we used to go skiing, and the next thing I knew he booked a reservation for us in Tahoe Thanksgiving weekend. I'm sorry."

"But Haley, Val has already agreed to come up. We'd planned on cooking together."

"I know and I'll still be there on Wednesday to help cook and have Thanksgiving dinner with you guys, but I won't be able to stay the whole weekend." Having her with me for the weekend was a big deal for me. I had planned on us walking around and seeing the Christmas displays in Union Square, and I'd dropped way too much money on non-refundable tickets for Beach Blanket Babylon. Being divorced sucked. Damn Jay. "Please, don't be mad. This is a big deal for Dad."

"Did it cheer him up?"

"I guess, but last night he broke out a bottle of whiskey. I wish you could find a way to be friends with him. It would be nice if we could have dinner together or at least spend a little time in the same room."

"It's hard for me."

"It's hard for us, too."

"Does he know you're talking to me now?"

"No, he's playing golf with Richard."

Jay wasn't my husband to worry over anymore. He was going skiing with Haley and golfing with his buddy. He'd figure it out, but Haley was my concern.

"I'm obviously disappointed, but I understand. I'm just glad you'll be spending Thanksgiving Day with me, and maybe the three of us can have dinner soon."

"Thanks, Mom. It really means a lot to me."

And my daughter meant a lot to me. I didn't want her tugged between me and her father. If the three of us having dinner made life easier or a little happier for Haley, I could do it.

Haley didn't waste any time telling Jay about our conversation. Consequently, I received a bouquet of flowers from Jay the next day, followed by a phone call to set a date for dinner. He and Haley were both free on Sunday. Cooking for one wasn't very inspiring, and I had some new recipes I wanted to try out, so we agreed to an early dinner in San Francisco at my apartment. He'd bring the wine.

Coincidently, I also received the promised text from Joshua. Wednesday was his day off, and since moving to San Francisco, he'd put off buying furniture and hoped I wouldn't mind lending a female eye. I was left a little fuzzy as to whether he considered it a date.

—

Joshua was particularly in the market for a dining table and chairs and something to sit on in his living room. I had anticipated wandering through stores like Crate and Barrel and Macy's or making the drive to Emeryville to hit the Ikea, but his tastes leaned toward vintage.

We met on Union Street, where numerous second-hand shops and antique stores wedged between high-end clothing boutiques and gift shops. He greeted me with a peck on the cheek; it seemed we were out of the friend zone.

I asked as we strolled down the sidewalk, "You've been in the city a couple months, and you're just now buying furniture? Why the wait?"

"I crashed with Paul until I could find a place, and up until a couple weeks ago, I'd been working seven days a week. Paul and I usually get to the restaurant late morning to prep for dinner, and most nights it's midnight before I get home."

"You've been doing that six to seven days a week?"

"We close early on Sunday and Monday, but yeah. Paul plans to bring on more staff, so I should start having two days a week off soon."

"You must really love your work to be so committed."

"I'd say it's more of a passion, which means sometimes I want to hurl a pan, but yeah, I love it. And working for Paul is great. He gets final say on what makes it on the menu, but he encourages me to experiment and be creative."

"Do you feel like you wasted your time going back to college?"

"Sometimes. I know most people go to college to find themselves and figure out what they want to do with their lives, but I lost myself for a while.

I stopped following my heart, and my confidence got seriously shaken, like I was nineteen again or something."

It hit me what was so different about him. It wasn't that he had physically changed so much, but that he conducted himself with much more confidence and surety of movement. "Are you following your heart now?"

He stopped walking and peered down at me with a sly, playful smile. "I am." He took my hand and kept walking. "College wasn't a total waste though. I'm a better writer than I used to be and probably know enough about the French Revolution and Robespierre to write a book."

I chuckled. "That's something at least."

"Actually, I wrote the menu descriptions for De Noche."

"I'm impressed. They were very clever, and I practically tasted flavors as I was reading."

"Thanks, it means a lot coming from a professional." He squeezed my hand. "I've started my own blog, too. It's called *Tales of the Kitchen.*"

"Great name—sort of a take on Maupin's *Tales of the City.*"

"Exactly, I knew you'd get the reference. Who knows, maybe I'll be famous someday, like Anthony Bourdain?"

"Now that would be awesome! *No Reservations* was one of my favorite shows."

"Sweet, it was one of mine too. So sad about him. He was awesome."

We stopped at the first shop that looked promising. It had an eclectic mix of art deco, mid-century modern, and contemporary kitsch. Joshua gravitated to a shiny red plastic table with leopard-spotted chairs shaped like a woman's high heel arranged around it.

He slid into one of the chairs and grabbed the table to keep from tipping over. "What do you think?"

We both laughed. "You'd need to practice with those heels. It may be difficult to eat if you can't let go of the table."

We kept moving and I spotted a beautiful mid-century Danish teak dining table with sleek lines and eight matching chairs in mint condition. The table was stained and polished just enough to enhance the wood without over-glossing or obscuring the grain. It was a work of art and would fit perfectly and look stunning in my old Davis house. I had moved our table and chairs with me to San Francisco and wondered if Jay had replaced them yet.

Joshua walked over. "This is really nice, but too big for my kitchen. I need more of a dinette size."

"I guess most city apartments are on the cramped side."

"Yeah, but this is a beautiful set." He bent over and peeked at the price tag. "Whoa, that's only a few grand out of my price range."

I supposed it was two or three grand out of most people's range. I'd been spoiled by Jay's paycheck, but I couldn't splurge on anything that pricey anymore either. It occurred to me I really didn't care if I no longer could afford it. I'd been no happier with Jay after we'd had money than before. As far as money was concerned, all I really cared about was having a decent place to live and a little cash in my pocket.

"A bit over my budget, too," I said.

Joshua took my hand and we moved on. We joked and chatted while we hit a couple more stores. I enjoyed his company. He was fun. I liked him holding my hand and gazing down at me with his big hazel eyes.

Eventually, we found him a turquoise and chrome dinette set from the 1950s, complete with sparkly vinyl upholstered chairs. By the time he'd paid and arranged for delivery, it was three o'clock and my stomach growled with hunger. If I planned to spend time with him, I'd have to adjust to his clock. Since he worked late, he slept late. His breakfast time was around eleven and lunch was closer to three or four in the afternoon.

I suggested a small Italian restaurant close to my apartment, but by the time we got there, the eatery had stopped seating until dinner. I figured what the heck and invited him to my place for a bite to eat.

When we got to my building, Joshua said, "Wow, you live here? Nice address."

I hadn't really thought about it. "I love the location and it's safe," I said, taking his hand and leading him up the stairs to my apartment.

When I inserted my key into the lock, Joshua took my hand, leaving the key dangling in the deadbolt. He turned me around, placed his other hand on my cheek, and stared into my eyes. My stomach majorly whooshed as he bent down to kiss me. His lips were gentle, his hand warm on my cheek. As he slid his hand to the nape of my neck, he eased his tongue into my mouth. It was an extraordinarily nice kiss. I dropped my purse, grabbing hold of his shoulders. Somehow, I ended up flush to the wall with Joshua pressing into me. We kissed for what felt like a long time. Good thing my neighbors worked during the day.

Separating for a breath, he grinned down at me. "I thought we should do that before we went inside."

Blow me over with a feather, he was a good kisser. He left me lightheaded, tingling all over, and wanting him. "Why before?"

"Just in case it changed your mind about inviting me in."

"Oh." If he kissed me like that inside, I don't know if I'd have the will power to put the brakes on. "I see what you mean."

He leaned his shoulder against my door. "You have to know I really like you."

"I know and I like you, too."

"So, I'm not going to come in today."

"Very mature of you."

He chuckled and pushed away from the door. "I *know* and I'm already regretting it, so I'm going to go." He bent down, pecked my lips, and asked with his lips still close to mine, "I'll see you soon, right?"

"Sure, I'd like that."

I wanted to ask when I'd see him next because I did like him, but at the same time, dating him felt riskier … scarier … than going on a blind date. The age difference aside, we meshed more than I had with anyone other than Jay. My handful of dates since moving to San Francisco had been colossal duds. My relationship with Kevin had been based on sex—both of us recklessly rebounding. Joshua was different. The fact that he wanted to wait told me he thought what we were doing could be special, but I wasn't sure if I was ready for a potentially serious relationship. On the other hand, the last thing I wanted was another relationship based on sex.

My questions were answered sooner than expected. Joshua called minutes later having scored an invitation that evening to the soft opening of Simone's, a chichi new restaurant South of Market. The owners had hired one of the top chefs in the country. Internally, I warred with seeing him again so soon, but in the end, caved to my love of good food—okay, *and* my desire to be kissed breathless again.

Chapter 21

ARKING IN FRONT of my building was harder than scoring tickets to the national tour of *Hamilton*. Joshua texted that he was circling the block and asked if I could meet him in front. Grabbing my coat and purse, I hurried down, hoping to catch him before he had to make the block again. I didn't know what kind of car he drove, but as soon as I saw a blue Mini Cooper with racing stripes and a white top coming down the street, I knew it had to be him. Sure enough, the car stopped in front of my building. I hopped in and Joshua gave me a quick kiss while the car behind us honked.

"Cute car," I said.

"Convenient is more like it. I used to have a Jeep but parking that beast in the city was a nightmare. I can squeeze this baby in just about anywhere."

"Except my neighborhood."

He laughed. "Yeah, your neighborhood is definitely a challenge."

"Well, I really like it. I've been thinking about trading in my Volvo SUV for something smaller. Maybe, I should get one, too."

"If you'd like I can loan you my car for a day so you can see how you like driving it."

"That's very nice of you to offer. Thank you, I just may take you up on it."

"Told you I was a nice guy," he joked.

"You are," I agreed, and asked, "So what exactly is a 'soft opening'?"

"When a new restaurant opens, they usually only seat half the tables for about a week before they advertise the opening. That way the staff gets a chance to work out glitches with the restaurant management system, timing, you know that sort of thing before they get slammed with a full house. It's basically a dress rehearsal."

"Makes sense."

"Anyway this is the first night of service for Simone's. Paul knows the owners, and they want a friendly crowd tonight. As special guests, all the food will be comped and alcoholic beverages will be half-price."

"I think I'm going to like hanging out with you."

He chuckled. "Restaurant work comes with long hours, but it has its own community and some nice perks. Though they would like us to write a Yelp review if we like it."

"I can manage that."

"I figured it wouldn't be a problem."

It began to rain—thankfully, Simone's offered valet service. We hustled into the restaurant, and I finally got a full view of Joshua. He cleaned up exceptionally well in his black suit and charcoal dress shirt sans a tie. He looked like a hot, sophisticated urbanite—far from the boy he'd seemed at Nugget with his flop of dark hair.

After helping me off with my coat, his eyes scanned me head to toe. "Wowza, you look fantastic."

Feeling fantastic, I returned the compliment. "So do you." I was rewarded with a kiss on my cheek.

He checked my coat and then ushered me to the hostess desk. While we waited to be seated, he kept me close with his arm around my waist. He whispered, "You smell good."

"I'm wearing Chanel," I said, and we both got the giggles remembering our clandestine kiss in the parking lot.

"Think I'll ever be able to tell you that you smell good without you laughing?"

The hostess arrived to show us to our table, and we managed to compose ourselves. She let us pause to admire the spectacular main dining room. The back wall had a floor-to-ceiling water feature backlit with a soft blue light and three-foot-high crystal vases filled with tall palm leaves and calla lilies surrounding the base. The rest of the décor was very sleek with ebony furnishings and crisp white tablecloths. Bluesy-jazz instrumentals played in the background, putting the finishing touch on the chic ambiance. She showed us to a small table for two and handed us menus.

I couldn't help smiling and shaking my head. "This is so not what I expected."

He cocked his brow. "Why? I told you this was an upscale place."

"Not the restaurant. I meant being with you in a place like this. It's just so incongruent with the person I thought I knew in Davis. You're much more ...."

He frowned. "Grown up?"

"No, although I suppose that's part of it. Developed as a person, I guess. You're much more interesting than I gave you credit for."

He tapped my foot under the table. "Let's face it, in Davis, we barely knew each other. I'm glad we're getting to know each other now. The more time I spend with you, the more interesting you are to me, too."

Most of the items on the menu included absurdly complicated reduction sauces and ingredients like fennel pollen, za'atar, and the like. This was Joshua's area of expertise, so I let him do the ordering. The evening was going great. The food was amazing, and the wine well worth the hundred-dollar price tag after the discount. Best of all, Joshua was good company, keeping me entertained with anecdotes from his culinary school days.

Then the waiter brought us each a gooey, molten chocolate cake with handmade ice cream and cappuccino for dessert. From nowhere Joshua asked, "So what else do you write, besides the column?"

"As a freelancer, I sell pieces to a few different women's magazines, but I doubt they'd be the kind of thing that would appeal to you. Middle-aged women are the target audience."

"I would never have guessed that kind of writing was so lucrative."

"What do you mean?"

He looked adoringly at me. "If you can afford to live in North Beach and drive a Volvo, you must make a pretty good living with that sort of thing." His smile faded. "Hey, smile. I didn't mean to offend you. It's impressive."

I hadn't been aware of making a face, but I was cognizant of an uneasiness in my chest. It never had been my intent to mislead him. "I do okay as a writer. I suppose I could completely support myself if I had to, but I can afford the apartment and car because my ex-husband provides spousal support."

The truth was my alimony payment had barely covered the Davis house mortgage, utilities, and general upkeep, but it more than covered my rent, leaving me in a comfortable financial situation.

"Is spousal support the same thing as alimony?"

"Yes, does it bother you?"

"I don't know how I feel about it yet. You're a smart, very together woman, and you don't seem unhappy, so I assumed since your daughter is grown, being divorced meant you had severed ties with your ex-husband."

"I have."

"I don't see how that's possible if he supports you."

Because I took spousal support, I wasn't *a smart, very together woman*? I was still tied to Jay? I tried to squelch my indignation by reminding myself that he was young; he hadn't experienced building a life with someone only to have the other person pull out halfway through construction. There was a buyout the deserting party had to pay. Besides, Jay had vowed always to take care of me. I had supported him through law school; he had promised to support me as a writer.

We both stirred our cappuccinos, not looking at each other. I took a sip and said, "We'd been married for eighteen years when he left me. We obviously have a history, but we're legally divorced. I've only seen him once since moving to San Francisco."

"Huh," he grunted, contemplating me with a confused expression. "I guess I'd assumed you left him, or it was at least mutual."

"He left me. We had a house and some other assets."

"What does he do for a living?"

"He's a very successful litigation attorney."

"Huh," he grunted again. I could see his wheels turning. "The Porsche you drove for a while, was it his?"

"The car became mine when the divorce finalized, but it's been sold." I didn't think it necessary to tell him Jay had sold it for me, or that the proceeds paid for my move and left a nice cushion in my bank account.

"So did you have a nasty court battle—he got the house in exchange for alimony?"

"No, he didn't object to anything I wanted. We agreed to continue joint ownership, but he's responsible for upkeep and the mortgage. He would actually give me more if I asked."

"Generous guy," he murmured before taking a bite of his cake, which had cooled and consequently, looked less deliciously gooey.

Both he and my dessert seemed less appetizing. I sipped my cappuccino to fill the silence. "I'm not a bitter bitch trying to take him for everything he's worth."

He winced and set his fork down. "That's not what I was thinking. You should try the cake before your ice cream melts. It's exceptional."

"I really don't appreciate being judged when you know nothing about the situation."

"Hey now, I'm not judging, but how about we go someplace where we can talk with a little more privacy?"

I was determined to grab the check, but Joshua snatched it out of my hand and insisted on paying. After collecting my coat, he helped me into it but didn't take my hand or put his arm around me. I wouldn't have let him if he'd tried. It was still raining, and we stood huddled under an awning not speaking or touching while we waited for the valet. Joshua was a mistake. As much as I liked him, he was too young to understand certain things.

Once in the car, I said, "Just take me home." Of course home was a fifteen to twenty-minute drive without traffic.

He headed north toward my neighborhood. After a minute he said, "I'm sorry I came off as judgmental. It wasn't my intent. The terms of your divorce aren't any of my business."

No, they weren't. "Thank you for the apology."

"You're welcome, but I would like to explain what's bothering me."

He had apologized; I cared enough about him to hear him out. "That's fair."

"I have a hard time believing things are final with your ex-husband. I don't buy it's over for him."

"How can you say that? You've never met him."

"Call it a gut feeling or unclouded guy sense. I can't see any guy, no matter how much money he had, forking over a monthly payment unless he was forced by a judge or wanted to keep the door open to get back together."

"Maybe he's honorable and feels obligated to a financial commitment."

"If that were the case, then why wouldn't he just come up with a lump settlement and walk away? I'm sorry, but I can't help thinking he's intentionally keeping you tied to him."

I couldn't dismiss everything he had said. Jay wanted me in his life, just not as his wife. "So do you think as long as I'm taking his money, I'm not letting go either?"

"It certainly complicates things. I'm not saying you don't deserve it, but the financial arrangement must be something you'd consider before getting seriously involved with anyone. I can't imagine he'd be so generous if you got engaged or moved in with someone."

He was right about that. Jay's generosity would come to an abrupt halt if he thought his munificence was supporting another man. I wouldn't blame him either.

"To be honest, I haven't given it much thought."

He glanced over at me. "Look, we've barely started seeing each other, so it seems too early to be having this heavy of a conversation, but I think we should put our cards on the table so no one gets hurt."

I didn't want to hurt him or be hurt. I liked the idea if we moved forward, it would be from an honest place. "I'm good with that."

"If you were anyone else, I'd cut bait. Your situation freaks me, but I think we really click. Being around you makes me happy. I'd like to see a lot more of you, but not if you're yo-yoing with your ex-husband. I don't want to feel like I'm competing with him or be your boy-toy while you're waiting for him to come back."

Ouch. He made me sound like a dirty old lady. "I'm not going back and forth with Jay—I'd never use you like that. I'm not that kind of person."

Joshua flipped the turn signal and turned right. Halfway down the block he said, "I'm sorry, I shouldn't have made the boy-toy comment. I know you're a good person. It had more to do with my own insecurities than anything you've done or said."

For some reason, his confession brought a smile to my face. "Are you always this honest?"

He chuckled. "I suppose I am."

"It's a very attractive quality. I really respect you for it."

"Thank you." He squeezed my hand. "Jay? That's his name?"

"Yes. In the spirit of honesty, I'm having dinner with him and Haley this Sunday." He let go of my hand and gripped the steering wheel with both hands again. "What I need you to understand is that Jay and I fell in love when we were sixteen. We have a shared history; we share a daughter. I'll never be able to cut him completely out of my life, but I can't see us getting back together either." I blinked back a sudden rush of tears.

Joshua reached over and gently stroked my cheek. "He really hurt you, didn't he?"

"Yes, he did." *And I don't think I can ever forgive him.*

We rode in silence the rest of the way. I had underestimated Joshua, again. He impressed me with his perceptiveness and maturity. He understood much more than I had given him credit for earlier.

When we made it to my neighborhood—no surprise—there were no vacant parking spaces. Joshua pushed on his flashers, double parked in front of my apartment building, and walked me to the front door. Thankfully, it had stopped raining.

He sighed and looked down at me with an uncertain smile. "This isn't exactly the way I pictured the night to end, but it's good we talked."

"I agree. You've given me some things to think about."

"So where does that leave us?"

"I'd like to see you again; I guess it's up to you."

Joshua's lips pressed together and turned up at the corners. He nodded before wrapping his arms around me, hugging me close. He was a good hugger; he put his whole body into it. I tilted my head up, ready to be kissed senseless. Our eyes locked, and I couldn't breathe while his gaze held me.

Then red flashing lights grabbed my attention, and he jerked away. A police officer got out of his squad car right behind Joshua's Mini Cooper.

"*Shit,*" he said under his breath and raced to his car calling out, "I'm moving it."

Luckily, he didn't get a ticket, but our night ended without the kiss I'd been looking forward to all night. *Heavy sigh.* He sent me a text saying he'd call me in the morning.

———

As promised, Joshua called the next morning with profuse apologies for his hasty departure. I assured him no apologies were necessary. Relieved, he invited me to an after-hours party at the restaurant Sunday night. I agreed, figuring Haley and Jay would leave no later than eight. Then, we talked and talked and talked.

He told me about growing up in Ann Arbor, and the year in high school his family spent in France while his father was on sabbatical. (His father was a French Literature Professor at the University of Michigan; hence the pressure to get a degree.) That threw me; he seemed so much like a native Californian. On the other hand, he had lived on the West Coast for eleven years. He said he only went back to Michigan once a year to visit his parents.

He asked, "Where did you grow up?"

"Not far from here. I was born and raised in Petaluma."

"Ah, the Egg Capitol of the World."

"That's the place."

"You can get some amazing goat cheese from a farm up there."

"Of course, you would know," I teased.

He chuckled. "So you must see your parents all the time, since they live so close."

"Not as often as you might think." I hesitated to provide more details. I didn't want to ruin our lovely chat by dropping a stink bomb about how I had humiliated Dr. and Mrs. Kirby by getting knocked-up in high school. They practically had gloated when Jay left me; it proved they'd been right that our marriage had been a mistake.

"Oh hey, I'm sorry," he said, "I didn't realize what time it is. I gotta get to work, but I want to hear about your parents so hold the thought for next time. See you Sunday night."

I hung up and realized we'd been on the phone for over an hour. I needed to get to work, too but couldn't concentrate. I kept thinking about some of the things Joshua had said the night before and about him in general. I liked him a lot. It was more than a physical attraction; talking to him was effortless, as if I'd known him for years. He was intelligent, had a good sense of humor, and a genuine warmth.

He was also insightful, raising some questions about Jay and my alimony that I couldn't dismiss. When Jay had first left, I hadn't thought twice about him paying our bills. Haley hadn't left for college yet, we carried a hefty mortgage, car payments, et cetera. When it came to our divorce settlement, both my parents and my attorney had advised securing life-time spousal support, which made me feel unbelievably pathetic—as if they thought Jay was the only man who would ever love me enough to marry me, as if I were incapable of caring for myself. I had bowed to their advice and asked for more than made me comfortable because I had this cracked idea that if I forced Jay to part with more than he'd planned, he'd halt the divorce.

Joshua was right, most men would have fought. Jay made way more money than me, but I was an educated woman. I had a skill set to support myself. I didn't even have debt, since Jay assumed responsibility for everything we owed. No doubt Jay's reasons were complicated.

In addition to being a surgeon, my father came from a moneyed family. He would have paid for me to attend any school I'd wanted, no matter how expensive. I'd made him proud with the grades and SAT scores to get into a top school. I'd been Daddy's Little Girl until Jay Braxton came along. Dr. Kirby wasn't pleased. He'd thought we were too young to be spending so much time together. When I got pregnant and announced my intent to keep the baby and marry Jay, it'd been too much for him. He took my car, my trust fund, jewelry he had given me, everything. I'd been ordered out of the house with only the clothes on my back. My mother hadn't come to my defense; as usual, she had deferred to the Doctor.

Eventually, he'd relented enough to let me pick-up my clothes and stay on his insurance plan, but I never stayed another night in his house. He had paid for Haley's preschool, which had been a godsend, but never given a dime to me directly. We were on speaking terms, and occasionally saw each other, but our relationship never recovered.

For a long time, Jay had felt tremendously guilty. Those early years had been difficult, but Jay had stood by me. He chose an area of law with a high earning potential because he had wanted to replace the comfortable life I'd lost. In exchange, I had loved him unconditionally and supported us while he attended law school. I'd viewed it as an investment in our future. Later, when my grandmother passed away, she left me an inheritance. It hadn't been a huge sum, but it'd been enough to pay off Jay's law school loans and help us get on our feet.

I'm sure Jay hadn't forgotten any of those things, so yes, a part of me felt absolutely justified in taking the spousal support. In addition, I had supported Jay at home, which had freed him to get on the fast track at the firm. If I hadn't spent so much time being a wife and mother, I could have put more effort into my writing career or branched into another field.

Now, I was free to do more. I had stepped up my efforts a bit, but not as much as I could have—not as much as I would have if I didn't receive a direct deposit from Jay every month. Logically, he should have been encouraging me off his payroll. Instead, he routinely asked if I needed anything. Joshua had been spot on about Jay wanting to keep me under his guardianship. The big payout from the Conway case afforded him the option to buy me out, but he hadn't offered. After the way he had looked and behaved the weekend before, I had to wonder if he wanted to get back together.

My answer would be no. I still loved him. I had loved him too deeply for too long not to love him, but my love was for the faded memory of the boy he had been. How could I love the man he had become, the man who shuns love? All I had for that man was pity. Joshua had been right about something else, too: Jay struggled with our separation. Maybe he needed my dependence to make his efforts feel worthwhile.

I wasn't sure, but I was certain his generosity wouldn't last forever. Once he finally adjusted to our separation, or if I fell in love with someone else, or he remarried for that matter, the dynamic would change. Someday, Jay would fight the spousal support, and he was a tough attorney to beat.

As long as he supported me, my fate was tied to him, like it or not. In the back of my mind, I always had known but hadn't wanted to deal with it. It gave him a fair amount of power he could wield over me if he ever chose. Who knew how long his generosity would last? I didn't want to confront a day when I was at his mercy the way I had been at my father's all those years ago. This time I didn't have anyone but myself to fall back on.

Something else nagged at me. If I didn't want to get back together, then why was I accepting his largesse? What did it say about me? It was one thing when I thought I was waiting out a mid-life crisis, but that wasn't the case anymore. If our financial situations were reversed, I wouldn't want to support him until death do us part. I wished I didn't need his money anymore, but I was locked in a twelve-month lease.

The more I thought about it, the clearer it became that I needed an exit plan if I was ever going to be free to move on with my life.

Chapter 22

JAY AND HALEY arrived at five o'clock Sunday afternoon. Haley used her key to my apartment and walked through the door calling out, "Hey, Mom, we're here!" I walked out of the kitchen and greeted them in the living room. I immediately noticed Jay looked healthier. The black rings under his eyes had faded.

After taking turns hugging me, Jay handed me a bag. "I couldn't decide which to bring."

I pulled out a bottle each of Stag's Leap Cabernet Sauvignon (The Leap Napa Valley) and Petite Sirah. "Wow, thank you. You brought the good stuff."

"I know how much you like Stag's Leap." Jay smiled at me with so much affection radiating from him that it unnerved me. Then his eyes scanned the room.

"Haley, why don't you give your dad a tour while I open a bottle?"

"Sure, Mom."

Shaking my head, I walked into the kitchen feeling foolish to read so much into a smile. Jay was always extra glowy whenever he scored a big win; he would consider me cooking a family dinner a major victory. I told myself not to think about the alimony or Jay's motives. Tonight, I didn't want to fight or cause waves. I was determined to have a pleasant evening with my daughter and think of Jay as an old friend. I put the Sirah in my tiny countertop wine cooler, opened the Cabernet and began washing potatoes and dropping them into a colander. A few minutes later Jay wandered in by himself.

"Where's Haley?"

He waved his hand dismissively. "Oh, she's in the living room texting someone. You'd never believe how much that girl texts."

I laughed. "Oh, I know. Getting her to actually talk on a phone is near impossible."

"Tell me about it. By the way, I really like your apartment," he said. "The rooms are small, but nice, and I like how you've decorated. You've always had great taste."

"Thanks, it's taken a while to get used to the smaller space, but I like it now and can't beat the location. The fact it came with an actual dining room really sold me."

"If you don't mind me asking, how much are you paying for it?"

I did mind. "A little less than the mortgage, but the rent includes utilities and a parking space. Trust me, it's a great deal for this neighborhood."

"I believe you, and you need parking. Hales and I had to park three blocks away." He held up his hand. "Not that I'm complaining. Anyway, after seeing this place, I was worried the rent was a lot more. So you really are doing okay?"

I rolled my eyes. "Yes, *Dad*, and I save ten percent of my paycheck every week just like you told me."

"Smart ass," he said with a laugh. "Whatever you're cooking smells great." He lifted the lid of the Dutch oven sitting on the stove and took a whiff. "Mmmmm, beef bourguignon?"

"Yep, it's a recipe I've been wanting to try. It has a three-day prep, if you can believe, and I had to flambé it with cognac. Want a taste?"

No asking twice. He grabbed a wooden spoon from the utensil jar and dug in. "Wow is that good. Man, have I missed your cooking."

What could I say? Your choice, buddy—so sad, too bad for you. "I actually don't cook very much anymore." I shook the colander and pulled the potato peeler out of the drawer.

"Oh, here. Let me," Jay said, taking the peeler out of my hand. I don't think it was my imagination that his hand lingered on mine.

My kitchen was a small alley design all the way in the back of the apartment. I had to nudge him over to make room for me to prep the carrots, which I intended to sauté with French butter and fresh thyme. I had thought

Haley would be the one helping me, while Jay watched football or something in the living room. Where was that girl? It was difficult to maneuver around the kitchen without bumping into him.

Finally, Haley appeared. "Need any help?"

"There isn't room for the three of us," Jay said.

Unfortunately, he was right. "Honey, why don't you take over for your dad?"

"It's okay. I got it," he said.

I raised my brow.

He grinned. "What? I like peeling potatoes."

"Since when?"

He shrugged with his grin widening. "Since now." He turned back toward the counter and intentionally bumped into my butt.

Haley giggled. "I'll be in the other room."

As she turned around, I called to her, "Finish setting the table, then. Please."

"Yes, Mother dear," she said not turning around.

"Plates and everything are on the sideboard."

"Saw them already," she called back.

I had Jay cut the potatoes into chunks. Once they were boiling on the stove and the carrots were doing nicely in the sauté pan, I got a chance to relax for a few minutes.

"The wine probably has breathed long enough." I pointed to the high cupboard next to the sink. "Would you mind getting down a couple wine glasses for us?"

"It would be my pleasure," he said.

I leaned against the counter and watched while he reached for the goblets and poured us each a glass. I'd always loved the way his body moved. He was wearing the Levi's I'd picked out for him the day we went shopping and a closefitting sweater that emphasized his Y-shaped physique. I squelched a knot of lust growing in my stomach and was left with a hollowness in my chest. Here we were, behaving the way we had when we were married, but I wasn't free to touch him or allow myself to feel any kind of attraction.

He handed me a glass. "About last Saturday—"

I held up my hand. "Just leave it alone—I want a pleasant evening."

"Let me say one thing, then I promise to shut-up about it for the rest of the night."

I knew I would regret hearing it. "Okay."

"Up until I upset you, it was the best day I've had in a long time."

I tried to laugh it off and joked, "Maybe you should go suit shopping more often then."

Jay gave me a knowing smile. He had made his point. So what if spending a few hours together had been enjoyable? The day had ended with him hurting me, again. The flowers last week and the expensive wine were his way of apologizing, but I didn't know what the hell he was angling for. Was he hoping to keep me on a back burner until he got tired of screwing other women? Did he think he could turn on the old Braxton charm and get me to do things I'd done when we were married: buy his clothes, cook him dinner … give him an occasional blow job? I clamped down on the anger building inside of me.

All I had to do was get through dinner, and I wouldn't have to see him again for at least a couple months. I asked, "How's work going?" The topic kept us out of emotional minefields while we finished getting dinner on the table.

We automatically assumed our old seating arrangement: Jay and I opposite each other with Haley to my left. Jay said grace as had been our custom. We all behaved as if nothing had changed with Sunday family dinners being the norm. Jay helped himself to seconds, and we lingered after we finished eating and visited just as we used to do.

Haley was excited about going back to school. "I'm still not one hundred percent sure I want to be a lawyer, but I'll be ready to go back next term. I already feel refreshed and appreciate school so much more after working at the firm."

"Sometimes it's good to take a break and get a little distance; it can put things in perspective." Jay glanced at me with a wistful smile and then said to Haley, "It's a technique I use all the time when working on cases."

"Well, I miss taking classes. Can you believe?"

"Actually, I can," I said.

"Your mom loved school," Jay said to Haley and smiled at me again. "I muscled through it, but she loved it. You get that from her, right Babe?"

Our eyes met. The façade of normalcy had cracked with an innocent slip of the tongue. He gave me an *I-didn't-mean-to-say-it* look, and I gave my head a little *no-worries* shake.

Haley glanced quickly between us and restarted the conversation. "So Mom, Dad and I wanted to talk to you about Thanksgiving."

If they thought we would be spending Thanksgiving together, they were sadly mistaken. I had plans that didn't include Jay. In fact, I was considering inviting Joshua since he didn't have family in the area.

I steeled myself and said, "I thought Thanksgiving was settled. You're spending Wednesday and Thursday with me and then you're going skiing with your dad."

"That part hasn't changed. You get Haley and I'll go to my sister's house," Jay said in a conciliatory voice. "Hales and I would like you to join us in Tahoe."

"Oh, really?" Unexpected as the invitation was, I wasn't completely surprised either.

"Hear me out," Jay said. "The resorts were all booked, and I ended up renting a cabin that sleeps eight. It has three bedrooms and two bathrooms. You'd get your own room."

"I really want you to come," Haley added. "Dad likes to go on runs that are just crazy. Besides I'd like someone to hang out with if I don't feel like skiing. It'll be fun. We can make hot chocolate and popcorn and watch old movies at night, like old times."

It sounded great, but the last time we'd taken a trip like this Jay and I had snuggled while watching movies with Haley, and then had made love in front of the fireplace after she had crashed for the night. It wouldn't be like old times.

Her big blue eyes begged me to say yes, and Jay's big pleading eyes did the same.

"I have theater tickets that weekend."

Haley asked, "Can't you exchange them for another night or give them to someone?"

"And Valerie will be here," I said.

Jay asked, "Isn't she gong to visit her parents?"

"Yeah, Mom. Isn't that why you're planning to eat early on Thanksgiving—so Aunt Val can make it to her parents for dessert?"

Talk about feeling ganged up on. "Honey, would you mind starting the dishes?"

Haley checked with Jay, and he nodded. "Sure," she said.

Jay and I silently picked up our wine glasses, and he followed me to the living room. We sat down on the couch, and he said in a hushed voice, "I told Haley not to get her hopes up."

"This was her idea?"

"Yes, but I support it. I'd like you to come. You know me, I'll spend every minute possible on the slopes. I'll only be around at night, and we can take separate cars if you want. What do you say?"

I shook my head. "What exactly are you hoping to achieve with this little weekend?"

"Not collide with a tree, have fun, unwind—you know, usual vacation stuff."

I narrowed my eyes at him. "That's it? Why do you want me there?"

"Well, it would help me with Hales. She's right, I like more challenging runs, and she could use the company." He chuckled. "I swear, I don't have any nefarious plans. You can lock your bedroom door if you don't trust me."

"If I go, I'm not cooking—not even breakfast."

"That's fine, I can manage breakfast and we can go out for dinner."

I scrutinized his face. He had a smug grin, but I believed him. I took a sip of wine, feeling my tension ease. Maybe he didn't have any ulterior motives, and I did miss Haley.

"Okay, I'll think about it."

His dimply grin widened to a full-on smile. "Excellent."

I raised my brows. "I didn't say yes."

"I know, but the fact you're considering it makes me happy. Maybe you're finally forgiving me a little bit?"

He should have quit while he was ahead. "I need to help Haley with the dishes."

He stopped me from getting up. "Please, don't. Shit, Kimmy, the last thing I wanted was to upset you tonight."

He hadn't said or done anything bad so why was so much anger bubbling inside of me? I supposed his confession about not wanting to see my love for him still stung.

"I know and I'm fine. Let me help Haley; then we can have dessert. I made a mocha-fudge cheesecake and picked up some coffee freshly roasted this morning."

"Sounds great, but you cooked, so you sit. I'll help Haley."

"Thank you, that's very nice of you."

"It's very nice of you to let me be here," he said with that sad, lost air he'd had the last time I saw him.

I stretched out on the couch and closed my eyes. Guilt gnawed my stomach as I listened to the clink-clank of dishes and pots and pans being washed. Jay was trying to be a good guy; his desire to be forgiven was natural, but for some reason, the more blatantly he asked, the harder it was for me to forgive him. Maybe I didn't want to let go of the little bit of power I had over him. Whatever the cause, I didn't want the evening to end on a sour note. For once, I wanted to part without one of us being hurt or ticked off.

I found Jay in the dining room, wiping off the table. "Hey, I meant to ask you. Have you replaced the dining room furniture yet?"

He stopped wiping. "Not yet. I've shopped around but haven't seen anything I like. Why?" He gestured to the table. "You don't want this?"

"No, but I came across a beautiful 1950s era Danish teak dining set that would be perfect for the house. I can give you the name of the antique store if you like."

"That'd be great. I'll give them a call and order it next week."

"Don't you want to see it?"

He tilted his head and asked tentatively, "Do you want me to?"

"It's really up to you."

"I can come back next weekend and you can show it to me."

Somehow the subtext of our conversation had taken a weird turn and Jay eyed me equally uncertain if we were talking about furniture. "NO," I said more emphatically than I'd intended. "It's perfect."

Jay stared at me with wounded eyes. "If you say so, then I'm sure it is." He leaned over and continued wiping the table.

Damn it, I hadn't meant to hurt his feelings. "I'd be happy to ask the store to hold it and e-mail you the contact information."

He straightened with a forced smiled. "It would be very nice of you to do that for me."

"And I'm sorry I laughed at you."

"What are you talking about?"

My heart pounded. I wanted to ease his guilt and pain but feared irritating another sore spot. "When we were married and you told me about things you wanted to try and wanting a motorcycle again, I laughed at you. I shouldn't have, and I'm sorry."

Jay's eyes got watery, and he blinked a few times. "The motorcycle was a dumb idea but thank you."

We continued our evening with dessert and coffee in the living room. Having Haley with us kept things light, and we managed to avoid touchy subjects and awkward moments.

I didn't realize how late it was until Gina knocked on my door wearing a shimmery, body-hugging dress that barely covered her assets and bright pink lipstick. I blinked and mentally inventoried my closet for a party dress; then quickly dismissed the thought. Good lord, where did she think she was going, clubbing in Vegas?

"Hey, ready to go?" she asked. Paul had invited her to the party at De Noche, and we'd planned to share an Uber to the restaurant.

"Sorry," I whispered, "Jay and Haley are still here."

Her eyes brightened and she barged around me into the living room, not giving me a chance to tell to go ahead without me and I'd catch up with her later.

Jay and Haley both stood, and Haley greeted Gina with a half-hug. Left with no choice, I introduced her to Jay.

Batting her eyes at Jay, she asked with an am-I-curious-about-you inflection, "So you're the ambulance chaser?"

"Uh, I guess. That would make you the bleeding-heart neighbor Haley told me about?" he asked sounding taken aback.

She laughed, smiling up at him. "That I am."

Was she seriously flirting with Jay … in front of Haley? Wasn't there some sort of unwritten gal pal rules about exes? I had found her vivaciousness entertaining, but not when she directed it at Jay in front of my daughter.

Haley glared at her.

Jay raised his brows at me in a what-the-hell manner, and asked, "Are you going somewhere?"

"Just a party, but there's no rush," I said, not wanting him to feel unwelcome.

I could see Jay puzzling over a party on a Sunday night. Our Sunday nights used to be about family time and resting up for the work week. Who went to parties at 8 o'clock on a Sunday night? "No worries—it's getting late anyway, and I have an early start tomorrow." He turned to Haley. "Hales, time to go."

We said our goodbyes. On the way out the door, Jay kissed my cheek and whispered, "Please think about Tahoe."

Gina waited while I touched up my make-up and swapped my flats for a pair of high-heeled boots. What she'd done seriously bothered me, and not because I was jealous. There was nothing to be jealous about. It had more to do with the inappropriateness of her behavior—the blatant lack of respect. I didn't know her well enough to talk about it. I considered her a friend, but how close could we really be after only knowing each other a couple months? She hadn't known Jay and me as a couple. She'd only met Haley twice. I'm sure her perception of me was informed by my column, but half the content was exaggerated for the sake of a sexier, more titillating read.

I decided to let it go, but would limit our interaction going forward, which made me a little depressed. Making new friends and building a new life was just so f-ing hard. Two steps forward and one step back, always. For once I wanted to take two steps forward and then another two steps without any backward slide.

I pushed the incident aside and focused on seeing Joshua again. We hadn't spoken since our lengthy conversation the other morning, but earlier he had sent me a text to confirm I still planned to come. I'd thought his invitation had been for a date, but then Gina had been invited, too. Paul had told her there would be a large crowd, and it would be a good networking opportunity for her to connect with the Latino community. It made me think I would be just part of the crowd *hanging out*.

Even so, I looked forward to seeing Joshua's adorable, familiar face. After my odd evening, the thought of being around him was inexplicably comforting. Who knew, maybe I'd be treated to a great kiss?

Chapter 23

WHEN WE ARRIVED at De Noche, the restaurant had already closed to the public and a large crowd was assembling. Paul had hired a DJ, and the tables had been rearranged to create a long buffet table and what I presumed to be an area for dancing. I spotted Joshua across the room. He wore his work clothes and was talking to a stunning blond who kept touching his arm. Jealousy rumbled in my stomach. Before I could catch his eye or walk over, Paul greeted us.

"*Buenas noches, senoras bonitas,*" he said, "I'm so glad you both could make it, especially on a Sunday night."

"I never sleep much anyway." Gina laughed. "Saturday, Sunday, what's the difference?"

Paul laughed, too. "In my world, weekends don't mean much, but since we normally close early on Sundays, it made it the best night to host a party."

I asked, "What's the occasion?"

"I'm wooing potential clients for catering gigs and holiday parties; plus I love parties."

"My kinda guy," Gina said. "Smart thinking."

An elbow bumped my arm, startling me, and I peered up at Joshua's smiling face. He said hello to Gina; then whispered in my ear, "Follow me."

He guided me through the crowd to the back of the restaurant and into what appeared to be a storage room. As soon as the door shut, his mouth descended on me. No doubt about it, he was a world class kisser. His tongue was addictively caressing, and he had a way of fitting against me that made me want to melt into him.

Just when I was beginning to feel an irresistible urge to undress him, he drew back. His eyes were slightly out of focus, and we were both breathing hard.

He grinned with his arms still around me. "Hi."

"Hi, yourself."

"I felt cheated not getting to kiss you the other night."

"Me, too."

He laughed. "I have to get back to the kitchen. Want to help?"

Seeing him do his thing was a no brainer. "I'd love to see you in action."

He grabbed an apron from a rack. "Here, you should put this on." He slipped it over my head and tied it for me. "Most of the food is already out, but there are a couple things I have to finish up. It shouldn't take us that long and then we can join the party."

I followed him to the kitchen, and he introduced me to Sal, a cook who was working the deep fryer. Joshua pulled a bag out of a freezer and gave Sal some instructions; then he led me to a stainless-steel worktable. Balls of dough and a bowl of some sort of filling sat on the table ready for assembly.

I asked, "What are we making?"

"Appetizer-sized empanadas." He scooped a spoonful of the filling and held it up to me. "Try a bite."

I tasted a salty-savory pork offset with some sort of sweet potato. "Mmmm. What is it?"

"Fried pork and cassava. It's a recipe I came up with based on traditional South American ingredients."

He expertly rolled out the dough, quickly cut out rounds, and dropped about a tablespoon of filling in the middle of each circle followed by a sprinkling of cheese. Then he showed me how to fold and seal them without the filling pushing out the sides. His fingers were dexterous, and he worked quickly. The dough was much harder to work with than I'd expected. I had to throw out my first few tries, but I finally got the hang of it.

"You got it," he said. "Do this a couple hundred times and you'll be faster than me."

I laughed. "I doubt that. You have some serious skill. I'm truly impressed."

He glanced at Sal, who had his back to us, and gave me a quick kiss. "Thank you. I wanted to impress you."

I smiled at him. His lack of artifice was so refreshing after the evening of veiled conversations with Jay. "It worked."

The kitchen door swung open behind me, and a female voice said, "Hey, Josh. I came to see if you needed any help."

I turned around and faced the blond he had been speaking to earlier. She was young, probably only twenty-three or twenty-four, and very pretty with big doe eyes and radiant, youthful skin. I sensed immediately she liked Joshua, really liked him. It showed all over her face and the way her body gravitated toward him. I had to wonder what he saw in an old lady like me when he could be with someone like her.

Without bothering to introduce us, he said, "I appreciate it, but we got it covered."

"Okay, I'm gonna go get a drink then. Can I bring you something?"

"Oh, no thanks. I'm not sure how long I'll be."

"But I'll see you later?"

"Yeah, I'll probably join the party when I'm done."

My good mood deflated as I realized the girl hadn't registered Joshua and I were together. Was it my age or was Joshua not as open as I'd thought? Just how many women was he currently seeing? I had no claim on him, and he was free to see whomever he wanted.

After she left, silence hung between us as we continued to assemble the empanadas.

"Her name's Zoey. She was a hostess here for about a month," he volunteered, keeping his eyes focused on his handiwork.

"She really likes you."

"I know. I was hoping you wouldn't notice."

"She's beautiful."

"You're beautiful." He paused with his work. "Look, I didn't know she'd be here. We've hung out a few times."

I picked up one of the rounds and carefully folded it over, making sure none of the filling squished out. "Meaning you slept with her a few times?"

Filling plopped out from the piece in Joshua's hand. "*Shit.*" He tossed it in the garbage. "Yes, but it was a very informal thing between us. I should've introduced you. I'm sorry for being rude, but I didn't want to hurt her by rubbing in her face that I'm into someone else. I'll clear things up with her tomorrow, but this isn't the place for it." His big eyes locked on me, and he gazed at me with unnerving focus, making me quake inside. "When we're done, would you mind if we cut out of here? I want to be alone with you."

After my day, I wasn't in a party mood. "I'd like nothing better."

"Right on." His face brightened. "Let's get this shit done and get outta here."

His fingers flew, and we left the empanadas with Sal to oversee the baking. While Joshua changed out of his work clothes, I found Gina with a margarita in her hand chatting it up with Paul and a couple other men.

"I'm exhausted, so I'm heading out," I said.

"You don't mind if I stay, do you?"

"Of course not, have fun."

I didn't see the need to tell her I was leaving with Joshua. I met him in the kitchen, and we slipped out the back door.

He took my hand and led me out of the alley and to a parking garage a couple blocks away. I assumed he had a plan, but when we got into his car he said, "The entire walk over here, I've been racking my brain about where I can take you that's private, but I got nothing. It's too cold for the beach, and I don't have any living room furniture yet."

I laughed. "We can go to my apartment."

"You sure?"

"Absolutely. I have left-over beef bourguignon if you're hungry."

"Perfect. I could use a break from Latin food." He started the engine and chuckled. "Let's hope I can find a place to park."

───

Luckily, Joshua was able to squeeze the Mini Cooper into a spot less than a block from my apartment. Walking into my living room, he glanced around with his eyes widening. He paused on an oil painting Jay had bought me for my thirty-fifth birthday. "Wow, this is really nice." He added jokingly, "Glad I didn't bring you to my place. It might have scared you off."

I crossed to him and took his hands. "It's just stuff. You're smart and talented and kind. It's going to take more than an unfurnished apartment to scare me off."

He grinned. "Thanks for that. No wonder I like you so much." He gave me a brief kiss, and asked, "How about a tour?"

Considering the size of my apartment, it didn't take long, and we finished in the kitchen. I heated a plate of leftovers for him, opened the Stag's Leap Petite Sirah, and seated him in the dining room. He ate while I sipped on a glass of wine. I ignored a twinge of guilt serving Joshua the wine Jay had given me, but Jay and I were never going to drink it together.

"It's so cool you have a dining room," he said.

"Right? It's why I took the apartment."

"Do you entertain much?"

"I don't know very many people here, but in Davis, I used to entertain all the time. I hope to again someday."

"I knew you'd be a great cook. No bullshit, this is first rate."

"Thank you. It's been a while since I made anything so involved. It's hard to get excited about cooking for one."

"I can empathize. When it's just me, I end up eating scrambled eggs or something easy, like a grilled cheese." He took another bite and washed it down with a drink of wine. "Mmmm. This wine is great, too. Stag's Leap?"

"Yep." I don't know why, but I confessed, "Courtesy of Jay."

"Huh." He stared at the glass and then shrugged, shaking his head. "Still good." We both chuckled. He asked cautiously, "How was dinner with him and Haley?"

"Incredibly surreal. We were all on our best behavior. In some ways, it was easier and more enjoyable than I'd expected, but underneath was this sort of wistful hollowness."

"You used to be a family. Dinner must've felt like a fragile façade."

"*Façade,* exactly the word that popped in my mind when we were eating. 'Fragile façade' is a perfect description. There we were having a family dinner, visiting as if nothing had changed, but we all knew nothing was the same."

He reached over and stroked my cheek. "You okay?"

I nodded. "I've been thinking a lot about what you said the other night. I don't want to be under Jay's umbrella for the rest of my life. I don't have a plan yet, but I'm working on one."

He softly pressed his lips to mine. We held together, leaning over the table, kissing with just our lips for a while.

"Your food is getting cold," I said with a smile.

Grinning, he picked up his fork and took a bite. "Mmmm. This is about the best beef bourguignon I've ever had, and remember, I lived in France for a year."

"Coming from you, I take it as a huge compliment. It's a Julia Child's recipe."

"Can't beat Julia. The woman knew the secret of great cooking: bacon, butter, and booze make everything better."

"Now that's a motto to cook by." We both laughed and compared notes on our favorite Julia recipes.

Talking to him was so effortless. We never seemed to struggle for conversation; something about his easy, open manner and soulful eyes soothed me. I liked that he was so different from both Jay and Kevin. They were such Alpha guy-guys. Not to say Joshua wasn't masculine—he was—but in a much less aggressive, non-macho way.

When he finished eating, we migrated to the living room. I caught a glimpse of my bedroom clock on the way. It was after eleven. I didn't want him to leave yet and hoped he hadn't noticed. We sat closely on the couch, angling our bodies toward each other.

Joshua took more than a sip of wine before setting his glass down. He took my hand and ran his thumb back and forth over the top of it.

"One of the reasons I wanted to be alone with you is because I wanted to talk to you about something," he said. "I wouldn't be bringing it up yet, but after the Zoey thing—"

"Joshua, you don't owe me an explanation."

"I know, but I want you to know where I'm coming from. I'm worried you got the wrong impression about something."

"You're a young, good-looking guy. I understand if you see other women."

"*Kimberly* ..." He exhaled loudly. "What I'm trying to tell you is I don't want to see anyone else. I know you want to take it slow, and I'm down with it. I just want you to know ever since we bumped into each other at City Lights, you're all I've thought about."

No wonder I liked him so much. "That makes me very happy to hear."

A warm glow enveloped me, and a similar glow radiated from him. I never had this feeling with Kevin, but I'd had it with Jay. I wasn't in love with Joshua yet, but with time, it seemed possible.

He scooched closer and wrapped his arm around me. Elated but at the same time apprehensive of jumping into a committed relationship, I gingerly snuggled into him. His body might have been on the slim side, but he was all muscle. A faint scent of cumin, garlic, and chili—De Noche aromas—lingered on his skin. I was beginning to associate the scent with him, and I breathed him in.

"There's just something about you that feels right," he said, holding me a little tighter.

Something about him felt right to me, too. If only he was a little older. Right now, age wasn't a problem, but at some point, it could be. We needed to take it slow, and I figured we'd had enough heart-baring talk for one night.

"By the way, I'm not interested in seeing other women either."

"That's a relief." He laughed. "Hey, are you going to write about us?"

I intentionally batted my eyes up at him. "I don't know. Are you going to give me something to write about?"

In a nanosecond, I was on my back with him grinning playfully on top of me. "I'll give you something." Our eyes locked, and the humor in his eyes shifted to unadulterated desire. His mouth swooped down on me as he wedged between my legs, pressing perfectly against me. We just kissed for a while. I luxuriated in the weight and warmth of his body, his soft hair in my hands. Then he drew back, leaving my lips numb and my tongue missing his caress. His mouth explored my neck while he unbuttoned my blouse with one hand. In the back of my mind, I kept thinking I should stop him.

He slipped my breasts out of the cups of my bra and murmured, "Wowza, look at you. God, your breasts are beautiful." His tongue and fingers teased my nipples. Again, I thought I should stop him, but his tongue moved faster, swirling around my nipple, making me want him even more; then a tingly sensation raced south with an astonishing jolt.

"Joshua," I gasped, while my body convulsed with the most unexpected pleasure.

He rested his head on my breasts, and I clasped him in my arms while I recovered. I wanted to keep him against me the rest of the night.

I ran my hand through his silky hair. "Definitely a first, but I can't write about it."

He sniggered. "Maybe not, but it's nice to know I was your first for something." He pushed off me and sat up. "Sorry, I'm kinda cramped. Besides, I should go."

I asked, "Why? Did I do something wrong?"

"No." He smiled and shook his head. "No, I'm trying to take it slow for you, but it's hard." He slightly flushed. "Pun not intended." We both laughed. He softly kissed me, eased my breasts back into my bra, and sighed. "It's getting late."

I so, so wanted him to stay—I knew he wanted to stay—but if he did, we would end up in bed. I adjusted my blouse, and we both stood.

What was I doing? He cared about me. I cared about him. He wasn't interested in anyone else. I wasn't interested in anyone else. We were going to sleep together whether it happened tonight or a few nights from now.

I tugged him to a stop. "Stay the night with me."

He turned and cupped my face in his hands. "Sure you're ready?"

I nodded. "The hell with going slow."

Chapter 24

*M*Y BEDROOM CLOCK said it was three in the morning, but I was wide awake. Joshua and I had made love twice but stayed up talking. I laid on my back while he lightly ran his fingers over my stomach and breasts.

"You have such a beautiful body," he murmured. "I could stare at you all night."

"Aw, I bet you say it to all the girls," I teased.

"No, just you," he said and kissed my stomach. "I used to watch for you when I worked at Nugget way before you ever noticed to me," he said, continuing to caress my breasts while he talked. "I'd see you and hope you'd come to my line. One day you did, and I went as fast as I could to get to you, but just as I reached for your cart, another checker tried to snatch you away. I was like *ah, hell no* and grabbed you back. You looked me in the eyes for just a second and that's the first time I felt like you really saw me."

I rolled on my side and propped up on my elbow. "I remember that day and you're right. I thought you had the most beautiful eyes."

He chuckled. "I hear that a lot."

I laughed. "I bet you do, but it wasn't just your eyes that I caught my attention. After that day, I kept an eye out for you, too. Did you know you made me a little nervous?"

He gave me one of his sweet smiles. "You were attracted to me back then, too?"

"I was, very much so. It made me feel like a dirty old lady."

"Do you still feel that way?"

I stroked his chest. He was confident and strong, and far from inno-cent—so different from my earlier impression. "Not now, not when we're together like this."

"But you still worry about being too old for me?"

I nodded. He could have his pick of beautiful young things without the baggage I carried.

He tilted my chin to look into my eyes. "Don't go there. There's nothing about you I would change." He kissed me with his soft lips moving slowly with mine as he eased me back down on the bed and his hand caressed down my body.

"Joshua, I don't think I can do it again tonight." His tongue did a little thing to my ear and his fingers applied a delicious pressure, and I wanted him again.

He made love to me slow and easy with no air between our bodies. Blow me over with a feather, was he an exceptional lover. He seemed to approach lovemaking with the same creative thinking he used for cooking: letting things simmer, adding a pinch of spice here and there, and having fun with combinations of flavor. He was so good with rhythms and knew how to use his fingers and tongue in surprising ways. He hadn't made me crazy with lust the way Jay had, but Joshua had plenty of finesse.

Afterwards I draped over him with my head on his chest, feeling immensely sated and close to him physically, mentally, and emotionally. I asked, "How did you get so good at this?"

"I study pornography on a daily basis."

I lifted my head in disbelief. "What?"

He smiled. "Joking." He gently coaxed my head back on his chest and ran his fingers through my hair. "Like anything else—practice."

"You've slept with a lot of women?"

"Yeah, I guess I have, and a long time ago, I had an affair with a woman who was much older than me. She took me under her wing so to speak."

"How old was she?"

"She never gave me a straight answer, but I guessed she had to be around forty."

"So the fact I'm older really doesn't bother you?"

"Nope, and I wish it didn't freak you so much. You shouldn't worry about what other people might think. Besides, you look like you're in your twenties."

I could kiss him for saying it. I did and noticed his eyes struggled to stay open. "You need to get some sleep." I rolled off him, and he reached over to turn off the bedside lamp. "Wait," I said. "I want to look at something first."

He flopped back onto the bed. "My body is an open book."

I picked up his foot to examine the tattoo on his ankle. "*This too...,* what does that mean?"

"It's short for *This Too Shall Pass.*"

"Is that biblical?"

"No, just an ancient adage. I got the tattoo when I was going through a really hard time a few years ago. I wanted something to remind me that phases of life are transitory. The idea for me is if everything is great, I should really appreciate it and enjoy the moment. If I'm sad or depressed or whatever, I won't be forever—you know, I'll live through it."

"I don't know if that's comforting or depressing," I said.

He sighed. "It depends on the moment, but I find it more comforting than anything else. Ready to go to sleep?"

I turned off the light, and he snuggled me into the crook of his arm. He murmured close to my ear, "Being with you feels different than it's been with anyone else. I think that's the reason why everything was so good tonight."

He was far from the fresh-faced innocent kid I'd thought. In many ways, he had more experience than me. I now knew he'd had numerous affairs, traveled throughout Europe, spent time in Southeast Asia in addition to working and going to school, and this was his second stint living in San Francisco. He hadn't been married or had children, but he'd packed a lot into his twenty-seven years.

I whispered, "The more time I spend with you, the less your age matters to me."

His arm tightened around me. "So spend lots and lots of time with me."

"Sounds like a plan." Of course, given his *This Too* philosophy, who knew how long he'd want me. His grip lessened, and he breathed evenly next to me. I wasn't sure if he was asleep, but asked, "What happened with you and the older woman?"

"I just didn't fall in love with her."

I understood. I had ended my relationship with Kevin for the same reason. I wondered if his "hard time" had anything to do with a broken heart. "Have you ever been in love?"

He mumbled, barely finishing his thought before dropping off to sleep, "Of course. Falling is easy. It's staying that's hard."

⌒

I WOKE UP EXTRA warm the next morning with Joshua half on top of me, naked and sound asleep. In the bright light of day, the dirty old lady feeling crept over me as I ran my hand over his bare buttocks. I loved that there was no looseness to his young body. His muscles were attached to his bones in way that couldn't be replicated with sweaty gym sessions, and his skin was smooth and firm and perfect. I yanked the sheet, trying to cover my stretch marks, the telltale sign of having gained and lost weight that no miracle cream could fade, and now seemed even more noticeable with sunlight streaming through the window.

Joshua's eyes blinked open, and he rolled off me. "What time is it?"

I glanced at my clock and pulled the sheet up to my chin. "Ten."

He sat up and ran his hand through his hair. "Shit. I'm due at the restaurant at eleven. I don't have time to go home and take a shower."

"You can shower here," I said.

"Sure you don't mind?"

"Of course not."

While he showered, I made coffee and whipped him up an omelet. He washed quickly, not bothering to shave, and came out looking yummy with wet hair and a shadowed face. Before, I'd thought he was cute, but now he seemed hot as all hell to me.

"Do you take milk in your coffee?"

"No, black is great. Is that omelet for me?"

"It is. Hope you have time to eat."

"You sweetheart," he said and pecked my lips. "Thank you, I'm starving." He bent over the counter and wolfed it down in about a minute. "I hate to eat and run, but I really gotta go."

"I know," I said and began walking him out. I had work to do, too. Looming in front of me was a deadline for an article I was writing about the role of children in today's San Francisco lifestyle. The piece needed polishing—plus, I owed Wendy a submission. I wasn't even sure what I was going to write about. Writing about Joshua was out; my feelings for him were too intimate and new for any kind of perspective. Bottom line, I needed uninterrupted thinking time.

When we got to the door, he cupped my face in his hands. "When can I see you next?"

I wanted to tell him tonight, as soon as he got off work, but worried it would make me appear over eager. "How about Wednesday?"

He smiled with a little sigh. "I was hoping for tonight since I get off early, but Wednesday works."

I laughed. "Okay, tonight then. Come over when you get off."

"You sure?"

"Yes, I'm sure."

He opened the door, and then turned back to me. "I should warn you I'm going to be a terrible boyfriend when it comes to texting. I can't text while I'm working, but it doesn't mean I won't be thinking about you."

Music to my ears on multiple levels. I smiled. "That makes you just about perfect."

Grinning, he rolled his eyes and kissed me one more time before jetting out the door and down the stairs. I closed the door with a happy sigh. I officially had a boyfriend, and I loved that he didn't play coy games.

Not only that, but he gave me an idea for my next post: *To Text, or not To Text, That is The Question, or The Upside of Textless Dating*. It was a subject that Wendy and my readership would eat up. Besides, I had personal experience with an on-line dating service that came with an APP so potential suitors could text me. After experiencing a couple incessant texters, who had absolutely nothing to say in person, I'd deleted the APP from my phone.

I revved up my laptop and wrote like a madwoman for the next few hours. My flow was interrupted by someone buzzing my door. A minute later, a deliveryman handed me a dozen gorgeous long stem red roses. I didn't have to read the card to know they were from Jay. Sure enough, it read, *"Thank you for dinner last night, Jay."*

What the hell? He'd already sent flowers thanking me the week before, and red roses to boot, but no *Love, Jay* or *XOXO, Jay*—just *Jay*. I had an urge to chuck them straight into the garbage, but they were too beautiful to waste. Instead, I arranged them in a vase and set them in the middle of the dining room table. I wished he would tell me what the hell he wanted so we could hash it out and move on. After all the years we'd spent together, one would think he could be honest about his feelings. On the other hand, he might not know what he was feeling.

My feelings were crystal clear. I had a great new boyfriend, and I didn't want Jay mucking things up. The flowers reminded me I'd promised to contact the antique shop and have them hold the dining set for him. I didn't have time for it but went to the store anyway and took care of it. When I got back, I sent Jay an email with all the particulars.

He e-mailed back: *Thank you for looking out for me. I'll call the store before I leave the office. Did you get the flowers?*

I responded: *Yes, they're gorgeous. Thank you*

He replied: *You're welcome. Wanted you to know how much I appreciated you hosting dinner. It was great seeing you, and I sincerely liked your apartment. Have you thought about Tahoe?*

No, I hadn't. All I had thought about was Joshua and work. I doubted Joshua would be cool with me going with Jay to Tahoe for a weekend getaway. I could picture him grunting *huh* with a puzzled expression if I told him.

I typed: *Very generous of you to include me, but I must decline. Maybe Haley can bring a friend? In any event, I'm sure you two will have a great time. Best -Kim*

Better not to make an excuse or offer any kind of explanation. If I did, he would argue or counteroffer. He didn't respond, and I went back to writing, determined to get as much done as possible before Joshua showed up. Then around eight o'clock Jay called.

After the general hellos, he asked, "How was the party?"

"Good, but I didn't stay long." No way was I going to get into a conversation with Jay about my night after he and Haley had left. "Is there a particular reason you're calling?"

"About Tahoe—"

"Jay, I've made up my mind and don't want to talk about it."

"Kimmy, please, let me explain." I didn't interrupt and he kept going. "It was my idea to invite you."

"Why didn't you just tell me? Why the ruse?"

"Because I knew if you thought it was my idea, you wouldn't come."

"I'm still not going, so I don't know what you thought you were accomplishing."

"Obviously, it got me nowhere, so I'm going to be honest. Being back in the house, seeing you last week and then again yesterday …." Jay's voice cracked. He paused and sucked in a breath before saying, "It's made me really feel what I've lost. I miss being a family."

His confession and the ache in his voice hurt, really hurt. I swiped at a tear. Not wanting to inflict more pain but knowing what I had to say would, I said as gently as possible, "We're not a family anymore; spending a weekend together won't change that. For me, it feels so hollow and false. I can't pretend, please don't ask me to."

"I understand—Tahoe's off the table. I felt the weirdness too, but it doesn't have to be that way. If I came down this weekend, would you be willing to see me?"

My heart gave a twist. "What do you want from me? And don't you dare tell me you want to be friends. We both know that's not true."

"Honestly, your apology for laughing at me made feel hopeful for the first time in a long time. I guess I'd like us to spend time together and see how things go."

He didn't want me. He wanted forgiveness. He was feeling nostalgic being back in the house, but those feelings could pass any time, just as his love for me had passed. He could go back to chasing Brittany or Tiffany or whoever made his tail wag. He'd played havoc with my emotions last summer, and I couldn't allow him to do it again.

"You shattered me."

"I know and I'm sorry. You've no idea how sorry I am. You have to believe me."

"I do, but after what you told me the day we went shopping, I don't think I can ever love you the way I did."

"If you can find a way to forgive me at least a little bit, maybe you could."

"I can't trust you to accept my love. I can't trust you not to shatter me again; so no, I'm sorry, it's not going to happen."

I could hear him breathing and waited him out. After a long beat, he said with his voice full of pain, "I don't have an argument for that."

"I didn't think you would."

I hung up with tears trickling, hurting as much for Jay as myself. If he had wanted to reconcile last summer or even a month ago, I would have. Not now, and not because of Joshua, but because of what Jay had confessed. If he had kept that little tidbit of information to himself, my answer would have been different. It became clear I had to sever the last ties with Jay: no dinners, no shopping, and no financial support. My to-do-list had to include inviting Wendy to lunch to pick her brain about other income opportunities and my lawyer about negotiating a settlement with Jay that didn't include monthly payments.

I headed to my bedroom, longing to curl in a ball and cry it out, but a knock on my door sent my thoughts flying to Joshua. Oh, how I wanted his soothing presence to calm the turmoil in my chest.

Opening my door, Gina breezed past me. At least she brought an opened bottle of wine. She followed me to the kitchen, chatting away while I got down a couple wine glasses.

"You missed a great party last night, but I guess you were having your own private party," she said with a suggestive titter. "So, tell me about Joshua."

For a second, I thought she'd said *tell me about Jay*. I couldn't concentrate with my insides aching and my mind wrapped around Jay. "Was it that obvious we left together?"

"No, but he sent Paul a text saying he was leaving with you."

So much for being discreet. "Oh, I thought he'd wanted to slip out without anyone noticing." Glasses in hand, I headed back to the living room with Gina still talking.

"I bet he did. Paul said there was a girl there Joshua had gone out with a few times. Apparently, she's still gaga for him." She paused as we passed the dining room. "Ooo, roses?"

"Not what you're thinking. They're from Jay—a thank you for dinner." I didn't want anything reminding me of him. "Want them?"

She laughed. "Sure, I'll take them. Your ex-husband is a looker." She picked up the flowers, and we went to the living room. "So dinner with him was a little more serious?"

"No, not at all. The evening was more for Haley." I didn't want to discuss Jay with her. "Did you pick up any clients last night?"

"A couple prospects, and I got some good dirt on Joshua."

I wasn't sure if I wanted to hear it, but my curiosity won out. "Oh, yeah?"

"Apparently, he's quite the little Casanova. According to Paul, he's broken a lot of hearts. He completely devastated an older woman when they were in culinary school."

I'd heard enough third hand gossip. "Is this a friendly warning?"

Her eyes popped at me. "No—at least not in that way. Paul said he's never seen Joshua hung up on anyone the way he seems to be with you. He's worried this time Joshua will be the one left with the broken heart."

I couldn't stop a smile from spreading across my face. "Thanks for that." We both laughed and I asked, determined to divert her attention from Joshua, "How's it going with Paul?"

"He's making me dinner tomorrow night, so we'll see." My buzzer rang. This time I knew for certain who it was. Gina asked, "Joshua?"

Gina, the flowers, and half empty bottle of wine disappeared behind her door just as Joshua reached the top of the stairs. He had a messenger bag hanging from his shoulder, a paper bag in his hand, and glowy smile on his clean-shaven face.

I kissed him as soon as he walked through my door.

"Wow, best greeting ever—better than I'd hoped," he joked as he handed me the paper bag. "I brought us some pumpkin-queso tamales for breakfast."

I asked with a straight face, "Oh, were you planning to stay the night?"

He grinned, not buying it. "Uh, I was hoping. I came prepared this time." He dropped the messenger bag and wrapped his arms around me. Pressing me close, he whispered in my ear, "I couldn't stop thinking about you today."

"I thought about you a lot, too." After holding it together in front of Gina, having his warm body molded against me, melted my defenses. My tears welled and tumbled out, making his shirt wet.

"Oh, hey, hey, Sweetie," he said, "What's wrong?"

I wanted to tell him I was crying because Jay left me feeling vulnerable and raw, but I was afraid if I did, he would turn around and walk out. I clung to him, saying nothing. He squeezed me tighter, letting me have my freak out moment without pushing for an explanation.

This Too Shall Pass. I took a deep breath and murmured, "Please, don't break my heart."

He lifted my chin and gazed into my eyes. "I know you've been seriously hurt, but I'm asking you to have a little faith in me just like I'm having to trust you."

What if we didn't last? What if in a couple months, I was alone again? I wasn't twenty-something. I was thirty-seven-flipping-years old, standing in the arms of a man ten years my junior. I didn't want to be alone or for my bedroom to have a revolving door. I didn't want a new lover every six months. What was I getting myself into?

Fully aware that I was jumping into the relationship deep end, I nodded. "I can do that."

Chapter 25

Late November

THE WEDNESDAY BEFORE Thanksgiving, I woke to the happy sight of Joshua strolling into my bedroom with a big grin and a breakfast tray in his hands. "Happy Anniversary, Sleepyhead," he said. "Come on, Lover, sit up."

"It's not our anniversary."

"Sure it is. It's been two months since we bumped into each other at City Lights. I've been a one-woman man ever since. Shouldn't that count?"

He thought we should start counting our time together with the night Gina and I'd had dinner at De Noche. I thought we should start with the night of the De Noche party since I'd agreed to see him exclusively that night. He'd won and now seemed to be changing the date, but I didn't care. We were still in a honeymoon stage and had been spending three to four nights a week together since we made things official. I'd been to his apartment a few times, but most nights he stayed at my place. I yawned and stretched. I hadn't quite adjusted to his schedule but couldn't afford to sleep in with Val and Haley coming.

I shifted a pillow behind me and sat up. "I suppose. You sweetie, what did you make?"

"Crab cake eggs benedict, rosemary potatoes fried in duck fat, fresh squeezed orange juice, and cappuccino," he said, setting the tray in front of me.

"Yummy. You know I've gained five pounds since you've started feeding me."

He chuckled and got in bed next to me. "Gives me more to love." He hadn't said *I love you* yet, but he'd danced around it a lot the last few days. "Share a bite?" I cut him a piece and held it up to his mouth. "Mmmm. Damn, I'm good," he joked.

"You're the best."

"No, you're best." We both laughed. "What time is everyone getting here, again?"

"Haley should be here around one and Val about three, depending on traffic."

He brushed my hair to the side and nibbled my neck. "So we have the morning alone?"

"Slow down, lover. I've got a ton to do." Not only were Val and Haley coming, but Joshua and I were hosting Thanksgiving for a large party, including Wendy and her husband, Paul, and some of Joshua's friends. "Sure you don't want to stick around and meet them today?"

He stopped nuzzling my neck. "Uh, no. I'll wait until I know back-up is on the way."

I giggled. "Aw, are you scared?"

"I'd be an idiot if I wasn't. I'll leave you to your girl's day, but I'll help with whatever you need this morning."

Having a boyfriend who was a whiz in the kitchen was the best. He could slice and dice, and whip eggs like no one's business. By noon, I was well ahead of schedule. Joshua had a quiche in the oven for lunch and was at the sink washing dishes. Wrapping my arms around his waist, I pressed against him, resting my cheek against his back.

He turned off the water and dried his hands. "Thought we didn't have time."

"Can you be quick?"

In a spilt second, I was pinned against the wall with his body. His mouth swooped down on my lips; then he hitched my leg up to his waist and grinded against me. His lips barely left mine to ask, "Bedroom?"

"Dining room's closer."

He hoisted me up. With my legs wrapped around his waist, I ran my tongue up his neck and around his ear while he walked us into the dining room. He abruptly halted and dropped his hands from my butt.

"Mom?"

I slid off his waist, turning at the same time; he barely caught my arm before I tumbled. "Haley, you're here." My eyes darted from Haley to Joshua. Based on the red faces and mortified expressions, it was a close tie who was more shocked and embarrassed.

Joshua recovered first. He held out his hand to Haley. "Hi, I'm —"

"Joshua," Haley said, ignoring his outstretched hand. "Yeah, I kind of figured that out."

"Right." He dropped his hand. "Please know I have great respect for your mother."

Haley's mouth pinched. "That's more than I can say."

That shook me out of my stunned haze. "HALEY BRAXTON, *enough!*"

Joshua turned to me. "How about if I finish fixing lunch while you two talk?"

"That would be very nice of you. Thank you." I said to Haley, "I'd like to speak with you in the living room."

As soon as we sat down, she said, "*Fuck*, mother, how old is he?"

"Watch your mouth—and I told you before he's twenty-seven."

"Seeing you together is totally different. Robbing the cradle a bit, don't you think?"

"*Little miss*, you need to stop right there. Now, I'm sorry you saw something that was embarrassing for all of us, but it gives you no right to be disrespectful. I'm still your mother; this is my home, and I won't tolerate it."

She pouted in silence for a minute. "I'm sorry. I do respect you. I was just shocked. I've never seen you with anyone other than Dad."

"He's dated women younger than Joshua."

"But I haven't had to witness it with my own eyes." She looked away and then let out an uncomfortable giggle. "You were all over him."

"I wasn't expecting you for at least another hour. You should have called me."

"I did and I texted you! You never pick up your phone."

I'd forgotten that I left my phone charging in the bedroom, where I couldn't hear it. "Okay, I'm sorry, but you shouldn't text while you're driving. It's dangerous."

"Jeeze Mom, *I know*. I was at a stop. You need to get a landline again."

Ugh, that again. "I'll think about it. Truce?"

She nodded, and we both heard Joshua drop a pan in the kitchen. "He looks familiar. Where did you meet him?"

"In Davis, but then we bumped into each other at City Lights. He makes me happy, and I'd really appreciate it if you would give him a chance."

Haley sighed. "I promise not to be rude."

About ten minutes later Joshua walked in and announced lunch. He had set the table for two with a wine glass at each setting. A salad bowl and the quiche sat in the middle. I usually didn't drink at lunch, but today seemed like a good day for an exception.

Joshua poured me a glass, then smiled at Haley. "Would you care for some?"

"Haley doesn't drink," I said.

"Yes, I do."

"You drink?"

Joshua laughed at me. "She spent a year at college. Besides, it's no big deal in Europe."

"He's right, Mom. I can handle a glass of wine. Come on, you were married at my age."

"That argument is getting old." Joshua raised his brows at me. "But I'm fine with it since you're done driving for the day."

He poured Haley a glass, and she said, "Thank you, and I'm sorry for being rude earlier."

"No worries." He winked at her. "How about we forget about it and start over?"

"I'm down with that," she said with a smile. He was winning her over.

"Great." He turned to me. "I'm going to take off so you can enjoy your girls' day."

He grabbed his coat and messenger bag from the bedroom, and I followed him to the door. "I'm so sorry about everything."

He pecked my lips. "Don't worry about it. Not exactly how I envisioned meeting your daughter, but we all survived. If she'd arrived five minutes later, it could've been a lot worse." We both snickered. "Did you know you have a really scary mom voice?"

I chuckled. "So I've been told."

He laughed. "Alright, have fun. See you tomorrow."

After a quick kiss, I went back to the dining room. Haley already had helped herself to salad and a piece of quiche. "This is an awesome salad, and the quiche is great, too."

Yep, my guy had serious talent. "Joshua made everything, including the salad dressing."

"Impressive and it was really nice of him to fix us lunch." She took another bite and swallowed. "He has nice eyes. He kinda looks like Chace Crawford—only with dark hair."

"Chace who?"

"You don't know who Chace Crawford is?"

"Uh, no. Should I?"

"Guess not but look him up on IMD sometime. You'll see what I mean."

"At the risk of sounding completely old and clueless, what is IMD?"

She laughed at me. "It's a website. I'm sure Joshua knows, but I'll show you later."

We ate in silence for a few minutes. After having had such a big breakfast, I wasn't very hungry, but Haley had quite an appetite. I asked, "How's your dad doing?"

I hadn't spoken to Jay since the night he'd called about going to Tahoe and exploring a reconciliation. My attorney had sent him a request to renegotiate the terms of our divorce a few weeks ago, but he hadn't responded, which was worrisome. I'd anticipated at least a phone call.

Haley put her fork down and crossed her arms. "I'm not getting in the middle of it."

"What do you mean by that?"

"I know Dad told you he wanted to get back together, and you said no."

"That's not exactly how the conversation went."

"Whatever, I'm just telling you the same thing I told him. I'd obviously like to see you together, but it's between you two. I'm not going to be a double agent passing intel back and forth. I don't want to be caught between you or be accused of taking sides."

It was a relief to hear there would be no reporting back about Joshua. "So what we do in San Francisco, stays in San Francisco?"

Haley gave me an impish grin. "Pretty much."

"Good. Do you want to have a few drinks with Val and me tonight?" So I was being a less than ideal mother. It seemed an innocuous way to earn a little loyalty.

She laughed. "Uh, yeah. You two are hysterical when you're drinking."

———

"Oh my god, Aunt Val, I was like *my mother is a nymphomaniac.* You should have seen her—she was devouring him," Haley said, laughing. The good news was she was laughing; the bad news was the girl was drunk. One glass of wine, she could handle. Three glasses, she'd hit her limit and became quite silly.

Val exploded with laughter. "Oh that poor boy. He must've been mortified." She and Haley laughed so hard tears ran down their faces.

Haley got control of her giggles. "After his initial reaction, he was pretty cool about it."

"He's not a *boy*," I said, cracking a smile.

"Sorry," Val said still tittering. "I can't get over you and Checker Boy are an item."

"Checker boy? What do you mean?" Haley asked.

"Valerie is referring to the fact that he used to work at Nugget. It's where I met him."

Haley's eyes bugged with recognition. "I totally know who he is now. I met him one day when I was at the store talking to Hunter. Remember Hunter? I was crazy about him." Haley's eyes got a little dreamy. "I wonder if he's visiting his parents in Davis this weekend. Think I should text him?"

Val and I both laughed and said in unison, "No."

"Honey, Auntie Val is going to give you some really good advice, ready?"

"Yeah," she said. "Lay it on me."

"Always have your Uber driver verify your name before getting in the car and never text or call a guy when you're drunk. Oh, and use condoms."

"Val!" I couldn't believe she'd said that.

"What? It's true."

Haley laughed. "Don't worry, I do."

I sobered fast. "You're not a virgin?"

She let out a nervous giggle. "Guess I should add don't drink with my mom to the list."

It was a shock, but of course she could be sexually active. I had been since turning seventeen, and she was nineteen and a half. I held up my hands. "We don't have to talk about it … unless you want to talk about it."

"Don't want to talk about it," she said, shaking her head. "What happens in S.F., stays in S.F., right?"

If Jay and I were still together, I couldn't make that promise. As things stood, I held up my pinkie. We shook and said together, "Pinkie-swear."

She yawned and asked Val, "Sure you don't want the bed?"

"Positive, you take it. I'm good with the couch."

Haley went off to bed, leaving Val and I at the table with the remains of our second bottle of wine. Val lifted the bottle. I put my hand over my glass. "I've had enough."

"Me, too," she said and corked the bottle. "Have you heard back from Jay yet?"

"No, no response to the buyout proposal. My attorney thinks I'm nuts letting him off the hook with six months of support up front and my share of equity in the house. I'm guessing Jay questions the Zillow estimate and is having the house appraised."

"Well, I'm really proud of you," she said. "I know what you're doing isn't easy, but you're keeping it together and making things happen."

"Thank you. I won't be able to keep this apartment, but by adding food writing and web content to my workload, I'll be fine. Plus, I'm plugging away on the novel."

"Good for you. I liked the short stories you wrote in high school." She downed the remainder of wine in her glass. "I remember the first couple years

I was out of college. I had some really broke times, but it felt so good knowing I was standing on my own."

"That's the same way Jay and I had felt, and here I am, doing it all over again."

"Come on, admit it—it's different this time."

"What do you want me to say, 'I am woman, hear me roar?'"

"No, I want you to scream it out your window and *roar*."

We both laughed. "It's different," I admitted. "This round no one will be able to pull the rug out from under me, and let's face it, I'll have a sizable nest egg from the house. And who knows, Joshua and I could move in together."

She looked at me surprised. "You're joking? Isn't he just a little hottie you're having fun with? You've only been dating him for what, a month?"

"About two, and I don't mean now." If Joshua and I made it to the year mark, living together seemed possible. I shrugged. "He's surprisingly mature."

Val nodded and I decided to call it a night. After my bathroom routine, I dropped into bed. It felt very empty and cold without Joshua's warm body next to me. Amazing how quickly I'd become accustomed to him being there. I couldn't resist calling him.

"Hi, Lover," he answered. "Have fun tonight?"

He sounded sleepy. "I did. I'm sorry, did I wake you?"

"Uh-huh, but I don't care. Tell me about your night."

"I got my daughter drunk and found out she's not a virgin."

He chortled into the phone. "Well, you're a very sexual person. You shouldn't be surprised if your daughter is too."

"You think I'm sexual? I thought I was on the puritanical side."

He barked a laugh. "You're very orgasmic. Believe me, you are not uptight in bed."

Making my voice husky I said, "That's because you make me want to do things."

He groaned. "Stop, or I won't be able to get back to sleep."

"Okay. Are you still on schedule to be here early tomorrow?"

"Yep, turkey is brining, sweet potato gnocchi are all done, and the appetizers are ready for the oven. How are you doing on your end?"

"All prepped, but I have to get up early to make the rolls."

"Let's get some sleep then," he said just like he would if he were next to me. "The sooner morning comes, the sooner I get to see your face. I love your face."

"Love your face, too." I hung up wondering how much longer it would take for him to say those three little words. He was so close.

Chapter 26

M Y ALARM WENT off at six. I jumped to hit the off button before the beeping woke Haley and Val, wriggled into slippers and padded to the kitchen. After making coffee, I got busy mixing dough for the Braxton Family holiday crescent rolls. It was Jay's grandmother's recipe, passed on to his mother and then to me. Despite the hour and barely sleeping the night before, I hummed with nervous energy. I hadn't hosted a dinner party in a long time, and this would be the first time I cooked for a crowd without Jay's help. He'd never been much of a cook, but he'd always been great about washing up behind me as I worked and making last-minute grocery store runs.

The first time I'd prepared a Thanksgiving dinner was the year we bought our house. Jay's mother ceded her hosting duties in consideration that we had a larger home and a dining room that could accommodate the entire Braxton clan. Maggie, Jay's mom, had arrived the day before to teach me how to make the rolls and walk me through all the little things I needed to do to ensure our bounty of dishes hit the table warm and delicious. I truly had loved my mother-in-law. When I married Jay, her love had wrapped around me like a big warm blanky, making me feel like I was as much her daughter as Jay was her son. She'd been that way with everyone in the family, making each of us feel loved and important. Jay had a lot of her qualities.

My throat tightened, remembering the day Jay had come home from work just before noon; him trying to be strong, and telling me that Maggie had passed away. She'd woken feeling off and thought fresh air and a brisk walk would set her aright. After setting out with Lucky, her funny mut of a dog that she'd rescued from the pound, she had collapsed on the sidewalk less than a block from her front porch. By the time the paramedics had arrived and transported her to the hospital, she was gone. Jay didn't cry, so I cried for both of us. We sat together with broken hearts, me with tears streaming, and Jay too grieved to speak. God, I missed Maggie … I missed the whole Braxton clan. I wished they were here.

I swiped at a tear before my sorrow contaminated the dough and shook my head, clearing my thoughts. Thanksgiving and making these rolls had me thinking of the past. I had to look forward. Today, Joshua would be cooking beside me, and a new group of friends would be gathering.

There wasn't room in the kitchen to roll out the dough and shape them into perfect little crescents, so I moved my operation to the dining room table. Joshua and I had made love on it more than once, and I cringed knowing Haley would never eat on it again if she'd caught us on it. She had to know I wasn't celibate, but it concerned me that she thought I lacked morals. Her comment about not being a virgin worried me even more.

I heard her stumble out of bed. She had to cross through the dining room to get to the kitchen, and I caught her. "Want to help?"

"Sure, let me get some coffee first."

Coffee was also new. Sugary Starbucks concoctions I had known about, but I didn't know when she had started drinking regular coffee in the morning.

She came back with a giant mug and sat down. "Oh, are these Grandma's rolls?"

"They are."

"I love these. How come you didn't make them last year?"

"I wasn't much in the mood last year." We'd had a very skimpy Thanksgiving with only the two of us. It had taken all my energy to make the most basic Thanksgiving dinner.

"Guess not. You seem so much happier now, like you're back to normal."

"I am happy. Thanks for noticing." I rolled out a big circle of dough and cut it into triangles while Haley sipped on her coffee. "Ready?" She set down her mug and helped me roll them up and set them on buttered cookie sheets to rise. "I'm glad you're up early. I wanted to talk to you before Val got up."

She eyed me nervously. "You're not preggers or something?"

"Uh, no." As she was well-aware, that would be a miracle. Where would she get such an idea? "I was surprised to hear you're not a virgin."

"Oh." She took a drink from her mug. "Thought we didn't have to talk about it."

"Sorry, mom's prerogative. I'm concerned. As far as I know you've never been in love or been too serious with anyone."

"Why does that matter? I'm an adult now. You, of all people, should understand I don't need to be in love to have sex."

I stopped working and stared at her. Technically, she was an adult, but she had a lot of growing up to do. She knew so little about life.

"Why me of all people? I was insanely in love with your father. At the time, I believed he was my one true love, and we'd be together forever. All those emotions had been incredibly intense and overwhelming. I thought I would literally die without him." For a while after he'd left me, I had thought I was dying.

"But I'm older than you were when you got pregnant. I can handle it and haven't been overwhelmed. Besides, you have sleepovers with Joshua. You're not serious about him, so I don't know why you're so concerned about me." She looked me in the eyes. "He has a drawer in the bathroom, and I saw you together."

I'd put his things in a drawer in effort to be discreet. Damn it to hell, she thought I was being a hypocrite. To disabuse her of the notion would require admitting Joshua was much more than a casual affair, but I wasn't ready for that conversation.

"Being intimate with Joshua isn't something I engage in lightly." This conversation was supposed to be about her, not me. "Someday you'll understand there's a difference between making love and having sex. It's so different when it's meaningful to both of you. I don't want you to feel used or get hurt; that's all."

Her eyes widened. "It's *meaningful* with Joshua?"

I danced around an answer the same way Joshua danced around saying I love you. "He's my boyfriend."

"Thought you said you were too old for a boyfriend."

Ugh, she exacerbated me. "My point is I care about him."

I could see Haley read between the lines. She was a smart kid, and her eyes became accusatory. "But you and Dad still really love each other."

"Oh my god, Haley, why would you think that?"

"The night we had dinner together, it was so obvious. I could feel it between you."

Jay's presence had pulled on me, just as it always had. After having loved him the way I had and spending so many happy years together, how could I not be affected on some basic, unconscious level?

"It's too early, and I need coffee," Valerie said walking in, saving me from having to answer. Haley must have been relieved too because she went to the kitchen to help Val.

An hour or so later, my phone beeped with a text from Joshua: *Hate your f-ing neighborhood, can't park.*

I texted him back, letting him know the gals and I would meet him in front. He double parked and all three of us raced down to unload his car. I sent Haley and Val back upstairs and jumped in with him.

"Gina's out of town until Saturday. She won't mind if you take her parking spot. Sorry I didn't think of it sooner." I directed him through the alley to the back of the building and used my key pass to get him into the tiny garage. As expected, her car was gone. She and Paul had fizzled out, and she'd opted to go to her parents' house for the holiday rather than join us.

He turned off the engine and unbuckled his seat belt. "Can we sit for a minute?"

"Of course." He reached over the console for my hand and brought it to his lips. We took a minute to decompress, him from his parking frustration and me from Haley's general ill-temper since our mom-daughter chat. When I sensed his tension had eased, I asked, "Ready?"

"Not yet. I want to be alone with you a little longer." He angled his body toward me and gazed into my eyes. The sweetest smile spread across his face. "You know something?"

"I know a lot of things," I joked, "but tell me anyway."

"This last month or so with you is the happiest I've ever been."

His blissful glow engulfed me, making me more downhearted than delighted. Happy as I'd been with him, I couldn't reciprocate the sentiment. If I had, it would've been a lie. I wished so badly it were true. I kissed him instead.

He pulled back and leaned his forehead against mine. "I love kissing you. I could kiss you all day."

"You're sweet, but we better go. We've got people to feed."

———

Preparing a Thanksgiving feast in a tiny alley kitchen had its challenges. (I couldn't have done it without Joshua charting out the exact order for prepping and cooking each dish.) However, the smallness of the room had its advantages. Since only two people could work in the space, and Joshua and I were the cooks, he was relatively safe from Haley and Val until other people arrived. I asked him to keep PDAs to a minimum in front of Haley. He respectfully kept his hands off me, but snuck in loving looks, pecks on my cheek, and an occasional body brush.

Val and Haley stayed busy setting up a drink station in the living room and making the apartment festive. Their artistic streaks tapped, they went wild with flowers, turkey feathers, mini pumpkins, small gourds, and assorted candles. Every now and then one of them would poke her head in the kitchen to see what we were up to and pump Joshua with questions.

Val had asked, "Where'd you get the kicks you were wearing last summer?" Joshua had no clue what she was talking about. She clarified. "The florescent Converse with the drawings."

"Oh, they were a gift from a girl I was hanging with. She's an artist. I wore them for her, but not really my style."

Haley had asked, "So how often do you crash with my mom?"

I could've killed her, but Joshua answered unruffled, "As often as she lets me."

At one point, we heard them talking in the dining room. Val said, "Checker boy looks like Chace Crawford, don't you think?"

I winced, hoping Joshua hadn't heard, and continued piping crab and egg yolk filling into egg white shells for the deviled eggs.

"That's what I told Mom. Can you believe, she didn't know who he was? So I told her to look him up on IMD, and she didn't know what that was either," Haley said.

They both laughed at my cluelessness, and Val said, "Did I tell you I met Chace a couple months ago?"

"No way! Oh my god, tell me everything. He's so fucking hot."

I cringed. Did she think my Checker Boy was f-ing hot, too? I did not want to know this. I didn't want Joshua to know this. When had she started dropping the f-bomb?

Joshua leaned over and whispered in my ear, "*Checker Boy*, huh?"

I peered up at him. "Sorry, she knows I met you at Nugget. She's just being silly."

He smirked. "Guess it's better than *Bagger Boy*."

After that, I turned up the volume on my Spotify stream of *Funk You! '60s and '70s Funk Superstars*. Busting out random, crazy dance moves while we cooked kept Joshua laughing and distracted.

The closer time came to company arriving, the more anxious I became. Knowing the food I'd prepared would give my friends and family pleasure was extremely gratifying, but at heart I was an introvert. I wasn't shy; I didn't fear people. However, I'd forgotten how much I mentally had to gear up for hosting. When Jay and I had entertained, he'd taken the lead as gracious host. I found myself wishing he were here again, knowing I'd be able to count on him to keep conversation flowing, refill glasses and see to the miscellaneous needs of our guests. I shook the thought out of my head. Everything would be fine. I would have Joshua by my side.

A little before two Haley, Val, and I went off to change while Joshua kept an eye on things in the kitchen. Val had brought some clothes for Haley, and I could hear them laughing in Haley's room. I had a hard time deciding what to wear. Since some of Joshua's friends were coming, and I hadn't met them yet, I wanted to look extra nice. I'd bought a dress for the occasion, but now it seemed too body conscious and youthful. I finally settled on a simple sheath Val had given me. I felt sophisticated and pretty in it, and pretty had to do.

After I finished fussing around with what to wear and certain my appearance was guest worthy, I went to the living room to do one last tweak on our bar set-up. A few minutes later Val and Haley came in all smiles, and I about dropped the wine glass in my hand.

Val had transformed Haley to movie star gorgeous. She appeared years older. The vibrant blue dress made her eyes pop and showed off her flat-tummy-curvy-girl figure.

Grinning, Haley struck a pose and asked, "What do you think?"

My daughter looked hot to trot, that's what I thought. It made me extremely uncomfortable and a bit irked at Val. "You look beautiful, but a little over-dressed?"

Val laughed. "Told you, Haley. Why don't you put on the outfit I brought you?"

"Oh, okay," Haley conceded. "But can I keep the dress?"

"I brought it for your mom. You'll have to fight it out with her."

I felt better knowing the dress was never intended for Haley and wanted her out of it before Joshua joined us. She turned to go just as Joshua walked in.

He stopped short and his eyes flickered. "Don't you look nice," he said. He had changed and looked especially good, too—the definition of hip-urban-hot in his dress clothes.

Haley giggled. "Thank you," she said and sashayed off to change.

Seeing them standing next to each other, all young and beautiful, shook me. What was he doing with someone my age? His reaction had been fleeting and natural, not so visibly different than my own had been, but it still prompted unsettling notions to flit through my head.

Then his attention focused on me, obliterating my disconcerting thoughts. His eyes radiated so much affection and desire that it unnerved me even more than my previous imaginings. He wore a positively dopey expression. "You look fantastic."

I quivered, very aware of Val watching us. "Thank you. So do you."

He gravitated to me, took my hands, and pecked my lips.

Val cleared her throat. "Can I help with anything?"

Apparently, Joshua had forgotten she was in the room. I dropped his hands and scooted around him. "Let's open some of these wine bottles."

"I'll be in the kitchen," Joshua said, sounding slightly wounded, and wandered off.

As soon as he was out of the room, Val whispered, and not with a so-happy-for-you tone, "That kid is in love with you."

I couldn't deny it since I thought he was too. "First of all, he's not a kid, and you have to stop calling him *Checker Boy.*"

Val held up her hand. "Sorry, the age thing isn't the issue. I'm more concerned you've only been together a couple months."

"He likes me. I really like him, but the L-word hasn't entered the conversation."

"What I know of Joshua, I like. I really do, but please don't rush into anything." The door buzzed and she squeezed my hand. "Be careful with him."

She hadn't said anything I didn't already know.

———

We had an eclectic group squeezed into my dining room: Wendy and her husband, Dick, who was also a writer, Joshua's couple friends Alec and Carlie, who ran some sort of web design business out of their home, two of his single male friends, Max and Adam, who were in an Indie band but also waited tables, and then Val, Paul and Haley. Much to Haley's chagrin, I had Joshua seated at the head of the table opposite me. It had been Jay's spot, but it seemed appropriate since Joshua was co-hosting. He suggested Haley sit between Max and Adam, which somewhat appeased her, and placed Val opposite her and next to Paul.

Once again, I found myself thinking of Jay—what he would look like sitting opposite me at the end of our dining table, the little wink and nod he would give me that said *well done, so proud of you.* Then he'd say The Lord's Prayer and we'd all take turns saying what we were grateful for before digging in. I had to stop thinking about Jay. I blamed it on the holiday.

Joshua stood with a glass of wine in his hand—no prayer or preamble. "Thank you all for joining us on this day of giving thanks. It's been a serendipitous time for me. First reuniting with my buddy Paul, who helped me get back to what I love doing. Thank you, Paul."

Paul smiled, nodding an acknowledgement.

"Then by pure chance, I ran into Kimberly at City Lights. As you all know, we met in Davis, but this time she saw me in a different light." His eyes locked on mine. "I am so thankful you took a chance on me." He raised his glass and surveyed the table. "To our hostess, my beautiful, amazing girlfriend, who has welcomed us into her home today," he paused, beaming at me again. "And to our first, of what I hope to be many, many Thanksgivings together. Cheers."

"Cheers," and clinking crystal echoed around the room, as well as curious smiles and raised brows. Gauged by the reactions, Joshua's toast had taken everyone by surprise, including me. Paul and Val were the only ones who didn't seem taken off guard. Haley politely raised her glass, but her pinched up mouth told me what she thought.

For the most part, the rest of the meal went smoothly given the diverse personalities and age differences of our guests. It helped that the food was sublime. Joshua kicked everything up to a higher level.

Val asked Paul, "How did you get out of cooking today?"

Paul laughed. "If I'd had dinner with my parents and family, I would be. I'd rather be here eating *his* food. I might own the restaurant, but Josh is the more creative chef."

"Not true," Joshua said modestly.

"It is and you know it. I'm more a businessman, which is why Josh will be taking over as Chef next week; then I'll be able to focus on the business side of the restaurant."

She asked Paul, "Has that always been the plan?"

"The plan was just to stay open." We all laughed. "No, I never planned to be the chef, but the first chef I hired backed out at the last minute. Luckily, Josh was available."

"But I hadn't been in a kitchen for a while and needed to get up to speed," Joshua added.

"Now he's in the zone, and it's great." Paul picked up a roll and said to Joshua, "These are crazy good."

Joshua smiled proudly at me. "I take no credit. Kimberly made them."

"They're my Grandma Braxton's recipe," Haley pointedly said.

Joshua looked at me and raised his brows. I shrugged. He knew I had a life before I met him. I wasn't going to apologize for using a family recipe.

"I love it. A couple that cooks together and writes together," Wendy said, jumping into the conversation. "You two should collaborate on something."

Joshua shot me a less than glowy questioning look; then turned to Wendy. "I don't consider myself a writer. The blog is just something I do for fun."

The conversation moved on, but a few minutes later, Joshua got up and whispered in my ear, "Can you help me in the kitchen?"

I rose and followed him. He was mad at me for the first time. He asked in a hushed voice, "Did you show Wendy my writing?"

"Yes," I answered, also whispering. "I was just helping you get noticed."

"If I want your help, I'll ask for it."

"Okay, sorry. Won't happen again."

I turned to go, but he grabbed my arm. "Hey, I'm sorry, too. I know you meant well, but I don't want to be beholden to you for—"

I put my hand over his mouth. "Trust me, Wendy never would've said a thing if she didn't like your writing."

We rejoined the party and by the time dinner was cleared, our guests had divided into two camps. Haley, Max, Adam, Carlie, and Alec were holding their own lively debate about Marvel characters versus mythological gods and whether Thanos could take down Zeus. I listened for an opportunity to jump into the conversation.

"Are we seriously having this conversation?" Max questioned. "Zeus is a god. Thanos is a comic book character."

"Oh, come on, a lot of critics are comparing the modern superhero to Greek Mythology," Haley said.

"If you're comparing to Marvel, then sure, you could make an argument that superheroes are our modern mythology," Joshua argued. "Marvel's heroes are both relatable and fallible, but DC's characters are way too flawless and idealistic to compare them to the Greeks."

"Alright, alright," Carly interjected, "let's just say hypothetically, Zeus vs. Thanos, hurts my heart, but Thanos is going down with a supercharged lightning bolt—Boom, baby!"

Adam jumped in, "Hold up, Thanos may not technically be a god, but damn, he has godlike powers. All he has to do is …" He snapped his fingers. "Know what I mean?"

I didn't have a clue what he meant. The older crowd was discussing the best little-known wineries in Napa. That was a conversation I could confidently partake in. Joshua's attention was split between the two, and I wasn't sure which he preferred.

Haley asked, "Hey Mom, do you mind if we watch some You Tube?"

I nodded my consent and watched Joshua eye them as they got up from the table. He glanced at me, and I nodded again. He mouthed, "Thanks," and followed them out. I wished he had just gotten up if he had wanted to go. He didn't need my permission. I was undecided if that or the fact he'd rather hang out with the younger crowd bothered me more.

Eventually, we all crammed in the living room to watch a couple videos of Max and Adams' band. Seating was limited, so Joshua tugged me onto his lap. Even though Carlie was on Alec's lap, I wasn't comfortable with it and squirmed back to my feet.

While Joshua launched a discussion of local bands and the best after hours' clubs, I went to the kitchen to start coffee and set out pies for dessert. Minutes later, Wendy, Dick, Val, and Paul migrated back to the dining room. It was rather obvious Joshua had abandoned me to hang with the kids. Paul was kind enough to help get everything out and displayed on the sideboard.

I went to the living room to announce dessert. Joshua and his pals were all laughing and having a good time. Haley fit right in. I felt much more like Haley's mom than Joshua's girlfriend. In my head, I asked in a cheery mom voice, *"Hey kids, ready for treats?"* My real voice announced, "Dessert and coffee are served. No rush, whenever you're ready."

I halfway expected someone to say *Thank you, Mrs. Braxton.*

Joshua jumped to his feet and walked out with me. "Sorry," he whispered, "My bad."

"It's fine," I said even though it wasn't. Did he have to say *my bad*? It was such a juvenile expression. "Paul helped me."

He grabbed my hand and yanked me into my unlit bedroom. "It's not fine. You haven't been fine all day. We can talk about it later, but right now, I need to know we're okay. I need you to kiss me."

He pulled me extra close with his hand pressed into the small of my back and his firm stomach muscles flush to my middle. His chest expanded and contacted as he breathed against me. Then he lowered his mouth to mine and gave me one of his great, knee wobbling kisses. When I was alone with him like this, all my qualms about us disappeared. I clung to him, not wanting to let go, and he kept holding me close with our bodies swaying.

"I love you," he whispered.

I love you, too caught in my throat. I remembered Joshua telling me that for him, falling in love was easy; staying in love was the challenge. For me, falling in love was hard and incredibly painful in its own exquisite way—so many doubts and fears that a wrong move could shatter the fragile beginning, but once rooted, letting go was near impossible. But maybe that had more to do with knowing what it was like to love someone to the very marrow of your bones and deepest depths of your heart. That kind of love stayed with you. I couldn't say the words and mean it the way I had with Jay. I really, really liked Joshua, but did I love him? If I couldn't bring myself to say the words, then I wasn't there yet.

"I love you," he repeated more clearly, as if he thought I hadn't heard him the first time.

Before I could respond, a light tapping on the door had me jumping out of his arms. I opened the door, and Val said, "Sorry, but I need to slip out and get to my parents' house before it gets too late." With hugs and promises to talk soon, she left.

Her departure prompted the slow exodus of our guests. Wendy and Dick were next.

Wendy said to Joshua, "I really did enjoy the writing samples Kim sent me. You have a very natural, engaging style. I meant it when I suggested you and Kim collaborate. I'll e-mail her about it next week."

Dick said to both of us, "Best Thanksgiving dinner I've ever had. Thank you so much."

Max and Adam left equally enthused, making jokes about food babies. Max made us promise to come hear them play soon and to bring Haley. He'd had his eyes on her a little too much all evening. He was too old for her, and no way would I double-date with my daughter, but I smiled and nodded as if I couldn't wait for us all to get together soon.

"Everything was so good, it was like an orgy in my mouth," Alec said as he helped Carly into her coat.

To which Carly added, "Totally gastrogasmic." Then she turned to Alec and asked, "Can I tell him?"

Alec busted out a wide grin and said, "Carly's pregnant."

"Oh my god, that's why you weren't drinking today. I'm so happy for you," Joshua said, giving Carly a big hug. He patted Alec on the back. "You're going to be a great dad."

"You will, too someday," Alec said, and they both laughed.

Joshua walked them downstairs. He was still smiling when he came back. I wondered if he was imagining what it would be like to be a father. I visualized him walking down the street with a baby strapped in a snuggly—a super, hands-on dad. I, on the other hand, had raised my daughter and had no desire to start over with a baby. It was too much to think about, and I pushed the thoughts aside.

By seven everyone had left except Paul, Haley, and Joshua. They helped me clean up. Once things were in relative order, Paul left and Haley said, "I should get going, too."

"Sure you don't want to stay the night?"

"No, Dad wants to leave insanely early tomorrow to beat the Tahoe rush."

Joshua offered to escort Haley to her car, but I wanted a little time alone with her. Besides, she'd only parked about a block down the street. He waited at the entrance of my building, insisting to watch us and make sure we were safe. I had no idea what he would do if we were attacked, but it was nice knowing he was there.

I asked Haley, "Did you enjoy yourself?"

"I did. Josh's friends are hella cool."

"What do you think of Joshua?"

"He's awesome, but why do you call him Joshua? Everyone else calls him Josh."

"I don't know." I'd have to think about that.

"Anyway, I like him, but I'm rooting for Dad. Don't give up on him."

"Oh, Haley, I waited over a year for him to come around, and he didn't." There were other issues, too, but she didn't need to know. "I don't know what he told you, but he never said he wanted to get back together."

"He may not have said it, but I know he misses you. He's going to love this." Haley held up the bag of leftovers I had packed to send home with her, including extra dressing I'd made as a peace offering for Jay and a dozen of the Braxton rolls. She popped open the trunk to load in her things. "Shoot," she said and picked up a brown file folder, the kind with a flap and elastic band around it, from the trunk floor. "Dad asked me to give this to you."

I took it, assuming it was the response to the settlement request. "Thank you. Be sure to call or text me when you get home."

She promised and gave me a hug. Just before she got into the car, she said, "He's going to ask about Joshua. What do you want me to tell him?"

"Tell him I met an awesome guy who makes me happy."

Chapter 27

JOSHUA'S OUTLINE ACTED as beacon in the distance drawing my focus. As I approached him, and his face became more and more distinct, the less clear I was about him, about us as a couple. Seeing him with his friends underlined all the reasons our relationship could never go to the next level. How could I have been so optimistic the night before and so uncertain now?

He smiled as I reached him. His soulful eyes sought mine, and his affection for me shone all over his face. Why was I questioning my good fortune? Joshua was awesome. He was kindhearted, had a generous soul, looked like Chace Crawford and cooked like Gordon Ramsey. What new couple doesn't have periods of adjustment? I really liked him. It didn't matter that I wasn't completely head-over-heels yet. I was well on my way to falling in love with him.

He grasped my hand and asked, referring to the folder in my other hand, "What's that?"

"Legal documents from Jay about the house."

"Huh," he grunted, leading me up the stairs. When we walked through the door he asked, "Isn't your divorce settled?"

I tossed the folder on the coffee table. "Just a few loose ends." We hadn't discussed the financial terms of my divorce since the night we dined at Simone's. I saw no reason to start now. Exhausted, Joshua dropped onto the couch. I plopped onto his lap and toed off my heels.

"Oh, so now it's okay to sit on my lap?"

I covered my eyes with my hand. "Thought you were letting it go."

"Nope, not letting it go." I moved to scooch off him, but he yanked me back. "You don't have to move. I just want to know what was up with you—you were pushing me away all day. Then you were pissed because I didn't help with dessert, but I didn't even know what you were doing. All you had to do was ask and I would've helped."

"I know, and I'm sorry. I freaked out with Val and Haley being here. They knew about you, but thought you were just …."

His face hardened. "*Checker Boy,* your little bed buddy?"

"*No,* and I told her not to call you that anymore." I cupped his face in my hands and made him look at me. "I'm incredibly lucky and proud to have you as my boyfriend."

"Thank you." He pecked my lips. "So why were you freaked?"

"They've never seen me with anyone other than Jay. I'd worried they'd think you were too young for me. So there was that, and Haley still hopes Jay and I will get back together."

"Understandable, but she seemed okay with me by the time she left."

"Yeah, she thinks you're 'awesome' and your friends are 'hella cool.'"

He chuckled. "That's hella awesome, don't you think?"

"Totally dope," I joked, and then admitted, "I felt old around your friends. I didn't know what to say to them and worried they viewed me as a mom more than your girlfriend. I don't want you seeing me that way."

He lifted my chin to look at him. "They thought you and Haley looked like sisters. You're too young and way too sexy to be my mom. Keep your mothering to Haley, and it won't be a problem."

"That's fair. Is that why you got mad at me for showing Wendy your writing?"

"Somewhat, but I'm over it."

"Good." I draped my arms around his neck and kissed him but didn't get his usual response.

"Did you know when I made the toast, you looked at everyone except me?"

"I'm sorry. Your toast was lovely." I kissed him again, but his lips remained stiff.

He leaned back and searched my eyes. "I meant what I said earlier."

"About what?"

"You know …."

I did know, and it hurt to see the uncertainty in his eyes. "You have to know that I really, really like you."

"But you don't feel the same," he said, almost as a challenge.

"I didn't say that."

"So this is the part you need to take slow?"

"Yes," I affirmed. "I want to be with you, but it's what I need. Are you okay with that?"

He nodded, and I snuggled against him with my head resting against his chest. I thought we were moving on until he said, "This morning when I told you I've never been happier and could kiss you all day, you dismissed me like I was an over-eager puppy."

I cringed, ashamed of how I'd treated him. He deserved so much better. "I'm sorry I made you feel that way. Like I said, I was on edge with everyone being here."

He shook his head, not buying it. "Not to sound egotistical, but I'm used to women wanting me more than I want them. With you it's the opposite. It always feels like I want you more than you want me."

That was exactly the way I had felt the last couple years with Jay. It may have been true, but I so, so didn't want him to feel that way. "Joshua, look at me." He gazed into my eyes, and I murmured, "I want you." I kissed his lips. "I want you," I murmured again and kissed his neck.

I repeated those words, kissing my way down his body, as I slid off the couch and knelt between his legs. Holding his gaze and without saying a word, I unbuckled his belt, unbuttoned and unzipped his pants, and freed him from his briefs. He gasped and ran his fingers through my hair, while I demonstrated just how much I wanted him.

Afterwards he lifted me onto his lap, cradled me in his arms and whispered, "How did you know that's exactly what I needed?"

It was something eighteen years of marriage had taught me, something which had been successful with Jay countless times, and no doubt, women around the world had discovered would put their men in a happy place without fail. I didn't view it as a trick, rather simply giving him what he needed more than words of assurance. It gave me great pleasure to do it for him.

I smiled into his chest. "Did it make you happy?"

"Being in the same room with you makes me happy; that sent me flying." He chuckled. Still holding me, he staggered to his feet and carried me out of the room.

———

An hour later, I laid partially on top of Joshua while he peacefully slept and ran my hand over his smooth stomach. His love making had been so different from even a couple nights prior. Tonight, he had been much less technical, less in control—as if he'd stopped worrying about impressing me with his sexual knowhow and just loved me. I had enjoyed it more than when he'd consciously played my body; although that had been pretty good, too.

Did he want me more than I wanted him? He had said *the first of many, many Thanksgivings* in his toast; he was thinking of the future. I was too, but more like a few months ahead, not years, so he likely had been right about that.

Was that part of the reason why he was crazy about me? He'd said he was used to women wanting him more. I'd seen the way his girl had gazed at him at the restaurant in Davis, and the way Zoey had gravitated toward him at De Noche. He had flirted with me aplenty while working at Nugget, and he'd been about to ask me out while his girlfriend watched through a window at Crepeville. From everything he'd said, and I'd heard and seen, he had been an operator. Maybe he liked that he had to work for my affection.

Jay had taken me for granted, and I had let him. I'd been so paranoid about appearing needy that I had let him get away with giving me less. Maybe the secret to keeping a man was not to give him quite as much love as he gave you. Give him just enough to keep him happy, but not enough to get comfortable.

It was a depressing thought. I hated to think the day I loved Joshua as much as he loved me would be the day that I started to bore him.

Joshua groaned, lifted his arm out from under me, and rolled on his side. Poor guy had been up extra early and had a huge weekend ahead. According to Paul, the Friday and Saturday after Thanksgiving would be their busiest days at the restaurant outside of Valentine's and Mother's Day, and they'd be slammed all the way through New Year's with parties and catering events. My sweetie would be working twelve to fourteen-hour days and needed his sleep.

I kissed his cheek and gingerly slid out of bed, careful not to wake him. Craving pumpkin pie, I snatched the last slice from the refrigerator, brought it to the living room and curled up on the couch feeling content. I'd had my first dinner party in San Francisco. It could have gone better, but overall, dinner had been a hit. A man who adored me—thought he loved me—slept in my bed, and we'd navigated our first rough day without crashing. There was a possibility of a writing project with Joshua, and I didn't have to share my pie with Jay, who had a thing for cold pumpkin pie and always gobbled it up before I could get a second piece.

Since Joshua was out for the night, it seemed a safe time to review the documents Jay had prepared. He'd gone along with everything I'd asked for in the past. I saw no reason why he wouldn't this time provided the appraisal was fair.

I opened the flap and pulled out the contents. Instead of legal documents, the folder contained a short letter, more like a note, and pages and pages of photos, chronicling our life together, taped to regular printing paper with handwritten captions under each picture.

As I read the note, my face heated and my heart sped up. Jay unequivocally wanted me back. He wrote: *The day I walked out, you said you wouldn't let me go without a fight. Well you should know I intend to fight to win you back. Since you don't want to see me, I put together some pictures that I hope will change your mind. I want us to spend a weekend alone together. If after that, you still want to make everything final, I'll sign off on whatever you want.*

I set the note down and picked up the pictures. The first was my seventh-grade class photo. The caption read: *I remember watching you walk into health class the first day of seventh grade. I thought you were so pretty. I was too scared to talk to you, but you were my first crush.* The next was of me in eighth grade. My image had been cut out of a larger photo. Jay had written: *California Junior Scholastic Club. I swiped this one from Yearbook class and cut your picture out. I kept it hidden under my mattress. I used to stare at it and daydream about you.*

The photos kept going: Jay and me at the beach, homecoming, prom, our wedding day, the day we came home with Haley, birthdays, Thanksgivings, and Christmases. There was even a picture of Leonardo DiCaprio and Kate Winslet from Titanic with a notation. *I would give anything to see you look at me the way you did after we saw this movie. I would even sit through the movie again.* He drew a little smile next to it.

There were photos from every year we had spent together and ended with the picture he had taken of Haley and me just before I drove her to the airport the morning that he'd left me. The caption read: *The day I made the biggest mistake of my life, walking away from my other half and love of my life.*

Tears had been trickling down my cheeks; now they flooded, and my chest heaved. I ugly sobbed with my whole body shaking, the way I had the day he'd left. I hated Jay for making me relive it. The pain had been buried, but not gone. I took deep breaths, trying to regain some control. Before I could, Joshua walked in wearing only his pajama bottoms.

He took one look at me and the pile on the coffee table and knew what had happened. His face was unreadable as the silence grew. Then his eyes softened, and he squatted in front of me. I fell against him, with my face smashed into his bare chest. He enfolded me in his arms and whispered, "I'm here. I gotcha. Just get it all out."

He held me and rubbed my back until I was empty. Grabbing my pumpkin pie-smeared napkin, he used it to wipe up my nose and the mess I'd made on his chest and led me back to bed. Without questions or accusations, he straightened first the sheet, then the blanket, and finally tossed my comforter on top of me, adjusting the edges neat and even. He scooted in beside me, adjusted the covers one more time, and spooned me securely against him.

⁓

I woke to Joshua fully dressed and sitting next to me with a cup of coffee in his hand. I hoped to God he wasn't pulling a Kevin. He wasn't happy, but he didn't seem angry either. He asked, "How are you feeling?"

"Like I've been through an emotional meat grinder."

"You look about that way," he said with a slight smile, "but you're still beautiful."

"Thanks for that." I sat up. He handed me the coffee and I took a sip. "And thanks for this. I really need it this morning."

"I figured you would." He tucked my hair behind my ears and grimaced. "I shouldn't have, but I looked at the pictures and read Jay's note."

I set the cup down. If he hadn't been so great the night before, and I wasn't feeling so guilty, I would've been outraged. "Oh." Damn Jay to hell. He had to do this to me now?

Joshua's eyes rolled upward, and he mumbled, "Shit," under his breath. "I take it the documents, whatever they are, completely sever you from him?" I nodded and he said, "Do it—spend the weekend with him."

"I can't believe you're so calm about it—that you're encouraging this."

"Face it, he's a barrier between us. You obviously have deep feelings for him; otherwise, you wouldn't have been so upset last night."

"We have a complicated history. That doesn't mean I want to be with him anymore."

"The photo of you sitting on his lap in front of a Christmas tree really got me." His voice cracked, and he shook his head. "You two looked so in love it glowed off the page ... I've never seen you look that happy and fuck, he goddam has dimples—"

"Joshua—"

"I can't compete with him."

I cupped his face and made him look at me. "Hey, I'm not asking you to do anything."

"It's not just him. It's the whole life you shared with him." He took a deep breath and exhaled. "I'll give you a free pass to figure it out. Sleep with him if that's what it takes, and I won't ask questions."

I dropped my hands from his face and hugged my knees, feeling off balance with the entire conversation. I did have feelings for Jay—a jumble of conflicting, twisted up emotions, but I also had feelings for Joshua and didn't want to hurt him. I searched Joshua's eyes. "Are you sure you're okay with me seeing him?"

"It's bullshit and I fucking hate it, but I don't think you can fully commit to me unless you do it. Obviously, I hope you close the book on him. If you do, you have to promise no more Jay. No beef bourguignon dinners, no sending home leftovers for him—"

"Hold on, they were for Haley."

"Your daughter doesn't like dressing, but half of it went home with her." I thought he hadn't noticed. He added, "Or buying him furniture."

"You know about that?"

"Uh-huh. Haley mentioned it. I mean nothing, no seeing him outside of what's unavoidable for Haley. He can't be a part of our life. I won't do this a second time."

He meant it. After what he'd witnessed the night before, I couldn't blame him. Hearing basically the same message from Kevin and now Joshua, I couldn't argue either. "I promise."

"See him this weekend. Hopefully, I'll be too busy to think about what you're doing."

"Or not doing," I insisted.

"*Not* sounds really good to me." He leaned over and pecked my lips. "Come have breakfast with me. I have to head out to work soon."

I followed him to the dining room, feeling guilty that he'd made me breakfast after everything that had happened. We ate and talked about the specials Joshua had planned for the weekend menu, completely avoiding the Jay subject.

On his way out, I asked, "See you Sunday night?"

He shook his head. "I'm going to say goodbye now."

"Joshua—"

His hand covered my mouth. "Don't." He gave me a full body hug and whispered, "I told myself I wasn't going to tell you I loved you until Christmas, but I don't regret it. I knew the risk I was taking when I got involved with you. Please don't call me unless you're coming back to me. Whether I see you again or not, I'll be okay. I don't blame you for anything."

He kissed me as if it were for the last time. I tasted salty tears and wasn't sure if they were his or mine. As soon as he pulled away, he jetted down the stairs without looking back. I shut the door with my body shaking and tears streaming, not wanting it to be the last time but knowing it could be.

There was no denying Jay had ignited feelings I'd thought were stamped out. We'd had far more good times than bad, and there were times I craved my old life. I missed my big, cheery yellow kitchen, walking to Farmer's Market, and relaxing on our patio. I missed family dinners and the adrenaline rush I used to get every time Jay walked through the door after work. I missed being with someone who didn't need an explanation for why I laughed at some things or cried over others; someone with whom our shared experiences made us like minded.

I had Joshua now, though; my life in San Francisco was fuller and better every day. I was making friends and becoming involved with the writers' scene. Joshua was introducing me to the various neighborhoods and clubs and little cafes I never would have found on my own. Since moving to the city, life seemed more colorful and faster—a never ending stream of images and snippets of overheard conversations that sparked ideas for stories. I loved city living and couldn't see myself going back to a life in Davis.

I gathered up the strewn pages on my coffee table, studying them as I arranged them in chronological order. So what if we hadn't had a perfect marriage; the pictures were empirical evidence we'd been genuinely happy for a lot of years. And Jay wanted me—unequivocally, he loved me and wanted me. *I intend to fight to win you back.*

He'd blindsided me again, making my insides a mass of buzzing nerves. Not just my insides, but my hands shook, and my throat was tight. The tables had flipped; now I had the upper hand. The knowledge gave me pause. When I called him, I wanted to be in control, no voice cracking with emotion. I showered, styled my hair, and put on make-up. (Not that Jay could see me, but it gave me confidence.) Only then did I call Jay. It occurred to me this was a bad weekend since he and Haley were already in Tahoe. He might rather ski.

He didn't. "I told Haley I might be called away on business and not be able to stay. I figured you wouldn't want her to know what's going on."

"Thank you, I'd rather her not. I don't want her to get her hopes up."

"Does that go for me, too?"

"Especially you. I feel like I'm being blackmailed into this."

"You are. You didn't leave me a choice." He chuckled, and asked sounding buoyant, "How soon can you be home?"

"I am home."

"Come on, you know what I mean."

If I met him in Davis, he'd be at an unfair advantage. "Won't Hailey be with you?"

"She ran into a group of kids she knows from high school. I'm sure she'd love to keep the cabin for herself and her friends. She can catch a ride back with them."

Now that I knew Haley wasn't the angel I'd thought, her staying in Tahoe with icy roads and a group of kids worried me. "No, I'd rather her not be there by herself."

"Okay, I'll come to you. How about if I get us a room at the Mark Hopkins? I can be there in time for dinner and take you on a real date."

Neutral territory sounded good. Moreover, an evening in a public place would keep things safe and civil, but a hotel room? "Only if I get my own room."

"Same room with two beds? I promise not to crawl in with you unless I'm invited."

"Alright, Mark Hopkins and two beds." If worse came to worse, I could always go home. "But why don't you stay and get in at least one day of skiing? We can meet tomorrow."

"I'm coming now. I'll pick you up no later than six."

Chapter 28

I SPENT THE AFTERNOON packing up my fine china and hauling it back to the storage closet in the basement, doing laundry, mopping floors, and anything else I could think of to stay busy. If I truly was going to honor Joshua's trust to do what I had to do to move on, reuniting with Jay had to be a possibility, as was shutting that door forever. Of course, Jay could regret asking for a reconciliation before the night was over. I couldn't see any way around one—possibly all—of us being deeply hurt before the weekend was over. No wonder I felt nauseous and jittery all day.

By the time Jay called at five-thirty to let me know he was over the bridge, I was determined to be open to wherever the evening led us. I chugged down the glass of wine I'd been sipping, dabbed on some lipstick and ran down to meet him. He pulled up in a shiny new silver Mercedes. I threw my overnight bag in the backseat and jumped in.

"Nice wheels," I said. "When did you get this?"

"Couple weeks ago. My one indulgence since getting the Conway payout." He glanced over at me and smiled. "I'll buy you one, too if you come home with me."

"Sorry, can't buy my love."

He laughed. "Worth a shot."

"Not a bad one, but can I ask a favor tonight?"

"What's that?"

"We both know the reason for this weekend, but can we not talk about it tonight? Can we shoot for a pleasant evening and get readjusted to each other first?"

"I like that idea a lot."

When we arrived at the hotel, I watched him checked us in and allowed myself to appreciate him anew. He was aging well and looked great in his jeans and leather jacket. I couldn't help a little pride creeping into my chest. Jay had come from a working-class family and here he was an impressively successful attorney, checking us into one of the nicest hotels in the city, not looking or seeming to feel out of place.

He arranged for the bellman to deliver our things to the room, and we stepped out into the nippy San Francisco air. Neither of us was dressed up or in the mood for a formal dinner. He suggested *Cosi Fan Tutte*, a cozy trattoria just down the hill, which we had stumbled on years ago. The food was classic homey Italian and very good.

As we began our descent down Powell Street, I tripped on my boot heel. He caught me and took my hand. He asked, "Does this bother you?"

Maybe it should have, but it didn't. "No, it's nice."

He didn't let go until we were seated at a small table in the corner, and then only reluctantly. We chose the Prix Fixe for two, and Jay selected an unpretentious bottle of Valpolicella. Ordering gave us something to focus on, but once done, we were on our own.

Jay fiddled with his fork, and I asked, "Are you nervous?"

He chuckled. "More than I was on our first date. Honestly, I'm sweating bullets here. I'm scared I'll say something that will screw things up."

"I don't think you will. I want to be here."

He cracked a genuine smile. "I'm glad. You know, you're more beautiful than ever. You're actually more attractive now than you were in your twenties."

I laughed. "Now that's going a bit over the top, don't you think?"

"No, you're still the prettiest girl in the room," he said with the sweetest sincerity.

My cheeks heated from the unbridled affection in his voice. "Thank you."

The waiter brought our wine, and I took the opportunity to switch topics. "How was Thanksgiving at your sister's?"

"About what you'd expect—football and beer all day followed by dry turkey."

"How's Pops doing?" His dad had struggled since Maggie passed away.

"He's better; didn't cry once. He really appreciated the birthday card and sweater you sent him. It was very thoughtful of you to remember."

"Of course, I love Pops."

"He loves you, too." He chuckled. "You should have heard him grumbling all day about how I'd divorced the best cook in the family." He quickly glanced at me, unsure if he'd stepped on touchy ground.

I didn't care; I was the best cook. "That wasn't always the case. Remember the first dinner we hosted your parents? What a disaster." I'd attempted to fry chicken and ended up with a pile of greasy, burnt pieces that were raw in the middle. I had burst into tears, and Pops had gone out and bought us KFC. Later, Maggie taught me how to fry chicken, bless her heart.

We laughed and Jay said, "You were just a teenager, my beautiful child bride."

"We were so young. Looking at Haley now, I can't imagine her being a wife and mother for at least another five or six years."

"Try ten, but we were more mature than her at that age."

"You know, I think you're right. She has a lot of growing up to do."

"Being parents forced us to grow up fast." We were getting awfully close to dangerous territory. Jay veered us another direction. "What's this I hear about you writing fiction again?"

"How did you know about that?"

"I stopped by to say hello to Val's parents last night before I headed back to Davis." He shrugged. "Anyway, Val was there."

He knew she would be. I wondered what else she'd told him, particularly about Joshua. "Val's parents, huh?"

"Sure, I've always liked them." He picked up his glass and took a sip. "Not bad." He set it back down and leaned toward me. "So tell me about what you're writing. Is it a novel?"

We went on that way, catching up while steering clear of emotional topics that would be inappropriate in a public place. It wasn't unpleasant but didn't move us any particular direction. Then the waiter brought tiramisu for two.

Jay snickered and that got me giggling. Apparently, Jay also remembered our creative use of tiramisu one night while on one of our Napa get-a-way weekends. We had to leave an extra big tip for the maid afterwards.

Our eyes met and Jay stopped laughing. "I've really missed you."

The pain and longing in his eyes and voice squeezed my heart. "I've missed you, too."

He smiled and reached across the table for my hand. "Should I ask for a to-go-box?"

A tug of lust built low in my stomach. I met his smile and held his gaze. Then I picked my fork and took a bite. "No."

"Tease," he joked and lightly bit the palm of my hand before letting it go.

After that, Jay's frisky vibe was on. He held my hand again as we walked back up the hill to the hotel. While we waited at a crosswalk, he put his arm around me and rested his lips against the top of my head. Half of me wanted him—really wanted him. I wanted to know what it would be like to make love to him again and if the sparks would fly just as they had the last time he'd kissed me. I wanted to feel his skin against me and taste his tongue in my mouth.

The other half of me fought to bolt. What if I fell crazy in love with him again only to have the same thing happen? Only next time I would be even older, and it would be even harder to start over. I'd lose Joshua and a huge, huge part of me didn't want to lose him. A huge part of me wanted to jump in a cab and go to De Noche just to see his face.

When we walked into the lobby of the hotel, I balked. Jay felt it and his face flashed with disappointment. He recovered quickly and asked, "Want to go to Top of the Mark?"

I agreed and we stepped into an empty elevator headed to the nineteenth floor. Jay put his arm around me and said close to my ear, "Try to relax. I promise not to push you."

The hotel sat at the top of Nob Hill, and the bar took up the entire top floor of the hotel; consequently, it offered spectacular views of the city. We found an empty high-top by the window facing north. We were underdressed, but no one seemed to care. Out of the one hundred martini choices, I selected pomegranate and he ordered a Macallan 18 neat.

We listened to a Jazz band with a female singer crooning American standards like *Someone to Watch Over Me* and *It Had to Be You*. It was so different from the bars I'd been to since our divorce. Club Violet, where I had met Kevin, and The Hideout, an after-hours club Joshua recently had taken me to, were a world apart from the posh sedateness of Top of the Mark. It was lovely.

Jay silently took my hand and led me to the dance floor. I fell into an easy step with him as he smoothly maneuvered us around the other couples. We were one of the youngest pairs dancing.

"I don't care if it makes me an old fart," he said, "I'll take this over a loud, crowded nightclub any night of the week."

I wholeheartedly agreed. "Aren't you glad I made you take dance lessons with me?"

"It's a good skill to have." He gave me a little twirl that ended with a dip, making me laugh. When he pulled me up, he gripped my hand close to his chest. I could smell his cologne—the same cologne I had sprayed on my pillow after he'd left. The fragrance had mingled with his skin creating the unique Jay scent I had loved for so long. I inhaled deeply, and my body automatically fitted into his embrace. He'd only held me a couple times since he'd walked out, but the weight of his arms, dents and curves of his muscles, and fluid movement were still achingly familiar.

We had another cocktail and danced until the band ended their last set. I'd had more than enough alcohol for the night and didn't have any excuse to put off going to our room. When we got there, Jay fumbled with the key card, dropping it twice before opening the door.

Chapter 29

*W*HEN WE WERE married, sharing the sink while brushing our teeth and getting ready for bed had been common. Tonight, I went in first and then got into the bed closest to the wall while he did his bathroom routine. Jay came out wearing his pajama bottoms and t-shirt. He glanced at me, hesitated, got into the other bed, and turned off the bedside lamp between us.

A lack of muffled noises from the adjacent rooms and hallway magnified the silence. Jay was too motionless and wasn't making the little noises he made when he slept.

Jay cracked first. "Will you get in bed with me? Promise, I won't try anything."

The wine and cocktails should have knocked us out, but we were never going to sleep with so much to say between us. His nearness pulled on me, too. I slipped in beside him and cuddled next to him. "Better?"

"Much better." He put his arm around me, and I snuggled closer. He said in the dark, "I've missed this more than anything else. It's so lonely sleeping alone. This whole time, I haven't slept with anyone else."

"What about all your little girlfriends?"

"You'd know I was lying if I told you that I didn't have sex, but I never stayed the night with anyone. I always went to their place and came home afterwards."

"How come? Didn't they want you to stay?"

"Some did, but it didn't feel right—besides, I didn't consider any of them my girlfriend. I always got turned off before it got that far."

"Just how many women did you have sex with?"

"Oh Kimmy, you don't want to know, and it doesn't matter. I didn't love any of them."

The image of hundreds of women crawling all over Jay's naked body made me shudder. I didn't want to know. "Is that why you left me?"

He rolled over and turned on the light. Then he rolled back and rested his head on the pillow facing me. "What? So I could have sex with other women?"

"Yeah, is that why?"

"It wasn't the main reason, but I was curious about what it would be like to be with someone else. Weren't you a little curious, too?"

"Maybe for half a second, but I always only wanted you. I was so mad at you for putting me in that position."

"Are you still angry?"

"Not about that, but yes, about other things. So how was it? Live up to your fantasies?"

"No. I don't know what I'd expected. It was never as good as it was between the two of us. Nobody else knows me as well as you do."

For crying out loud, was he back for the sex? I couldn't help laughing. "Is that why you want me back? You miss the way I lick your dick and suck your balls?"

He snorted with laughter. "Are you drunk?"

Saying something dirty and a tad shocking cracked him up every time. It had been our private joking-in-bed thing since we were teenagers. "Only a little bit, and don't worry, I'm only raunchy with you."

"God, I hope not with anyone else." He bumped his pelvis against me. "I've missed it, but it's not the only reason I want you back."

"Alright," I said seriously, "Tell me, what has made you do a one-eighty?"

"It's hard to explain."

I gave him a light slap on his chest. "Try."

"Okay, okay, but I don't have a simple answer. It's a compilation of things that made me realize how much I still love you. I'm not sure where to start."

"Then start at the beginning. Were you happy when you first left?"

"More like exhilarated. I'd been under so much pressure for so long, and the instant I walked, it felt like the weight of the world was off my shoulders."

"What do you mean? We'd finally gotten to a point where money wasn't a struggle, and Haley was going to college. You left when everything should have gotten easy."

"Yeah, but it felt like there was even more pressure to be this dream couple … to prove to your parents and everyone else that we'd made it. I know you felt it too."

"I wanted us to do well, but I never felt like we had to hit some arbitrary gold standard."

"That's not true. Why was it so important to you to have the house just so? Or that we had to be somehow more in love than our couple friends?"

"I wanted to give you a nice home because you worked hard and deserved it. For God's sake, I loved you. I never thought the depth of our love was a competition." Thinking back, there had been times when I'd been defensive of our marriage, but mainly, I'd wanted a stable and loving home for our little family. "I admit, the first ten years or so that we were married I felt like I had something to prove, but I swear I let that go. I'm sorry I made you feel that way."

"It wasn't all you; I put a lot of pressure on myself. Anyway, the high faded fast."

"What did you do when you were free?"

"Embarrassing shit, things you would expect from someone half our age."

"Like …?"

"Like when I ran out of clean underwear, instead of doing laundry, I bought new."

"How long did that go on?"

"About a month." He scowled. "That got expensive."

I couldn't help shaking my head. "Okay, what else?"

"One time I left dirty dishes in the sink for a week."

"Eeewwww, gross!"

"It was. Now I know why you'd always insisted on dishes being washed before we went to bed. I used to resent you for it, but now I'm a believer."

"Hallelujah and praise the Lord," I joked.

"Ha ha. The thing is all my little rebellions never lived up to the expectation in my head."

I propped myself up on my elbow and contemplated him. "If that's all it was, you would have come around sooner. You didn't leave me because you wanted to go crazy for a month."

"No, I didn't but that was the beginning of me waking up." He stared out in space thinking for a while before he said, "You know that feeling when you move into a new house, and it takes a while before it feels like home?"

"Yeah, I know the feeling."

"It's the way I've felt."

"You did move into a new apartment."

He propped up on his elbow and stared into my eyes. "But I still have that feeling all the time. I keep waiting for it to go away, but it hasn't happened. I haven't been able to get into any routine—nothing feels right. When you moved out of the house and I moved back in with Haley, I expected my life to normalize. I really thought I'd get my equilibrium back, but I haven't. It's been a year and a half since we split, and I still feel so disoriented. It's like I've been driving in a circle and can't find my way home. I don't think I can without you."

I reached up and stroked his cheek. "I've seen that lost look you get, but I didn't know what it meant."

"Don't feel sorry for me. I did it to myself." He dropped back on the pillow and stared at the ceiling. "After my mom died, I really thought I was keeping it together. Truth was I went a little crazy. I wasn't thinking clearly. I kept seeing my life coming to end, and I never got a chance to be young … somehow, I got it mixed up in my head that you were holding me back from living, and yeah, part of that was going to bars, getting drunk, and you know …."

Oh, I knew. Boinking cocktail waitresses with big tits.

He turned to me and gripped my hand. "All of those things aside, your apology for laughing at me made me really rethink everything. When you had mocked me, it had felt like you didn't respect me … like you were rejecting me. I was so angry with you for it, but now, I know you'd been trying to keep me grounded. I'm sorry, I'm so sorry for getting so angry with you." Jay's eyes welled, and he took a deep breath.

"We both made mistakes, not just you. In retrospect, I think I didn't want to talk about our problems because if we didn't talk about them, I could pretend they didn't exist. I never meant to belittle you. I do respect you."

"Thank you. You seem to be happy and doing fine, though." He cracked a small smile. "How ironic is that?"

"For a while I wasn't sure if I'd ever be fine again, but I've finally found my balance. I know you will, too. This last month I've been happier than I've been in a long time."

Jay sat all the way up. "The guy you've been seeing, Joshua, how serious is it?"

I sat up too, unsure how to answer. Joshua and I hadn't been together long enough to predict anything. "Serious enough he stays the night."

"What, like every now and then?"

My pulse sped up. "No, more like a few times a week."

He asked stone faced, "Does he know you're spending the weekend with me?"

"Yes. He doesn't like it, but he thinks it's something I need to do to resolve things with you." Jay didn't need to know that Joshua had left with no expectation of our relationship resuming. "He's giving me a free pass this weekend."

"You're kidding?" His face grimaced and his body tensed as I watched him piece everything together. Then he grunted, "Fuck," and got out of bed, pacing around the room. "Please, tell me this whole finalizing thing isn't because of some kid you met at Nugget."

I got out of bed too. "First of all, he's not a kid. He's a talented chef and a grown man who conducts himself with more maturity than some thirty-seven-year-olds I know."

Jay stopped pacing and took it on the chin like a man. "Okay, I deserved that."

"Secondly, no. It's not because of him. I would be doing it anyway."

"Then why?" he asked bewildered. "I have no problem sharing my income with you, so I don't see why you would unless there was someone else."

"Because, as long as I take your money there can't be *someone else*. I'm tied to you, and I don't want to be the discarded wife dragging on your coattails, dependent on your largesse. If we're not going to be together, then I need a final break to get on with my new life."

"Your new life can't include me?"

I shook my head as tears trickled down my cheeks. "No. You'd always be between me and another man. I don't want to spend the rest of my life alone. The money isn't worth it."

"Hold on. Are you saying either we get back together, or I'm out of your life completely?"

Jay stared me down, waiting for an answer. It was one thing to contemplate in a theoretical sense; it was another to tell him to his face. How do you cut out someone so entwined with you and not feel the loss to your very core?

Shaking, I swallowed hard. "Yes."

Jay got his determined, no-way-in-hell-am-I-going-to-lose glint in his eyes. "I'm not going to let that happen." He cupped my face and wiped my tears with his thumbs. Then his eyes drilled into me as if he were trying to reach the very center of my being. "I can't let that happen. I made a massive mistake, but I'll fix it. I can't lose you forever."

"I don't think you can fix it."

Jay's eyes welled up again, and this time he couldn't blink back his tears. "I know I hurt you. I would do anything to start the last two years over again. You're still angry, but I know you love me. What we shared doesn't go away. I love you. I've always loved you. I just lost my head and blocked it out for a while."

I jerked away. "*How could you block it out?* Do you know what that feels like to hear? To know you had sex with me night after night, but couldn't look at me because you couldn't stand to see the love in my eyes? It hurts *too much* and, yes, I'm angry. I'm so flipping mad at you for everything you've done! If I was a guy, I'd punch your lights out." I shook my head in disbelief. "You think all you have to do is say you love me, and it'll all go away?"

"No, but what else do expect me to do? You know how sorry I am, and I'd do anything to make it up to you. Hit me if you want." He took my hand and balled it into a fist. "Just get it over with and hit me—punch me as hard as you can if it'll make you feel better."

"I'm not going to *hit* you." I yanked my hand away and sank onto the edge of the bed.

"You're just going to have to find a way to forgive me, then. You have to. Please, don't make the same mistake your father made."

I gaped up at him. "What the hell does my father have to do with it?"

"He's never forgiven you for marrying me. It cost him his daughter and you lost your father because of it. Don't punish us the same way."

For the first time I had an inkling of the hurt and betrayal my father must have felt. Could I ever forgive Jay after the depth of pain he had inflicted—a pain I could not live through again?

I shook my head and whispered, "I can't."

He knelt in front of me and took my hands. "Forgive me, please, just forgive me. I'll do whatever it takes. I'm begging you to give me another chance. Kimmy ... please forgive me ... please." He broke—the same way I had the morning he'd left. Tears streaked down his cheeks, his chest heaving and convulsing, and he dropped his head on my lap.

I slipped down beside him and wrapped my arms around his quaking body. He grabbed onto me and buried his head in my breasts. I rocked him, ran my fingers through his hair, and soothed him as I would a child.

"I need you, Kimmy. You have no idea how much I need you. I don't know how to live without you."

"Shhh ... it's okay. I'm here. Everything is going to be okay."

"I love you, Kimmy. I love you so much."

"I know."

"Okay. I just need you to know."

"I know."

"Okay, okay then ... okay."

With his head against my breasts, I continued to hold him while his trembling subsided and breathing evened. I knew the exact shape of his head and the way his hair smelled. He smelled the same since the first time he'd held me. His arms were still strong and his body warm and solid just as it always had been. I had never wanted his arms to let go of me and now he was back ... wanting me ... needing me ... loving me.

In my heart, I knew his capacity for love, and deep down he was a good man. He was my first love, the father of my child; he'd held me and comforted me when I'd had no one else, and stood by me, supporting and encouraging me as I'd grown into being a woman, a wife, and a mother. We had shared too many profoundly personal things for anyone ever to replace him. He'd hurt me, but he'd wounded himself just as deeply. I could find happiness and live without him, but I loved him. I'd always loved him.

I didn't want to be like my father. For Jay and me to have a chance, I had to let go of my anger and resentment, and in that moment, I made my choice. All the pain I'd locked up bubbled to the surface and released. My own body convulsed, and a low moan came from somewhere deep inside of me. I clung to Jay as tightly as he clung to me.

"I forgive you, Jay. I do. I forgive you. And I love you. I love you so much."

Our mouths found each other, and we made our way back to the bed. I braced for him to turn off the light, but he didn't. He laid me down and eased on top of me. He gazed into my eyes and said, "I love you, Kimberly Braxton"

Jay's weight on me was home. His weight, his scent, his taste in my mouth, all the things I had needed and craved; like a woman deprived of food and drink, I was starving for him. It was Jay, my Jay, who buried his head in my neck. It was my husband's back that my hands ran over. It was my husband who reached down and slipped off my pajama bottoms. Finally, it was my husband, thick and hard, who joined and became one with me, filling me in a way no one else could, moving with me in perfect rhythm, and as I cried out his name, my husband's eyes locked on mine just before he burst inside of me.

"Kimmy, oh my god, Kimmy, I've missed you so much," he murmured still inside of me.

"I've missed you, too."

He started to shift.

"Stay, don't move yet, please."

"I don't want to crush you."

"I don't care. Stay inside me, *please*."

"I'm not going anywhere. I swear I'll never leave you again."

The arm draping over my back was extra heavy, and it took a second to register that the arm wasn't Joshua's. Jay and I had made love one more time before falling asleep. We'd taken our time the second round, exploring and getting reacquainted with each other's bodies. Ripples flitting through my stomach warned me not to trust everything that had transpired. I'd been caught up in Jay's heart squeezing confessions; the lateness of the hour combined with the alcohol in our systems had heightened the drama. I rolled onto my back. Jay adjusted his arm on my tummy but didn't wake up.

He blocked his love for me. It was possible. To move on, I'd had to bury my love for him. I never should have allowed Jay to shortchange our relationship. It had to have made him think less of me. How can you love someone you don't respect?

Jay rolled onto his back and his eyes flickered open. A small smile played on his lips. "Morning, Babe. Sleep well?"

"Not bad. Yourself?"

"Like a baby." He stretched and put his arm around me. "How about we order room service and spend the day in bed, what do you say?"

I sat up. "Just because we made love last night doesn't mean everything is settled."

His smile slipped and his brow creased. "I know we have issues, but things will be different. I promise, I'll go to marriage counseling or whatever you want. We're already being more honest and talking—the way we used to. If you really have forgiven me, I know we can work things out."

"I have, but I have to ask you something—and I swear no matter what your answer is, I won't get mad."

He sighed and sat up, too. "Okay, what is it?"

"Is it *me* you really want or just *someone*? Are you afraid of being alone the rest of your life and that's why you want to get back together?"

"I thought you were going to ask a tricky question." He chuckled. "I've had plenty of time to think about it." He took my hand and played with it, so I knew he was nervous despite his confident laugh. "I'm sure I could've found someone else by now if all I wanted was companionship. I didn't seriously try because I think subconsciously, I knew no one could ever replace you. I want *you*, only you." He lifted my hand to his lips to make his point. "I think I'm like my dad. He always said he was only capable of having one great love in his life and that was my mom. You're it for me."

I knew what he meant. Jay was my one big, great love. It didn't mean I was incapable of loving someone else, but I could never love another man in the same, earth-shattering way. I nodded. "Remember that night you came over after the Conway win?"

"Of course."

"What was going through your head?"

"I didn't plan to seduce you, if that's what you're asking. I was excited about the win and making partner. Then you got upset, and everything went to shit. Next thing I knew, you were kicking me out."

"That's because I couldn't allow myself to be used by you."

"I realized that after I left. At the time, I was rattled by how out-of-my-mind turned on I was, and I knew what it would mean if we slept together. I couldn't sleep that night. I kept thinking about how much I missed coming home to you after work."

"Damn, I was hoping you were up all night with blue balls."

He barked a laugh, "Oh my god, I can't believe you said that."

I snickered, "Anyway, you were saying?"

"I was saying that I got up the next morning determined to talk to you about exploring a reconciliation, but—"

"When you got there, Kevin …."

"Yeah." Jay closed his eyes and ran his hand through his hair. When he spoke again, his voice was low and laced with regret, "I thought you'd already moved on. I was hurt and pissed off, so I didn't say all the things I'd planned."

"I broke up with him after you left."

"I didn't know that until weeks later, and by then you'd moved to San Francisco and didn't want to see me. I was waiting to make my move until you to stopped being so mad at me, but when you asked for a final settlement, I knew I couldn't wait any longer."

"I was angry *and hurt*. Seeing you was too hard and now … now …."

He put his hand on my cheek and searched my eyes. "What? What's worrying you?"

"You're going to have to forgive me for some things, too," I whispered.

He knew I was referring to Joshua. "Do you love him?"

"No, but I was really close." It was a selfish thing to admit. I guess I wanted him to know that I had choices. He wasn't the only man who valued me.

My dart hit the bullseye and anguish burst from his eyes. "It's my fault," he said and crushed me against his chest. "I can't believe how close I've come to losing you forever."

I immediately regretted hurting him to no purpose. Joshua posed no threat to Jay. Joshua had known before I did who I would choose. I hoped Joshua was right about his ability to easily fall out of love. Please God, let his feelings for me and mine for him fade quickly.

"Let's order room services. I need a shower and coffee before we talk about how this could work."

By the time I emerged from the bathroom, food had arrived. A table next to the window had been elegantly laid out with a tablecloth and dishes set just as if we were in the hotel restaurant. Jay had ordered enough food for three people. Our choices included eggs benedict, a crab and lobster omelet, lemon-ricotta pancakes, bacon and fresh fruit.

"Little hungry?" I asked.

"You gave me a workout last night." He grinned. "Actually, I was just covering my bases. I figured you'd like the omelet and pancakes."

He was right. I sat down and poured the coffee. Black for Jay and with cream for me. "You're spoiling me. Setting the bar rather high, don't you think?"

"It's been a rough year." He shrugged and offered a lopsided grin. "We deserve a treat."

We ate in silence for a few minutes. The omelet was delicious, made with fontina and a generous amount of lobster. Joshua would love it and undoubtedly could replicate it if he wanted. *Joshua*. Letting go of him wasn't going to be pain free. He had crept too far into my heart to ease out unnoticed.

After allowing the coffee to work its way through our systems, I sat up straight and said, "I want you to know how happy I am to be sitting next you—just looking at you, knowing I'm free to touch you."

He smiled and squeezed my hand. "Me, too."

"But we have some things to work out."

"Do you think getting back together would be a mistake?"

"No, I don't."

"Good. I'm willing to negotiate everything else. Tell me what you need."

I took a deep breath and stated as firmly as possible, "I won't move back to Davis. Living in the city has freed my mind in a way that's hard to explain. It's like I'm seeing the world through a different lens."

Jay's brows knit together, and he sighed. "I had a feeling you wouldn't want to move back. Based on the few times I've seen you and what Haley's told me, you thrive on city living."

"I do. I love it here."

"You've become, I don't know … more sophisticated, stronger. Whatever it is, it suits you, so sure, I get it. Besides, I think we need a fresh start. I love our house, but I haven't been comfortable since I moved back."

"Why do you suppose?" I asked, genuinely curious.

Jay shook his head and stared out the window. "Every time I walk in a room, I can't help wondering if you and that fireman … you know?" He shuddered.

I couldn't help laughing. "We didn't have sex all over the house if that's what's bothering you."

"I don't want to talk about him. Bottomline is I'm ready to let go of the house, and I have a plan that I think you'll like."

Due to the Conway win, Jay was close to convincing the other partners of the law firm to open a small satellite office in the Bay Area that focused on Intellectual Property. He could continue with Construction litigation while he built up the new department.

"We could live in the city, but we won't be able to afford the size of house we had in Davis," he added.

"I love the idea and I'm fine with a smaller place," I assured him. "When we bought the house, we thought we'd have more kids. That house was for a different set of dreams."

"Agreed. So new dreams?"

"Travel more, explore the city … make life an adventure."

Jay busted out his dimply toothpaste ad smile and tears crept to the brims of his eyes. "That's exactly what I was trying to explain to you the night of Haley's graduation."

I leaned over, wrapped my arms around his neck and kissed him. "I get it now. Sorry it took me so long."

Jay pulled me out of my chair and onto his lap. "Any more conditions?"

"Swear that you'll never leave me again," I demanded.

Jay looked deeply into my eyes, holding my gaze until nothing else in the room existed. There was only Jay, my husband and soulmate. "I swear."

"And promise that you'll tell me you love me at least once a day and really mean it."

A small smile played on his lips. "If I skip a day, can I double up on the next?"

I scowled and shook my head.

He chuckled. "Easy promise because I really do love you. I'll say it ten thousand times a day if you want."

Laughing with happiness unfurling inside me, I said, "I want."

"I love you, I love you, I love you, I love you, I love—"

I shut him up with a kiss and then settled against his chest with his strong arms wrapped around me. Our breathing synchronized, and I listened to his heartbeat drown out the last of my doubts and fears. His love reached my very core, warming me, making me feel like we shared one heart. At least for the moment, our love was strong and in equal proportion. I cherished the moment, fully aware that we would have our rocky days, but certain my husband was back and would never leave me again.

Acknowledgements

I would like to express my gratitude to Carolyn Waggoner and Kathy Williams for their insightful feedback and encouragement. Special thanks to David Sutton for his sharp pencil and keen editing eye and Adam Russ for sharing his extremely valuable male perspective. I'd also like to thank Scott Evans for his hospitality and allowing me to share early pages with the Blue Moon Writers group.

Many, many thanks to my husband, Ted, for telling me he loves me every day and putting up with me disappearing into my office to write and to my daughters, Annie and Katie Mac, who are unending sources of inspiration and love.

About the Author

Ten Thousand I Love Yous is Lisa Slabach's second novel. She is currently working on her third full-length manuscript and on a collection of short stories inspired by her experiences growing up in a small farm community in Washington's Yakima Valley. In addition to writing, Lisa works for a Fortune 500 Company, managing financial institution relationships. She is a long-time resident of Northern California and lives with her husband, one-hundred-forty-pound puppy and numerous goldfish. In her free time, she enjoys wine tasting, shopping with her daughters and cooking in her pink kitchen.

Under the working title *Broken,* the first chapter of *Degrees of Love* was published in the *Blue Moon Art and Literary Review*. *Broken* won the 2012 Merritt Contest for Women's Fiction and was awarded Second Place in the Fire and Ice Contest for Women's Fiction. Prior to publication, *Degrees of Love* was recognized as a Best Book of 2014 by Kirkus Review. *Degrees* made its full-length publishing debuted December 1, 2017 and was nominated for a 2017 Reviewer's Choice Award by RT Book Reviews.

www.lisaslabach.com

Degrees of Love

June, 2006

Chapter 1

I fired up the engine of my BMW and listened to it purr while I inhaled the leathery new car scent. Last week, I'd come home in love with my handsome ride, but ever since I'd felt guilty about the indulgence. Not so much anymore. I wanted one minute, a mere sixty seconds, simply to sit and savor my success, but I had to go. I'd promised my boys I'd cook dinner. I also had to break the news of my promotion to my husband and hoped he wouldn't object.

Putting the car in gear, I drove out of the San Francisco International Airport parking lot and wedged my way into the stream of commuters nudging south. It took about an hour to drive the paltry thirteen miles to my home in San Carlos. After a long day of travel and meetings, I was too tired for any kind of TGIF joie de vivre.

I stepped out of the car just as Micah ran out the front door. "Mom's home!" Jason followed close on his heels. "Mommy!"

I hugged them close. The boys were getting so big, and I wondered how much longer they would race to meet me or call me *Mommy*.

"Hey, give Mom a chance to get inside before you tackle her," Matt half-heartedly ordered from the doorway. He stretched over the boys and pecked my cheek as I passed him.

As soon as we walked into the house Micah asked, "So what's the dinner plan?"

I was fried and really wanted to order a pizza, but I'd already used my free pass the night before with Chinese takeout. Rallying energy, I threw on an apron and dug red bell peppers, zucchini, and chicken out of the refrigerator while my guys settled around the kitchen table.

"Glass of wine?" Matt already had a bottle of Sangiovese sitting on the counter.

"Love one." My stomach clenched, but I went for it. "I got the call."

Matt paused with the wine in one hand and the corkscrew in the other. "What call?"

"The job." I took a breath. "I was offered the promotion."

"Oh." He glanced at me as if surprised and returned his attention to inserting the screw.

"I don't have to accept." I tried to sound as if it wasn't a big deal, but it was. I'd worked hard for that promotion and in the marrow of my bones needed a change for reasons I couldn't even begin to explain.

Matt meticulously poured an equal portion into each glass and handed one to me. His lips bent up, but his eyes weren't smiling. "Take it. Sounds like a great opportunity."

"You sure?"

He took a drink, and his smile became more genuine. "Absolutely. Congratulations."

"Thank you." I took a gulp from my glass and the lump in my throat receded.

"So, what will your new title be?"

"Senior Vice President."

"Impressive. When do you start?"

"Monday, since I'll already be in New York, and I'll meet my new boss." I knew almost nothing about Reese Kirkpatrick. Monday was his first day with Global Security. I didn't want Matt to know I had any qualms and asked, "How was your day?"

"Dad said we're going camping 4th of July." Micah looked at Matt. "Right, dad?"

Jason's face lit up. "Yeah, he said we'd catch fish and eat s'mores at night."

"Oh, really?" I raised my eyebrows at Matt.

Matt shrugged and this time he changed the subject.

After dinner, Micah and Jason wandered off to watch a movie while Matt twisted in his chair. He knew he was in the doghouse for promising the boys we'd go camping.

"How's work? Did you get your test results?"

The left side of his mouth lifted. "Yes, the preliminary reports are very promising, but I won't bore you with details you don't understand."

His superior attitude grated on me. Still, I probably wouldn't understand. Matt's work was difficult for most people to grasp. As a computational biologist, he studied genetic sequences in proteins. His work chemically linked the relation between depression and chronic illness, and was equal parts biology, mathematics, statistics, and computer modeling.

Funny, I understood when his colleagues explained what they did.

"I'm happy for you." I emptied the remaining wine into his glass. "So, camping? What happened to La Jolla and the Cove? Snorkeling and a condo with indoor plumbing?"

"I found a campsite along the Truckee River with great trails and fishing. It has flushing toilets and showers." I didn't bite and he threw me a bone. "You don't have to go."

He knew I wasn't big on camping, our vacation time was limited, and now I would be the bad guy if I didn't go. "Some choice you've given me."

"I thought it'd be nice to go someplace where you couldn't use your laptop."

He looked at me with his wide blue eyes and I melted. My vacations were never truly vacations. I always kept up with e-mail and joined important conference calls. Knowing the level of dedication expected by my company didn't alleviate the mom guilt. "You're right." A surge of affection for him filled me. I sat on his lap and kissed him.

He leaned his forehead against mine. "So you'll come?"

"Will you clean the fish?"

"Always do."

"Then I'll go." I kissed him again; then moved to get up. He tugged me back on his lap and hardened underneath me. "The boys are awake."

"They're watching a movie," he murmured close to my ear.

This was not Matt's typical behavior, but I liked it and my body responded. I led him by the hand to our bedroom. Before the door shut, Matt had his shoes kicked off and was unzipping his jeans. I locked the door and undressed too. I pictured a pre-show of tasting and touching before the main event. Matt had a different agenda. He thrust his tongue in my mouth and thrashed it around as if we were having a tongue war. The strange thing was it didn't feel like it stemmed from passion. It was habit. I pulled away.

No matter how many times he did the crazy tongue thing, or how many times I jerked back, Matt never clued in that I hated it. I wanted to tell him just how much I hated it but was afraid of wounding his ego. In a blink, he mounted me and a few blinks later, he collapsed on my chest. He pecked my cheek and murmured, "That was great." Then, he went to the bathroom. No kissing, no cuddling, no post-coital chat.

A weight on my chest kept me down. I should be happy. I'd just finished having sex with my husband. It hadn't been great, but not horrible either. At least we had sex.

Matt walked back in the room. "You tired?"

"A little bit."

He pulled on his boxers with his back to me and looked over his shoulder. "Think I'll watch the movie with the boys. You mind?"

"Go ahead." They were watching *Cars* for at least the hundredth time. I got up, finished the dishes, and went to bed.

———

The next morning, Matt slept snoring beside me while I lazed in bed daydreaming about the guy who worked at the Safeway fish counter. He had deep dark eyes and, while not great looking, exuded manly sexuality. I imagined how our first contact would be made.

"May I have four trout fillets, please?" I asked.

"You got it! Do you have a good recipe for trout?"

"No, I thought I would just throw them on the grill."

"If you'd like, I'll write one down for you."

"That's very kind."

"My pleasure." He handed me the recipe with a rakish wink.

Instead of a recipe, it's a confession that he watches for me. If I'm interested, call him.

Silliness. Even though it was Saturday, and my bed was comfy, I got up. Maybe I could get through at least one cup of coffee in peace before Saturday morning cartoons started blaring from the television. I made a pot of coffee, poured a cup, and headed for the back porch. The cool air bit my skin, but curling up on a lounge chair, I was comforted by the early sun on my face. As I sat enjoying the morning, sipping coffee, my thoughts wandered back to my increasing awareness of other men.

Last week, I had even caught myself checking out a Safeway bagger's butt. He couldn't have been more than twenty, but his chinos looked good on him. I imagined myself as Blanche DuBois. *"Young man! Young, young, young man...I just want to kiss you once, softly and sweetly on your mouth!"* How pathetic. I shook my head clear.

Everyone who knew Matt and I would attest we were happily married. We didn't fight. Neither of us indulged in excessive bad habits. Matt wasn't abusive. He didn't cheat. As my mother repeatedly said, I was lucky to have a man like Matt. So polite, so steady... so reliable.

He'd changed very little since we'd met while attending Northwestern University. I was getting my master's in Acting, and he was getting his in Biological Engineering. One day I decided to eat in the cafeteria. When I couldn't find an empty table, I hunted for any open seat. Then I caught Matt staring at me. He was sitting alone, and he was pretty darn cute.

I walked up to his table and smiled down at him. "I saw you looking at me. Would you like to invite me to sit down?" He chuckled and turned a deeper shade of red. I noticed the serious pile of books on the table. "It's too noisy in here to study anyway."

As long as I could remember, I'd had a weakness for smart men. The fact that Matt was blue-eyed and blond was a bonus. His eyes were pools of clear blue water, and they crinkled adorably when he smiled. After half a dozen coincidental meetings, he asked me out. I'd thought it was fate, but Matt later confessed he sought out places where he guessed I might be. He thought I was exotic with my dark features and second-hand-store-chic clothes. I never considered myself particularly unusual; however, being an actress, I had been *dramatically* different from the women he had dated. He had been different for me too.

There was never any great passion between us, but we were compatible in our way. His apartment became my haven from the craziness of my theater friends. He calmed me. My roommate, Serena, thought he was a looker, but *flat*. That's what she called him. "Flat." As in absence of fizzle. If being even-tempered and reliable was *flat,* then it was good with me.

I was twenty-three when we married. At the time, Matt loved me, adored me even. I remember the moment I sensed a shift in him. It was at our wedding reception. I had envisioned us inseparable as we celebrated our big night, but Matt wanted to catch up with college buddies.

"I have the rest of my life with you. I just want to talk to my friends."

Not wanting to appear needy or selfish, I kissed him and let him go. Subtle though the change was, a moment of absolute clarity hit me. I had transformed to a fixture in his life that no longer required special attention. We were married, and I would be there when he finished with other things. I supposed that's what marriage was. I just never thought it would happen so soon after we exchanged vows. It didn't mean Matt stopped loving me. Things simply had changed.

Now here we were, thirteen years later. Lucky thirteen. Last week our wedding anniversary came and went without much fanfare. After the boys had gone to bed, I presented Matt with a watch. He gave me nothing, not even a card. The next day I bought the BMW on impulse. I told him it was an early birthday present for me.

"Mom, where are you?" I turned and Micah stood all of three feet from me.

"Right here." I knew what he wanted.

"Oh. What's for breakfast?"

"French toast and bacon sound good?" It was a rhetorical question.

"Mmmmm. Thanks, Mom. Can I watch cartoons?"

"Sure, but keep the volume down. Daddy and Jason are still sleeping."

Less than a minute later, the television blasted. I jumped up and followed the noise.

"Micah, turn it down." He didn't respond. "Micah, that means now."

I think I was louder than the television. His face scrunched, but he did as told. I went to the kitchen to start breakfast and heard Jason stumble out of bed and make his way to the family room. A minute later, Matt loped in looking sleepy eyed. He headed straight for the coffee.

He took a sip and smacked his lips. "Good coffee." I dropped a slice of battered bread in the pan, and it made a pleasing sizzle. Matt leaned over and inhaled the scent of vanilla and cinnamon wafting from the skillet. "Mmmm, smells delicious."

His unexpected compliment brightened my mood. "It's such a beautiful day. Let's take the boys to Bean Hollow Beach this afternoon. We haven't been there in ages."

Matt looked at me a bit confused. "We're going to the A's game."

"You didn't tell me, but it sounds fun. What time do we leave?"

Matt looked at the coffee mug in his hand and then back at me. "I only got tickets for the boys and me. I thought we'd have a boys' day. You don't mind, do you?"

How could I object? Matt went to the bedroom to get dressed. I fought an urge to fling the spatula in my hand at him, but I flipped the French toast instead, wiping a tear before it dripped into the pan. I shouldn't be so angry and hurt. I wanted him to be a good father, but I *was* hurt. The game was something I could do with them, too.

I told myself it didn't matter. A week's worth of laundry waited for me. Besides, since the guys would be gone all day, I could treat myself to a shopping trip in San Francisco. Recently, I'd recommitted to an exercise plan and lost fifteen pounds. None of my suits fit properly, and I wanted to make a good first impression when I met my new boss.

After breakfast, I helped the boys find their A's caps and baseball gloves, and then lathered them up with sunscreen. Just before they climbed into Matt's Honda minivan, I gave everyone a hug, including Matt. I was still upset with him as they drove away. I hated that minivan. I had encouraged him to buy an SUV or Jeep.

Once inside, I missed the noise that had worked my nerves only moments ago. The quiet wasn't peaceful. It seemed inexplicably loud. I turned on the radio to drown it out, and a familiar tired restlessness crept over me while a weight settled in my chest. As I moved from room to room, gathering laundry, I kept expecting the impatient, heavy feeling to go away. It didn't until I walked into Neiman Marcus, my place to go when I really wanted to splurge.

Beyond pleased that the size 6 suit hung unattractively on my body, I asked the salesgirl to bring me a size 4. It was perfect. "I'll take it," I declared and started to get undressed.

She gathered my selections and asked, "Anything else I can help you find?"

"I could use something for going out. Not for Business." I don't know where that came from. I didn't have plans to go anywhere.

She was back in a flash with an armload of clothes. After I dismissed her first few suggestions, she held up a printed wrap dress. It reminded me of something my mother might have worn in the seventies when she was a young divorcee on the hunt for a new husband.

"Who's the designer?"

"Diane Von Furstenberg. You've got a rocking figure and can pull it off."

Flattery always helped. I put it on, and she was right. The dress was low cut and emphasized my newly flattened stomach and slenderized waist. I turned for a side view.

She studied my reflection. "Have you ever tried a push up bra?"

Okay, that was not flattering. My breasts weren't as perky as they used to be. Breast feeding two boys and gravity had taken its toll. I tried the suggested miracle bra with the dress.

She echoed my thoughts. "It's very sexy, but still sophisticated."

I had to hand it to her. She was good. I floated out of *Needless Mark-up* on heady shopping high with two suits, a dress, a bra with the matching underwear, and two pairs of shoes.

I hustled home to put my things away before Matt saw them. It wasn't because of how much I'd spent. Matt handed me the bills years ago when I started making more money than him. Other than the car, I'd always handled our money responsibly. It wasn't the money. It was the dress. I was embarrassed by how provocative I looked in it and wasn't sure what possessed me to buy it. If I wasn't comfortable modeling it for Matt, why did I bother?

I knew. I thought about it while I packed the dress in my bag Monday morning. When I looked in the fitting room mirror at Neiman Marcus, I saw who I used to be, and maybe still was under my standard little sweater sets which I accessorized with my little pearl necklace. After Matt and I had married, I changed my style to please him. I wanted one night to please myself.

One night to have fun and pretend I wasn't the suburban soccer mom. The dress was my "costume."